"Nuzo Onoh is a wordsmith who has earned the moniker The Queen of African Horror. *Where the Dead Brides Gather* is a creepy, well-crafted thrill ride powered by Nigerian mythology, haunting imagery and an unforgettable protagonist's otherworldly nightmares inextricably woven with her deeply human heart."

TANANARIVE DUE, winner of the Bram Stoker Award® and *Los Angeles Times* Book Prize for *The Reformatory*

"A heady, addictive horror delight that will keep you up at night for all the right reasons."

IRENOSEN OKOJIE, award-winning author of *Butterfly Fish* and *Nudibranch*

"At times hilarious, at times terrifying, always gripping, Nuzo Onoh's excellent novel joins sharply observed domestic conflicts and complications with deftly portrayed supernatural menace. With the assurance of a master, Onoh brings to vivid life characters who confront a frightening menace. *Where the Dead Brides Gather* is the latest triumph from the ever-impressive Nuzo Onoh."

JOHN LANGAN, Bram Stoker Award®-winning author of *The Fisherman*

"A powerful ghost story whose beating heart is a living girl. Bata is a character readers will fall in love with instantly—a haunted child who holds onto her kindness and gentle spirit amidst terrifying events."

A. C. WISE, award-winning author of *Wendy, Darling* and *Hooked*

NUZO ONOH

WHERE *the* DEAD BRIDES GATHER

TITAN BOOKS

Where the Dead Brides Gather
Print edition ISBN: 9781835410561
E-book edition ISBN: 9781835410622

Published by Titan Books
A division of Titan Publishing Group Ltd
144 Southwark Street, London se1 0up
www.titanbooks.com

First edition: October 2024
10 9 8 7 6 5 4 3 2 1

This edition is published by arrangement with African Literary Agency.

A CIP catalogue record for this title is available from the British Library.

Printed and bound by CPI Group (UK) Ltd, Croydon, CR0 4YY.

To my beautiful cousin, Mrs Monica Amuchechukwu Igbokwe, the new custodian of our stories and my beloved and cherished family whose fierce independence continues to inspire me every day. "Rock on" dearest Auntie Monica xx

Yesterday, our rich in-law, Bongo, brought a horse to my uncle Gabriel's house. It was a pre-wedding gift for my cousin, Keziah, who was soon to become his wife. The horse was a truly impressive creature, big, black, and powerful. It stood the height of two grown men and the girth of five fat women. Its white-streaked mane was long and thick, just like its sleek neck and bushy tail. The muscles in its torso rippled when it neighed, and its hooves kicked with manic frenzy, keeping all away from its vicinity. Everybody that saw it said that Bongo had done well, that he had given his in-laws a gift fit for a king. They also agreed it was a good thing the horse would be killed for the wedding feast. It had certainly earned the butcher's knife and the soup pots with its unruly behaviour.

From the time it was dragged into my uncle's compound and tethered to the mango tree, the black horse neighed with incessant panic. It screamed and groaned so much that we all were forced to abandon it and its mesmerising beauty in order to save our eardrums. Even we village children, normally used to extreme ruckus, found ourselves unable to withstand the terrifying screams of that great horse.

And its cries were truly chilling. It was an eerie whine that was shrouded with human anguish and terror. In my ten years of existence, I had heard the voices of countless creatures, from the chirpy songs of birds to the raging howls of rabid dogs. Yet nothing prepared me for the unearthly sounds of raw terror coming from the gaping mouth of the black horse. Even from the modest distance of my father's compound, its piercing shrieks filled our ears and chilled our hearts. My skin involuntarily gave birth to little, hard rashes that came in shuddering waves as the black horse screamed through the endless hours of the morning and afternoon.

"I swear, that horse must be infected with madness," my stepmother, Ọla, complained later that evening as the deafening din continued. "Its screams can be heard across all the compounds in this village. Someone should do something about it."

"Perhaps it's been bitten by a snake and is in a lot of pain," my mother suggested, her eyes filled with the habitual compassion that made her a target of my stepmother's manipulations. I could hardly recall a time when it wasn't my mother feeding my three half-brothers. Ọla was always too busy with one thing or the other to care for her triplets, and Mama never complained about being taken advantage of by her.

"We can't let the poor children starve," Mama would always say whenever my big sister, Ada, complained about my stepmother's laziness and non-existent maternal skills. "It's not their fault that their mother is a Pancake-Face rather than a nurturing mother. After all, that's one of the reasons your father married her: to appreciate her beauty rather than her cooking skills. At least she's done what she was brought in to do, and has given your father three sons in just one pregnancy. What else can we ask of her?"

'Pancake-Face' was the term used to describe a well-powdered and made-up face. It was a beauty practice peculiar to beautiful women in our village. They would coat their faces with thick powder several shades paler than their skin, slap bright blue eye shadow on their lids, and colour red circles into their cheeks with lipstick. My stepmother was one of the biggest practitioners of that beauty regime and there was no denying that she was beautiful. With her tall slenderness, smooth ebony skin, and striking features, Ọla was a sight to dazzle every eye in our village—men, women, and children. Despite her not being my blood-mother, my dream was to be as beautiful as Ọla when I grew up.

Ọla pushed her glamorous, beaded braids away from her face, frowning in irritation as the black horse continued to groan. Its screams were getting louder and more terrifying as the night drew closer, and my heart continued to thud in involuntary panic.

"I heard that horses know when they're going to die and will cry and mourn their impending death till the minute the butcher's knife slices their throat," my big sister Ada said, cracking her knuckles absent-mindedly as was her habit.

"Who told you such evil?" Ọla shivered delicately, shaking her head reproachfully. "This girl! I've never seen anyone that tells more outlandish tales than yourself. That's how you convinced us that Keziah's period was stolen by a witch, only for us to discover she was pregnant, hence this speedy marriage tomorrow, huh!" Ọla screwed up her beautiful face in disgust.

"I'm not lying, this woman," Ada retorted. "Go ask Papa if you don't believe me. I heard Papa telling Uncle Gabriel that horses can sense their death and will kick and bite anyone that comes near them, as well as cry non-stop until they're killed. And I wasn't lying about Keziah's period, either. She told me herself that a witch had stolen her period; that's why she didn't even know she was pregnant till her tummy started swelling." Ada's voice was as fiery as her eyes. My big sister was known across the clans to have a temper that rivalled the fury-wind itself.

"Whatever." Ọla waved a dismissive hand laden with sparkling rings. "I just wish someone would stuff something into that vile horse's mouth, so we can get some rest. I don't know how we're expected to sleep tonight with all that din." She leaned down and turned up the volume of the small transistor radio by her feet. My stepmother never went anywhere without her transistor radio and Mills & Boon book.

Instantly, the familiar happy lyrics of the FESTAC '77 song filled the air: "*Festac '77, 77 is here; Festac '77, 77 is here!*" Over and over, the song repeated the joyful chorus in a never-ending loop.

"I'm sick of this useless song," Ada bit out viciously, glowering at the radio. "That's all they ever play these days, wretched 'FESTAC '77' non-stop, as if there's no other song in this world."

"What is FESTAC '77?" I asked from my mat. Ọla looked down at me and patted the empty space beside her. I quickly scrambled from the floor to sit next to her on the wooden bench.

"FESTAC '77 is the festival of arts and culture currently taking place in the big city of Lagos," Ọla said with that wistful tone of voice she had whenever she spoke of her beloved Lagos City, our country's capital. "Every famous African from the world is taking part, even Miriam Makeba; you remember Miriam Makeba, don't you?"

I nodded eagerly. "She's the one that sang 'The Naughty Little Flea'."

"Exactly! She's in Lagos City even as we speak. Heaven knows I'd give an arm and a leg to visit Lagos City again for this festival and—"

"What will you do there when you visit, eh?" Ada cut in with a voice dripping with mockery and spite. "Perhaps you'll dazzle them with your Pancake-Face and read them a stupid story from your precious books, eh?"

Ọla gave her a withering look of disdain and coolly returned her attention to me.

"Bata, I told you I schooled in Lagos City before I married your father, didn't I?" My stepmother smiled at me. I nodded enthusiastically again. I couldn't recall the number of times Ọla had drooled about Lagos City to me and everybody that cared to listen. "Lagos City is like nothing you've ever seen," Ọla continued, her eyes glowing dreamily. "The houses are so big and tall they cover the skyline. As for the roads, they're so wide that ten cars can drive on them and still have space to spare. And come see the cars, Jesus Almighty! You'll think you're in New York in America. Everywhere you look are white people and rich people." Ọla sighed wistfully.

"What's the big deal about white people, eh?" Ada snapped. "If I want to see a white person all I have to do is wait for Christmas when Engineer Tip-Toe returns with his German wife and almost-white son," she hissed loudly, cracking her knuckles angrily.

Engineer Tip-Toe was the only man in our village who had visited the white man's country and got a university degree under the government's sponsorship for gifted students. Since his return from Germany with his white wife and little son, he had been working in Lagos City and rumoured to be almost as rich as our village chief. He owned the second storey-building in our village, with the first one belonging to our chief.

In the background, Uncle Gabriel's black horse released another chilling screech, instantly drowning out the FESTAC '77 song.

"That's it! I'm done with this blasted horse. I'm going to complain to Our-Husband right now about it." Ọla stood up from the bench and sauntered away with her trademark slow and swaying walk. She left a heady scent of her perfume behind.

My stepmother was the only woman in the entire village that used perfume. It was in a bottle hidden inside a pale blue package with the bold title of 'Charlie'. She told me that it was how white women smelled and that only the rich African women living in Lagos City used that powerful scent. I had once sneaked my way close enough to Engineer Tip-Toe's German wife to smell her body, but she smelled nothing like Ọla's perfume. She just smelled of breastmilk.

When I told Ọla my observations, she explained that the African hot weather had likely drained the scent from her. It seemed every white woman that came to our country soon sweated away their natural perfumed odour. This discovery created a natural pity for Engineer Tip-Toe's German wife in my heart. If only she knew what would happen to her, maybe she wouldn't have followed Engineer Tip-Toe back to our village after all. I promised myself that as soon as I became educated and rich like my stepmother, I would acquire the white women's body scent in its special Charlie bottle.

I watched Ọla head over to Papa's parlour. I wanted to follow her to see what Papa might do, but I knew I would get a scolding from both my big sister and my mother, not to mention my father.

"Huh! Let's see what the foolish woman will achieve," Ada muttered, eyeing my stepmother's departing back with icy malevolence. It was no secret that my stepmother and my big sister heartily despised each other. "Does she expect Papa to tell Uncle Gabriel to kill the horse before tomorrow's wedding, eh? Well, she'll soon find out that this is one time her beauty can't perform miracles for her, huh!"

"Ada, watch your mouth," Mama admonished gently, eyeing my three half-brothers as she spoke.

Not that Mama needed to bother. The three little hogs were too busy stuffing their faces with boiled corn and coconuts to notice either their mother's departure or my big sister's insults. Even at their tender age of five, the triplets, or Ejima as they were collectively called, had already built a fearsome reputation in the village for unrivalled gluttony. The clanswomen knew to stuff their faces to get them to behave, and Mama never let them leave her presence with empty stomachs, as rare as it was to encounter them with non-protruding tummies.

I knew Ejima once had individual names, but I was sure neither they nor their mother remembered those names. They were called Ejima from birth, meaning twins or triplets. Much worse, they were so identical that it was impossible to tell one from the other. They even managed to confuse their own mother at times. When they heard their name called out, they would answer with uniform synchronicity, knowing that whatever occasioned the call related uniformly to them, be it a new shirt, a sweet treat, a warm bath, or bedtime stories. Being their constant playmate, I was the only one they couldn't trick in the entire village. There was a special glint in their individual eyes that revealed their very soul to me, coupled with the tone of their voices. Ejima-Three cried constantly while Ejima-Two giggled with irrepressible mischief. The big bully, Ejima-One, the oldest of the triplets, already walked with the puffed-arms swagger of a midget dictator, as if he ruled the entire world and heaven.

We waited for several minutes for Ọla to return to the communal space where the family was gathered for our usual evening meal. I didn't really expect her to come back anytime soon, as Papa was known to enjoy her company to the exclusion of all else, save Ejima's. So, we were all pleasantly surprised when Ọla returned within the space of minutes.

"So, what did Papa say?" Ada asked before Ọla could sit down. "Did he get rid of the horse? I swear, I can still hear the horse's screams, can't you, Bata?" She turned to me for confirmation, her eyes brimming with malevolent humour.

I quickly nodded, before turning to Mama for affirmation. I figured Ọla wouldn't be displeased with me if Mama agreed with my sister and me. Despite her gentle nature, Mama was still Papa's first wife and Ọla owed her respect, especially when Ada was around. Ada would kill anyone that disrespected our mother in her presence.

"Your father is a fool," Ọla muttered with uncharacteristic viciousness.

"Don't call my father a fool, you stupid woman," Ada raged, squaring up to Ọla. Mama got hurriedly to her feet too. She placed herself between Ada and Ọla, as ever determined to prevent another fight between her first daughter and her sister-wife.

"Our-Wife, watch your words around the children," Mama admonished, shaking her head at Ọla. "How can you insult their father in their presence, eh?"

"I wasn't insulting him," Ọla snapped. "I was only speaking the truth. Where his big brother, Gabriel, is involved, that man will never see reason. Anything Gabriel wants, Gabriel gets. And now that his daughter is marrying into wealth, he expects the world to bow down to him; not minding she's marrying a man old enough to be her father, and even worse, a man whose two wives died funny deaths. You know I speak the truth, Our-First."

Ọla hissed loudly, her red lips pursed in vexation. "Now, Our-Husband has asked us to go and spend the night in Gabriel's compound, to help with the wedding preparations. I don't know about you, Our-First, but I'm telling you now, I'll only spend an hour there before coming back to my own bed." Ọla kissed her teeth as she motioned her sons over. "You three pigs, come along now. Time to sleep, and don't you dare ask me for anything else to eat tonight. I'm too tired for your nonsense, so be warned." Ọla turned back to Mama. "Our-First, will you ask Ada to keep her eyes on Ejima and Bata while we're gone?"

Mama nodded. "Of course she will." She turned to me. "Bata, follow your brothers to bed and don't give your big sister any trouble tonight, alright?" There was a significant tone in her voice which I recognised with a sinking heart. "We'll be back very soon from your uncle's house."

I nodded slowly, rising from the floor where I'd been sitting eating boiled corncobs and coconuts. Ada looked mutinous, but there was nothing she could do about her new responsibilities. At sixteen years, she was the oldest child in the family and the one usually lumped with the childcare duties whenever both Mama and our stepmother were simultaneously absent.

"Before I forget, make sure Bata doesn't sleep with her head towards the door," Mama said to Ada, before turning to look at me pointedly. "We don't want you having more nightmares and waking up everybody when we're gone, do we?"

I lowered my head in embarrassment. My nightmares were legendary in our family. Rarely did a night go by without my waking our household with my screams. I would start off sleeping on my thin mattress on the floor, and end up outside our L-shaped bungalow, shouting and gasping for air, my face drenched in terror-sweats. No matter how much Mama prodded, I could never recall my dreams in detail. All I was left with was the impression of a thick forest shrouded in mist, and chalk-coloured women who smelled horribly, ghastly in their unearthly paleness, chasing after me with unbelievable speed. They sprinted on all fours like dangerous beasts of prey, shrieking rage into my ears as they drew nearer, reaching for me with their white claws... *closer... closer...*

I would stumble into wakefulness, screeching and running like somebody chased by a pride of lions. It was the same dream night after night, and all the rosaries Mama placed around my neck before I slept failed to keep away my sleep tormentors.

Mama said the nightmares arrived on the day I survived the fall into the deep ravine along the route to the village stream at the age of five years. According to the witnesses, I stopped breathing for so long they were convinced I had died from my head injuries. I woke up just as they arrived back to our compound, bearing my prone body in readiness for a burial. Save for a slight grogginess, I seemed to be just fine, speaking normally and recognising faces. And apart from the bump on my head and some small cuts and bruises, there were no other visible signs of my terrible accident. In no time, I was back to my boisterous play.

My recovery was declared a miracle from God, and Mama purchased several candles for thanksgiving prayers at our local Catholic church.

Her gratitude was short-lived.

That same night, I experienced the first attack of the nightmares that would go on to blight my life and the tranquillity of our home.

2

When I was six years old, just slightly older than Ejima were now, Papa took me to the shrine of the village medicine-man, Dibia, to cure my nightmares. That was after our local priest, Father David, had exhausted all his holy water and novenas on me following Mama's entreaties. Papa, who wasn't a believer of the Christian faith, dragged me to the medicine-man's shrine after one particularly bad week of shrieking and sleep disruption.

Dibia had discarded Mama's rosaries with a contemptuous snort and replaced them with a string of charmed cowrie beads. He also prescribed that I lie on my mattress with my head facing the wall instead of the bedroom door.

"If the child sleeps with her head facing the door, she will absorb the negative auras of all the wandering supernatural entities that walk the roads at night while the rest of humanity sleep," Dibia said, massaging powerful oils and herbs into my head. "However, if she sleeps with her legs facing the door, it'll allow her to run, and even fly, should her dreaming-self encounter other itinerant spectres with malevolent intentions."

Papa and I left the medicine-man's shrine with little hope and great anxiety. After all, we had tried every other remedy possible to no avail. There was no certainty that Dibia's juju would work.

The same night following the visit to the medicine-man, I slept with my feet facing the door as instructed. And for the first time in my life, the pale spectres did not torment my sleep. Mama was so happy that she prepared a celebratory feast for the family and even took baskets of food gifts in secret to Dibia to avoid offending Father David. For several weeks afterwards, I continued to sleep peacefully with my feet facing the door, while the rest of our household enjoyed untroubled slumber as a result.

My respite expired three months following the visit to Dibia's shrine. I went to sleep with no thoughts of my erstwhile ghostly tormentors. Halfway through the night, I woke up shrieking, running, and flailing my arms wildly as if to push away something unwholesome and terrifying. Once again, our household was in turmoil and Papa was threatening again to send me away as a domestic servant in a big city, a dire fate normally reserved for difficult children such as myself.

The older I grew, the worse my symptoms became. With each attack, Papa's irritation with me increased till the previous tender indulgence he had for me vanished, gradually replaced with frowning impatience. Save for my stepmother's intervention, Papa would have surely carried out his dire threat. Thankfully, Ola needed my errand-girl and playmate duties for her triplets. So, she used her Pancake-Face magic on Papa, thereby ensuring my salvation from expulsion. In gratitude, I redoubled my efforts to keep Ejima busy with all types of games and foodstuff, leaving their mother free to pursue her numerous interests. Ola was only happy when she shopped for clothes in the big city and kept company with her horde of fawning female friends, especially her best friend, Teacher Uzo, the village spinster. I knew that as long as I carried out my nanny duties well, my stepmother would ensure my security in our home. Ọla was the only person with the powerful magic to bend Papa's iron will.

Later in the evening, Mama and Ọla left for Uncle Gabriel's house to assist with my cousin Keziah's wedding preparations. I followed Ada into the house and was soon curled up on my mattress in the same old position, with my feet facing the door. Everybody knew it was now a futile ritual, but we kept hoping that one day, the medicine-man's magic might be reignited and bring us a peaceful night again. Ada ensured I recited my 'Hail Mary' nightly prayer before leaving our shared bedroom for Ejima's bedroom, where she was to remain till our mothers returned.

As always, my heart started racing as soon as my head rested on my thin pillow. I clutched my charmed cowries with desperate fingers, mumbling prayers underneath my breath— "Oh please, Mother Mary, don't let the raging ghosts come to my dreams this night. Please don't make me wake up and wake Papa up; please… please…"

I kept my eyes wide open for as long as I could, fighting sleep with desperate grit. Even when my lids became heavy, I used my fingers to prise them apart. I held them open till my fingers grew as weak as my eyes, and my brain grew as foggy as Ọla's smoky kitchen. The last thing I remembered was yawning for the umpteenth time and thinking, *I'm sooo tired…*

Then sleep came; and once again, they came for me.

When next I regained wakefulness, I was sitting cross-legged in front of my cousin Keziah's room, with my back pressed hard against her shut door. The wide corridor leading to her room heaved with stunned kinsmen and clanswomen, and the din was mind-stealing. Beyond them, Uncle Gabriel's black horse continued its infernal shrieks, magnifying the mayhem in the place. My mother was amongst the horde gathered around me, and she wailed the loudest.

"What has happened to my child? Who has done this evil to my poor child? Oh, Jesus! Oh, Holy Mother!" Mama's voice was a pitiful dirge that quickly roused the wails of the gawping clanswomen. She rushed over to scoop me up in her arms.

I pushed her away, fighting her embrace. My actions were instinctive, a strange rejection of a mother I loved beyond all humans. Before I could dwell on my odd act, something else grabbed my attention.

I saw my hands—my very white hands—*Oh, Mother Mary, save my soul!*

I shrieked and raised my arms up. My mouth formed a wide O. I stared slack-jawed at my thin arms coated with white paint, right from my shoulders to my fingertips. A quick scan showed me that I was as naked as the day I exited my mother's womb. Not even a pair of knickers covered my nudity. Every bit of my slight body was coated in a brilliant white paint that contrasted sharply with the rest of my gloomy surroundings, lit up by kerosene lamps held high by the gathered kin. When I tried to wipe the paint, it stuck firmly to my skin.

I started rubbing my body with manic frenzy, whining softly like a whipped puppy. Soon, the women joined me, using their wrappers and headscarves to wipe me down. Their actions were as desperate as my frantic fingers and beads of sweat quickly glistened on their skin.

All to no avail.

The more they wiped my skin, the whiter I glowed. It was as if somebody had dipped my body into a pool of white diamond molasses and brought me out in my unearthly, crystalised whiteness.

"Oh, Jesus, save us!" a woman screamed. "It isn't white paint on the child's body! It's her real skin. Look! Even her hair and eyes have turned white! What evil is this?" She rapidly weaved the sign of the cross, flinging the demon over her shoulders with her arms as she shrank away from me.

The crowd in the corridor quickly imitated her actions with terror-widened eyes. Mama was wailing inconsolably, while Ọla stared at me with goggled eyes. In my entire life, I had never seen my usually unflappable and indifferent stepmother so stunned. Ọla's face, more than anything else, sent limb-quaking terror to my heart.

I began shaking violently. Visions and images started whizzing through my mind in a kaleidoscope of vivid and terrifying colours—*Oh, Mother Mary, save my soul! The raging ghost-women! They finally caught me in my nightmare! But why am I here instead of our house? And my white skin; oh, Mother Mary, have pity! Am I now a ghost?*

"Bata, come, my child." Mama tried again to lift me from the floor where I remained with my back pressed hard against Keziah's door. "Let's take you to Father David at once. Our holy priest will know what this evil is and help us return you to your proper colour."

Again, I shoved my mother away with such force that she stumbled. I stared at my arms, as stunned as the rest of the crowd—*Where did such power come from? Why am I pushing Mama away? I want to go with Mama. I want Father David to remove this horrible white skin. I want to leave this place and return to our house. Please... somebody, please...*

Even as the thoughts ran through my mind, I tried to rise from the floor. I pressed my palms to the ground, trying to heave myself upright. But it was as if I had been moulded into the flooring with concrete. No matter how hard I tried or pushed, my body remained glued to the ground.

I started to cry. Great balls of tears crawled down my face, and my whole being heaved with the force of my sobs. But no sound came from my lips. It was as if my tongue had been sealed inside my mouth by the same invisible force that held me prisoner on the floor outside my cousin's bedroom. My terror almost stole my sanity, and my heart pounded so hard I thought I would surely die—*But I don't want to die! I want to go home... I want to go with my Mama...*

"Somebody send for Dibia at once," I heard a deep male voice command. My eyes flew towards the direction of the voice— *Papa! Oh my wicked luck! Papa will kill me for causing more trouble! Oh please... please...*

The terror in my heart was so great it killed my tears. Slowly, with great determination, I forced myself to calm down. The effort hurt the back of my throat where the sobs bunched up in a hard knot. Even my hiccups felt like hammer blows crushing my chest—*It's okay, Bata. It's okay. Don't cry so that Papa doesn't get angry and send you away as a house-servant in the big city. Maybe Papa might even sort out this evil skin you wear. Papa is strong and wise. He'll take care of everything. Please, please, don't let Papa be angry with me... please.* Slowly, with great effort, I gradually swallowed my tears and stopped my panicked arm-flapping, fixing my eyes solely on my father's strong and harsh face. I willed myself to take strength from his strength.

"Hello? What's going on out there? Can someone help me open my door? I'm stuck inside the room and the door won't open." My cousin Keziah's whiny voice pierced the night air.

Once again, pandemonium ruled as the crowd resumed their panicked shouts, triggering the horse's frantic neighs.

"Mama-Ada, get your cursed child away from my daughter's door," Keziah's mother screamed at Mama, her eyes wild with rage and terror. Everybody, save Ọla, called my mother by the name 'Mama-Ada', since her first child was my big sister Ada. But to my stepmother, my mother was simply 'Our-First', a respectful title to recognise Mama's status as Papa's first wife. In return, Mama called

Ọla 'Our-Wife', to show she was welcomed warmly and without resentment into the family as a sister-wife. Otherwise, everyone else called Ọla 'Mama-Ejima', the exalted mother of triplets.

"Shut up, woman!" Papa's voice brimmed with repressed rage as he glared at Keziah's mother. The knife scar down the side of his right cheek pulsed with menace. "Can't you see that we're all dealing with something beyond our human experience? This is no time for your woman-foolishness." He turned to the gathered crowd. "Everybody, just calm down till Dibia arrives. He'll soon sort this evil out. Keziah, be patient and wait inside your room. We should have everything resolved soon."

Papa's voice was the magic that was needed to bring sanity to the unruly crowd. And when his eyes caught my terrified gaze, I saw an unexpected gentleness in their familiar hard glint that brought unbidden tears to my eyes once again. The last time I had seen that look in my father's eyes was a few years after my fall, when I was six or seven years old perhaps, before the nightmares killed his affection for me. Papa broke away from the men and strode towards me. From his great height, he stared down at me, his face grim. Then he stooped low and took my hands in his, my white-paint hands that trembled as violently as my father's large hands.

"Be strong, my daughter." Papa's voice was the gentlest I had ever heard, and his eyes were filled with unfamiliar pity and kindness. "We'll soon fix this evil that has possessed you. Dibia will be here in no time, and I promise, I'll give your mother money to buy you a new dress tomorrow, alright?"

I nodded, letting my tears run freely down my cheeks. Papa wiped them with the same uncharacteristic gentleness and my heart flowered—*I don't care if I remain white forever if Papa will continue being kind to me...*

Dibia arrived with the delegation that had gone to summon him, armed with his familiar juju-bag that contained all the divination tools of his trade. As soon as they saw his trademark blood-splattered face and feather-littered body, the crowd parted for him, drawing back in alarm. It was a known fact that malevolent entities clung to the medicine-man's body as a result of his astral journeys to the realm of the dead. Nobody wanted to risk body contact with him in case a mischievous spirit jumped from the sorcerer's body into their own.

Dibia sat down in front of me, adopting the same cross-legged lotus position as myself. Like the rest of the crowd, I shrank back from him instinctively, terror widening my eyes. I was aware of his fearsome reputation and the rumours surrounding his supernatural exploits. As a result, I now suffered the same terror his presence invoked in the villagers.

"Child, do you know who I am?" Dibia asked after staring silently at me for several intense minutes.

I nodded. I opened my mouth to speak, but once again, no words came from my lips. The medicine-man's eyes suddenly squinted into hard flints.

"You have lost your speech, am I correct?" His voice was as hard as his eyes. Again, I nodded, my heart racing like an antelope.

"Hmm; just as I thought," Dibia murmured under his breath. He reached into his raffia bag and brought out a red Kolanut, the famous Ọji-Ikéngọ̀ used for divination with the ancestors and spirit-world. With a stentorian voice, he chanted invocations in an unknown tongue that layered my skin with sudden goosebumps. He rolled the Kolanut on the ground, flung it into the air, bounced it between his palms before finally coating it with the fresh blood dripping from his shaved head.

"Here, hold this Kolanut," he commanded, reaching for my right hand and pressing the Ọji-Ikéngọ̀ into it. Then he fixed me with a terrible gaze that reached beyond my soul and began to shout commands into my face. He shook the iron bell gripped in his hand with the violent frenzy of a possessed human.

"Whoever, whatever you are, I command you to show yourself," Dibia shrieked at me, sprinkling salt and white Nzu powder on my head. "If you are a malevolent spirit, show yourself now or face my wrath. There is no hiding place for you. The charmed Ọji-Ikéngạ̀ will reveal your hidden evil and devastate you before the eyes of mortals and spirits. However, if you are a good spirit, then release the child's tongue and reveal yourself. I command you in the mighty name of Amadioha, the greatest of gods, and in the fearsome names of our ancestors whose powers you cannot withstand. Speak, now. Speak! Speak! Speak!"

The medicine-man's shrieks pierced my ears, filling my body with an indescribable heat that brought sudden swoons to my head. My breathing came hard and fast, and I struggled to inhale air into my lungs. Everything around me was swimming and I found it difficult to hold onto the faces of the people around me. Even Papa's face refused to show his features to my terrified and blurred gaze.

From a distance, I heard the screeches of the crowd as doors and windows started to slam with violent force. A great wind swept through the house, winking out the lights from their wick-lamps and plunging the compound into instant darkness. Inside my head, an unearthly presence observed the chaos with icy detachment, an ancient and powerful presence that sent the real me, my Bata-soul, cowering in a dark space in my overheated body. All sounds started to slowly die; the screams of my kinsmen and even the frenzied neighs of the black horse, which now resembled the fading whines of a mouse. The fury-wind withered into stale air, till suddenly, all was darkness and silence.

3

When the lights of consciousness returned to my eyes, I found myself all alone. The crowd had vanished, together with my parents and the medicine-man. Save for the shrieks of the black horse, a deathly silence shrouded my uncle's hamlet in creepy solitude. There were no sounds of laughter, chatting, or singing, not even the barking of the rowdy Ekuke-hamlet dogs.

I noticed that I was still sitting in the same lotus position before Keziah's bedroom with my back pressed against her door. The air was now cold, an unnatural chill that turned my breath into white smoke. Yet, I did not shiver despite my nakedness. My body trembled in neither cold nor terror. My heart was calm and my breathing steady. It was as if I were looking at myself with a third eye, a cold eye that observed my insignificant human form with icy detachment. I was no longer the Bata I knew, the snivelling little girl who was terrified of her own shadow. This was a different me, a calmer and stronger me that neither cried nor feared her unearthly transformation. My skin was still chalk-white, and I clutched tightly to the red Kolanut that Dibia had pressed into my palm before I sank into the dark.

I inhaled deeply and exhaled with a loud whoosh. Once again, I watched the smoky air whirling around my face with fascination. It was a strange phenomenon for me, one I had never witnessed in myself or anyone else in all my ten years of existence. I exhaled again, transfixed by the wonder of my smoky breath—*Does it mean that everything in me is now white, from my skin to my breath? Maybe my blood is white as well, and my piss and poo and…*

I didn't have time to finish the thought.

A figure materialised before me, a ghoul from the deepest depths of Satan's hell. It glowed with a terrible light that should have blinded me. But my ice-white gaze calmly held its gliding form in its ghoulish monstrosity, my heartbeats steady and calm— *Why am I not afraid? Why am I not shrieking and scrambling up from this floor and running from this unspeakable horror?*

Even as the thought left my mind, a new thought superimposed it—*We meet again, foul spirit!*

The abomination gliding with silent menace towards me was no stranger. It wore the familiar ghastly mien of the raging spectres that had terrorised my dreams for as long as I could remember. From the top of its head to the tips of its toes, it gleamed a dazzling white colour that imitated my own skin. The red gash of its lips stretched in a malignant smile that promised me instant death. I flexed my neck and eyed the ghoul with cold detachment as it steadily advanced. And I noticed something I had never seen in my previous dream-encounters with its kind— *It's a bride! It's the ghost of a dead bride!*

The spectre was dressed in a long, white wedding gown which was made of a sequined lace material with flowered motifs. The gown was stained with mud and flecks of blood. It trailed to the Ghost-Bride's feet, exposing silver-tipped shoes underneath. The veil on its head was longer than the gown, its lush organza falling all the way to the ground behind it. A strange odour seeped from its body, a vile stench that reeked of a combination of raw chicken, wet dog, rotten eggs, and bad breath. I would have gagged from the stench before my transformation.

When our gazes clashed, I was stunned to see that its eyes glowed a normal human black. Somehow, I had expected it to have eyes the same colour as its skin, just as my new crystallised eyes. As it drew closer, I felt rage and hatred emitting from every invisible pore in its translucent body. It bred an icy resolve in my heart. I held its angry gaze as I began to address it.

"Anene Eze! Abominable spirit!" I thundered, my voice an unfamiliar deep timbre that resonated beyond the walls of my uncle's house. "Prepare for your annihilation, foul being!" I held my sitting position before my cousin's shut door as I spoke. Raw power emitted from the deep resonance of my voice, forcing the Ghost-Bride to pause its glide in mid-air.

Something rustled by my side. I looked down and saw a sea of red silk flowing past my feet. In that instant, the magnet holding me chained to the ground broke. I rose from the floor in a fluid motion, like one pulled effortlessly by a puppet-master's strings. I raised my arms and stretched.

Then I stretched again—and again. With each stretch, my body lengthened and grew until it almost tripled my normal height. Had my stepmother stood before me in her tall slenderness, I would have stared down at Ọla with eyes set three feet above hers. I noticed that I was now dressed in a long red kaftan of dazzling beauty. The gown covered every part of my chalk skin, and on my head a red gauze veil covered my face, making me a blood-bride in my terrifying redness. The veil extended past my feet as it flowed down the wide corridor, crawling and swishing with a life of its own. A dazzling red light shrouded my body, illuminating the corridor with its intense hue. With grim determination, I stood sentinel before my cousin's door with my arms outstretched, blocking the malevolent Ghost-Bride from gaining entrance.

The sight briefly awakened the cowering Bata-me from my dark space. Terror gripped my heart, sending shudders to my body. Suddenly, I wanted to see my face underneath the dense veil—*Surely, this tall bride can't be me? But if not, then where am I? Who is this tall, new person? Is she a Ghost-Bride too? Where am I? Oh, Mother Mary, where am I?*

"Anene Eze! I repeat, prepare for your annihilation!" the tall-me roared, pointing a threatening finger at the slowly advancing Ghost-Bride. "You cannot have this bride. No matter your greed, you can never steal another bride's groom. Everything ends here for you tonight, foul spirit! Have you forgotten the past already? Have you forgotten your debt to me, accursed spectre?" My voice echoed down the long corridor, a drumful of fury and power.

In a blink, a reel of dazzling images started spinning inside my head like a Technicolor film on Papa's television set during the rare occasions we had electricity in our village. I felt another mind intruding into the vision, a foul mind I wanted to reject and eject. I didn't need to be told that it belonged to the evil Ghost-Bride. But the other-me, the blood-bride, allowed it in, letting it share the ghastly visions she weaved inside my mind-screen.

I saw the evil Ghost-Bride as she once was in her lifetime, a beautiful mistress to a rich man unwilling to end his marriage. Determined to marry her lover, she hired assassins to kill his wife in a staged robbery-murder that went unsolved for many years.

The Ghost-Bride gasped softly as more pictures reeled in rushing sequence, exposing the dark secrets of her old life. She remained suspended a few feet from Keziah's door, her head cocked, black eyes blazing with pain and rage as she followed her life's story. More images flashed inside my head. I saw the Ghost-Bride dancing inside a dingy little room, laughing wildly and toasting her imminent rise to wealth and status once she married her rich, newly widowed lover. Her black eyes glittered with arrogance and desperate greed.

As the images grew fainter, I saw the Ghost-Bride on her final day on earth, dressed in a white wedding dress of flowered organza lace. Her veil trailed softly behind her as she walked down the long flight of stairs to join her waiting groom for their wedding. Her face beamed with pride and smug triumph. The beautiful bouquet of flowers she clutched enhanced the dazzling beauty of her wedding trail.

Halfway down the stairs, a bright red light suddenly materialised behind her. In a blink, it slammed hard against her, a powerful force that instantly unbalanced her.

She tripped, stumbled, and started falling—*Oh, Mother Mary!*

I shut my mind's eye from the ghastly vision, my heart pounding. After several panicked seconds, I opened my eyes once again when my curiosity overcame my fear.

I wished I hadn't.

The Ghost-Bride was still in free-fall. Down endless marble stairs she fell, screaming, head crushing, limbs breaking, blood spurting, staining and painting everything a cheery red colour— veil, dress, stairs, and her once beautiful face. The final image I saw was the pale ghost of the dead bride, separating violently from her crushed and bloodied body sprawled at wrong angles at the bottom of the stairs.

With a shriek of rage, her spectre flew across the vast hall with the fury of a hurricane wind. Her long veil billowed behind her like the white wings of a great bird of prey and blood dripped heavily from her smashed head.

"Why? Why? Why?" she screamed with raised fists, as she cursed the fates that had denied her the chance to become a bride.

She dived down from the ceiling and floated towards her grieving groom. Instantly, a bright red light repelled her, shrouding him in an impenetrable shield. It was the same red orb that had pushed her down the stairs to her untimely death. From my hidden space, I felt an icy chill clutch my heart, squeezing terror into my soul.

Over and over, the Ghost-Bride tried to get close to her devastated groom still in his smart white suit, now bloodied, as he crouched next to her crushed corpse, weeping inconsolably. But she could not reach his side. The dazzling red light kept repelling her, and within its bright glare, I saw a sight that brought a soft gasp to my Bata-lips.

The glowing ghost of the groom's late wife stood sentinel over her husband. Her mien was fierce and terrible. Garbed in her traditional red Bubu kaftan and sparking fiery eyes, she was a fearsome sight to behold in her sizzling fury.

"Anene Eze! Vile murderer! Fear for your accursed soul!" the ghost-wife shrieked at her murderer. "Bongo will never be your husband in this life or the next. Despite his infidelity, I'll not send him to his death; at least, not yet. His innocence in your vile crime, coupled with our two young daughters, has saved him from my rage—for now. As for you, vile creature, only your soul-obliteration will quench my thirst."

A bolt of deadly red flames spun towards the terrified Ghost-Bride. She ducked and took to the ceiling once again in panicked flight. The vengeful ghost rose in swift chase. Pulsating with righteous rage, she flew after her killer, shooting deadly bolts of sizzling flames from her hands, lips, and eyes. Their fierce battle took them over the high ceilings, as they flew and crashed against the walls, chairs, and balustrade in their bitter combat. The punishing bolts of red flames continued to torment the evil Ghost-Bride, and her shrieks sent shudders of icy chills to the Bata-me still lurking inside the tall sentinel standing guard before my cousin's door; a terrible sentry I finally recognised with bone-crushing terror—*Oh, Holy Mother, save my soul! I've been possessed by a dead woman!*

In the midst of my new terror, another sudden illumination hit my panicked mind—*Bongo! The groom my cousin Keziah will marry tomorrow is the same Bongo as this grieving groom!* In that instant, I knew that Keziah's hope of marrying Bongo was a doomed one unless the imposing sentinel guarding her door kept her safe from his dead mistress's ghost.

Then, the pictures winked out, just as unexpectedly as they had started. The Ghost-Bride shook her head like one in a daze. Her body jerked violently as if stunned by an electric shock. I could see that the vision of her tragedy had deeply affected her. Fiery sparks flew from her black eyes as she let out an unearthly howl in a discarnate voice that instantly curdled the relentless screams of the black horse. Once again, she resumed her furious glide towards Keziah's door, intent on possessing my cousin's soul. The malodorous stench oozing from her pervaded the entire corridor like Satan's hell-funk.

The tall sentinel-me smiled coldly at her. I flexed my neck, every muscle in my body rippling in readiness for our supernatural battle. The Ghost-Bride dived towards me with a suddenness that would have taken me by surprise had I not been ready for her. The flash of a red bolt from my left hand sent her stumbling backwards. In a furious backward flight, she wheezed out of the corridor, instantly disappearing through the thick walls. I followed her, gliding out of the house with the speed of the fury-wind. I was just in time to see the vile ghost vanish into the body of Uncle Gabriel's great black horse, sending it into a screeching frenzy as it bucked and shuddered in manic terror.

The horse turned a terrifying white hue that brought loud screams to the lips of the gathered villagers already grappling with my unearthly transformation. A second bolt from my hands sent the Ghost-Bride scrambling out of the tortured body of the great horse in panicked flight. The animal collapsed to the ground, foaming from the lips as its life rapidly ebbed away. Still, even in its death-throes, the great horse continued to shriek with relentless grit as had been its habit.

I abandoned it and its ghastly screams and pursued the fleeing spectre back into the house as again it sought to gain entrance into Keziah's room. Once more, the deadly fiery bolts from my hands sent her crashing to the floor mere steps from Keziah's door. With a slow glide, I approached her, my eyes emitting sparking darts of hate. The Ghost-Bride scrambled to her feet in elevated flight, terror and rage flashing in her dark eyes as she took to the high ceiling. In a blink, my long red veil swished a deadly chase, wrapping itself around her legs and dragging her back to me. She was still screeching when I opened my hand and shoved the Ọji-Ikéngà into her gaping mouth. It was the same charmed Kolanut the medicine-man had given the Bata-me earlier that night. My actions were instinctive, guided by the entity in possession of my body and an unknown knowledge that knew the devastation to expect.

With dispassionate eyes, I watched as the sacred nut began to wreak its deadly vengeance. Just as the powerful medicine-man had threatened, the Ọji-Ikéngà began to take its ghastly toll on the foul spectre. From my hiding place, I recalled Dibia's words as he pressed the Kolanut into my palms—*"If you are a malevolent spirit, show yourself now or face my wrath. The charmed Ọji-Ikéngà will reveal your hidden evil and devastate you before the eyes of mortals and spirits."*

The evil spectre started to shriek and convulse. She clutched her neck and retched, trying to vomit the charmed Kolanut. But it worked itself past her throat and into her gut. With frenzied hands, she freed herself from my imprisoning veil and started to levitate once again, her body swaying clumsily in the air. She didn't get far. Her ghastly flight halted in a spasmodic motion that left her suspended in mid-air before my towering frame.

As I watched, the Ghost-Bride began to wither and age. Her face grew streaks of black and red veins that crawled down her neck and arms like bloated worms. Her glow started to dim rapidly with her sudden deterioration. Soon, her features—eyes, ears, nose, lips, cheeks, and chin—began melting, becoming almost liquid in their foul decay. She was shrieking in pain, struggling to escape her dire plight. But her flight was dead, and in a blink, she fell to the ground, writhing, howling, melting.

I lifted the red veil covering my face, a face that belonged to Bongo's murdered wife, just as I suspected. My Bata-self shuddered in terror at the sight of my body-possessor's terrible mien. The grim smile on her face spelled the doomed fate of her assassin. She hovered over her killer, staring down at the decaying spectre with hard, unforgiving eyes.

"Anene Eze, foul being!" she cursed, her eyes boring into the still-raging ones of the rapidly disintegrating Ghost-Bride. "Once more, you've come in your unremitting greed to marry a rich groom, my husband yet again. But not on my watch. Do you hear me, you wicked woman? Not on my watch! Today, we end it all for good. I shall wipe your accursed name from the memories of men and the spirits. Not a strand of your hair shall remain in existence in the realms of both mankind and the spirits. Even the grave that holds your putrid corpse will vomit you out as a cat regurgitates a ball of hair. Your evil will finally be known and your body burnt to unholy ashes. Long have you evaded my vengeance, but your greed has again exposed you. Now, we end this cursed fate for good."

And with a sustained blitz of intense red flames, the ghost-wife obliterated her murderer to a pile of powdery ashes. Instantly, my body started to tremble violently as a sudden chill froze my flesh and bones. Something invisible, fast, and powerful, exited my body like the rapid gush of a raging river. From a long distance, I heard the terrifying shrieks of Uncle Gabriel's black horse. It sounded as if the butcher's knife had finally found its throat. Then it fell silent.

A great weariness instantly overcame me. I felt myself shrinking, diminishing, till once again the roof appeared very high above me. With a low groan, I slumped to the ground into the deepest sleep of my life.

4

I was lying on my mattress when I woke up, back in the room I shared with my big sister Ada. As soon as I opened my eyes, I experienced intense joy on being in the safe familiarity of our bedroom. I couldn't explain why I felt such happiness, nor did I bother dwelling on the unusual emotion. Instead, I allowed myself to wallow in its bliss.

I stretched luxuriously, enjoying the weakness in my limbs. It was the warm and cosy feeling of a tired body enjoying a well-deserved rest. I yawned widely as I contemplated whether to rise from the mattress. As always, my mind did its usual morning check to see if I could recall the familiar nightmares that plagued my sleep—*Did I run outside again? Did the raging ghost-women in my dreams catch me again? Will Papa be angry with me today?*

But no memories formed in my mind. As hard as I pushed, I couldn't remember my dream. Stranger still, the usual apprehension that followed me on waking up every morning was absent from my heart. Before I could make sense of things, the door opened and Mama came in, closely followed by Ọla and Ada. The unusual sight of all three of them inside my room sent panic-thuds to my heart. I quickly scrambled up from my mattress, jumping to my feet in guilt.

"Bata, lie down, child." Mama hurriedly guided me back to my bed with urgent hands—*Uh? I stared at them in confusion. Am I sick? But I don't feel ill. Why are they all looking at me so weirdly as if there's something wrong with me?*

"Are you hungry?" Ọla asked, her eyes bright with a mixture of repressed excitement and puzzlement. "Tell me anything you want to eat, and I'll get it for you."

My heart started pounding. A hard knot formed behind my throat—*Oh, Mother Mary! Something horrible has happened to me, otherwise, how can Mama-Ejima of all people offer me food? She never cooks, and food is the last thing she'll offer anyone, even her triplets.*

I shook my head.

"It's alright, daughter." Mama's voice was gentle, and her face wore its familiar kindness. "You don't have to do anything today. Just lie down, okay? Sleep and rest till you feel strong enough to get up."

"But I'm strong, Mama," I said, quickly jumping up from my mattress again. A sudden dizziness almost toppled me. I caught myself just in time. "See, Mama? I'm well. I'm not sick. Can I go outside and play with Ejima?"

I saw them all exchange significant looks before Mama took my hands in hers.

"Tell me, daughter, do you remember anything from last night at all?" she asked quietly, looking at me intently.

I frowned, started to shake my head, then stopped—*Last night?* I forced my mind to go over my activities the previous night with detailed precision. "After you and Mama-Ejima went to Uncle Gabriel's compound, I went to our bedroom, while Ada went to sleep with Ejima," I said, looking at Ada for confirmation. She nodded, but in a distracted manner. "Then I said my prayers and went to bed. I just woke up, and then you all came in." I shrugged.

Again, they exchanged significant looks. "Does the name Anene Eze mean anything to you? Have you heard that name mentioned anywhere before?" Mama asked, an odd look in her eyes, as if she faced a ten-headed ghost. I was surprised by this look of terror in my mother's face since she was rarely afraid of anything, what with being covered by the blood of Jesus and the love of Mother Mary.

Anene Eze? I shook my head. "Who is Anene Eze?"

"No matter. Did you have your usual nightmare?" Mama persisted with her strange interrogation, holding my hand so tight it hurt. "Do you remember your dreams at all?"

I shook my head again. "I don't think I dreamt last night," I said with reluctance—*What if they think not dreaming is a sign of illness? After all, there's never been a night I haven't dreamt.* "I mean, maybe I dreamt, but I can't remember anything. Didn't you bring me inside the house last night as usual? Didn't I run away from my nightmare as always?"

Mama shook her head. "No, child." Her voice was quiet, her face solemn. "You didn't scream in your dreams or run away from the house last night. Something else happened though. Come; let's feed your tummy, and then you'll go to your father who will explain everything to you."

"What? What happened, Mama?" My voice was raised in sudden panic.

"I can't discuss it with you, at least, not till your father has spoken with you." Mama started to walk out of my bedroom, pulling me along. I found myself struggling with an inexplicable tiredness that brought waves of dizziness in its wake. "Come now; your food is getting cold."

We all trooped out of my room. I noticed that Ọla and Ada kept looking at me queerly, as if I were a strange creature that had wandered into our compound. I quickly looked down at myself, wondering if there was something bad that I couldn't see. But all

I saw was the familiar sight of my ten-year-old self with my legs and arms in their skinny normality. Still, the strange fatigue and dizziness persisted—*What is wrong with me? And why are they all looking at me so strangely?*

At our communal eating place, I saw the triplets already seated on the straw mat eating their breakfast of Akara-beanballs and Akamu-corn cereal. They smiled cheerfully at me as they hurriedly made space for me on the mat. Their smiles reassured me—*At least Ejima are treating me normally. So, maybe there's nothing wrong with me after all.* I sat next to the boys, waiting for Mama to serve me my breakfast.

A sudden thought popped into my mind. "Mama, when do we get ready for Keziah's wedding? Hey, listen, everyone! Can you hear the silence? Uncle Gabriel's horse isn't crying anymore. Do you think they've now killed it for the wedding stew? I wonder what horse meat will taste like? Does it taste like cow meat or goat meat?"

A loud noise drowned my voice as Mama dropped the empty tin-bowl in her hand. It danced a twisting tango on the cement floor before coming to a rest by her feet. She looked at me with terror-widened eyes before exchanging that strange look again with Ọla and Ada.

"They said the horse died the very minute you fainted last night and… uh-uh—" Ada stopped mid-sentence, covering her mouth with her hand. Mama glared angrily at her, while Ọla shook her head, making disapproving tuts.

"I keep telling you your careless tongue will land you in trouble one day," Mama scolded Ada, avoiding my eyes and my questions. And now, more questions were whirling inside my head, but I was too frightened to voice them—*When did I faint last night? Where did I faint? Is that why they're all being kind to me? And why did the black horse die? Did I do something bad to it in my sleepwalk?*

Mama served me my breakfast, then started bustling around

the kitchen with manic zeal. I felt she didn't want to look at me, unlike my stepmother, who couldn't seem to keep her eyes away from me. Several times, I caught Ọla's eyes staring at me with that same puzzled expression I had seen on their faces since I woke up—*Something is definitely wrong with me, but what? What?*

Papa sent for me before I could finish my breakfast. I heard his deep voice shouting my name and dropped my spoon in panic.

"Quick, go answer your father. I'll keep your food warm for you." Mama helped me to my feet.

"We'll go too," Ejima chorused in happy unity, quickly abandoning their empty plates with loud squeals.

"We'll go eat goat meat with Papa," Ejima-One said with bossy greed, his voice ringing with the familiar authority of the first-born triplet.

"And pig meat too," Ejima-Two chimed in with his usual gleeful mischief.

"And cow meat too. I want cow meat." Ejima-Three was already whining, ready to cry for his food and everything else as was his habit.

"You'll go nowhere, you greedy hogs," Ada said, forcing them back to the floor. "Why don't you boys ever ask for chicken meat, eh? Is it because chickens aren't big enough to feed your greed? It's always cows and goats and pigs you demand. I won't be surprised if one day you ask for an elephant too," she hissed loudly, glaring down at them.

"Is elephant meat sweet?" Ejima-One asked, his eyes alight with the familiar greed.

"I want elephant meat." Ejima-Three's voice was all wobbly. Ada's frustrated curse was the last thing I heard before Papa's loud voice cut it off.

"Look, your father is getting impatient. Hurry now," Mama urged.

"I'll take her to Our-Husband," Ọla offered, rising languidly to her feet.

"We'll go with Mummy," Ejima squealed, dashing over to their mother. The triplets addressed their mother as 'Mummy' instead of 'Mama', as Ada and I did. Being an educated woman, my stepmother insisted they use the name the white people used.

"You know you can't be there." Mama gave her a piercing look. Ọla looked disappointed, her lips pursing petulantly. "This is the time for the men, first. They'll let us know everything later. Let's start getting ready for the wedding, so we're not late."

Ọla shrugged and nodded, sitting back on her wooden bench. She twirled her long braids with bored indifference, while Ada cracked her knuckles with vicious grit. Mama turned back to me.

"Go on, Bata." She gave me a reassuring smile. "We won't go to the wedding without you. And listen, child, no matter what you hear from your father, don't be afraid, alright? There's nothing wrong with you. You're just blessed, that's all. You're very blessed by Our Holy Mother, okay? Don't you forget that. Off with you now."

Mama waved me away. My legs suddenly became too weak to carry my weight—*Oh, Mother Mary! What is wrong with me? What will Papa tell me? What does Mama mean by her strange words?*

Despite my terror, I managed to make it to my father's parlour, where he received visitors and took his afternoon nap on days he wasn't at work. Papa owned one of the largest stalls in our village, where he sold wholesale foodstuff, from dry fish to bags of rice, beans, and salt. He was sitting on his favourite cushioned sofa when I entered.

Papa wasn't alone. The room heaved with almost every male member of our clan, including my uncle Gabriel, whose daughter, Keziah, was getting married later in the day. In the corner and separate from everybody sat Dibia in his fetish glory. The sight of all the men with their unsmiling faces sent my heart pounding and my limbs quivering—*What have I done now? What wickedness have I committed? Oh, Mother Mary, save me!* I managed to curtsy low to Papa as was our habit, my siblings' and mine. The unfamiliar dizziness washed over me anew.

"Good morning, Papa." I straightened, forcing myself to hold my balance even as I averted my eyes from his gaze. Of all his children, Papa was the strictest with me due to my bad habit of disrupting his sleep when the nightmares struck. I therefore tried my best to avoid him as much as I could. I didn't want him to remember his former threat to send me away as a domestic servant in the big town, just in case he decided to carry it out one day.

"Akuabata. Come, child." Papa urged me closer, smiling kindly at me—*Oh no! Now I know for certain that I'm sick! Papa has never smiled at me in this manner!* "Come and sit at my feet. Don't be afraid. Everyone here is your kinsman." He stretched his arm out to me. Papa was the only one that called me by my full name, Akuabata, instead of the abbreviated name of 'Bata' used by everyone else.

I hesitated before taking the offered hand. My body trembled and I bit my lips hard to stop myself from crying. Papa pulled me gently down till I sat next to his feet on the linoleum flooring, facing the stern faces of my kinsmen.

"Dibia, the child is here," Papa said, clearing his throat as he turned to the medicine-man. "Feel free to speak with her."

The other men murmured noisily amongst themselves until the medicine-man coughed discreetly, signalling his readiness to commence the meeting. Silence fell in the room. All I could hear was the raspy breathing of the men and the distant shouts of the children from the nearby compounds.

And suddenly, the last place I wanted to be was inside my father's crowded parlour.

5

The medicine-man looked at me for a long time, his eyes narrowed in suspicion. I squirmed on the floor by Papa's feet, struggling to hold his gaze. After what felt like countless, torturous hours, he finally spoke.

"Bata, do you know why you're here?" Dibia asked.

I shook my head, too frightened to speak.

He nodded slowly, leaning close to me till our faces almost touched. His expression was grim and his eyes probing.

"Do you remember what happened to you last night?"

Again, I shook my head—*Why does everybody keep asking me about last night? What did I do?*

"It's just as I thought," Dibia said, nodding and giving the gathered men a meaningful look. "The spirits used the child as a vessel last night. That's why she can't remember anything from the time she was possessed till they left her body."

"But is it usual for her to lose her skin colour during a possession?" Papa asked, pressing his hand hard on my shoulder. "I've heard of spirit possession in the past. We all recall when the vengeful spirit of Ogodo possessed his wife's lover, causing him to strangle her to death as they were having sex on the very marital bed she'd shared with her late husband before she poisoned his soup. Her lover spoke in a voice that was identical to Ogodo's own and even walked with Ogodo's distinctive limp when he was arrested. He didn't even remember his own name or his kinsmen anymore. That is what a possession is. Akuabata's case was unlike anything we've ever witnessed. You all saw what I saw, didn't you?" Papa turned to our kinsmen. "Correct me if I'm wrong, but what we witnessed yesterday seemed to go beyond a mere possession. The child was white from her hair to her toes. Even her eyes were white. She grew taller than the mango tree in Gabriel's compound. We heard the voice that came out of her mouth when she spoke. That wasn't my child speaking; that wasn't Akuabata's voice I heard last night. And now, you can all see her with your own eyes. The child is back to her normal size and self; her skin is again the normal brown of a living human. She has no recollection of what happened to her yesterday." Papa turned back to the medicine-man as our kinsmen nodded vigorously in affirmation. "Dibia, what evil is this, and why is it happening to my child? More importantly, how can we keep it from happening again?"

The parlour filled with the voices of the clansmen as they all demanded answers from the medicine-man. Nobody was paying attention to me, which was a good thing, as to my shame, I pissed on myself—*Oh, Mother Mary! Mother Mary! Mother Mary!* I couldn't seem to think of another word and my head was about to explode with limb-freezing terror. I found myself recalling my dream, the final nightmare I had the night before they brought the screeching black horse to my uncle's compound—*Oh my bad luck! I remember now! One of the raging white ghosts finally caught me in my dream! For the very first time ever, the chasing ghost-women caught me, and now I'm doomed! Papa will surely send me away to the big city if he ever finds out...*

"Okeke, I hear you," Dibia said, addressing Papa by his first name. "Indeed, you are right. What we witnessed last night goes beyond mere possession. We all saw how Gabriel's great horse stumbled and died the minute the child collapsed. We heard the fury-wind that blew from Gabriel's house towards that doomed horse, just before it cried its last. That was when the spirit left the child's body. Save for that horse, it would've surely possessed someone else and killed them on the spot, or it would have remained in Bata's body for as long as she could withstand the possession before dying. Let us be thankful to the ancestors that the horse was there to receive the departing spirit."

The medicine-man turned to me and all eyes followed his own—*Oh please, don't make them tell me to stand up and see my piss stain! What will I do? Mother Ma—*

"Bata, I need you to listen carefully, child." Dibia's voice cut into my panicked thoughts. I looked up startled, nodding frantically, over and over like a grey lizard—*Smile, Bata! Smile nicely at everyone! You must endear yourself to all of them so they don't punish you for what you did. Uncle Gabriel must be very angry with me for killing his great black horse, and Papa will surely send me away now for bringing disgrace to his compound. Smile at them, Bata; go on, smile nicely so they won't be very angry...*

"Did you ever meet a stranger anywhere?" Dibia's voice broke into my frantic thoughts. "I want you to think very carefully: did you ever speak to anyone that seemed unusual in any way?"

I shook my head vehemently, my bright smile fixed to my face. My body continued to quiver like leaves in a thunderstorm.

"Okay. At least we know she wasn't fed witchcraft that turned her into a ghost-carrier," Dibia mumbled, turning back to face me. "Now, I want you to tell me about the nightmares you've been having. I know that you've been prone to night-terrors from when you were little. I myself gave you charmed cowrie beads to ward off the evil. But your father tells me they still plague your sleep. Can you tell me what exactly it is you dream that causes you to run from your bed screaming every night?"

Even before Dibia finished speaking, I felt all eyes on me as my kinsmen started murmuring loudly amongst themselves. By their startled expressions, I could tell that my night-terror was news to most of them.

"Speak child; don't be afraid," Dibia urged. "What do you see in your dreams?"

I looked up at Papa, and he nodded encouragingly at me. His eyes still held the unfamiliar gentle kindness in their dark depths, and the sight calmed my terror; somewhat, just a little bit. My heart was still thudding, just not as fast.

"I s-see chalk-skinned ghost-women in my d-dreams," I stammered, feeling the familiar unease my nightmares wrought in me. "Th-they smell horribly and are always angry and scream in rage as they chase me on their hands and feet, just like animals run. Then I wake up when Mama brings me inside the house." I hung my head, shamed by exposing my curse before the entire clan—*What if they tell my other cousins and everyone starts laughing at me when I go to school? What if it reminds Papa of the troubles I bring and he decides to ignore Mama-Ejima and send me to the big town after all?*

"Are you telling us you have the exact same ghost-dream every single night?" My uncle Gabriel's voice was incredulous. The other kinsmen also gasped their shock.

I nodded, afraid to meet their eyes. The uric stench of my shame filled my nostrils and I prayed desperately that nobody else smelled it. I wrung my hands with manic frenzy as I awaited the heavy rock of adult disapproval to fall on me. Instead, I felt Papa's hand on my head. He stroked my hair in a gentle, repetitive motion like one calming a fussy baby. I looked up sharply, stunned by it. He smiled down at me, his knife-scarified face filled with a new compassion that brought hot tears to my eyes.

"It's alright, my daughter," he said in that unfamiliar kind voice. "Nothing bad will happen to you. Don't be afraid. Your papa is here and Dibia will find a cure for you, I promise."

I continued to look at him with shock-widened eyes, until the medicine-man's voice dragged back my attention.

"It's just as I thought," Dibia said with a grim smile. "The child is a night-flyer, one of the charmed ones who can traverse both the spirit and ancestral realms. By some unfathomable miracle, she's been touched by the same divine hands as myself, and has become a vessel for the spirits." He turned to Papa. "Okeke, you are indeed blessed. Your ancestors have deemed it fit to choose your daughter as their tool. I too witnessed what happened in Gabriel's house yesterday and did my divination with the ancestors and deities afterwards."

Dibia leaned forward and fixed Papa with intense eyes. "Okeke, do you know what sits there at your feet?" he asked in a grave voice. Papa looked perplexed, same as my gathered kinsmen. All eyes returned to me again, and I squirmed uncomfortably—*If only I could disappear, or turn into an ant and crawl away without being seen...*

"You're looking at a high priestess of unrivalled powers! Your daughter is now a charmed Bride-Sentinel," Dibia announced in a stentorian, yet excited voice. Papa looked at him, startled. "Yes, Okeke; your daughter, Bata, now holds the power to protect brides from the malevolent attacks of Ghost-Brides before their wedding day. I've heard of such charmed entities but have never seen one in my life till now." Dibia stared hard at me before returning his gaze to Papa. "Okeke, you were right when you said it wasn't a normal possession. Bata wasn't merely possessed. Instead, she became a ghost herself to fight the malevolent spectre. As our people say, you need a demon to fight a demon. This special child before us has become the living ghost that vanquishes dead ghosts."

Papa and the clansmen gasped, and I almost pissed on myself again—*Oh my bad luck! What curse is this? I'm a ghost! I am both dead and alive, just like Lazarus in the Bible story!*

"Yes; you are all looking at a wondrous phenomenon beyond anything even I have ever encountered," Dibia continued, eyeing me with great approval. "Okeke, your ancestors have given this child the sight to see the ghosts of girls who died before they could become brides to their beloved grooms. Such unfortunate ghosts labour under the yoke of their unfinished business, roaming pathetically in their pale realm, unable to transcend to the ancestors' realm. Most of them are filled with the fury of their early demise and unfulfilled dreams. They crave for any opportunity to become brides once again and complete their derailed destinies. Their thirst is a blind one, usually driven by no malevolent agenda, save the desire to say 'I do' before a religious man or officiating clansman. They usually return to their ancestors in peace once the wedding ceremony is over, leaving the real bride confused by her reactions at her own wedding."

Dibia paused, before stuffing his nostrils with a pinch of Awulu-tobacco powder. His face creased up as he released a mighty sneeze.

"May demons not call your name in vain," chorused the kinsmen in solemn unity.

"Same to you," Dibia said with a grim smile. Everyone knew that sneezing, even one occasioned by tobacco powder, signified a person's name being called by either spiteful humans or malevolent spirits.

"As I was saying," Dibia continued. "Some of you have seen brides who display strange and unexpected behaviours at their weddings. They cry excessively or laugh hysterically. Others might even burst into songs or demonstrate excessive affection for their grooms. That is the Ghost-Brides showing their joy at finally fulfilling the dreams they were deprived of by their untimely deaths. The human brides go on to live happy lives with their husbands, unaware that they briefly harboured the ghosts of these doomed souls in their bodies on their wedding day."

Dibia paused again and passed his snuff box around. Some of the kinsmen accepted the tobacco while others, including Papa, declined. Dibia's voice reclaimed my petrified attention once more.

"However, once in a while, as happened last night, a Ghost-Bride may have a malevolent agenda. These are brides with corrupt and vengeful souls, accursed ghouls whose intentions are to permanently deprive the human brides of their bridehood and even their very life force. They don't leave the brides' bodies after the wedding, and instead stay on in our world, wreaking havoc on the unfortunate grooms, their families, and the wider communities. The poor grooms quickly realise that their brides are no longer the women they loved and courted. These poor women appear to have morphed into terrible strangers that confuse and frustrate their husbands and in-laws. The Ghost-Bride that came for Gabriel's daughter last night was one such evil ghost."

Everybody gasped again. Gabriel's eyes almost popped from his sockets. Dibia looked him straight in the eyes. "Yes; this is the truth, Gabriel. Save for the intervention of this blessed child, your daughter would be dead to you as you knew her. By this morning, Keziah's soul and body would have been devoured by a truly malicious spirit that came with a deadly agenda. The dead bride of Keziah's groom, the vile city woman that went by the name of Anene Eze in her lifetime, came for your daughter's soul last night. You heard the child call Anene Eze's name in the unfathomable voice that was not of our realm as we waited outside in the compound. You all saw how Bata regained her child-height and her skin morphed back to a normal human colour after she vanquished the malevolent Ghost-Bride. That's why she remembers nothing of what happened, because she was a ghost herself, battling another ghost. You owe her a cow at the very least, Gabriel. I know she's your niece but consider her a high priestess whose status supersedes yours and every other person in this village, save myself. Thanks to her, the vile truth about Anene Eze is now out and I'll be informing her village medicine-man, so they can dig up her grave and dump her vile corpse inside their own Ajọ-Ọfia, the evil forest of the accursed dead."

The men cheered their approval loudly as Dibia filled his nostrils with more tobacco powder. This time, even though his face crinkled, he resisted the sneezes. Before I could blink, my uncle Gabriel fell on his knees before me, bowing his head to the ground over and over. He grabbed my two hands, squeezing them tightly, frantically. Tears streamed down his face and when he spoke, his voice was no longer the harsh authoritarian voice I'd been used to since my infanthood.

"Our child! Blessed gift from our ancestors! Your uncle thanks you from the bottom of his heart." Uncle Gabriel's voice was tremulous. "Forgive me for any harsh words I may have used on you in the past. Name anything you want—anything whatsoever—and it shall be yours."

I shuddered, wrapping my arms around myself—*Uh-uh. I don't want to be a ghost or this horrible Bride-Sentinel thing.* Other clansmen soon joined my uncle. They too fell on their knees before me, showering praises on me and asking me to protect their daughters, granddaughters, sisters, and nieces come their time to wed.

"Let the child be," Papa said, standing and pulling me up from the floor. I wanted to resist. I didn't want them to see and smell my fear-piss. But I had no need to worry. They were too engrossed in their panic to notice my uric shame. "Dibia, is there anything we can do to keep Akuabata safe?" Papa's voice was filled with a terror I'd never heard in his voice in all my life. "You heard her narrate her dreams. God forgive me, I had no idea the anguish this child endured when those accursed ghosts tormented her sleep. Can you guarantee that they won't harm her, especially now they know who she is?"

"Have no fear, Okeke." Dibia smiled, rising from the floor. "Bata is protected by the ancestors. Nothing can harm her, neither ghosts nor demons. She is one of them now, even though she shares your human blood. Bring her to my shrine later today so that I can purify her and wash away any lingering residues of the evil ghost she battled last night from her aura. We don't want it draining her energy any more than it did during their encounter."

He smiled at the group of kinsmen. "I bid you all good-day and health. I know your clan has a wedding to attend and will now leave you to enjoy your festivities."

"Dibia, you speak as if you're not invited too." Uncle Gabriel admonished him gently as he rose to his feet, together with the other kinsmen. Dibia laughed humorously as they all headed out. Soon, only Papa and I were left inside the parlour.

"Come, my daughter; let's return you to your mother," Papa said, still holding my hand in his as if he were afraid a Ghost-Bride might steal me away if he let go. "Did you understand everything Dibia said?"

I nodded, still too stunned by all I'd heard to marshal the wild thoughts crawling around inside my head like scattered ants— *I'm a ghost! Oh, Mother Mary, save my soul!*

"Are you afraid?" Papa held my frightened gaze with his new kind eyes. I nodded again. "Don't be. You heard Dibia. You're protected by both our ancestors and the gods. Yes, even Jesus himself, who you and your mother pray to, protects you. That's because what you did last night at your uncle's house was a great miracle. Your papa is very proud of his wonderful daughter, and from now onwards, you must make sure you spend enough time with me whenever I'm back from work, do you hear?"

Again, I nodded—*Oh, Mother Mary, thank you for making Papa like me again, like in the past, even though I've now become a ghost. Hopefully, he won't send me to the big town when I dream the bad dreams again.*

"Do you feel ill?" Papa asked, halting his steps. Worry lines furrowing his forehead. "Do you feel any different at all? It's important you let me know at once. You heard what Dibia said about ghost residues, didn't you?"

I nodded. "I just feel a little tired and dizzy, that's all. I'm not sick, I promise. I can still go to the wedding, honest."

Papa gazed at my face for a long, hard minute before grunting. "Hmm; we'll see. But as soon as the wedding is over, you must accompany me to Dibia's house for your cleansing, alright?"

I nodded again, feeling a semblance of normality slowly return to me after the strange experiences of the day. As long as I was allowed to attend Keziah's traditional wedding, I was willing to go anywhere with Papa afterwards. I loved weddings, the beautiful brides in their wonderful wedding gowns, the exciting grooms with their wondrous gifts, the delicious foods, joyful festivities, and the excitement of dressing up in my Sunday best. Best of all, Keziah had promised to make me a flower-girl at her church wedding later in the month. I could barely contain my anticipation.

Papa returned me to Mama and Ọla, who stared in stunned disbelief at the sight of him holding my hand. Everybody knew how much I irritated my father, and how stingy Papa was with any overt display of affection except when Ọla or Ejima were with him. The gentleness in both his voice and his face as he released me to their care left them both slack-jawed. Even before he called them over to his parlour to update them with the new situation in our compound, I knew my fate would never be the same again.

6

Ọla dressed me up for Keziah's wedding as if I were attending the wedding of a king. She had insisted on preparing me for the event, and being the beauty expert, Mama happily surrendered me to her capable hands. Ọla hurriedly ushered me into her large bedroom, as if she feared Mama might change her mind.

"Make sure you don't touch anything on my dressing table, you hear?" Ọla warned as we entered her room. "They're not playthings and I don't want to quarrel with your mother if you damage my stuff, you hear?"

I nodded fervently. "Mama-Ejima, if you like, I can clean the dust off your beautiful shoes you'll wear to the wedding," I offered with an eager smile. I was determined to be the best-behaved child in the world for my stepmother. We had always gotten on well, Ọla and I. A part of my heart told me she liked me the best amongst all the kids in our clan, even more than her triplets whom she rarely interacted with.

"Good girl." Ọla gave me a distracted smile, patting my head approvingly as she started gathering the secret weapons that would give me a Pancake-Face to rival her own. "So, what did your father and the clansmen say to you when he called you into his parlour?" Ọla's voice sounded disinterested, but I saw the tension in her rigid shoulders.

I felt the old unease douse my excitement—*Not again! How many more times will everybody question me today?* I had already been grilled by Mama, Ada, and a few relatives, and felt a return of the heavy concrete in my heart on hearing Ọla's words.

"They told me what I did at Uncle Gabriel's house last night," I mumbled, picking up a pair of sequined pink shoes lying by the yellow bookshelf. I started wiping them gently with the hem of my dress. The dress was already due for laundry and I thought I was doing it a great honour by letting it wipe its manky material on Ọla's beautiful shoes.

"And?" Ọla prompted.

I shrugged. "Uncle Dibia said I'm now a Bride-Sentinel and the clansmen asked me to protect their clans-brides when they get married." I shrugged again, feeling embarrassed by my own words.

"That's what I heard as well." Ọla took the pink shoes from me and held my hands in a feverish grip. "Bata, promise me that when my little sister, and my best friend, Teacher Uzo, finally get married, you'll be their Bride-Sentinel and won't let any evil Ghost-Brides steal their souls. Do you promise?"

I nodded slowly, reluctantly. Since my meeting with the medicine-man and our clansmen, my new power was all everybody could talk about. It kept me in a perpetual state of anxiety that caused my heart to jump at the slightest sounds—*If only things would go back to how they used to be. I'll even welcome a hundred nightmares rather than become this horrible Bride-Sentinel thing.* Ọla beamed at me and returned to her dressing table. I picked up the pink shoes again and resumed polishing them.

Soon, my gaze began to wander around my stepmother's hallowed bedroom with the same wide-eyed fascination of my previous visits. As the mother of triplet sons, Ọla's room was the largest in the house, even though Ejima didn't share her room with her. Unlike all the other rooms, it was plushly furnished, with a wide double bed, a white standing wardrobe, and a dressing table whose wide mirror reflected the vast array of cosmetics and jewellery it housed. On the wall, a large calendar featuring the Jackson 5 displayed the date—5th February 1977. Each of the twelve pages of the calendar exhibited a different photo of the famous boy band and I never ceased to admire their handsome and elusive aura, these wonderous young men with overblown afro hair that were like no other men I had ever seen in my village.

Overflowing with beautiful clothes, shoes, bags, jewellery, cosmetics, and decorative ornaments, Ọla's bedroom was so different from every other room in our house that it could have been imported wholly from a foreign land. For one thing, it was the only bedroom that had a carpet, a gift from her city-bred family when she married Papa. Even the smell was different from the rest of our house. While Mama's room smelled of food, Ejima's bedroom of piss, Papa's parlour of tobacco, and Ada's and my bedroom of… I don't know, Ọla's spacious bedroom delighted the nostrils with the heady fragrances of Charlie, scented soaps, and body creams.

But the best of all the furnishings inside Ọla's bedroom was the small bookshelf lined with an array of colourful books. The three-tiered shelf stood slightly taller than me and was painted a bright yellow colour that mimicked the oil-painted walls of the bedroom. Nobody I knew had as many books as my stepmother, not even my school teacher. The bookshelf laboured under the weight of the neatly arranged books that all seemed to have a common title—Mills & Boon. I had tried numerous times in the past to count the number of Mills & Boon titles on the bookshelf and always lost count when I reached sixty-three or seventy-two. Ọla had never allowed me to touch those precious books on the yellow shelf no matter how hard I begged.

"Those are big people's books, Bata," she would say with a laugh when I asked to read them. "Of course, there aren't any big people that can read in this house of illiterates, except me."

"I can read too," I would say, proud to share the same exclusive skill as my beautiful stepmother. My big sister Ada had never hidden her contempt for the written word and preferred learning the industrious art of dressmaking. Most days, she worked part-time in Papa's store when she wasn't learning how to sew dresses from the village seamstress. Ada hoped to open her own tailoring stall eventually.

"Ha! You can indeed read, my little mini-me." Ọla would laugh again, ruffling my hair affectionately. "But you're not an adult, are you? However, if you continue to learn everything that I teach you, as well as what you learn at school, then when you're a bit older, I'll make you a gift of all these books. How does that sound to you?"

It sounded just perfect to me, together with her pet-name for me. I loved being called Ọla's mini-me. It made me feel special and beautiful like my stepmother. I knew I was the daughter Ọla wished she had. We shared a girly bond which I never had with my mother, who preferred Ada's sensible company to my childish ramblings. I was always the first to admire my stepmother's latest fashion or hairdo, even before Papa. I hung onto Ọla's every word and tried hopelessly to imitate her deliberate speech, her swaying walk, her aloof smile, and her penchant for holding books. I hoped to one day own a transistor radio like hers too.

Ọla was secondary school educated, a rare attribute in our village womenfolk, who generally never went beyond primary school, if even that. Ada said Ọla only pretended to read the books to impress Papa and other gullible villagers she wanted to dazzle with her superior education. My big sister always told me off for imitating the phony habit and cuffed my ears each time she saw me with one of my Ladybird storybooks. But I didn't care;

Ada's sneers and fists did not douse my determination to become my stepmother's clone. Instead, I would carry the second-hand picture books Ọla always bought for me during her frequent shopping trips in the big city with her best friend, Teacher Uzo, ignoring Ada's scowls and Mama's amused looks. My mother's eyes always held a quizzical and humorous look whenever they rested on me, as if she were unsure of my origins.

"Okay, let's remove this dirty rag and turn you into a perfect princess," Ọla said with a little chortle, speaking to me in English. Hearing myself addressed in that precious, exclusive language filled my heart with warm gratitude, once again strengthening our special bond. I quivered in excitement as she tied her blue and silver voile material around me, weaving it around my thin body in a way that made it appear like a full dress. Then she put her sparkly trinkets on my ears, wrists, and neck, before decorating my corn-rowed hair with colourful ribbons and glittery hair clips.

"That's more like it," Ọla murmured with smug satisfaction, bringing me before her wide mirror. Looking at my reflection, I marvelled at this new girl I beheld. It was as if I had added three years to my age. My eyes shone brighter than I'd ever known them to, and my face seemed to radiate with a secret glow all of its own.

"See how beautiful you look now," Ọla said, adjusting my wrapper before spraying perfume on me from the Charlie bottle—*Oh, Mother Mary! I finally smell like a white person!* I was ready to go to paradise if St Peter had summoned me at that instant. "Anybody seeing you now will think you're my blood-daughter. That's why I call you my mini-me. I think we have to find you a new name instead of Bata. Let's see…" Ọla tapped the corner of her red lips with her equally red-tipped forefinger.

I waited in excitement, desperate to hear my new name. To be considered my stepmother's real daughter, by anyone, was the greatest compliment Ọla would've paid me. It wasn't that I loved her more than my mother—*Oh no! Never!* But I knew that even Mama would be the first to admit that Ọla was more beautiful than anyone else in the whole world.

"That's it; I think I have the perfect name for you." Ọla squealed, clasping her hands before her face. "We'll call you Amina, after the famous Nigerian queen. I studied Queen Amina's history at school, and I think it's a perfect name for you, our beautiful little warrior-princess. And remember you promised to be my sister's Bride-Sentinel, okay?"

I nodded enthusiastically this time. I was so happy with my new look that I would have done anything for my glamorous stepmother, even the detested Bride-Sentinel chore.

"Great! Now I won't worry anymore because I know my little Amina will take good care of us. And you mustn't forget to be Ada's Bride-Sentinel too when she gets married; that's assuming that rude girl ever finds a husband that'll tolerate her attitude, huh!" Ọla twisted her lips in derision.

Once again, I wished my big sister and my stepmother would be friends instead of the eternal antagonists they were. But they both seemed to thrive on their squabbles and got easily bored when either one was absent. If Ọla wasn't asking, "Where's Ada?" it would be my sister asking, "Where's that Pancake-Face disappeared to this time?" Then, as soon as they saw each other, they would welcome one another enthusiastically with hearty greetings and even occasional brief hugs before reverting to their bickering within minutes.

Mama praised me when Ọla finally brought me out of her room to show off her handiwork.

"What are my eyes seeing?" Mama's eyes widened as she turned me round and around for her inspection. "Is this my little Bata or a stranger, eh?" She turned to Ọla. "Our-Wife, you've outdone yourself this time." She hugged my stepmother gently before turning to Ada. "Look at your little sister. Isn't she beautiful?"

Ada nodded, hugging me close and whispering into my ear, "Don't let any idiot man propose marriage to you today, my beautiful little sis." She laughed and straightened up as I punched her playfully, faking a frown. My sister's words confirmed to me that I was indeed looking the best I'd ever looked in my life—*If only I didn't feel this weird tiredness.* Still, I couldn't wait to get to Keziah's wedding to show off this dazzling new me—*Keziah!*

The name brought back unwanted thoughts to my mind, dousing my happy mood with icy gloom—*I bet everybody now knows what I did last night. Will they stare at me funny or curse me or maybe thank me like Uncle Gabriel did? I hope nobody ever mentions that horrid name Anene Eze again or asks me to be their stupid Bride-Sentinel.*

"Look how beautiful your dresses are. My two daughters will be the envy of everybody at the wedding today." Mama wore a gentle smile as she linked her arms with Ada and me. In her green lace wrapper, matching headscarf, and shiny cheap jewellery, Ada looked almost as glamorous as my stepmother, if not as beautiful.

"And my three sons will be the bane of everybody's life today by the time they're done stuffing their faces." Ola eyed the triplets sourly, as if she weren't their mother. In many ways, she wasn't. The boys spent so much time with Mama that it wouldn't have surprised me if they one day confused her for their blood-mother.

Soon, we were all headed to my uncle Gabriel's compound to welcome Bongo, our rich in-law, who was coming from the big town to finally make my pregnant cousin, Keziah, his bride.

The scene I had dreaded unravelled in its most horrendous display as soon as we entered Uncle Gabriel's compound. I was instantly besieged by villagers, all screaming their pleas into my face, pulling me here and there, and inflicting bruises on my arms.

"Bata, you remember me; I'm your cousin Ikem's wife. Please, come and protect my daughter next month when she gets married."

"Bata, I have a beautiful dress already waiting for you in my house if you book my daughter for protection next week."

"Bata, it's me, your best friend Ngozi's mum. You know Ngozi's big sister is getting married in a few weeks' time. You won't let anything happen to your best friend's sister, will you?"

Over and over, they screamed their frenzied requests into my face till Ada lost it with them. My sister unleashed her notorious temper, shoving, punching, scratching, and even biting one persistent woman's hand till they all gave me room.

"My sister won't do a thing for you wretches unless you leave us in peace," Ada yelled, her eyes flashing fury. "We came here for our cousin's wedding, and by God, we'll enjoy this wedding without you idiots ruining it for us."

"That's our girl! Give it to them!" Ola cheered loudly, clapping and nodding approvingly at Ada, who smiled back at her in brief camaraderie.

"Ada! Watch your language before your elders," Mama admonished gently before taking my hand firmly in hers. "Come; let's go find a seat somewhere before the wedding starts," she said, pushing past the crowd.

Mama led us into Uncle Gabriel's house, sweeping past the chairs arranged under the canopies in the compound. The first people we saw as we entered the large living room was the famous white woman in our village, Engineer Tip-Toe's German wife and her almost-white son, born with the white people's pale skin and the black people's kinky hair. The great engineer had made the special journey from Lagos City to attend Keziah's traditional wedding. Usually, he only visited our village during the Christmas festivities to great fanfare. The villagers would gather at his large compound to be regaled with fantastical stories of Germany and Lagos City by the flamboyant engineer, decked out in flowing Babariga and Agbada attires, which he twinned with his blonde-haired German wife. The sight of the tall, white woman garbed in our native fashion never ceased to amaze, fascinate, entertain, and please our villagers.

On several occasions in the past, Ọla had taken me along to Engineer Tip-Toe's compound, and together with the other village women, we would stare in awe at his white wife as she breastfed her almost-white son who was already walking and talking. I reckoned the boy was almost the same age as the triplets, four years old at the very least. Yet his mother would breastfeed him shamelessly before the gawping villagers.

"Ancestors have mercy!" the women would repeat over and over, shaking their heads in bafflement. "Whoever heard of a talking-walking child still getting breastfed? Hey, Oyibo white woman, why don't you have another child for your husband if you're so desperate to breastfeed babies, eh?" they would shout out with humorous mischief.

The German woman would smile coolly back at them, not understanding a word they said. Later, she and her husband would take another one of their infamous walks around the village as the villagers lined the paths to watch them in perplexity.

"There they go again, walking aimlessly with no destination in mind." The men would shake their heads with disdainful bewilderment. "That's what happens when a man marries a white woman and loses his senses and his balance. Whoever heard of a person taking a walk without a destination or purpose? It's not as if they're visiting relatives or going to the market or the farms. Engineer Tip-Toe says it's something called 'Exercise' that he learnt in the white man's land while studying there, together with that crazy walk of his."

Like the other villagers, I used to follow behind the odd couple and their almost-white son whenever they took their infamous evening walks across the village, marvelling at Engineer Tip-Toe's peculiar gait. The famous engineer didn't walk in a flat-footed and balanced fashion like other normal men did. Instead, he lunged forward on the tips of his toes as if ready to start a race at the blow of a whistle. Engineer Tip-Toe called his unique gait 'The German Success Walk'. He said that was how the German people walked, on the tips of their toes in a brisk and purposeful manner, unlike the calm and leisurely steadiness of our people's pace. Apparently, The German Success Walk had led those lucky citizens to spectacular success and world-wide dominance, resulting in the creation of the Mercedes-Benz car, which was the ultimate brag of success in our society. Engineer Tip-Toe and Chief Omenga were the only people lucky enough to own the German status car in the ten villages comprising our community.

Many of the children in my school practised that famous walk and a lucky few, mostly the boys, were already masters at it. They tilted so forward when they walked that it was a miracle they managed to hold onto their balance. I too tried walking like the great engineer to acquire the special German walk, but Ada had smacked my head and warned me never to try out 'that lunatic-walk' as she called it. The next time I attempted the walk in the secret of our back garden, I fell flat on my face and bruised my knees. I decided then that my big sister might have a point after all. The German Success Walk was indeed a lunatic-walk on the legs of a small, village girl like myself, who had never seen the marvellous shores of that great city of Germany. I figured it was a special walk best left to the boys.

Engineer Tip-Toe's wife was once again dressed in our traditional Bubu kaftan and her scarf was so high I wondered how she managed to stop it from toppling from her blonde head. She smiled warmly at us and she and my stepmother soon started chatting in English. The curious villagers lurking outside the open doors and windows gawped at my stepmother's proficiency in the white people's language and once again, my pride in my stepmother was great. Seeing Ọla and Engineer Tip-Toe's wife chatting together made me more determined to become educated like her—*If only this horrible Bride-Sentinel thing will let me.*

Just then, my cousin Keziah entered the living room with a crowd of women. She saw me and shouted my name with enthusiastic joy as she waddled over to me. She hugged me so tightly that her pregnant tummy almost squashed my face. In all my life, I'd never been hugged by my big cousin, and I found myself overwhelmed by intense shyness.

"My wonderful little cousin!" Keziah held me away, tears trailing down her plump cheeks. "I never knew just how much you loved me till last night. How can I ever thank you? Who would've ever thought that something so little like you could be so powerful? You're truly the little cooking pot that put out the great fire!" She pulled me back into her arms for another suffocating hug. "Listen; after my traditional wedding today, you must come to the big city and spend your holidays with us. I'm determined to spoil you the way you deserve to be spoiled, you wonderful child."

Keziah's mother also rushed up to me and enfolded me in her arms. To my surprise, Mama dragged me away from her, eyeing her bitterly.

"Ha! Now you want to thank my child for saving your daughter," Mama sneered. "Who was it that called her a cursed child last night, eh? If my memory recalls, you called Bata my cursed daughter."

Keziah's mother looked shame-faced, lowering her gaze and giving a pained smile. She wrung her hands frantically like one washing off dirt. "Mama-Ada, it was the devil speaking through my mouth last night," she pleaded. "All of us were terrified when we saw the child turn into a ghost, her skin, hair, and eyes, all white. Can you blame us? Nobody knew then what we now know: that she has been blessed by the ancestors. Forgive your fellow clans-wife, please. Let me thank this wonderful child properly for saving my Keziah's life."

Mama finally relented and allowed Keziah's mother to hug me and heap blessings on my head. I received the praises with my familiar shyness and an unfamiliar pride. I'd never been one to have any attributes to make me or anybody else proud. All I was good at was singing Jesus songs or playing with Ejima and my cousins, as well as dreaming nightmares. That was all. This new attention was birthing a strange emotion inside my heart, one that made me want to hide and preen simultaneously—*Is this how Mama-Ejima feels when everyone praises her beauty?*

By the time the rich in-laws arrived, led by the flamboyantly garbed groom, Bongo, I had eaten enough assorted meats and eggs to fill up a king's plate. When I was first presented with the meat dish by Keziah's mother, a sudden thought had darkened my mood as I stared at the lumps of fried meats on my tin-plate—*I wonder if any of the meat on this plate is the poor black horse's meat?* I shuddered, feeling both guilt and repulsion. But for my actions, the black horse wouldn't have died such a horrible death— *What if its flesh is still tainted with the evil-essence of the Ghost-Bride?* At the thought, another involuntary shudder quaked my body. I wanted to ask if the horse meat was included on my plate, but I was too afraid. One could never tell what might trigger an adult's temper. Instead, I carefully picked out the meats that seemed familiar, mostly the chicken wings, cow muscles, and goat lungs, together with the boiled eggs. As I wolfed them down with an insatiable greed that rivalled Ejima's, I prayed desperately that I hadn't accidentally eaten a piece of the black horse. After everything that happened yesterday, I no longer wanted to taste horse meat—*Never, ever, forever, in Jesus's name, Amen!*

7

Later that evening, after the festivities ended in Uncle Gabriel's compound, Papa took me to Dibia's shrine for the purification ritual. I was grateful the medicine-man's house wasn't far from our house. The wedding had tired me more than I realised. Every step I took felt as if I logged a cow on my back. My head throbbed and my body shivered violently like one suffering from malaria.

"You didn't mention our visit to Dibia's shrine to your mother as I told you, did you?" Papa said, walking in front of me. "You know how she fusses over Father David and her church, so it's better to keep her in the dark about this."

I mumbled a reply, too tired to even talk. Papa must have heard something in my voice because he paused and turned around.

"Are you alright?" he asked, his voice laced with concern. Then his eyes widened in panic as he saw the heavy sweat pouring down my face. "Oh, my ancestors! Why didn't you tell me you're not feeling well?" Papa quickly scooped me up in his arms, holding me close.

His actions brought hot tears to my eyes. To be held in Papa's arms was a wonder I'd never experienced. At the same time, I felt so ill that I was convinced I was dying.

"It's alright, my daughter." Papa's voice was breathless as he sprinted towards Dibia's shrine like someone fleeing a lion's claws. "I'll get you to Dibia's house soon. I knew you shouldn't have attended that wedding. Good ancestors, please keep this child alive!"

Dibia rushed out of his house as soon as Papa shouted his name. He quickly guided us into his mud-shrine and stretched me out on his mat. He hurriedly assembled his divination tools, chanting invocations with hushed urgency. In seconds I felt my body smeared with warm liquids. I was too sick to open my eyes and look, but my nose smelled the distinctive cloying odour of chicken blood. I lay on the mat shivering uncontrollably, my teeth chattering. My breath was as hot as a sizzling stew pot, and I kept sliding in and out of consciousness. Soon, my eyes started to see things that had no business being inside the room.

A dense cluster of white cloud surrounded me. In an instant, I was swallowed in a whirling hurricane that resembled a kaleidoscope of white butterflies. Their delicate touch was icy to my skin, and my body shivered and trembled like one soaked in a pool of ice. In their birring multitude, I felt a deluge of tiny creatures darting at my body, buzzing and whining against my ears.

Except the sounds I heard were not the normal buzz of insect-life. It was a cacophony of ghastly voices from the coldest, dead realms. They babbled a torrent of frenzied words and manic messages into my head till I feared I would drown in a pool of naked insanity.

"Amadioha, save my soul!" Dibia screamed, stumbling away from me. His face looked ashen, and terror boggled his eyes. He stared at me as if I had morphed into a ten-headed ghost. "Okeke, why did you wait this long to bring the child over? Her body has now become the congregation place for restless ghosts. See how they swarm around her in their multitudes, draining her life force!" I heard Dibia's voice, but it seemed to be a long way away.

"Weren't you the one that told me she was protected, that nothing would happen to her?" Papa's raised voice was accusing. I could hear the fear fuelling his anger and his face was taut with tension.

"Yes, but I also told you that she carried the ghost residues from yesterday. Now, she has become a magnet for Ghost-Brides. They cling to her in great numbers, each of them determined to give her messages for their loved ones. Her body is too young and weak to endure their essence, and now, I fear they've drained her energy so much that it might be too late to save her."

I heard Papa's loud gasp, but I paid him no heed. Because for the first time, I was seeing the butterflies in their true forms— *Oh, Mother Mary! Oh, Mother Mary!* Where there should have been butterfly heads attached to the delicate white wings, my eyes beheld human heads instead, tiny heads draped in long white veils that floated gently behind them in their frantic flight. Their faces sent shudders to my body, chalk-white faces with the brightest silver-grey eyes and reddest lips. The mini-spectres dived low, screeching into my face and my ears. Some of them bared their sharp little teeth, biting, nipping, and gnawing my flesh in their unholy rage. Others wailed pathetically, plastering themselves against my skin, my hair, and even my face like sticky glue. I tried to swat them with my hands, but my strength was gone, stolen by their terrible and icy touch. I could only moan, my voice too feeble to be heard amidst their ruckus.

And now, my attention was no longer focused on the pesky sprites that swarmed around me. A greater terror materialised inside the shrine, sending dizzying waves to my head. I stared with horror and awe at the entity standing menacingly behind Papa, a towering female-like spectre whose body gleamed an oily black colour that rivalled the blackest night.

From her thick, braided hair to her bare feet, multiple thin lines of white paint streaked across her imposing height like a human zebra. She stood taller than Agu, the tallest man in our village. And just like a man, a long bush of hair flowed down her chin and below her exposed breasts in the longest beard I've ever seen. Her body was covered in multiple rings of the brightest ivory, and on her ankles and arms, she wore heavy ivory bands similar to those worn by the ruling class of Ọzọ peers. Several chains of Jigida, cowrie beads, were wrapped around her waist, and a strange necklace wrought from human teeth hung heavy around her neck. Numerous inscriptions covered her large breasts, tattooed in strange Nsibidi symbols I couldn't decipher. Next to her, my father, normally a very tall and big man, appeared no larger than a puny adolescent.

But it was her face that frightened me into quaking terror. My body shuddered in violent spasms as I stared at her multiple faces from underneath laboured lids. Like a cascading oily waterfall, different ghastly faces rotated on her head with dizzying speed— black faces, bloodied faces, white faces, red faces, skeletal faces, painted faces, tattooed faces, wrinkled faces, and even golden and silvery faces. Every frightening emotion known to humankind was painted on the myriad of terrifying faces spinning in bone-chilling rotation—rage, menace, hatred, anguish, even death. They continued to drop in a shimmering collage of terror, one petrifying face after another, till my heart almost exploded from the nightmarish vision—*Oh, Mother Mary, save me! Papa, help me!*

The faces froze their spin till only one fierce, black face stared down at me—a four-eyed female face. She fixed her quadruple black eyes at me, and my blood curdled in my veins.

I screamed.

Or at least, I made a sound that should have been a scream, but instead came out as a quivering whine. I prayed for blindness, for sudden sleep, or a fainting spell; anything to free me from the horror before my eyes. My body trembled violently as I stared with hypnotised terror into her eyes, the four black bulbs devoid of light. No matter what new face she wore, four terrible, dead eyes gazed down at me with the cold hardness of a lifeless statue, sending more shivers to my quaking body.

Then, her eyes dropped back into their dark sockets. In a wink, a plume of thick smoke poured out of the cavernous hollows where her eyes should have been, instantly fogging up the shrine—*Oh, Holy Mother! What is happening? Is it my imagination or is the shrine growing?* Before my stunned eyes, the shrine stretched so high that the thatched roofing seemed as tall as an Iroko tree. The mammoth spirit-woman was stretching too, soon reaching almost to the roof of the impossibly high shrine.

Papa started coughing, choking and gasping, overcome by the dense fumes. Despite my rapidly fading consciousness, I retained a faint awareness of my surroundings. I noticed Dibia looking briefly at Papa before quickly turning his attention back to me. Even though, like me, he wasn't affected by the smoke, I saw something in his eyes, a frenzied furtiveness that told me he too had seen the terrifying, mammoth phantom hulking behind my father. Papa was the only one blind to the ghastly presence inside the shrine.

"Okeke, you'd better leave this place at once if you want to live," Dibia said quietly to Papa, keeping his face averted from the chilling apparition.

"Akuabata... my child... I can't leave her." Papa stumbled towards me, overwhelmed by the hacking cough that stole his breath. His teeth rattled from the sudden intense chill inside the hut.

Dibia quickly waved him away. "Bata will be fine. Allow us to get on with this supernatural battle. Leave the shrine now before they do you more harm."

With a desperate glance at me, Papa stumbled outside into the fresh evening breeze. I heard him gasping and coughing, but it didn't sound as bad as it had been within the smoky hut. In my debilitated state, I marvelled at the fact that I wasn't choking from the fumes; I, who was always the first to run away from the kitchen when Ọla burnt yet another stew pot. The slightest smoke caused my eyes to weep and my nose to run. Yet, here inside the shrine, I exhibited no reaction to the smoke-attack by the multi-faced spirit.

"Child, can you hear me?" Dibia whispered urgently into my ear. I wanted to answer, but I was too sick to speak or even nod. I raised my right fingers weakly. "Good. Now, I want you to answer me truthfully. Can you see anyone inside this shrine with us? And I'm not talking about these troublesome spirits clinging to you."

Again, I raised my fingers. Dibia grunted grimly. "Do you recognise it as a Ghost-Bride?" he asked. I wasn't sure how to answer in the negative and opted for silence instead. "Raise your right hand for yes, and your left hand for no," Dibia instructed.

I raised my left hand. "Not a Ghost-Bride? Good. So, do you know this new ghost then?" Dibia persisted. I was about to answer when I saw the mammoth ghost glide towards me. In a blink, its great height hulked over us, sending sudden shivers to my body.

I shrank deeper into the mat, making pathetic whines that sounded like an irritable infant fighting sleep. Dibia turned his head to look and his eyes suddenly widened. In that instant, I knew he no longer needed an answer from me. He now faced the terror I beheld.

Teeth chattering, I squeezed my eyes tightly, shutting out the ghastly vision above me. The cacophony from my unwanted spectral companions was stealing my senses, and I felt my heart wilting, melting, dying…

"Eze-Nwanyi Mmuọ, king-woman-spirit, this lowly servant salutes you, even as he dares to ask what you seek in our human realm?" I heard Dibia's voice from a foggy distance. The medicine-man spoke in a trembling whisper, tempered with great respect.

"Do you know my name?" I heard the spirit ask. Its multiple voices sounded like thunder, rumbling and terrible. Had I been alone in the shrine, I know I would've surely died. But Dibia's presence imbued my dying soul with courage—*Uncle Dibia is a powerful medicine-man. Surely he'll know how to vanquish all these horrible ghosts.*

"How can a mere mortal like me know the sacred name of a great spirit such as yourself?" Dibia murmured again in the unfamiliar trembling voice that filled me with fresh terror—*If our powerful medicine-man is terrified of this ghost, who can save me from its malice then? Oh my bad luck! I'm doomed!*

"I am Mmuọ-Ka-Mmuọ, the ghost-collector of the spirit realm. I am she that keeps the ghosts of the ghosts. I am the guardian of the Ghost-Brides and the keeper of their gate."

"K-keeper of the ghosts of gh-ghosts?" Dibia stammered, his voice fear-hushed. "But how can ghosts have ghosts, great spirit?"

I heard the booming laughter of the spectre from its impossible height. "Do you think only humans yield ghosts when they die? Of course ghosts have their own ghosts too. There are endless layers in every living soul which can never be explored or comprehended in their mysterious totality. But that's not my concern right now. Do you know why I am here?"

I forced my eyes open on hearing its words, an effort that took the last of my dying strength. Through the narrow slits of my eyelids, I saw Dibia prostrated before the spirit, bowing his head over and over in humble obeisance before its striped feet.

"How can a mere mortal such as I dare to guess the will of a great spirit such as yourself?" Dibia whispered his familiar mantra, still knocking his forehead on the ground. I could tell that even the great medicine-man feared to look the mammoth spectre in its myriad of cascading faces.

"When the locusts fly, the plants quake beneath their dark shadow. They know their days are numbered, soon to be annihilated by the flying devastation above. Yet, the plants with seeds and those with deep roots are stoic under siege. They know they will rise again," the bearded spirit said, hovering over me.

But its close proximity didn't matter anymore. My terror had vanished. What remained was a pain beyond anything I had ever endured, a soul-pain that was slowly squeezing the life from my heart. Tears rolled down the sides of my face—*I'm dying... Mama, I'm dying; your daughter is dying. I'm so afraid... Hail Mary, full of grace... Papa, please save me... Papa... Mama...*

"Sometimes, the plants need humans to save their seeds for them before the marauding locusts arrive." The spirit's voice sounded so close that my ears vibrated from its rumble. "Today, I am the seed-collector. I have come to collect this child's ghost that she may live to rise another day. As long as she remains a Bride-Sentinel, the restless dead will give her no peace. She will remain a magnet to them, and they will eventually drain her life force. To save her from harm, she too must become a ghost. Only then will they leave her in peace. Therefore, I must take her spirit to our world so that she can acquire the ghost-essence that will shield her from future attacks from spirit entities. Have no fear; the child will not die. She has a great destiny to fulfil, after all. I shall return her spirit once she is successfully inducted into ghost-hood. Now move aside, good seer, that my job may be done without harm to yourself."

The great spirit's voice faded into a distant place that I could not reach. If it spoke other words, I did not hear them because, suddenly, I was remembering, seeing everything that took place at Uncle Gabriel's house in its terrifying ghastliness—*Anene Eze! How could I forget? Oh, Mother Mary, save my doomed soul!*

And in that instant, I died.

8

I looked down and saw my dead body lying on the thin raffia mat inside Dibia's shrine. I was hovering close to the high ceiling of the unnaturally tall hut, trying desperately to maintain my precarious balance. Terror almost froze my limbs into icy logs—*Oh no, no, no! I've gone and died after all! I'm dead... a ghost! Oh please, somebody get me down from here! I don't want to fly. Papa! Mama!*

I was crying. My shoulders shook with the force of my sobs, yet no tears fell from my eyes. Below me, I saw the bearded ghost catching and trapping the swarm of tiny Ghost-Brides that had drained the life from my body.

"Come here, you little wretches," she cursed in that multiplicity of rumbling voices that sent shuddering chills over my body. "Did you truly think you could escape me so easily? Now, see what you've gone and done. You've killed this innocent child in your foolish greed. Now you'll all have to answer to me. Get ready to face my wrath once I get you back to our realm."

As she spoke, the necklace of human teeth came to sudden, terrifying life. They clicked and rattled menacingly, as if ready to devour the tiny spirits. The rattling teeth cowered the fluttering ghosts, freezing their frantic flight. They hurdled beside my dead body in a quivering mass of white cloud.

The white lines streaked across the spirit's mammoth body began to sizzle and glow like electric rods, turning her flesh into a powerful magnet. In a blink, the cowering little ghosts were rapidly pulled into the blazing stripes by an invisible and powerful force. I heard their screeches and howls as they tried desperately to escape being captured.

All in vain.

The invisible magnet dragged them irrevocably against the hulking spirit. Her white zebra-streaks glowed fiercer and brighter till the truant ghosts were all reined in. Soon, her powerful body became a collage of shrieking, white butterflies. The Ghost-Brides wailed so pitifully that even I became sorry for them.

"Shut up, you little whingers!" the bearded spirit thundered, sending terror into my heart once again. The caterwauling Ghost-Brides instantly fell into shocked silence. "That's better. I'll have no more of your mischiefs. We'll save all that till we get home, and then, by the ancestors, I'll give you all enough reasons to regret this little jaunt you took today, trust me."

She raised her head and fixed her four terrible eyes on me—*Oh, Mother Mary! Oh, Mother Mary!* I surged upwards in a desperate flight, trying to get away, to fly higher and higher till I crashed through the thatched roofing and escaped into Papa's safe arms outside the shrine. But the more I tried, the lower I tumbled.

"Uncle Dibia! Uncle Dibia!" I was screaming with everything in me. "Save me! Please, save me! Call Papa; tell him to come and take me home immediately. I don't want to die! I don't want to be a ghost anymore. Oh please, Uncle Dibia, save me! Do something!" Dibia wasn't my blood-uncle, but like every well-bred village child, I called my elders by the respectful terms of 'Uncle' and 'Auntie'.

The medicine-man was deaf to my desperate screams. He remained in his prostrated position before the bearded spirit, who continued to look at me with those four terrifying, dead eyes.

"Don't be afraid, child," the mammoth ghost said, holding out two mighty arms to me. "I shall do you no harm. Come; we have a long journey to make. Don't worry about your body. It will be alright. I'll soon bring you back to it when we're done." Again, she beckoned me over.

Like the entrapped Ghost-Brides, I too flew helplessly into her magnet arms. A strong smell of burning wood and smoke filled my nostrils, reminding me of corncobs roasting under open fires during our Tales by Moonlight sessions in our compound. A hard knot formed behind my throat as she set me down gently beside her, before enfolding my hand in her large palm. Briefly, I wondered why I hadn't shrunk into a butterfly like the rest of the Ghost-Brides, but my attention was soon drawn back to my dead body stretched out on the mat. I looked as if I was sleeping, and save for a strange ashy colour to my skin, I would have struggled to accept my prone body was a dead one.

"G-great spirit," Dibia stuttered, raising his head briefly. I looked directly into his eyes, but he was blind to me. "How long will you keep the child's spirit with you? When will life return to her body?"

The spirit looked at me and then at my corpse. "She will spend thirty nights in our realm, which is how long it will take her to acclimatise to ghost-hood. In your realm, time passes more slowly, and only two hours would have gone by the time she returns to her body once again." In my distress, I wasn't sure if I heard thirty days or thirty years. Either way, it didn't matter. I was now dead and going to the land of the dead, never again to see my family and my human world.

Mmuọ-Ka-Mmuọ turned back to me. "Shut your eyes, child," she said in a voice that had more kindness than I had so far heard. "It's better that way. We don't want to frighten you with sights you have no business seeing during our spirit-journey."

I shut my eyes—*Oh, Mother Mary! Oh, Mother Mary! Oh...*

A terrifying sound filled my head: the thunder of a hurricane and fury of a cyclone. In a blink, I was lifted off my feet by a powerful whirlwind that pulled me faster and higher into a cloudy world devoid of life and light. I was screaming, gripping tight to my guide's hands with the strength of a hundred warriors. My body weighed the same as a hundred corpses and I feared I would drop from the great height and crash to the ground.

"Be calm, child." I heard her voice inside my head, away from the rage and fury of the whirlwind. "Shut your eyes and hold my hand. I will keep you safe. No harm will come to you. I am Mmuọ-Ka-Mmuọ, the ghost-collector of the spirit realm, she that keeps the ghosts of the ghosts. No spirit in my care will come to harm. Rest your soul now. Be still and become what you now are."

And in a wink, my terror died. A sudden calm descended in my heart—*I am with Mmuọ-Ka-Mmuọ, the ghost-collector of the spirit realm, she that keeps the ghosts of the ghosts. Nothing can harm me.*

With that thought, stillness fell. The winds suddenly died, and my body became a feather, light and free, just like the true ghost I now was. I inhaled deeply, again and again, holding tight to my guide's hand—*Please, Mother Mary! Keep me safe!*

Our journey seemed to be over in a blink. Before I could gather my senses, I felt my feet on solid ground. I opened my eyes to an unfamiliar world beyond the realms of humankind, a foggy terrain of dazzling whiteness, swirling with smoky air of great density. A loud shout escaped my lips, and I shrank deeper against my guide, forgetting my initial terror of her mighty form. Even as I looked, I saw the glowing light of her white stripes wink out one after the other, releasing the trapped Ghost-Brides from her body.

Instantly, they fluttered away, their voices shrill with frustration. Before my stunned gaze, they stretched into their normal heights and sizes, full-sized young women now shrouded in a brilliant array of the most dazzling colours. They glowed brightly in the thick fog of their white world, gliding in spectacular glory, their flight the pride of the peacocks, a rainbow of glorious colours, instead of the terrifying whiteness of the Ghost-Brides in my nightmares.

"Have no fear, child," Mmuọ-Ka-Mmuọ said again in her thunderous voices. "You have now entered our realm, *Ibaja-La*, the place where the dead brides gather. This is the sanctuary for grieving brides who died tragically before they could exchange vows with their beloved grooms. We welcome every bride here, save the ones in arranged and loveless marriages. Those ones are obviously not grieving the loss of their grooms, who were not their twin-flames. As you can see, there are brides of every colour, nationality, and race here. Regardless of where they died, this realm is their final destination, a solace for their broken hearts. It's a holding bay for them pending their release. Mind you, some of them never get released. You'll soon learn more about those unfortunate ones later. We also have the brides whose evils keep them trapped here for eternity. You won't find them in this section of our realm. Those are the ones you will fight and vanquish as a Bride-Sentinel, just as you did with the accursed one, Anene Eze, last night, even though then, your body was a conduit for another powerful entity."

Mmuọ-Ka-Mmuọ paused, but I wasn't listening to her anymore. Terror quaked my body and my legs buckled. Had I not been gripping tight to Mmuọ-Ka-Mmuọ's hand, I would have surely collapsed on the white floor. Instead, I pressed myself tighter against her mammoth frame, staring at the horde of angry Ghost-Brides now crowding around us with icy menace. This time, they made no sound, and an eerie silence hung over the foggy realm.

I saw some of them in the traditional white Akwete wraps and heavy carnelian beads of the Nigerian-Edo brides. Others

wore wonderful attires whose names I was later to discover—
magnificent Korean hanboks, striking Japanese kimonos, vibrant
Mexican chiapanecas, colourful Indian saris, and stunning red
and gold Chinese cheongsams. I also noticed numerous black,
white, and brown-skinned Ghost-Brides gliding in a haze of white,
their long lace gowns and flowing veils whirling around them like
angel wings. Never in my life had I seen such an exotic collection
of brides, not even on Papa's television set. Yet, in their many
differences, they all shared the same eyes, sparkling eyes of the
palest silver-grey, eyes that now glared at me with unbridled rage.

The sight stunned me into awed terror. Save for the ghastly
paleness of their dead faces and uniform silver-grey eyes, I would
have thought them the most beautiful and wonderous beings
in Jesus's world. But instead, I shrank away from the rage and
hatred oozing from their icy pupils, trembling against Mmuọ-
Ka-Mmuọ's powerful frame.

"It's alright, child," the great guardian said, looking down at
me with a grim smile. "They know you're the Bride-Sentinel, and
so they see you as the enemy who would keep them away from
their beloved grooms. That's why they attacked you so viciously
when they escaped. Give me a second while I wipe away their
memories of you."

Mmuọ-Ka-Mmuọ spoke some words which refused to let my
ears catch them. I saw her lips move, but for some inexplicable
reason, my hearing went dead in that instant. The gathered Ghost-
Brides must have heard her words though, for the menace in
their bodies vanished. I saw their silvery eyes return to a uniform
haunting sadness, while their interest in me instantly waned. Now
they observed me with a kind of apathetic curiosity that birthed a
new emotion in my heart—*Oh the poor, poor women!*

Intense pity and compassion for them overwhelmed me. The
feeling was the same kind of emotion I felt whenever Ejima hurt

themselves or some village kids said mean things to them. Even though the dead brides were all bigger than me, all I wanted to do was to hug them and coo softly into their ears in the same voice Mama used whenever I was frightened or sick with the fever. There was a pathetic vulnerability about them that brought a tight knot to the back of my throat, and it took everything in me to halt the tears brewing inside me. In that minute, their pain was my pain, their loss mine also to share—*Poor, sad brides! It's a good thing none of them showed up at Keziah's door. I would've happily let them all in, the poor things. Holy Mother, please give them back their grooms so they can be happy again!*

"I see we have some new faces here," Mmuọ-Ka-Mmuọ said, as my hearing returned. "Jeong-from-Gwangju, Emma-from-Quebec, Aaliyah-from-Dubai, and Guadalupe-from-Mexico, I welcome you beautiful brides to *Ibaja-La*. I pray your journey was smooth, and your sister-brides have made you welcome. Have no worries. You're now in a safe realm where no harm can touch you ever again. The minute your grooms are ready to let go and remarry, you'll all get your chances to finally become wedded brides and fulfil your destinies and dreams. After that, you will freely transition for your new reincarnations. In the meantime, make yourselves at home, and call my name if you have any problems."

The one called Jeong-from-Gwangju started sobbing gently and Mmuọ-Ka-Mmuọ gave her a look filled with pity. For a split second, her four stony eyes seemed to melt into soft, malleable orbs.

"Jeong-from-Gwangju, it is good you cry," she said, nodding her massive head. "Cry for your groom and yourself, so that the poison will leave your soul. I know you won't become a real bride ever again since your groom is also dead. But you'll find you're not the only one of your kind here. There are other brides like you who also committed suicide when they lost their grooms or tragically died together with their grooms. I'm glad to say that they've all settled well here. They will help you adapt soon. I know you'll quickly learn to love your new world, just as they do."

Mmuọ-Ka-Mmuọ turned to me again. "Child, you must now go and acquaint yourself with the rest of the brides. Have no fear; nobody will harm you. They don't know who you are anymore. Listen to them, open yourself to them, and learn their ways. Recognise each and every one of them. Know their voices, their faces, their scents, and their hearts, so that you can identify them even in your sleep. All the Ghost-Brides here are harmless; they're just grieving. The same can't be said for the ones at The Wastelands. They're the ones I mentioned, whose evils entrap them here for eternity. I think you already met those fiends in your dreams. I'll tutor you on them at a later time. But for now, follow your guide, Madison-from-Texas, and whatever you do, never, ever let them know that you are a Bride-Sentinel, are we clear?" I nodded fervently—*Never, ever, ever.*

"Good; off you go now. We'll meet again soon." Mmuọ-Ka-Mmuọ placed my hand into the outstretched hand of the beautiful African American Ghost-Bride, Madison-from-Texas. I turned to thank her but found myself staring slack-jawed at an empty space next to me.

Mmuọ-Ka-Mmuọ had vanished, just like a ghost. Madison-from-Texas was gliding away with me by her side. And I was flying, just like the rest of the Ghost-Brides around us—*Oh wow! What miracle is this?* I observed my flight with wide-mouthed wonder as I glided smoothly beside my new guide. Madison-from-Texas's sequined and beaded long wedding gown flowed behind her like the whitest angel wings, and the ashy hue on her brown face failed to ruin its translucent beauty.

"Come, honey," she said to me with a sad smile. "Come and tell me how a little child like you ended up among us dead brides, when you should be playing in your school playground or visiting Disneyland with your Momma and Poppa."

Her words brought home to me the reality of my plight. I started wailing. My body shook with the force of my sobs, and my voice was as sad and desperate as the rest of the Ghost-Brides. Once again, no matter how hard I cried, no tears dampened my face—*Mama... Papa... I don't want to die! I want to come home. Please, Jesus, make me alive again like Lazarus. Mama... Mama...*

9

Soon after Mmuọ-Ka-Mmuọ vanished, Madison-from-Texas guided me through a tall white gate that opened into the most wonderous place ever created by Jehovah God and His son, Jesus—*Surely, only God could have created such a dazzling world of stupendous beauty*. I found myself in a vast, silvery universe that seemed to spread and stretch into eternity. Gone was the dense foggy world beyond the high gates. Instead, everything here, from the trees to the birds, the sky to the soil, was a dazzling silvery hue that was both breathtaking and eerily terrifying.

I stared around me in awe, tiny ripples of bliss layering my skin in goosebumps. Everywhere I looked was a paradise of balloons, ribbons, confetti, twinkling lights, floral wreaths and bouquets, all glittering in the ubiquitous silver colour. There were multi-tiered cakes of all sizes, colours, and designs, adorned with tiny bride and groom figurines in sparkling crystals. Tea pillows, red envelopes, bowls of gold coins, sparkling jewellery, silver-labelled gourdes, jars, and bottles of palm wine, sake, Wayalinah, baijiu, beer, and every variety of wine layered the landscape. Other equally mesmerising ornaments in vibrant gold, red, and green colours were also on dazzling display. I was witnessing a stupendous, never-ending wedding banquet that was destined to last for eternity. The sight brought a tight knot to my throat—*I'll never get to attend Cousin Keziah's church wedding or become her flower-girl after all.*

From a distant part of the realm, I heard heady African drumming, harmonic singing, and wild clapping. Gradually, the muted strains of music from musicians across every culture took rotating turns to fill the festive air—Bob Marley, Mozart, Lata Mangeshkar, Teresa Teng, Fela, Carlos Santana, Umm Kulthum, Miriam Makeba, Hiroshi Kamayatsu, and Yao Lee. The list was endless. Save for the Jackson 5, Fela, and Miriam Makeba, I didn't know who the other singers were at the time or so many other strange mysteries and cultures I came across in *Ibaja-La*. All that knowledge came to me later. And as I listened to the haunting strains of the wonderful melodies I heard over the cool air of this incredible world, I knew in that instant that the music would never die. Their serene yet joyful refrains would charm and soothe the tragic citizens of this silvery realm for eternity.

My stunned gaze noticed numerous massive round tables spread across the vast realm. Countless crystal-studded chairs with elaborate carvings surrounded the tables. Each table was almost the size of a small village, and like everything else in this fantastical realm, they floated and rotated in a gentle motion that was both soothing and hypnotic. Under the bright lights, the tables and chairs shimmered a dazzling silver hue. There were rich wines and sumptuous cuisines from every part of the world atop each table, and I noticed countless wrapped gifts piled all around the vicinity. Tinkly, flowing fountains and fluttering white doves added to the heady extravagance of the bridal utopia, and the air smelled of heady scents and tasty foods.

I felt my body tremble with sudden hunger. I wanted to throw myself at the cakes and meats. I could literally taste them in my mouth. The gift boxes and parcels beckoned me to unwrap them and discover their exciting secrets—*How can they ignore all these foods and gifts? I wish I could take some of them back to Ejima!* At the thought of my three half-brothers, despair overwhelmed me afresh—*What's the use? I'm now a dead person. I'll probably never see any of them again.* This time, I allowed the tears to brew unchecked, though they failed to fall from my eyes or dampen my cheeks.

Through the misty lenses of my misery, I noticed that each vast round table was occupied by Ghost-Brides of various civilisations. Madison-from-Texas told me their tribes, from Native American to Australian Aborigine brides, Eskimo to Amazigh brides, amongst many other new ethnicities I had never heard about in our village. I was amazed to see that the brides sat on chairs that floated, just like the tables and the Ghost-Brides themselves. A round silver table hosted some African Ghost-Brides in their colourful traditional wedding Ashoke gowns, while another hosted several Japanese shiromuku-clad Ghost-Brides in their silent anguish. Further down, a colourful table groaned under dishes from India and sari-covered Ghost-Brides, while another table hosted European Ghost-Brides in their white gowns and veils. The huge quantities of foods and drinks went mostly untouched, and the exquisitely decorated tables and chairs hosted Ghost-Brides who wept rather than ate.

As my gaze settled on the European Table, I saw a sight that caused my jaw to drop. Two male brides, complete with beards and veils, glided amongst the other Ghost-Brides. Their faces wore the same apathetic, sorrowful glaze, while their equally silvery eyes observed their surroundings with languid disinterest. I noticed that even their nails and lips were painted a bright red, just like a woman's might be.

"Wh-why are those men dressed like brides?" I stammered out the question without thinking, pointing at them as I spoke.

"Because they're brides too." Madison-from-Texas smiled as she took in my shocked expression. "You mustn't point at people, honey. It's rude and we don't wanna make anyone here sad, do we?"

I shook my head in mortification and Madison-from-Texas smiled again as she ruffled my hair gently, her eyes filled with the compassion reserved for a child shivering with the malaria fever.

"You poor baby! Reckon you never heard about the homosexuals in your little African village? Well, I ain't gonna shock your littl' ears, honey. Let's just say that in some countries far, far away from your village, some men can become brides, not legally, mind you. But they can have themselves a kinda marriage ceremony with their husbands, just like us. There ain't many of them that have done so, but Mark-from-London and Paul-from-Frisco are brides like every other bride here."

I gawped at the two male brides, struggling to make sense of what Madison-from-Texas said. But no matter how much I turned it over inside the brewing cauldron of my mind, I just couldn't fathom it—*How can a man marry a man? Who will be the Mr and who will be the Mrs? Maybe the white people have some magic that helps them shed their skin and become male or female as they wish, just like the men that turn into antelopes and horses during the secret masquerade rituals in our village…*

At the thought, my confusion gradually vanished. Everything finally made sense. I'd heard about such stories of fantastical body-shifting from my cousins and friends. They said that during that famous Nshi Masquerade Festival, powerful men versed in the occult could change forms at will. One of my cousins said she once saw a horse dressed up in a three-piece suit, complete with a tie and hat, galloping towards the stream. She said she recognised the flowered bow tie as belonging to somebody whose identity she couldn't reveal. Her mother warned her never to call the human-horse by its true name otherwise the man would remain trapped in his horse form forever.

Now, as I observed the two male Ghost-Brides in their beautiful, flowing gowns, something told me that they were juju-women who had shed their skins and accidentally became trapped in their male bodies when someone called out their names during their shapeshifting. I felt intense pity for them and vowed to treat them with the greatest kindness I could summon.

Madison-from-Texas led me to one of the tables and sat me down next to a bride who was sobbing softly into her beautiful, flowered handkerchief. The two bright red circles painted on her cheeks drew my fascinated gaze. I instantly recognised her— *Jeong-from-Gwangju! She's one of the newly arrived Ghost-Brides. I guess she's just like me. We're both new to this world.*

"Welcome to the American Table, honey," Madison-from-Texas said with a smile, cutting me a large slice of cream cake.

I fell on the cake like someone starved for over a year—*Oh, Holy Mother! This is the bestest food in the whole world, ever!* I'd had cakes in the past, but never anything like this. Madison-from-Texas laughed when she saw how quickly I gobbled it up and cut me several more slices.

"Poor baby," she cooed, patting my head gently. "Eat all you can, okay? Just let me know anything you want to eat or drink, and I'll have it in front of you before you can say Teddy P!" She turned to the weeping Ghost-Bride sitting beside me. "Oh hi! You must be Jeong-from-Gwangju. So sorry about what happened to you, honey. I heard your late groom was American too, right? I guess that's why you're at the American Table rather than the South Korean Table. Just go right on and make yourself at home here. Every table is open to everyone here, so just use whichever table you feel comfortable at, alright?" She turned back to me. "By the way, this here is another new arrival, just like you. Her name is…"

Madison-from-Texas stared at me in confusion. While I knew her name, she never knew mine.

"My name is Ba—" *Oh no! I almost gave her my real name! Think! Think! What name and city can I claim? My village is a tiny one, and they might link me to it if I mention it! I wish I lived in Enugu town, just like my cousin Keziah and her husband… Enugu town! That's it!*

"My name is Amina-from-Enugu," I said, my heart racing— *Thank you, Mama-Ejima, for giving me Queen Amina's name!*

"*Annyeonghaseyo*, hello, Amina-from-Enugu," Jeong-from-Gwangju said, looking at me with red-puffed eyes. "But, aren't you too young to be a bride?" She spoke in her Korean tongue, her voice hesitant, yet cute, just like the triplets' voices. But somehow, I understood her as clearly as if I had always spoken in that foreign tongue. I found that in this realm, every language morphed into the single language of grief, and I was able to understand their souls rather than their words.

"I asked her the same question too," Madison-from-Texas said, giving me a quizzical look. "So, tell us, Amina-from-Enugu, how did you end up here? Were you a child-bride in your African village? That's so terrible, isn't it?" She turned an outraged face to Jeong-from-Gwangju before quickly turning back to me. "I mean, look at you, honey! You're little more than a baby, yet they forced you into early marriage to a horrible pedophile. Was that why you took your own life? Because you took your own life, right? Just like poor Jeong-from-Gwangju here. And who can blame you?" She shook her head sadly before folding me in a big hug. "Guess what, honey? I think you're better off here. In fact, I think we should ask Big Momma Mmuọ-Ka-Mmuọ to keep you here forever. I mean, I'm sure you're not desperate to return to the horrid pedo-groom you left behind, are you? You don't really want to go back and be anybody's bride, do you?"

I shook my head, inhaling the sweet scent of her perfume so different from Ọla's Charlie—*Thank you, nice Madison-from-Texas, for telling me my story. I know it's a sin to lie, but please, Jesus, forgive me because it's not really my lie. It's Madison-from-Texas's lie and she's only trying to help me. I think I like her very, very much!*

"That's what I thought," Madison-from-Texas said, nodding her veiled head firmly as she held me away from her, looking at me with fierce determination. I could tell I had given her a new purpose in ghost-life. "No more baby-brides, I say. What do you think, Jeong-from-Gwangju?" Madison continued, asking questions she already had answers to. "Do you think we should get all the other brides to join us in pleading for poor Amina-from-Enugu to stay here indefinitely? When you think about it, it just makes your blood boil to see how these little kids are treated just because they're poor. I'm sure you guys in Korea must have the same problems too since, you know, you've got your own poor people there as well, right?"

She shuddered delicately, and turned and patted me gently on the head. "I bet your poppa sold you to a very rich old man, just to make some money to feed your family. I hear they do such things in Africa and Asia. But don't worry, honey. I won't let anything bad happen to you here. I'm American and we don't take any bullshit. I'm not sure how much longer I have here because from what I heard from one of the new arrivals I used to know, Cedric—that's my groom I left behind in Texas—yeah, Cedric is planning a second wedding soon. So, I might yet get to become a real bride after all, yippee! Isn't that just wonderful?"

Madison-from-Texas clapped her hands in excitement. Her eyes glowed briefly with intense joy before she remembered my imagined plight once again. "Don't worry, honey, I'll sort out everything for you before I leave, and if I don't, I'm sure Jeong-from-Gwangju will help. You will, won't you, honey?" She turned to Jeong-from-Gwangju, who nodded shyly—*At least she isn't crying anymore, poor woman! I must remember that I'm a suicide, a child-bride forcefully married off to a rich old peedo-something… What was it that Madison-from-Texas called him? I guess it doesn't matter. A rich old man will do just as well. I guess I'm now a Ghost-Bride too. Oh, Holy Mother!*

The next day, after one of the deepest sleeps of my life on the softest pink bed Madison-from-Texas had made for me, I woke up to the wondrous sounds of birdsong and the gentle strains of the various world music. They hummed together with the poignant wailings of the Ghost-Brides, which rang with a lyrical quality that merged seamlessly with all the other exquisite sounds of *Ibaja-La*. In no time, after I had again gorged myself on cakes and meats, Madison-from-Texas resumed our tour of the Ghost-Brides' realm. In the dazzling silvery daylight, I noticed many other Ghost-Brides keeping themselves busy in various ways instead of feasting at the tables. Their main pastime seemed to be one of conjuring, from creating various items to cooking up even more sumptuous dishes. Incredibly, they did this just by the power of their thoughts and imaginations. It seemed to me as if they only had to imagine something for it to appear before them. Watching them at their mesmerising creativity, it quickly dawned on me that during their magical creative process was the only time the Ghost-Brides ceased their congenital wails, as well as when they were drunk on the copious amounts of wines on their tables. I saw numerous drunk Ghost-Brides either dancing wildly, singing loudly, wailing inconsolably, or just pining in morose silence. Observing my confused stare, Madison-from-Texas smiled and told me that each Ghost-Bride responded in their unique ways to alcohol. She said that she herself always sang boisterously when she was in the drinks. Something told me that Jeong-from-Gwangju would sink into silent depression should she ever get drunk.

I stared in awe at a silent gathering of over fifty Ghost-Brides swaying in gentle uniformity while seated cross-legged on the ground. Their eyes were tightly shut, their arms crossed in a uniform X-fashion across their shoulders, while their heads nodded in a gentle, repetitive eight-count sequence in perfect synchronicity. They sat in a wide circle near some gem-crusted silver trees as they created more astounding magic and added new glittery gems to the already over-adorned trees. They also manifested gorgeous eye-popping gowns and fulgurous fashion from their different cultures.

"This group is The Fashion Gathering, honey," Madison-from-Texas explained with a smile as she saw my glazed expression. She turned and nodded at a different group of Ghost-Brides sat in the familiar silent, circular formation, swaying crossed-armed to their mystical magic. "Over there is The Food Gathering; you could join if you want to manifest foods and drinks. I bet you'd love that, wouldn't you, honey?" She winked as she ruffled my hair playfully. "On the other hand, you might join The Book Gathering should you wish to magic the greatest books or magazines ever. I'm sure you'd love to have a storybook as big as you, with the cover encrusted with the shiniest gems—and I mean the real thing: diamonds, sapphires, rubies, emeralds, you name it. Or maybe a book with animals that come alive on the pages and speak to you as you read about them? Now, wouldn't that be something, right?"

My mouth opened wider as I stared up at Madison-from-Texas with disbelief.

"Is this true? Can I really make such a book?" I asked in a hushed voice. In my mind's eye, I saw the brilliant colours of Aladdin's jewel-fruits which he had plucked from the magical trees inside the cave. *Aladdin and His Magic Lamp* was one of my favourite books amongst all the books Ọla had bought for me.

"Of course, you can, honey." She smiled again in the desultory manner of the Ghost-Brides. "You're now in *Ibaja-La* where everything is possible. *Ibaja-La* gives you the magic that is embedded in its very soil and air. You now have the same powers we have and just need to join your favorite gathering to harness the group power for even greater magic. Mind you, nothing stops you from doing it yourself. You just have to shut your eyes, cross your arms as you've seen them doing, and nod your head eight times while visualizing whatever you desire, and boom! It's there before you can say Teddy P! The only thing you don't need to conjure up with the ritual is the flying. *Ibaja-La* gives you its flight once you enter, just as you're flying now with total ease. As I said, you don't need to join a gathering to manifest, but I think it's always nicer."

Madison-from-Texas's words brought warm waves of bliss to my body—*I can become a magician like Rumpelstiltskin and magic anything I like. Mama-Ejima would love it here! I think I'll magic the most beautiful Mills & Boon books for her, with the shiniest book covers in the whole wide world!*

During the following days as Madison-from-Texas continued our tour across the vast silvery realm, we soon came cross The Wedding Gathering. This gathering was the biggest of all the gatherings I had seen, with over five hundred Ghost-Brides in the great circle. This time, unlike the other gatherings, there was no silent conjuring. Instead, the brides applied themselves to grieving plaintively and re-enacting their doomed weddings, down to the tiniest details of their wedding tiaras. There were wedding costumes, veils, and bouquets of indescribable beauty, wondrous body-art, glamorous wigs and hairstyles, jaw-dropping wedding gifts and intricately designed invitation cards. All that was lacking were the grooms, and that was the one thing they wanted the most, and yet couldn't magic into existence like everything else. Of all the gatherings I had witnessed, I found this one the saddest and I couldn't wait to leave their space. Their agonised wails haunted me long after I had left.

As each wondrous day blended seamlessly into the next, my longing for my former world lessened, till I could barely recall a time I hadn't lived in *Ibaja-La*. The more I saw as I observed the workings of this incredible realm from my gliding position next to Madison-from-Texas, the less I grieved my past life—*Oh, Holy Mother! I've truly come to heaven! Surely, this is what heaven must look like, even if it's a brides' heaven. I wonder what children's heaven would look like?* Again, that delicious shiver coursed through my body. In that instant, I knew I wouldn't mind if I had to spend a long, long time in this beautiful new realm.

Madison-from-Texas was a wonderful guide, and under her wing I soon got to meet many of the Ghost-Brides and learn their tragic stories. Though I was quickly adopted as the realm's mascot, my core friendship group became the four brides that arrived on the same day as me, guided by the irrepressible Madison-from-Texas.

I gradually got to know their stories, while Madison-from-Texas readily shared the tragic story she had created for me with everybody in the realm. As time went on, I too started to believe that I was a child-bride who committed suicide when I was dragged away from my family to marry a rich, old peedo-man who had bought me from my poverty-stricken father. My face soon adopted the tragic look of the other Ghost-Brides, and even though I wailed at times when I missed Mama and my siblings, everyone assumed that I cried for the hardships I had endured in my past life and for my tragic suicide. I was fed so many cakes and assorted meats and given so many presents and hugs that in no time I ceased missing home, and started hoping I would get to live in *Ibaja-La* forever.

In time, I learnt that Madison-from-Texas had died from a sudden brain aneurysm the day before her wedding. She said she only remembered having her nails done at the salon when a mighty headache knocked her off the chair. The next time she woke up was as a Ghost-Bride in *Ibaja-La*. Of all the brides, she seemed the least affected by her tragedy.

"I know my Cedric well, honey," she said to me when I asked how she coped with life in *Ibaja-La*. "He's one sizzling hot dude, and the ladies just won't leave him alone. I know one of them Texas hoes has got her greedy claws on him now. But no worries. Come their wedding day, bam! I get my wedding after all!" Her grey eyes actually twinkled with glee as she spoke, and I was suddenly as excited as she was—*Please, Mother Mary, make the Texas hoe, whoever she is, marry handsome Cedric so that nice Madison-from-Texas can finally become a real bride, Amen!*

Jeong-from-Gwangju told me her equally handsome groom had died in a car crash on his way to their wedding venue. She had taken arsenic on her wedding day, still dressed in the beautiful hanbok she now wore in *Ibaja-La*. She was always either crying into her colourful handkerchief or regaling me with stories of her homeland, her fiancé, and their doomed dream of their American paradise.

Emma-from-Quebec died from cancer, tragically, the night before her wedding. She said her boyfriend of ten years, Greg, had proposed as soon as she was diagnosed, but she had refused. She believed she would beat the disease and marry him when she went into remission. She never went into remission and finally, towards the end, she agreed to marry her handsome Greg. Except she took a turn for the worse just hours before her bedside wedding at the hospice, and died before she could say 'I do'. Emma-from-Quebec would twirl her beautiful blonde curls with her fingers as she spoke, her voice a hushed cauldron of anguish. Until I met Emma-from-Quebec, I'd never heard of the word 'cancer', and prayed fervently that that horrid disease would stay away from me forever.

Guadalupe-from-Mexico was gunned down right outside her family compound on her wedding day. It was a revenge attack on her father who was a top judge. An ex-convict released from prison had opened fire at the wedding party, killing the bride and several wedding guests. She struggled the most to settle in the realm and spent most of her time on the Mexican Table, crying and telling her story over and over to anybody that would listen. I noticed she rarely left the Mexican Table, unlike the other Ghost-Brides who flitted across tables and fountains, sharing their grief and keeping themselves occupied with wedding preparations. Even when she was drunk, she continued to wail in grief. Between her and Jeong-from-Gwangju, I was never sure who cried the most.

After Madison-from-Texas, my most favourite Ghost-Bride was Aaliyah-from-Dubai. She reminded me a bit of my mother because she prayed a lot to God. But her god wasn't Jesus. She called him Allah, just like the Hausas in my human country did. Madison-from-Texas said a god was a god by any name he was called—Jesus, Jehovah, Allah, Buddha, or Teddy Pendergrass. I knew she was wrong because Jesus is the only god in the world. But I didn't say anything because she was older than me, and children shouldn't disrespect their elders by arguing with them, especially when the elders were ghosts.

Aaliyah-from-Dubai had the most beautiful wedding dress ever, although those of the Chinese brides rivalled its loveliness. It was a dazzling, long gold and green gown with wonderful beads embroidered into it. She called it a kameez, and her matching veil, a dupatta. Multiple bangles, necklaces, and rings adorned her henna-decorated body. I even saw a gold ring on her nose! Aaliyah-from-Dubai was so beautiful and glamorous she reminded me of Ọla, even though her religious piety also reminded me of Mama. Whenever I saw her, I missed my family intensely. She too had died before she could take her marriage vows. In her case, it was really a tragic accident. She was having what she called a Halal Bridal Shower on a luxury yacht belonging to her rich father, when she took an accidental tumble into the sea. She drowned before they could fish her out of the water.

I learnt about so many amazing cultures and peoples from my friends, and time flew by in a clockless serenity that required no ablutions. We neither defecated nor washed, yet our breaths and bodies maintained the sweet freshness of fruits and flowers. In time, I too learnt how to wish things into my existence with the power of my thoughts, just like the rest of the Ghost-Brides in the various gatherings. I was now in the process of completing my own Aladdin book, a shiny, beaded and sequined affair that would be the envy of every magpie in creation when completed. My only regret was that my stepmother would never get to see this wondrous book.

Occasionally, Mmuọ-Ka-Mmuọ would materialise literally from thin air to announce that a Ghost-Bride would be finally leaving for her wedding. Just like everything in *Ibaja-La*, I got used to her frightful visage and the strong smell of burning wood and smoke that clung to her. Gradually, her myriad of terrifying faces and four dead eyes ceased to send my heart pounding as in the past. On the contrary, she now appeared benevolent and reassuring.

"You're indeed a very lucky bride," Mmuọ-Ka-Mmuọ's multiple voices would thunder across the realm when she came for the latest bride. "But remember not to linger in the human realm after you've said your 'I do', otherwise the portal to your reincarnation will close. Are we clear?"

There would be loud cheers and louder wails as the chosen bride celebrated her sudden liberation with joyful squeals. The other Ghost-Brides would quickly gather to dress up the lucky bride, do her make-up and her hair, and celebrate her hen-night raucously. It was the only time I saw the Ghost-Brides smiling and singing without the aid of their wines. Then, they would all lead the bride to the tall gates to see her off with songs, good wishes, and happy clapping, before returning to their familiar wailing. In all my time in *Ibaja-La*, I never heard a Ghost-Bride laugh and I often wondered what their laughter would sound like.

I never saw those chosen brides again after they left *Ibaja-La* with Mmụọ-Ka-Mmụọ. Madison-from-Texas told me that the blue light-portal to their reincarnation only opened beyond the tall white gates, where Mmụọ-Ka-Mmụọ awaited their return from their weddings.

"Do they always return?" I asked, recalling Dibia's words in my father's house. I realised since arriving in this realm that Dibia knew nothing about the Ghost-Brides, just the tiniest tip of the spiritual ant-hill.

"Yes, everybody returns once they exchange their vows with their grooms," Madison-from-Texas said. "After all, we each want to hurry our reincarnation so we can be reborn to find our twin-flames again. This second time round, it will be an everlasting union that untimely death can't break up. Exchanging the wedding vows binds our grooms to us for eternity, ensuring they'll remember us when we meet up again in our next lives."

"But what about Cedric's new wife?" I asked, fascinated by her theory of twin-flames. "Who will be her twin-flame when she reincarnates, if you take Cedric away from her when you reincarnate?"

"Oh, don't you worry your littl' head, honey." Madison-from-Texas waved away my question with an airy hand. "Wives are different from us brides. They've already taken their vows and got married, so they ain't got no unfinished business so to speak.

They get to enjoy their husbands in their lifetime and we get to enjoy them in the next life-cycle. It's only fair, ain't it?"

I nodded. It was fair indeed. The poor Ghost-Brides deserved to exchange their vows and fulfil their destinies with their grooms in their next lives.

"Mind you, once in a while, we get some brides that refuse to return to *Ibaja-La* after exchanging their vows," Madison-from-Texas continued. "They're the selfish and greedy brides, and they just wanna possess the new wives forever. They don't care nothing about the rules and laws of *Ibaja-La* and just wanna wreak vengeance on their former fiancés for remarrying. Big Momma Mmuọ-Ka-Mmuọ has to go drag them back and banish them into The Wastelands as punishment." Madison-from-Texas did another one of her delicate shudders. "Trust me, honey, you don't wanna know where The Wastelands is or what goes on there. Lordy! I hear the brides there are pure evil, you know, like vampire-zombie-hoodoo kinda brides. They suck souls and other weird stuff, and Big Momma Mmuọ-Ka-Mmuọ never lets them out—except on very rare occasions, when one of them somehow repents and sheds the corrupt evil in their souls. As I said, it rarely happens anyway, and we have nothing to do with them, thank God!"

Listening to her and seeing the terror on her face, I also said my own silent prayers, weaving the sign of the cross in frantic repetition—*Oh, Mother Mary, may I never see the evil Ghost-Brides from The Wastelands! Please keep me safe from them forever and ever, Amen!*

10

Imet Gisèle-from-Paris while I was chatting with my new friends at one of the world tables in *Ibaja-La*. She appeared suddenly beside us, her long veil trailing several feet behind her. It was one of the longest veils I had seen since my arrival, and I stared at it with open-mouthed awe.

Then my eyes widened. Suddenly, I no longer noticed her extraordinary veil. Instead, my gaze was riveted at her feet. Rather than gliding gracefully in the air like the rest of the Ghost-Brides, her sparkling diamanté shoes walked solidly on the ground—*She's human! A human bride has come here! But how?*

I looked at her face and recoiled. My action was instinctive, unguided by any rational thought. All I knew was that I was repulsed by the cool smile on her pale face, her clumsy strides on her tottering heels, and the sleek curls of her blonde hair, so similar to Emma-from-Quebec's. And when I looked into her icy blue eyes, I knew my heart was right to reject her—*Why are her eyes blue when everybody here has silver-grey eyes? And why do I distrust her smile?*

"*Bonjour!* I'm Gisèle-from-Paris," she said in a husky voice, stretching out her hand languidly to be shaken. There was something about this new Ghost-Bride that reminded me of my stepmother. They shared an air of superior disdain which elevated them above others around them. But Gisèle-from-Paris lacked Ọla's kindness and charm.

Madison-from-Texas ignored the outstretched hand and looked around nervously as if searching for someone to tell her what to do. It was an odd reaction, considering Madison-from-Texas never needed any help on what to say or do. She was already the de facto leader of our friendship group of six, and we all looked to her for guidance. After several awkward seconds, she shrugged and shook hands reluctantly with the new arrival. Her arm seemed to take forever to stretch out, like one loath to touch a slug.

"Hi, I'm Madison-from-Texas," she said finally, her voice the coldest I'd ever heard. She quickly reclaimed her hand and turned back to us. "These are my friends, Jeong-from-Gwangju, Emma-from-Quebec, Guadalupe-from-Mexico, Aaliyah-from-Dubai, and little Amina-from-Enugu." She nodded towards us.

Everybody smiled nervously at the newcomer, though none of us shook her hand. I could tell my friends also disliked Gisèle-from-Paris. Madison-from-Texas never once called her 'honey'.

"So, I guess you must be a Repentant, right?" Madison-from-Texas asked, her tone cool, distant.

My heart skipped—*What's a Repentant?* I'd never heard that phrase since my arrival in *Ibaja-La* and wild thoughts danced around inside my head—*Does it mean Gisèle-from-Paris is a sinner? Only sinners repent. Will she go to purgatory? I knew as soon as I saw her that I didn't like her one bit. Sinners go to hellfire! I wonder what sin she committed?*

"*Oui-oui*, I'm a Repentant." Gisèle-from-Paris damned her soul before my shocked face. "Mmuọ-Ka-Mmuọ gave me my pass today." She shrugged, her blue eyes filling with tears that never fell, just like mine and the rest of the Ghost-Brides in this realm. For some strange reason, her words sounded garbled in my ears, as if she spoke several different languages at the same time. It took every power of concentration in me to understand her.

"So, how did you end up in The Wastelands in the first place?" Madison-from-Texas continued her interrogation, her eyes hard with suspicion. *The Wastelands!* Sudden terror doused my skin in a blanket of icy goosebumps—*Oh, Holy Mother! She's an evil Ghost-Bride from The Wastelands!*

Gisèle-from-Paris looked uncomfortable, doing another of her shrugs and fiddling with her veil. Her shoulders remained hunched, as if she struggled to stand in an upright position. When she spoke, we had to lean close to catch her hushed words. In fact, Madison-from-Texas had to relay it all to me later. For the first time since I arrived in *Ibaja-La*, I was witnessing a Ghost-Bride whose language I couldn't properly grasp.

"Well, I fell in love with my twin sister's fiancé, Julien, and as a result, he broke off their engagement," Gisèle-from-Paris said quietly. Her pale blue eyes stared into the distance with icy indifference. "*Alors*; a week before our wedding, Julien decided he still loved my sister after all. He'd found out that I'd lied about her having an affair while they were engaged." Gisèle-from-Paris shrugged again. Everybody was staring at her goggle-eyed, stunned by her horrible revelations, yet silently willing her to continue her tale. "Anyway, I threatened to commit suicide if Julien cancelled our wedding. He didn't believe me. I told him I was pregnant. Still didn't work, not even after I told him I'd taken an overdose of sleeping pills, *le petit bâtard*. He later found out I had lied. Anyway, I ended up taking the sleeping pills for real and phoned him. But he still thought I was playing *les jeux*, *oui*? I kept waiting for him to arrive and save me. He never did. *Et voilà!* I guess I died."

Gisèle-from-Paris paused, the cold, distant look still in her pale blue eyes.

"So, what happened?" Madison-from-Texas asked, startling the newcomer from her reverie. She gave a nervous laugh and another one of her indifferent shrugs. Her laughter sent shockwaves to my body. I had always wondered what the laughter of a Ghost-Bride would sound like. I had imagined it would be musical, mystical, beautiful. Gisèle-from-Paris's laughter didn't sound anything like what I'd envisioned. To my ears, it was the barking of dogs and the caws of a vulture.

"I guess Mmuọ-Ka-Mmuọ heard me threatening to kill my sister if Julien ever married her. She tried to bring me back to *Ibaja-La* at first, but I escaped into the first bride I saw. It took Mmuọ-Ka-Mmuọ a long time to capture me, and in the process, the bride almost died." Gisèle-from-Paris gave us a pleading look, begging our understanding. "I mean, I didn't want to be dead after all; none of us wanted to die in the first place, *oui*? I figured it was better being alive in someone else's body than being a ghost. And, by God, we made Julien's life a misery, my bride-host and I. We slashed his tyres and smashed up the windows of his house. Ha! Neither Julien nor the police could understand why this strange woman had such a deadly fixation on him. We even crashed our car deliberately into my sister's car, breaking her legs and arm. She's still in crutches and her wedding to Julien has been postponed till she can walk down the aisle unaided. Mmuọ-Ka-Mmuọ only succeeded in dragging me out when the woman ended up in a mental hospital after trying to commit suicide because she couldn't fight my possession of her any longer. *Et maintenant*, here we are!" She gave another little shrug. "Anyway, that's all in the past now. Please believe me when I tell you that I'm no longer the person I was then. I'm a real Repentant now. I know by the time I gain my flight and the correct eye colour in your realm, I'll be ready to have my wedding after all when Julien finally marries my sister."

Everybody was stunned into silence. They stared at Gisèle-from-Paris as if she had suddenly sprouted horns and claws.

"What? What?" I said, turning to Madison-from-Texas for explanation. Once again, Gisèle-from-Paris's strange language had failed to pierce through my brain. And when Madison-from-Texas told me what she had said, I almost collapsed on the ground—*Oh, Mother Mary! She's as bad as Anene Eze! She's an evil bride despite her repentance! That's why she can't fly in this good realm of nice Ghost-Brides and continues to retain her true human eyes that reflect her sinful heart. What if she's lying and plans on doing more harm to the rest of us?* The thought filled me with sudden dread. I shook my head violently—*Uh-uh! Surely, Big Momma Mmuọ-Ka-Mmuọ can see through everybody and will know what to do.*

I glowered at Gisèle-from-Paris, unable to hide my dislike. Just then, I noticed the scent, the unfamiliar odour that was unpleasant and cloying. It smelled of raw chicken, wet dog, rotten eggs, and bad breath combined. It oozed out of Gisèle-from-Paris in noxious waves that shrouded her in a sickening green cloud. There was something terrifyingly familiar about the reek, but I couldn't pinpoint it. It felt as if I should know that stench, yet everything in me recoiled from its corrupt funk.

I gagged, squeezing my nostrils—*Can't they all smell her? Can't they see the vile green fumes oozing from her body? Why am I the only one who can smell this rank odour in Gisèle-from-Paris?* Until I smelled it, I never realised that all the Ghost-Brides in *Ibaja-La* shared the same delicate fragrance of flowers and citrus fruits—*Why then does this Ghost-Bride smell so horribly different?*

And when I looked up, I found Gisèle-from-Paris observing me. The look in her icy blue eyes sent sudden chills across my body. Suddenly, I wanted more than anything in the world to be far, far away from her vicinity.

Mmuọ-Ka-Mmuọ came for me on my twenty-ninth day in the realm. I had no idea what day it was, or how long I had spent in *Ibaja-La*. Mmuọ-Ka-Mmuọ told me all that when she took me away from my friends to meet The Great Council of Guardians. The air was shrouded with the familiar smell of burning wood and smoke that followed the great spirit, briefly swallowing the delicate fragrance of *Ibaja-La*.

"Come, child," she said, leading me away from my astonished friends. "We have a journey to make." Her multiple faces cascaded down in the familiar shimmery terror. With her long braids and longer beard, Mmuọ-Ka-Mmuọ stood like a mighty zebra-tree in our midst, radiating immense power and strength. And just like Papa in the shrine, everybody appeared like tiny puppets around her.

"Big Momma Mmuọ-Ka-Mmuọ, please don't make Amina-from-Enugu become a true-bride, please!" Madison-from-Texas howled, flitting frantically around Mmuọ-Ka-Mmuọ. My other friends quickly joined the ruckus, darting here and there in their ethereal flight, blocking our exit. "Please don't make her go exchange vows with her groom. It ain't fair on her to be stuck to that old pedophile. I mean, she's only a kid. It ain't her fault her father was so poor that he had to sell her to the sick pedo to feed his family. She's not even a child-bride, more like a baby-bride, for chrissakes. It's a damned crime I think, what they've done to this sweet littl' kid. Please let her stay here with us, Big Momma. She's very happy here; ain't you, honey?"

I nodded fervently. Mmuọ-Ka-Mmuọ's cascading faces froze into a single baffled expression. Her four obsidian eyes looked from me to the wailing Ghost-Brides. They all crowded around me, crying for me instead of their lost grooms as was their habit.

I joined in their grief, feeling my lips tremble as intense self-pity washed over me. My mournful tears were invisible on my cheeks, but my body shuddered with exquisite agony.

In the midst of my weeping, I remembered that I wasn't a real Ghost-Bride after all, that I didn't have an old groom waiting to welcome me as his bride in our human realm—*Oh no! Mmuọ-Ka-Mmuọ doesn't know the story Madison-from-Texas created for me. Now she's going to punish me for lying!* My heart started racing, panic stealing my breath. This time, my wails were for my guilty terror.

Mmuọ-Ka-Mmuọ's lips twitched in a little smile. She looked at me and two of her four eyes dipped in a wink—*Huh?* Then she turned to my friends, her cascading faces once again wearing the stern mien of the fearsome sentinel of *Ibaja-La*.

"Behave yourselves, ladies, and don't scare the child," she scolded, though her voice lacked anger or volume. "I promise you, Amina-from-Enugu won't become a true-bride anytime soon. That's exactly why we're sending her back, because she had no reason to be here in the first place. It was a mistake which The Great Council of Guardians now intends to rectify. I'm sure you'll all be happy if she returns back to her childhood, rather than staying here for eternity."

My friends cheered loudly, attracting the attention of the other Ghost-Brides. Soon, several of the brides flew from their different tables and congregated before our little group. On hearing my news, they joined in the happy cheering, although some of them wailed at the prospect of losing their mascot. Their unshed tears brought on my wails again, and in that instant, I wanted more than anything to remain in *Ibaja-La* forever. I couldn't imagine a life where my beautiful bride-friends didn't exist.

"Please, Big Momma Mmuọ-Ka-Mmuọ, could I stay just for a little longer before going back?" I pleaded, sobbing my tearless cries. She gave me a startled look from a different frozen face.

"You want to stay here, child?" Her voice was incredulous. "You actually like this place that much?"

I nodded. She gave me a long, considering look. Then, she made a noise that sounded like a grunt.

"We'll see." She took my hands. "Now, come along. We can't keep The Great Council of Guardians waiting. You can come back and spend more time with your friends after the meeting. It's not as if you're leaving today anyway." She turned to the Ghost-Brides. "Ladies, keep yourselves busy while we're gone. The child will be back with you once we're done."

"Don't worry, honey." Madison-from-Texas blew me extravagant kisses. "I'll have the best cream-cakes waiting for you when you return."

The other Ghost-Brides echoed her words, promising me enough cakes and meats to feed ten villages. I noticed that Gisèle-from-Paris kept her distance from us, her face sulky and whiter than usual. I gave her little notice. She was not my friend and I didn't desire her goodwill. Since our first meeting, I had gone out of my way to avoid her and her garbled, incomprehensible words. The sight of her clumsy gait on her tottering heels was enough to send me flying in panic, even before I smelled her rank odour.

Soon, Mmuọ-Ka-Mmuọ and I glided through the tall silver gates, which shut behind us with a loud clang. I found myself once again at the very foggy spot we had stood the first time I arrived at *Ibaja-La*, what felt like a long, long time ago.

"I must congratulate you on your vivid story about yourself," Mmuọ-Ka-Mmuọ said, looking down at me with a broad smile on all her cascading faces. Even her skeletal face grinned a ghoulish grin. "You shrouded your identity well with intelligence and intuitiveness. Well done, child. I like your new name, by the way, Amina-from-Enugu. Hmm... I think we'll keep it for the job you'll be doing for us henceforth. Now come; let's go and see if you are ready for your destiny."

I wanted to tell her that I wasn't intelligent or intuitive; that Madison-from-Texas had invented my story; that I wasn't worthy of any great destiny she had for me. But my words stuck behind my throat. Panic began to grow roots in my heart—*Oh, Holy Mother! What is this job they plan for me? Most importantly, who are The Great Council of Guardians?* All I could see in my mind's eye was the gathering of stern kinsmen and Dibia in Papa's parlour, all there to judge me once again—*What if I've somehow displeased this important gathering of great spirits? Oh please, don't let me get into trouble again, especially in this spirit realm.*

"Hold tight to my hand, child," Mmuọ-Ka-Mmuọ said, looking down at me from her great height. "We're going on a new journey. It will be over before you can count the fingers of your two hands. Come, The Great Council of Guardians awaits us."

I began to count my fingers—*Otu mkpulu-aka, one seed of the hand, mkpulu-aka abuọ, mkpulu-aka atọ, mkpulu-aka anọ, four seeds of the hand.* Before I got to five fingers, a mighty roar filled my head. It was the sound I recalled from my first journey with Mmuọ-Ka-Mmuọ, the thunder of a hurricane and the fury of a cyclone. Once again, I was lifted off my feet by a powerful whirlwind that pulled me faster and higher into a cloudy world devoid of life and light.

In my terror, I forgot to count the rest of my fingers. Not that it would have made any difference, because before I could blink, I found myself inside a vast hall filled with light, string music, and the most incredible table ever created by Jesus, the holy Christ.

11

I stared around the great hall, mesmerised by the marvellous sight I beheld. A magical globe-shaped hall with walls of cascading, shimmering, rainbow waterfalls met my awe-goggled gaze. The roof stretched to eternity, making it impossible to see where it started or ended. A kaleidoscope of bright colours lit up the space in dazzling brilliance, and even the floor was the same riot of colours, layered with a carpet of vibrant flowers of every hue and scent. A delicate fragrance filled the air, bringing sudden tears to my eyes. The delicate emotions the scents wrought in my heart were like nothing I had ever experienced—a strange yearning, a poignant recall, a blissful dream, and a tragic pain. I couldn't understand how the memories came to be or what had caused them in the first place. They just were, an exquisite pain in my heart, awakened by the haunting fragrance of this great place.

In the centre of the great hall floated a massive golden table, shaped in a half-moon. Except it wasn't golden after all. Even as I watched, the table rapidly changed colours, becoming a fiery blood hue, then a moon-silvery sheen, and finally a dazzling bottle green, before reverting to its original golden glory. I gasped softly, my gaze riveted on the incredible beauty of the magical table. Like everything else in the realm, the table levitated several feet above the flowered ground in its shimmering magnificence. Its edges were encrusted with sparkling gems of every colour and size, and it harboured twenty legs formed of giant-sized, jewel-encrusted mythical creatures of every kind—flying lions, elephant-headed giraffes, multi-legged cobras, polka-dotted tigers, and eagle-headed zebras.

Before my awed gaze, the carved creatures came alive. Their eyes glowed like jewels and their gem-encrusted skin shimmered with the same colourful radiance of the magnificent table. As their mouths opened, the most incredible music filled the hall. The sound was magical and haunting, and the pure strains of the unearthly melody sent goosebumps to my skin. My chest tightened as I fought to suppress the emotional overwhelm that engulfed me on hearing the beautiful chorus. I knew that no amount of conjuring from The Music Gathering would ever come up with anything close to this sheer perfection of musical harmony.

A new smell twitched my nostrils, an overwhelming scent of burning wood and smoke—*Big Momma Mmuọ-Ka-Mmuọ's distinctive scent, just magnified tenfold*. Something flickered in the corner of my eyes and I quickly turned my head.

I gasped, my eyes and mouth in saucer-wide synchronicity. Seven bearded women materialised before the table in their terrifying mammoth visage. One minute, my gaze was dazzled by the beauty of the singing table; the next, I stared in speechless wonder at seven giantesses of various skin-hues, from brown to white, red to yellow, and pink to jet-black skin. They were all as tall, bearded, and powerfully built as Mmuọ-Ka-Mmuọ, and just like her, they all wore identical sets of cascading faces and quadruple black eyes that stared at me with stony detachment—*Oh, M-Mother M-Mary! The Great Council of Guardians!*

My hand flew to my lips as I quickly lowered my head. My heart started to pound like leather drums and my legs were ready to buckle under my quivering body. Before I could marshal my thoughts, Mmuọ-Ka-Mmuọ lifted me up to the sole levitating chair facing the singing table and its fearsome occupants. I squeezed my eyes shut, fearful of their intimidating presence.

"Don't be afraid, child," she said, her voice the familiar deep rumble. "We're not here to judge you, but rather to tutor you and give you knowledge that will preserve your life." Mmuọ-Ka-Mmuọ patted my head gently before joining the assembled spirits as the eighth member of The Great Council of Guardians.

Sudden silence descended in the hall. The mythical creatures froze into inanimate statues and their music instantly ceased. Save for my harsh breathing and the loud thudding of my heart, no other sound filtered through the air. I could have easily heard the sound of an ant's fart in the icy stillness had there been a farting ant nearby.

A loud bell clanged from the impossibly high ceiling of the hall, and with great reluctance, I opened my eyes and once again looked up into the fearsome cascading faces of the eight members of The Great Council of Guardians—*Oh, Holy Mary! What is this new wonder?* My jaw dropped and my soul soared. I stared with wonder at the eight guardians. Little delicate fingers of bliss slithered over my body and hot tears pooled again in my eyes—*Mama! Mama!* I wasn't sure if I spoke the words aloud or just wailed them in my head. My shocked eyes remained fixed on the eight wonderous faces before me.

For all the eight members of The Great Council of Guardians, including Mmuọ-Ka-Mmuọ, now wore a single, identical face— my mother's gentle, loving face. According to the golden plaque I saw before Mmuọ-Ka-Mmuọ, she represented the African region. The other golden plaques set before each of the remaining seven members bore identity labels too—The Asian Region, The Middle-Eastern Region, The Latin-American Region, The

Caribbean Region, The European Region, The American Region, and finally, The Pacific Region.

"Child, do you remember this face you now behold?" Mmụọ-Ka-Mmụọ asked, her voice uncharacteristically gentle.

"M-Mama… Mama," I stuttered, still gawping at the miracle before me.

The guardians looked at each other and nodded. The one with the golden plaque from The Pacific Region stretched out her arm towards me. My astonished eyes watched the arm elongating, growing to an impossible length like a great python, till her hand finally settled on my head.

I shuddered involuntarily, feeling sudden waves of fire and ice douse my body. The weight of her hand on my head was like a metal boulder. I started to sweat profusely.

"It is good you haven't lost your memories of your past life, child," Pacific Region said, her voice an identical multi-tone rumble to Mmụọ-Ka-Mmụọ's own. "We had feared you might lose your memories of your old life, but already we can tell that you're different. For one thing, you're the first in our long history to become a Bride-Sentinel as a non-ghost, and at such a tender age too. No living human being has ever become a Bride-Sentinel. You are indeed truly special."

The other guardians murmured their assent, beaming at me with my mother's loving face. Seeing Mama's familiar gentle expression slowly squashed my initial apprehension, and gradually I began to sit easier on my floating chair.

"Don't forget that when she died briefly as a child, she touched the realm of the dead before regaining her life," Mmụọ-Ka-Mmụọ said. "With the blind hunger of a new-born, her fledgling ghost had tapped briefly into our powers before we could stop her. She self-healed, enabling her to escape back to her body. We all saw the dazzling light of her tiny soul as she fled back to her mother's frantic calls in their human realm. But she was such an infant that we thought nothing of it, till her powers started to manifest."

There was another murmuring of assent as Mmuọ-Ka-Mmuọ spoke, and sudden icy claws trailed a delicate path along my spine—*Oh, Mother Mary! My childhood accident in the ravine! I really died on that day as Mama said!*

"Tomorrow, you will return to your world to carry out your destiny," Pacific Region continued, her hand still heavy on my head. "But first, we need to ensure that you're ready for your assignment, as well as equip you with the weapons to defeat our foes. As you already know, *Ibaja-La* is the realm of grieving dead brides. What you do not know is that every member of this Great Council of Guardians was once a grieving bride too."

Huh? My eyes widened as I stared at them slack-jawed. They all chuckled softly at the look on my face. "I know it's hard for you to comprehend that we were all once beautiful women who loved their grooms as intensely as every other bride in *Ibaja-La*, but it is true," Pacific Region continued, withdrawing her hand from my head. "However, we weren't ordinary women in our lifetime. We were what you humans would call witches, even though we called ourselves by a different name—Ndi-Ajuju, The Seekers. There have been countless Seekers throughout the ages in every corner of the universe and each of us serves different deities and spirits, no demons, just great gods and higher spirits. For the eight of us here, our grief brought us together in the supernatural realms when we each lost our grooms on the very same day."

Pacific Region paused, a pensive look on her face. My heart flowed out to all of them. The beloved face of my mother that they wore looked haunted and heart-wrenchingly sad.

"Don't pity us, child," Mmuọ-Ka-Mmuọ said, her eyes hard and distant. "It was a choice we all made of our own free wills. Our deities offered us eternal life and unrivalled powers if we sacrificed our grooms to them. Many of The Seekers declined the offer. We eight accepted, and on the appointed night, we offered the souls of our beloved grooms in exchange for unimaginable powers. We entered the next dawn following our great sacrifice and found ourselves transformed in every way, body, mind, and spirit." Mmuọ-Ka-Mmuọ paused, staring into a distant place I could not see.

"Yes, child, we are all powerful beyond imagination." Asian Region picked up the narrative in a rumbling voice that mimicked Mmuọ-Ka-Mmuọ's own. "We can create worlds and end worlds. We can give life and take lives. Every part of our bodies pulses with magic, from our eyes to our fingers. In fact, nothing, no feat, is impossible to our thoughts and desires." She turned to look at her companions who nodded in affirmation, their faces icy, remote. Never had I seen Mama's face look so fearsome and forbidding.

Mmuọ-Ka-Mmuọ once again resumed her speech. "Despite our great powers, we still nurse the wounds of our terrible choice on that fateful night. There is no joy in our hearts: guilt and pain are our unremitting companions. *Ibaja-La* is our conscience-project. We created this realm to give grieving brides the comfort and camaraderie we never had or deserved, and we take turns in guarding it and sustaining its magic. With our powers, we can reunite the Ghost-Brides with their grooms even though we ourselves can never be reunited with our own grooms." Once again, Mmuọ-Ka-Mmuọ paused, stroking her long beard with an air of distraction.

"We also created the antithesis to the utopia of *Ibaja-La*—The Wastelands." Caribbean Region took up the story. "We keep all evil Ghost-Brides of The Wastelands clothed in identical white wedding gowns and veils to make it difficult for them to hide. One might even say that we deserve to be in The Wastelands considering our diabolical past; but then, no great knowledge comes without sacrifices, and we believe *Ibaja-La* more than makes up for every past wrong we committed." Caribbean Region folded her powerful arms across her chest as she observed my trembling body on my floating chair.

I fought the tight knot in my throat—*Poor, poor women! How terrible it must be to live with their guilt forever and to be sad and ugly for eternity.*

"Now you know the history of *Ibaja-La* as every Bride-Sentinel should." Mmuọ-Ka-Mmuọ smiled wearily from Mama's face and the pity I felt for all of them was now magnified tenfold. "Amina-from-Enugu, you said you want to live in *Ibaja-La* forever, right?" Mmuọ-Ka-Mmuọ asked, fixing me with Mama's gentle eyes.

I nodded. "Yes please, Big Momma Mmuọ-Ka-Mmuọ," I said, my voice just above a whisper. Briefly, I thought of the family I left behind in the human realm, especially Mama, whose loving face I beheld on the guardians. I yearned to see my real mother, to be hugged by her and smell her unique scent of Dax hair pomade. But my long sojourn in the realm of the dead had dulled the intensity of my homesickness. Now, my fear of never visiting the wondrous world of *Ibaja-La* and its beautiful inhabitants drowned my hesitation.

"To stay in *Ibaja-La* forever, you must first return to your world to fulfil your mission as a Bride-Sentinel. Are you willing to do so, child?" Mmuọ-Ka-Mmuọ asked. "Are you ready to protect human brides from malevolent Ghost-Brides, and later abandon your world and all you hold dear for eternal residence in *Ibaja-La*?" There was an almost imperceptible inflection in Mmuọ-Ka-Mmuọ's voice that I couldn't read. It sounded as if she wanted me to answer both yes and no to her questions.

A sudden tenseness descended in the hall, sending my heart thudding hard and fast—*Oh, Mother Mary! I don't know what this Bride-Sentinel thing is. I only know what I heard from Uncle*

Dibia and the villagers about what I did for Keziah. But I really want to stay here and if being this Bride-Sentinel person is my route to eternity in Ibaja-La, *then so be it. Better still, I'll get to see Mama, Ejima, and everyone once again, so it's not too bad, I guess.*

"Will it hurt to become a Bride-Sentinel?" I finally asked, wringing my hands and biting my lips.

Mmuọ-Ka-Mmuọ made a choked sound that sounded like a chortle and the rest of the council mimicked her humour. The tense atmosphere relaxed and I felt the tightness in my shoulders ease.

"No, child, it doesn't hurt, though there might be some slight discomfort initially. But first, we have to conduct a test to see if you are ready to become a true Bride-Sentinel. You just have to answer a few questions and we'll take it from there, alright?"

"So, do we take it that you are accepting our offer to become a Bride-Sentinel and willing to undertake the test?" European Region asked, her rumbling voice reverberating in my head.

I swallowed and nodded. My heart was racing wildly, this time with excitement and anxiety—*Please let me know the answers; please don't make me fail the test and lose* Ibaja-La *and my beautiful friends and the delicious foods forever.*

Mmuọ-Ka-Mmuọ turned and nodded to the rest of the council, before folding her arms across her broad chest.

"So, tell us, child: what is one means by which you can identify a normal Ghost-Bride?" Pacific Region asked, before I could organise my churning thoughts. Once again, her arm stretched an impossible length to rest heavy on my head.

Oh no! The test has started! My mind started to scramble like panicked ants, searching for clues and recalling every minute detail of my interactions with my beautiful friends in *Ibaja-La.*

"Their smell!" I cried out triumphantly. "All the Ghost-Brides in *Ibaja-La* smell lovely like flowers and fresh fruits." I paused, a slight frown on my face. "Except for Gisèle-from-Paris. She smells horrible. Nobody else smells like her." I wrinkled my nose, recalling the foul stench of the ground-locked Ghost-Bride.

Again, the guardians exchanged significant looks and nodded.

"Well done, Amina-from-Enugu," Pacific Region said with a wide smile. "You have earned yourself my face."

Huh?

Before I could marshal my thoughts, Mama's face vanished from Pacific Region's mien. In a blink, the familiar cascading faces returned in their terrifying glory. Pacific Region began to chant mystic words that sent sudden heatwaves to my brain. My gaze became foggy. I blame it on what I saw next, the impossible sight of a flying face hurtling towards me from across the great table. It was a face to fill the greatest of warriors with terror, a face birthed from the deepest depths of Satan's hell.

I screamed, raising my hands to deflect the raging alien face. I felt a brief sensation of heat on my exposed arm before a warm blanket covered me.

Everything went black. A million tiny roots began to sink their soft claws into my head. I tried to dig them out; to scratch my face, my neck, my scalp. But my arms were suddenly frozen at my sides, and the invading face quickly found its new home. In a blink, my eyes began to see sights never seen by any of God's human creations, terrifying worlds and entities, impossible creatures and wonderous feats. And in that minute, I knew that I now gazed with the sight of the immortals.

"Amina-from-Enugu, you have earned *The Petrify Face*," Pacific Region said, her shimmering faces observing me in their familiar cascading multitude. "With this face, you can petrify your foes into instant immobility, turning them into lifeless statues. Use it well, and it will save your life." Her arm shrank back into her body like a snake coiling up.

I was shaking on my elevated chair, desperate to fly away from the great hall and its mighty occupants. But terror glued me stiff on my floating prison and I could save neither myself nor my face. A new face now shared my head—*The Petrify Face! Oh please... no... no... I don't want to look like Big Momma Mmuọ-Ka-Mmuọ...*

"B-Big M-Momma Mmuọ-Ka-Mmuọ," I stammered, fighting my panic. "Th-the face... will my face disappear? Will I look l-like you now?"

Once again, their collective grunt-chortles chased away my fears.

"No, child; you won't lose your face or look like me, I can assure you. Though I don't think it's that terrible to resemble your Big Momma, is it?" The teasing note in Mmuọ-Ka-Mmuọ's voice brought a reluctant smile to my lips as I heaved a sigh of relief. "Depending on your answers, you will receive The Eight Faces of Devastation from us today. The faces will remain hidden inside you till the need arises for them to emerge and fight for the Bride-Sentinel, okay?"

I nodded slowly, and once again the test commenced.

"Amina-from-Enugu, tell us a second way to recognise a true Ghost-Bride?" Asian Region asked, fixing me with Mama's gentle gaze. I was starting to realise that all the guardians spoke with the same multiplicity of voices. It took a while for her words to break through my fidgety thoughts. Her repeated question quickly brought me back to my senses. I shook my head with a guilty smile and forced my wandering thoughts back to the present.

"Th-they all have silver-grey eyes," I stuttered. "Apart from Gisèle-from-Paris, who has blue eyes, all the Ghost-Brides have silver-grey eyes like my own." I was starting to realise that Gisèle-from-Paris was becoming my yardstick in deciphering the traits of the true Ghost-Brides. "Also, the Ghost-Brides never laugh except Gisèle-from-Paris, who laughs like a dog and a vulture."

"Well done, Amina-from-Enugu. You have now earned my face, *The Soothing Face*," Asian Region said, smiling benevolently at me with motherly pride. "With this face, you can calm the most distressed hearts of Ghost-Brides and replace intense grief with calm serenity. Guard it well, child."

And just like The Pacific Region, she started to chant her mystic invocations; and once again, a new face hurtled towards me with terrifying speed. In seconds, I felt its familiar heat sear my skin. As its gentle roots burrowed into my head and neck, I didn't bother to fight it this time. My gaze grew brighter, seeing even more dazzling colours and incredible sights that once again filled my heart with indescribable bliss.

The rest of the guardians proceeded to ask me their questions, and with each correct answer, I was rewarded with a new face— *The Fire Face, The Skinning Face, The Melting Face, The Vanishing Face, The Healing Face*—till finally, it was Mmuọ-Ka-Mmuọ's turn to ask me the last question.

"Amina-from-Enugu," Mmuọ-Ka-Mmuọ said in her rumbling voice. She was the only one in the great hall still wearing my mother's face. "Tell us, child, what did you discover about the bride known as Gisèle-from-Paris?"

A sudden silence descended in the hall at her words and all the guardians now watched me with an intensity that filled me with panic. My heart sank to my heels. An unpleasant feeling washed over me—*Gisèle-from-Paris! What can I say about that horrible Ghost-Bride?*

"Gisèle-from-Paris smells rotten like spoiled meat," I said, my voice a low mumble.

"Is that all?" Mmuọ-Ka-Mmuọ asked.

"She speaks in a garbled tongue I can't comprehend, unlike the rest of the Ghost-Brides whose languages I easily understand. She's also the only bride that laughs. I don't like her laughter."

"Anything else?"

"Her eyes are different. They're blue, while everyone else has silver-grey eyes. Also, she can't fly like the rest. A vile green fume oozes from her body. It stinks. Nobody else sees it or smells her horrible odour, but I do and I hate it. I know she's a Repentant, but I still don't like Gisèle-from-Paris. She makes me want to run away from her." I lowered my head, suddenly ashamed to have spoken so uncharitably about a Ghost-Bride, even one as unpleasant as Gisèle-from-Paris.

The sound of loud clapping and cheering snapped up my head. All the eight members of The Great Council of Guardians were applauding with great fervour, their cascading faces shimmering with blinding intensity.

Huh?

"Amina-from-Enugu, you have exceeded all our expectations and proved yourself a prodigy beyond par," Mmuọ-Ka-Mmuọ boomed, beaming at me with immense pride. "You have encountered one of the cursed brides from The Wastelands and smelled her true corrupt soul. We deliberately let Gisèle-from-Paris into *Ibaja-La* to see if you would detect her. And while the rest of the brides only saw the visible signs of her difference, you saw the vile truth of her corrupt essence, hence your inability to comprehend her tainted words. As a Bride-Sentinel, should you ever come across her kind in future, you will know them by their unique stench, the same odious funk you smelled on Gisèle-from-Paris. And now, I bequeath you with the final weapon to fight and destroy evil as a true Bride-Sentinel, and, more importantly, a future member of this Great Council of Guardians come the ripe time, if you so desire."

Mmuọ-Ka-Mmuọ paused, holding my stunned gaze with Mama's loving eyes—*Did I just hear right? Did Big Momma Mmuọ-Ka-Mmuọ say that I'll become a member of their Great Council of*

Guardians one day? The magnitude of her words was impossible for me to absorb and I struggled to contain the myriad of emotions churning within me—*If I become a guardian, does it mean I'll get to live in the great hall forever? Will I grow as tall as all the other guardians? Will I have four eyes and grow a long beard too? Uh-uh!* I shuddered at the thought. I didn't think I wanted to grow a long beard, even for the treat of living in the wonderous hall forever. An eternity in *Ibaja-La* was enough for me.

Just then, Mmuọ-Ka-Mmuọ stretched out her impossibly elongated arm and placed it on my head, just as the other guardians had done. It rested heaviest of all the other hands I had already borne.

"Amina-from-Enugu, prepare to receive your final face," Mmuọ-Ka-Mmuọ's voice thundered into my befuddled head. "All the faces we bequeath you today will ensure you are never again possessed by any ghost or spirit as you were when you fought Anene Eze and lost your life. But most importantly, they will give you all the powers of the Bride-Sentinel—our collective powers. The Bride-Sentinel is all energy and spirit. It is a fearsome entity that has existed for centuries beyond count. We raised this powerful entity from our own blood and souls, using the secrets of our occultic arts and the powers of our deities. It was wrought to fight the powerful negative entities that fuel the malice of the evil brides consigned to The Wastelands, and others that still abound. The Bride-Sentinel will come to you in your hour of need. You and it will become one; you will also become one sacred entity with us until the battle is fought and won." Mmuọ-Ka-Mmuọ held my awed gaze fiercely. "In our long history, no human has ever worn The Eight Faces of Devastation till now. But you are the great mystery that defies logic, a living child touched by the hands of death. You have lived amongst the dead without losing your sanity or your memories. On the contrary, you have thrived in the realm of the dead. You are now ready to return to your own world to fulfil your destiny."

Mmuọ-Ka-Mmuọ paused again and turned to her peers for their consent. Each one of them nodded, their cascading faces grim.

"Know this secret, Amina-from-Enugu." Mmuọ-Ka-Mmuọ resumed her speech, bringing more wonder to my stunned heart. "Each time your body turns the white hue of the spirits in your human realm, it means that danger is nearby and the Bride-Sentinel has awakened inside you to fight it. But never forget this crucial lesson, Amina-from-Enugu: the Bride-Sentinel must never, ever harm a groom. Out of guilt, we took an oath never to harm a groom again after our great sacrifice. Should you ever harm a groom, the Bride-Sentinel will flee from you and you will be powerless before the evil entities you battle." Mmuọ-Ka-Mmuọ's hand on my head became a heavy ball of steel and concrete, crushing me into my chair.

"And now, I gift you my face, *The Annihilation Face*. With this face, you will reduce our foes to ashy dust and protect both our realms, the living and the dead, from harm. Of all the faces you now wear, this is the most dangerous and powerful. Wear my face with great care, Amina-from-Enugu."

Even before she uttered her last word, I saw the final face detach from Mmuọ-Ka-Mmuọ's head with whirling force. It was devoid of features, a blank face that pulsated with unbridled menace. Icy terror doused me in sudden sweat as it hurtled towards me at great speed. It slammed into my face before I could blink. I felt a great faint engulf me, stealing my sight. From a far distance, I heard the reanimated mystical creatures singing their glorious songs once again from the magical table. The last thing I saw before darkness overwhelmed me was the eight cascading faces of the great guardians, shimmering and whirring in their dazzling magnificence inside the great hall of impossible beauty.

When next I awoke, I was back in the familiar grounds of *Ibaja-La*, surrounded by my wailing bride-friends. Mmuọ-Ka-Mmuọ was nowhere to be seen and already, my visit to The Great Hall seemed like a distant dream.

The Ghost-Brides hugged me joyfully when I finally opened my eyes, and instantly began stuffing me with delicious cakes from all the different Region-Tables. They pestered me with endless questions about my visit with The Great Council of Guardians. Yet, try as I may, I couldn't recall any details of my visit to that hall of incredible beauty, save its haunting magnificence and the kaleidoscopic singing table with its stupendous mythical creatures.

12

Gisèle-from-Paris approached me as I glided across the realm sometime later that day, following my return from The Great Hall. I was aware it was my last day amongst my bride-friends and wanted to absorb as much of their world as was possible in the little time I had left. I knew the unique scents, sounds, and sights of *Ibaja-La* would stay with me for the rest of my life, and the thought of leaving it all for my human world left a gaping wound in my heart. I didn't know when next I would return to the realm and the uncertainty weighed heavily on me.

I was perched atop one of the many silver trees, its shimmering branches laden with dazzling gems, when a familiar foul scent suddenly assailed my nostrils—*Gisèle-from-Paris! Oh no! Where do I hide?* Even before the thought left my head, I sensed the Ghost-Bride close by. I looked down to where she stood in her familiar hunched position, her sequined wedding gown and impossibly long veil glittering beneath the bright silvery skies. Instantly, my spirit plunged even lower. I could do little to repress the sudden shudders of repulsion that overwhelmed my body.

"*Bonjour*, Amina-from-Enugu," Gisèle-from-Paris said in her husky voice, looking up at me with her icy blue eyes. Once again, the thick green fumes oozed from her body with their sickening funk, and I quickly covered my nostrils with my hand, ignoring all politeness.

"I hear you visited with The Great Council of Guardians, *oui*?" She sidled closer to the silver gem-tree, looking up at me with her calculating eyes. Her congenital hunched shoulders skewed her neck into an awkward position, making her appear like an ugly vulture. "How did your visit go, *ma chérie*? What did they say to you? Come; fly down from your tree, let's talk. We're all friends here after all, and should share secrets, *oui*? So, quick: tell me everything that happened at The Great Hall."

My heart started racing—*What to do? What to do? Maybe I should just fly away since she can't fly.* Despite the garbled quality of her words, I was able to understand the essence of her demands and something told me to put as much space between us as possible. As if she could read my thoughts, Gisèle-from-Paris suddenly reached up and grabbed my right foot, which was positioned at the lowest branch. She yanked so hard that I stumbled down to the ground before the stunned gasps left my lips.

"This is better, *non*?" She smiled down at me with malevolent satisfaction. "Friends should stay close together, don't you think? Now, where were we? Aahh! I remember!" She smacked her forehead. "*Alors*; you were about to tell me all about The Great Hall, *oui*?"

I wasn't, but she had me trapped. I could tell her a lie about it, but for the life of me, no ready lies popped into my mind— *Madison-from-Texas, where are you? Please come, I need you now!*

"Oh well, if you won't tell me, I guess you won't say no to Madison-from-Texas, will you? Right then, let's go find her." Gisèle-from-Paris eyed me sourly—*Oh, Holy Mother! I swear this evil bride can really read my mind!*

Before I could reply, she grabbed my hand and started dragging me towards the nearest Region-Table, which just happened to be

her people's table, the European Table. She grabbed a thick slice
of vanilla cake and began pulling me towards the cluster of silver
trees bordering the high walls of *Ibaja-La*. I had always been
drawn to the tall trees, curious about what lay within their dense
knot. But for some reason, Madison-from-Texas never glided
near them, same with the other Ghost-Brides. I had planned to
ask Madison-from-Texas about that mysterious forest, but other
wonders had overtaken my curiosity.

I resisted Gisèle-from-Paris's pull. I dragged my feet and
yanked my hand from hers. I tried to glide away but she grabbed
hold of me once again before I could escape.

"Why do you keep avoiding me?" she asked in her distorted
speech, frowning down at me. "Is it because I'm a Repentant? Is
that it, *oui*? It's not nice to discriminate against brides, you know.
I liked you and thought you were a lovely little girl, but I guess
I was wrong." She turned away from me, wiping tears from her
eyes. I gawped at her tears, another visible sign of her difference
from the rest of us in *Ibaja-La* who never shed water-tears no
matter how hard we sobbed. With great difficulty, I processed
her words, grabbing rapidly fading vowels and mangled letters
till I finally made sense of her speech.

Instantly, shame washed over me. Her words stung me like
wasps—*Oh, Jesus, forgive me! Bata, you're a hypocrite Christian,
that's what you are. Father David will force you to do a hundred
rosaries in penance if he finds out how uncharitable you've
been. Who are you to judge a Ghost-Bride when they're all poor
dead brides dealing with their own tragic deaths? You should be
ashamed of yourself. And she even likes you despite your meanness
to her.*

I reached out and took Gisèle-from-Paris's hand in mine. I
smiled at her and forced myself not to cover my nose from her
stench or withdraw my hand from the cloying softness of hers.

"I'm sorry, Gisèle-from-Paris," I said, looking up at her with an apologetic smile. "I'll tell you what I saw at The Great Hall, okay?"

She beamed me a wide smile and giggled happily. I felt very righteous for making her pleased and felt the urge to expand my charity. So, when she suggested we go to a quiet place where we wouldn't be disturbed, I willingly went along. Soon, we were seated underneath another silver tree far away from the Region-Tables as I regaled her with descriptions of the singing magical creatures, the floating rainbow table, the sweet fragrances, and the majestic glory of The Great Hall.

Gisèle-from-Paris listened with rapt attention, her eyes saucer-wide like a child listening to a fantastical fairy tale under the full moon. She kept asking me about The Great Council of Guardians, what they looked like, what they said to me, what we did inside The Great Hall.

"Come, Amina-from-Enugu, tell me exactly what the guardians said to you." She cut me off impatiently as I started to describe the powerful emotions wrought in me by the intoxicating scents in The Great Hall. Her eyes were clouded with suspicion. "Surely, they must have had something very important to tell you, otherwise Mmuọ-Ka-Mmuọ wouldn't have taken you along to see them, *oui*? From what I've heard, it's very rare for all the members of The Great Council of Guardians to gather in one place at the same time, so I know they must have told you some crucial secrets. Come, *ma petite*, tell everything now, okay?" Gisèle-from-Paris's eyes bore down at mine with hard insistence, a scheming glint lurking in their pale blue depths.

I opened my mouth to speak, but it was as if my mind had shut itself to both of us. Try as I might, I could neither recall nor recount my experiences save the basic descriptions I gave her. In the end, she gave up with a loud hiss and an impatient shrug. A deep frown furrowed her forehead as she eyed me sourly for several tense moments. Finally, she stood and pulled me up beside her.

"Oh well, no worries, Amina-from-Enugu," she said in her grating voice, flashing me a smile that didn't quite reach her eyes. "Next time, I guess. Anyway, now that we're friends, I'm going to show you a wonderful secret nobody else knows." She giggled again like one of my little cousins, as if she were my age rather than an adult. A flutter of excitement tickled my heart—*A wonderful secret? Yes-Yes!* I was thankful I had made friends with her before my departure the next day, otherwise I would never have had the good fortune to see the secret.

"Should we invite Madison-from-Texas and the rest of our bride-friends?" I asked—*It'll be wonderful to share the experience with my bestest friends.*

"*Non-non!* This is just for you and me," Gisèle-from-Paris snapped, her brows furrowing again. "Here, put this slice of cake into your pocket. Make sure you don't squash it now, okay? We'll need it for the secret later." She took firm hold of my right hand, walking as fast as her clumsy strides would allow on her tottering heels.

"Where are we going?" I finally mustered the courage to ask. She was leading me further and further away from the realm and deeper into the thick forest of tall silvery trees. I glanced behind us nervously, seeking my bride-friends or even any of the other brides. Despite my new resolution to be kinder to Gisèle-from-Paris, I didn't want to remain alone in her company for long. I couldn't explain why my heart couldn't be at peace with her, but it just couldn't. "Where is the secret? Is it far?" I tried to shield the anxiety from my voice. Despite my curiosity to finally see what lay inside the forest of silver trees, something in me recoiled from spending time in Gisèle-from-Paris's unsavoury company.

"You'll see," she said, quickening her steps till she was almost running. In that instance, I noticed something else strange about her. The faster Gisèle-from-Paris walked, the more hunched her body became. Soon, she stooped so low that she appeared like a white, hulking, four-legged beast of prey in her flowing wedding dress.

The sight sent icy shivers through my body, filling me with an inexplicable sense of dread. Once again, my heart started to race, causing me to breathe in short, hard gasps that had little to do with exertion. With firm resolve, I shook away my disquiet—*Uh-uh... It's alright. There's nothing to fear. Anyway, nothing will stop me seeing the wonderful secret before I leave* Ibaja-La *tomorrow. Who knows when next I'll have the chance to return here?*

I quashed my unease with grim determination. In no time, I was gliding in the air to keep up with Gisèle-from-Paris's turbo-speed. I looked around me in wonder, seeing tall silver tree after tall silver tree lined in perfect formation like the mighty warriors of an ancient, powerful god. They had no branches or leaves, just great silver trunks that stretched to infinity. Like everything in *Ibaja-La*, even the soil was silver-coloured while the sky lit up the forest with its silvery radiance.

Yet, despite its stark beauty, there was an energy in the silver forest that unsettled me. I couldn't identify what it was about it that brought sudden goosebumps to my skin. Perhaps it was the total absence of sound and smell, together with the feeling that we were being watched by invisible eyes. Whatever it was, I was greatly relieved when we finally exited the vast silver forest.

My relief was short-lived.

Before I could inhale the new air beyond the silver forest, I found myself facing a desolate landscape of mottled brown soil, dry dead shrubs, and stunted black trees devoid of living leaves.

💀

I stared around me in disbelief and dismay. Save for the black-coloured dwarf trees, this new landscape could have sprouted from any ravaged village in my human world—*How in Jesus's name did this bleak land find its way into* Ibaja-La? It had been so long since my eyes had viewed anything other than the pristine silver beauty of the bride-realm that I couldn't help the involuntary shudder of revulsion that quaked my body at the ugly sight I now beheld.

"I don't like this place." I tugged at Gisèle-from-Paris's hand. "I want to go back home." I started backing away towards the white forest we had just exited, but Gisèle-from-Paris pulled me roughly back to her side.

"*Non, ma petite.* You haven't seen the secret yet," she said with a tight smile. "You're now going to use that slice of vanilla cake I gave you to perform a miracle. Come, we're almost there."

Huh? A miracle with my cake? All thoughts of returning to the bride-realm instantly left my mind. I brought out the thick slice of vanilla cake from my pocket and stared at it with puzzlement. A sliver of excitement coursed through my body. I could barely wait to see the cake-miracle.

We had barely taken a dozen steps before Gisèle-from-Paris came to a sudden halt. I almost bumped into her because of the abruptness of her stop. A vast ravine opened up before us, a deep canyon that stretched so wide that it seemed infinite.

I gasped, stumbling away from the precipice, my heart pounding so loud I could hear it through the lovely hanbok that Jeong-from-Gwangju had created for me. I stared goggle-eyed across the canyon to a far land shrouded in dense, misty fog. Even from the distance, there was a sinister, waiting quality about the smoke-cloaked world across the ravine that filled me with an inexplicable terror.

"There's a blue frog that lives deep down inside the ravine," Gisèle-from-Paris said in an excited voice, her words rushed and even more mangled to my ears. "They say it's a magical frog that takes people across the ravine."

At her words, a sudden thrill coursed through my body as the images of the wondrous creatures I had seen inside The Great Hall flashed through my mind. Still, something about her words didn't sit well with me.

"But how can a small frog take anyone across the ravine?" I almost whispered the question to myself, but she heard me and giggled maniacally once again in the familiar childlike fashion I was starting to really dislike—*Surely a grown-up shouldn't laugh like a child. I wonder if she's making fun of me?*

"That's why it's a magical frog, silly," she said, her blue eyes glinting mischievously. "They say it only performs its magic if it's fed the cakes from *Ibaja-La*. But it will only eat the cake from the hands of a bride from *Ibaja-La* and nobody else. That's why I asked you to bring the vanilla cake. *Et maintenant*, call it and feed it the cake, let's see what happens."

Gisèle-from-Paris leaned close to the precipice to look into the great depths. She motioned me over with her hand and I approached cautiously. Despite my curious excitement, I feared the cavernous gorge. My unlucky experience as a child had created a permanent fear of deep ravines in me.

"Hurry, you," she said, waving her hand. "Don't you want to see what lies across the ravine? If only I could fly like you, I would fly right across, but I need the magic frog to get there. Now, shout 'AWOR' as loud as you can—that's its name. Then, throw the cake into the ravine; quick."

I obeyed.

"AWOR!" I shrieked, enjoying the freedom to yell as loudly as I wished without the unspoken restrictions imposed by the solemn, grieving atmosphere of *Ibaja-La*. I had almost forgotten how it felt to shout as I used to do as a human child playing with my siblings and cousins.

"AWOR! AWOR!" I shouted again gleefully. My voice echoed eerily across the ravine, over and over, till I was convinced other voices took up my original call. As I threw the slice of vanilla cake into the gorge, I watched it falling with great excitement and anticipation—*down, down, down*. It seemed to take forever falling and I cocked my ears to hear when the frog gobbled it up. But I heard nothing; no thud, no gulp, no rustle.

A sense of disappointment washed over me—*There's nothing like a magic frog there. Gisèle-from-Paris just made it up to trick me as punishment for my former meanness to her*. I turned and looked askance at Gisèle-from-Paris, but she was busy peering into the vast gorge. I shrugged and sighed wearily as I turned to leave.

A great rumble issued from the deep defile. The ground beneath me started to quake violently. I gasped. Gisèle-from-Paris screamed and staggered away from the edge of the ravine. Her eyes were terror-wide, and I felt my heart drop to my feet. Instinctively, I started to fly but she grabbed my feet and yanked me down beside her.

"Hey! Stay put, you," she shouted at me. "I told you there was a magical frog here, didn't I? Prepare yourself to see something amazing. I've never seen it either, but from the stories I've heard, it's an incredible sight. Just you wait." Her voice was pitched high in excitement, her eyes now bright with anticipation.

As I grasped the message in her muddled speech, my terror almost vanished, now replaced by the same high anticipation she displayed. My excitement returned in full force—*At last! The secret!* I inched closer to her, staring fixedly at the ravine from where the ghastly rumble issued. A dull light began to glow inside the canyon. In seconds, it became brighter, flashing an illuminous blue radiance that dazzled the sight. Something started to move inside the gorge. The ground beneath us quaked more violently than before. It shook so hard I thought the earth would explode and swallow us whole.

Then I saw it—*Oh, Holy Mother, save me!* Before I could swallow my scream, a great blue frog emerged from the vast depths of the ravine. It was so big that it dwarfed ten elephants combined. From its massive head, four bulbous black eyes stared at us with cold scrutiny, eyes eerily identical to those on Mmuọ-Ka-Mmuọ's cascading faces.

Gisèle-from-Paris gasped as loudly as me. Even as I stared slack-jawed, the frog began to expand and elongate, bloating so rapidly that in seconds, it morphed into a mammoth, pulsating creature the size of a hill. And by the time it ceased swelling, it had formed a massive blue bridge stretching right across to the distant foggy land lying at the other side of the ravine.

"Quick; let's run across while the frog-bridge remains," Gisèle-from-Paris said, dragging me along with her.

I held back, loath to step on the body of the giant blue frog— *What if it bites me or my weight breaks its skin and I sink into its body and suffocate to death? Maybe I should fly over instead...*

"Don't be afraid; it won't bite," Gisèle-from-Paris said, as if she'd read my mind. "Come on, we can't afford to waste time." She tugged harder and I followed her lead with great reluctance.

As I stepped onto the shimmering blue body of the giant frog, I gasped softly. My eyes widened in wonder—*Oh wow! It feels just like a normal road!* I stepped harder on the blue surface, stunned by the solidity of the frog's body. I had expected it to be soft and spongy, but instead, my feet connected with a flat, firm surface that sustained my balance. The dazzling blue light emitting from its body shrouded us in a soft blue haze, just like everything in the immediate vicinity. Soon, I was running along the blue frog-bridge with Gisèle-from-Paris, all my earlier fears clean vanished. My heart beat with anticipation as we drew closer to the foggy terrain—*I wonder what new secrets I'll see across the canyon?*

Another sliver of anticipation coursed over my body at the thought. If it was anything like the spectacular blue frog, then the journey would have been worth it in every way. I could hardly wait to share everything with Madison-from-Texas and the rest of my bride-friends. My steps quickened, and in what seemed like seconds I found myself stepping off the blue-frog-bridge and standing before a vast landscape shrouded in thick fog.

A terrible silence descended; not even a cricket chirped. An overwhelming odour assailed my nostrils, a stench that was repulsive and terrifying in its familiar funk. An icy shiver slithered across my skin, coating it in goosebumps—*Oh, Holy Mother! Oh, Mother Mary! I know this place! Oh, Jesus, save me! I know this cursed, foul land!*

13

An unwholesome smell oozed from the mist, a rank odour that reeked of raw chicken, wet dog, rotten eggs, and bad breath. It was Gisèle-from-Paris's distinct stench, except it was now magnified a millionfold. Little, hard rashes coated my skin with a blanket of terror. My head swelled into an overripe melon that threatened to explode, spilling a bloody, mushy gore of petrified brain-matter. I was breathing in short, hard gasps, and every bone in my body felt like baby mash. The freezing air brought on involuntary shivers and when I looked up at Gisèle-from-Paris, the icy malevolence in her pale blue eyes confirmed my suspicions—*Oh, Mother Mary, save me! I know this evil place!*

My mind finally opened, spilling ghastly memories long suppressed. In dizzying seconds, my childhood nightmares began to reveal themselves to me in their terrible clarity. The unwholesome stench that had always followed me into wakefulness finally brought comprehension to my stunned mind—*Gisèle-from-Paris's smell is the same vile pong I smelled in my nightmares! No wonder her stench always had an unpleasant familiarity to it!*

A great shudder quaked my body—*Does it mean she's come from my nightmare? Is she one of the ghastly ghosts that chased and tormented me in my dreams?* I glanced around fearfully, seeking the horde of chalk-white ghouls that used to hound my sleep in the human world—*Has Gisèle-from-Paris brought me here to kill me? Will she call on her friends to harm me? But why? Why do they hate me? What have I done to them? Who are they? Oh my bad luck! I'm doomed...*

"Welcome to The Wastelands, Amina-from-Enugu," Gisèle-from-Paris said, before bursting into manic cackles that echoed eerily in the silent, foggy expanse. "Aren't you happy to be the first Ghost-Bride from *Ibaja-La* to step foot in my world, *oui*? Come, *ma chérie*; I'll introduce you to my sisters. They can't wait to see you again." Once more, her laughter rang loud and gleeful in the sinister, foggy world.

I felt hot piss trail down my legs; at least, it felt like hot piss even though I knew such vile excretions were impossible in *Ibaja-La*. But I was no longer in that sanctified place, and when I looked down, I saw the damp ruin on my beautiful hanbok—*I really pissed... I really pissed! Oh, Mother Mary, I really pissed!* The sight magnified my terror. I would have voided the last drop of blood in my body if it were possible. Tears filled my eyes and this time, they trailed down my cheeks. For the first time since I entered the realm of the dead brides, I was shedding real human tears and stinky human piss, bereft of the protective magic of *Ibaja-La*— *The Wastelands! I'm in The Wastelands, the realm of the accursed Ghost-Brides! Mama... Papa! Somebody, save me... please...*

"Ha! I see you remember this place well." Gisèle-from-Paris cackled as she gripped my hand and began to drag me deeper into the foggy, corrupt world of my nightmares. Even through the mist, I could see the ravaged landscape birthing dead shrubs and stunted black trees. No flowers or ponds graced the realm and the air rang with the silence of a dead planet, a place devoid of living creatures. Yet, I knew we were not alone. I sensed the unseen threat through every pore in my trembling body.

With great force, I yanked my hand away from her grip and primed myself for flight.

But nothing happened: my feet remained rooted to the ground, and soon the evil Ghost-Bride had me in her hold once again.

"Ha! You thought you could still fly in our world, *oui*?" Her eyes glittered with spiteful malevolence as her fingers dug deeper into my arm. "Too bad, *ma chérie*. Here, you walk on your feet like the rest of us."

"P-please, Gisèle-from-Paris; p-please let me go," I stuttered between hard chokes and loud wails. "I w-want to go home. I'm s-sorry for being bad to you. I promise I won't tell anyone anything. I'll keep the s-secret, honest. Please l-let me go home…"

"Shut your stupid mouth before I do it for you," she snarled, her voice as ugly as the look in her eyes. "And my name is Gisèle Dubois, not your stupid Gisèle-from-Paris rubbish. I'll break your head if you call me by that stupid name again, *comprends*?" The sudden vitriol in her voice sent my heart racing. I was seeing Gisèle-from-Paris in her true horrible colours and terror deadened my limbs.

I stayed rooted to the ground, unable to move my feet. She cursed loudly and pulled me along as if I were Papa's Christmas ram forcefully dragged towards the butcher's knife. Once again, her gait was stooped, and she sprinted like a white-hued animal on four legs, her long veil trailing merrily behind her. The stench was now all-pervading, filling my mouth with nausea. My eyes stung from the thick fog and waves of dizziness washed over me—*Oh, M-Mother M-Mary! Oh, M-Mother Mary…*

A sea of white entities materialised out of the mist, encircling us like egg-white around the yoke. The new beings blended so well into their foggy terrain that it was difficult to see them clearly.

But not for long. Even in the dense fogginess of the bleak realm, their animal-like hunched forms pulsed with enough rage to annihilate a village—*The accursed Ghost-Brides!* My legs lost their bones as I collapsed on the dusty ground, shaking so hard I could barely breathe.

They surrounded us in their ghastly multitude, a sinister gathering of raging Ghost-Brides burning with vengeance and hate. They were all dressed in identical dirty, flowing wedding gowns and long veils, and like Gisèle-from-Paris, their bodies discharged thick green fumes that fouled up their world. I didn't need to look into their glittering eyes to know that their collective malice was directed at me. And when I looked up into Gisèle-from-Paris's face, the hatred in her eyes curdled my blood.

"Sisters, I bring you the vile one that killed our sister-bride, Anene Eze," Gisèle-from-Paris shouted triumphantly, kicking me viciously with her shiny silver shoe. The kick landed painfully in my side and I moaned softly, petrified of incurring her further wrath.

"She's the little interloper that kept sneaking into our world to spy on us," another of the cursed Ghost-Brides said, poking my cheeks with a claw-like finger. The long red-tipped nail cut my skin, drawing blood. I whimpered, rubbing my cheek with a trembling hand.

"So, you are fearless, right?" A tall Ghost-Bride with the shiniest tiara yanked me up from the ground. Her blue eyes, so similar to Gisèle-from-Paris's own, glittered with cold malevolence. "No matter how many times we chased you away from our realm, you insisted on returning. I guess The Great Council of Guardians sent you to spy for them. And now, you've ended up in our hands. Well done, Gisèle Dubois. Now we can deal with this little meddler who dared disrespect us with impunity." Her voice had the same garbled quality as Gisèle-from-Paris's and I was thankful I had spent enough time in that vile bride's company to now understand their mangled speech.

The gathered brides roared their joy, their shrieks filling my heart with terror.

As I stared with glazed eyes at their hunched forms, inhaled their malodorous stench, and heard their peculiar shrieks, I was immediately drawn back to my nightmares. Once again I was being chased by a horde of shrieking female ghosts, whose hunched white bodies pulsated with rage and malice. My arms instinctively wrapped themselves over my head as I cowered on the ground, sobbing softly and quivering with terror and the chilling freeze of the cursed realm.

"Where is Anene Eze?" the tall bride in the shiny tiara asked in a threatening voice as she yanked up my head. "She caught you the last time you were here and instantly vanished with you. She hasn't returned since then. Where is Anene Eze? What did you do with her? Speak before I strike you dead." She pushed her face into mine, her eyes glaring hatred.

I gagged, holding my nose to mitigate the effects of her stench. She slapped away my hand and kicked me viciously with her silver shoe that was identical to Gisèle-from-Paris's own.

"Do I smell, huh?" Her voice was raised in rage. "How dare you cover your nose when I speak, you rude little runt!"

"She did the same to me while I was in their precious *Ibaja-La*," Gisèle-from-Paris said, eyeing me savagely. "But I recognised her from her previous visits to our realm as soon as I arrived at *Ibaja-La*. The other brides there think she's a bride just like them, the fools. I say we kill her now."

On hearing Gisèle-from-Paris's words, my heart dropped straight to my feet—*She knows me! Gisèle-from-Paris knew who I was all this while! I'm truly doomed now.* This time, I could do little to control the loud wails that issued from my lips.

"P-please don't kill me," I cried, scrambling to my knees and holding tight to Gisèle-from-Paris's ankles. "I'll never disrespect you again. I'm sorry for holding my nose; you don't smell… It's the air that is smelly, not you. P-please forgive me and let me go home. I'll never, ever return to your world again. I thought I was dreaming. I didn't know I visited here for real. I'll tell Big Momma Mmuọ-Ka-Mmuọ to free me from being a Bride-Sentinel, I promise. P-please let me go, please…"

"So now you finally admit you're a cursed Bride-Sentinel, huh? You're going nowhere till you tell us what you did with our sister-bride, Anene Eze," the tall Ghost-Bride said, pulling me up again from the ground. I realised she was their leader by the deference the rest of the evil Ghost-Brides paid her. "Answer me quick: what did you do with Anene Eze? Speak now!"

Oh no, no! Idiot me has gone and revealed my secret! "Sh-she came to possess my cousin, Keziah, and… and…" I paused—*Oh, Holy Mother, what do I say? I can't tell them that I killed Anene Eze with Dibia's charmed Kolanut or they'll be very angry with me and kill me for real. They won't even believe me if I tell them I was possessed…*

"And what? Speak up, you disgusting child!" the leader ordered, shaking me hard.

"I'm sure she killed Anene Eze," Gisèle-from-Paris said bitterly. "That's what Bride-Sentinels do after all. They kill us whenever we try to become real brides. *Oui!* They hate us and never have any pity for our plight. The Great Council of Guardians called her away earlier today and no doubt gave her more instructions on how to destroy us when she returns to the living world tomorrow. She refuses to tell me what they told her and I don't think she'll reveal what she did to Anene Eze. I say we kill her now. I really can't stand her."

Even before Gisèle-from-Paris finished speaking, the rest of the gathered Ghost-Brides took up her call.

"Kill her! Kill her! Kill her!" Their shrieks filled the air, a cacophony of hate and rage. Hot sweat doused my body, terror stealing my breath. I tugged hard, trying to free my trapped hand and flee my attackers—*Fly, Bata! Fly from here! Just focus; ignore*

Gisèle-from-Paris's lies. You can do it! I delved deeper into my mind, straining, screaming silently as I tried to thrust my body up into the air with the power of my mind. I crossed my arms over my shoulders and shut my eyes tight, nodding rapidly eight times, over and over as I willed myself to fly.

But my efforts were in vain, and once again my feet remained land-trapped. It was as if my flesh were filled with concrete and my bones wrought of iron. The painful truth dawned on me with a deep feeling of despair—*Gisèle-from-Paris is right. In their world, I've truly lost my ability to fly, just like them.*

Gisèle-from-Paris's cruel hand yanked my hair, pulling my head all the way back till I thought my neck would snap. I screamed in pain, twisting my body to mitigate the agony. In a blink, I felt multiple hands on me, sharp-nailed fingers that ripped my beautiful hanbok with furious zeal. The first set of teeth sank into my wrist as I desperately tried to shield my nakedness. Before the howl left my lips, a second, third, and fourth set of teeth-nails mauled my body with the speed of rabid dogs. Angry hands and punishing feet inflicted tremendous pain on me, pinching, punching, scratching, squeezing, kicking, stamping, till my body grew damp with my own blood—*Mama... Papa... I'm dying. Your daughter is dying... Oh the pain... the pain...*

I felt waves of dizziness overcome me. My sight glazed and everything around me started to grow foggier than the cursed realm of my doom. I felt the salty taste of my tears on my swollen, bruised lips and the pain in my heart grew unbearable—*Mama, I'm sorry... Papa, I'm a bad daughter, please forgive me... Holy Mary, Mother of God, pray for us sinners now and at the hour of our death, Amen.*

As the darkness crouched closer, I felt something crawl its steely way into my body. A heat like none I had ever experienced suddenly seared my skin, bringing a sharp gasp to my swollen lips. My head started to burn up like a fire-roasted yam tuber. I screamed in agony, my voice an unearthly shriek that instantly stilled every other sound in the vicinity.

Sudden silence descended. I could hear nothing but the sound of my hard breathing. An inexplicable strength flowed into my limbs as if my blood had turned to lead. In a blink, all my terror winked out like a dead star in the sky. The burning inside my head vanished, replaced by a birring sound that filled my ears with sudden ancient knowledge.

A cold calm filled my heart. I smiled as I flexed my steel muscles with languid deliberation. I noticed the chalk-white skin of my limbs with icy indifference. In a fluid motion, I hauled myself up from the ground and turned to face my attackers. Horror filled their faces. They started to stumble away from me, screaming and sobbing, their eyes wide with terror. There was a beetle-like quality to their manic flight that brought a cold smile to my face.

And I watched them run. My multiple faces continued cascading and my four eyes rotated furiously inside their deep sockets, releasing invisible waves of death. With icy contempt, I watched the bride-vermin drop to the ground, one after the other, their bodies rapidly dissolving into fine dust on the desolate landscape of their accursed realm. And still, my cascading faces and obsidian all-seeing eyes watched their pathetic flight and their savage annihilation with detached disdain. Around me was a ghastly wasteland of vanquished Ghost-Brides, some petrified into eternal statues, others nothing more than small heaps of white dust. Their dying shrieks filled the air and my heart thrilled at the devastation I wreaked on my enemies. Briefly, I wondered if Mmuọ-Ka-Mmuọ was even now collecting their cursed ghosts, she that was the keeper of the ghosts of the ghosts.

A thought forced itself into my head—*Gisèle-from-Paris!* I swerved my neck and saw her running in her familiar hunched and clumsy motion, her long veil trailing wildly behind her. She glanced behind with terror-glazed eyes and saw me watching her with lazy contemplation—*Do I petrify her first into a living statue before reducing her to dust? Or perhaps I should burn her into cinders with* The Fire Face *or even melt her into mushy liquid with* The Melting Face?

With a tiny jerk of my neck, I pulled the deadliest of my eight faces and annihilated Gisèle-from-Paris into white dust. As she disintegrated, a sudden light flashed before me, almost blinding me with its dazzling intensity. I shut my eyes and raised an arm to shield my face. A dark shadow fell heavily over me and I opened my eyes.

Mmuọ-Ka-Mmuọ stood before me in her towering might. The multiple stripes on her body flashed like lightning rods on a stormy night. The chain of human teeth hanging around her neck rattled so furiously I feared they would fly to my neck and chew the life from my veins. Her plethora of cascading faces fell in a blistering speed that sent my head spinning. I saw the rage seething on her multiple faces, but I didn't care. Seeing her in her towering glory was all the balm I needed.

Relief flooded my body as my heart exploded with joy. The icy presence rapidly flowed out of me, thawing my heart and its inhuman ruthlessness. The shrill birring sounds ceased as my cascading faces melted back into my skin like palm oil on hot yam. Once again, I wore my own Bata face and my Bata cowardly heart.

"Big Momma Mmuọ-Ka-Mmuọ!" I cried—*I'm safe! Oh, Mother Mary, I'm safe! Everything is alright now!*

"Child! Oh, my poor child! What have we done to you?" Mmuọ-Ka-Mmuọ cried as she reached out her massive arms to me. "We should have waited before giving you The Eight Faces of Devastation. You're not old enough to control your powers. And now, it's too late! It can't be retrieved until you have fulfilled your destiny in your human realm. You poor, poor child! What a great burden you will have to bear."

And for the first time, I saw real tears fall on Mmuọ-Ka-Mmuọ's cascading faces. My tears joined hers, washing away the last vestiges of the fire burning inside my head.

With a deep sigh, I fell into Mmuọ-Ka-Mmuọ's waiting arms. And the world went black.

14

The next time I opened my eyes, I found myself stretched out on a thin mat on the floor of a very small room. Two men stared down at me from their kneeling positions, their dark faces stretched in terror. One of them, a big man with a scar down the side of his right cheek, had tears pouring down his face.

"Oh, ancestors be praised! She lives! Akuabata is alive once again!" The crying man swept me into his arms, squeezing me so tight I thought I would surely suffocate. His body smelled of Heineken beer, cigarette smoke, and sweat, and a sudden memory teased my mind. It quickly vanished though, and I sat up hurriedly, pushing away the strange man hugging me with frenzied arms.

"Where am I?" I asked, trying desperately to hide my panic—*Oh, Big Momma Mmuọ-Ka-Mmuọ! Where have I come to? How can men enter Ibaja-La? Where are Madison-from-Texas and my bride-friends? Where's Big Momma Mmuọ-Ka-Mmuọ?*

"Where am I?" I asked again, fighting my rising terror.

On hearing my question, the two men gasped loudly. They exchanged stunned looks before staring at me with the same horrified gaze I had witnessed when I first awoke.

"Dibia! What language is this she speaks?" the big man with the scarred face gasped in a hushed voice, his eyes wide with disbelief. "What is this terrible voice coming from my daughter's lips? And her eyes! Amadioha, have mercy! Look at her eyes! What evil is this?"

The man he addressed as Dibia, an older man of small stature, stern demeanour, and blood-splattered head, stooped low to peer into my face.

"Ancestors, have mercy!" he whispered in a voice as hushed as his companion's own. He grabbed my chin hard and tilted my head till his face almost touched mine. "What evil is this, eh? What demon has followed the child back from the realm of the dead?"

"What? What? What's wrong with me?" I asked, my voice raised in panic. Once again, both men gave me a startled look on hearing my question, but they gave me no answers.

"Dibia, do something this instant, you hear me?" The scar-faced man was almost apoplectic with anger, his eyes red-hued and hard. He hulked over the wiry man, who was still holding my chin, unrepressed rage pulsating the thick veins in his neck. "I brought my child to you for ritual cleansing, and instead, you killed her. Now, you've brought her back to life completely changed from the daughter I know. How can I take her back to her mother with such ghastly eyes on her face, eh? They're exactly the same eyes she wore during her possession yesterday at Gabriel's house. Have you ever seen any human with eyes completely white like this?" He stared at me aghast, his eyes glazed with terror. "You promised me everything would be alright but look at this now. Listen to her talk. What language is this she speaks in this fearsome tone that echoes with a multitude of voices? How can a single person speak with many voices at the same time? Dibia, I don't care how you do it, just return my child back to me as she was when I brought her to you, do you hear?" The big man was crying and shouting simultaneously as he shook the smaller man with fear-fuelled rage—*His daughter? Am I his daughter?* I stared intently at him, trying hard to place him in my memory. But no pictures formed in my mind. I knew neither his face nor his name, and his voice brought no memories of his place in my heart or my life—*Oh please, Big Momma Mmuọ-Ka-Mmuọ, come and take me away from this horrible place and return me to my bride-friends in* Ibaja-La.

I looked around the tiny, dingy room with its mud walls and thatched roofing and felt tears pool in my eyes—*Such a horrible place as this can never exist in our beautiful* Ibaja-La, *never!* I shuddered and hung my head, reluctant to see either my surroundings or the two men with me. My heart was thudding wildly and fearful thoughts whirled inside my head—*What next? What will they do to me now? And what's wrong with my eyes that's got them both in such a panic? Why can't they understand me when I speak to them?*

"Okeke, calm your heart, my good friend," the bloodied one called Dibia said, letting go of my chin. He straightened and stepped away from me, tapping his cheek as he fixed me with a hard, considering stare. I looked away, unwilling to hold his gaze. Despite being the smaller of the two men, there was a raw power and menace in his aura that filled my heart with unease. After several tense seconds, he turned his eyes back to the big man.

"Yes, Okeke. I think I know what happened to your daughter. In fact, I'm sure I now know what happened to the child and—"

"What? What happened to her?" the one that called himself my father cut in impatiently. "Tell me quick before my sanity and I part ways for good. I'm going crazy here."

"Hold your heart, my friend. If you remember, I told you everything that happened inside this shrine when your daughter died, right?" Dibia said, once again fixing his hard gaze on me. My father nodded. "And do you recall that the great spirit, she that goes by the name of Mmuọ-Ka-Mmuọ, had said that the child shall spend thirty nights in the realm of the dead before returning to us, right?"

Again, my father nodded.

"She said that the thirty nights will be the equivalent of two hours in our human time," Dibia continued. "However, as we both know, Akuabata was dead for almost three hours instead of the two hours expected. Therefore, something must have gone wrong in the dead realm which delayed her return. Such a long sojourn in the underworld always has consequences. Therefore, she has returned, still in the spirit state she was in while she resided with the dead." Dibia paused as my father gasped, staring at me with horror-widened eyes.

"It's okay, Okeke." Dibia patted him gently on his right shoulder. "Don't worry. It will take the child's spirit a little while to realise that it's back in the world of the living. But, trust me, it will happen. Give her a few days and you'll see that I'm right. Her eyes will return to their normal human colour and her voice will again be its normal mono. Within a matter of days, she'll forget the language of the dead and speak in our human tongue once again. You just have to be patient and allow nature and the ancestors to do their work, alright?"

My father did not nod this time. Instead, he fixed me with a stare as intense as Dibia's before shaking his head violently.

"What do I tell her mother, eh?" he muttered, still staring at me as one would an alien insect. "What will our people say when they see her, I ask you? You already know the stories circulating in the village after what happened at Gabriel's house last night. This new phenomenon will surely bring disaster on our heads. Just looking at the inhuman whiteness of her eyes sends chills to my soul. Can you imagine the terror she'll bring to her siblings, looking and speaking the way she does now? Can you even envision the pandemonium her appearance will cause in the wider compounds?"

"So then, do you want me to keep her here till she returns to her human form?" Dibia asked in an excited voice that indicated it was the very thing he wanted. "Okeke, I ask you again to let me have this child as my apprentice. Between the two of us, we will raise the greatest medicine-woman in the ten villages and beyond. Akuabata is a blessing from the ancestors. Let's not let her gift go to waste. Leave her with me and return to your family."

For several minutes, my father remained silent in deep thought while my heart raced so fast, I thought I would surely die—*I am a returned dead! According to them, I'm a ghost! What will become of me? I don't want to stay with Dibia or the one that calls himself my father. They're both strangers who fill my heart with fear. I want to go back to* Ibaja-La, *to Big Momma Mmuọ-Ka-Mmuọ and my bride-friends. What do I do? Oh my bad luck, what do I do?*

I started to cry. In seconds, my shoulders built up an earthquake of shudders, my face devoid of tears, just as when I lived in *Ibaja-La*. My body shook violently as I howled out the confusion, terror, and anguish that tormented my soul. Both Dibia and my father exchanged startled looks before my father stooped again and held me in his arms.

"It's alright, my child," he murmured. "Hush now; don't cry, okay? I'll not leave you with Dibia. Of course you'll go home to Mama. Your sister and brothers are all waiting to see you. I'm sure they're all back from Keziah's wedding by now. Come; cease your cries, okay? Do you want me to carry you home on my back? Here, climb now. Let's go home."

My father knelt down and turned his back to me. I scrambled up from the mat and stood before him.

"I can fly," I said proudly. "I'm not a little girl anymore. I'm a Ghost-Bride from *Ibaja-La* and we all fly in our realm. I'm ready to fly now."

I poised myself for my flight as I waited for him to lead the way. Instead, he looked helplessly at Dibia. The small man shrugged and gave him a pained smile.

"Patience, my friend," he murmured. "Her speech will come back soon, you'll see. Take her home since it appears to be what she prefers, and who knows? Seeing her mother and siblings might jolt her memory and speed up her recovery. It's a good thing evening has now fallen hard, so you should be able to navigate your way home without encountering many villagers. Just tell Akuabata to stay mute and keep her face down so nobody discovers her latest affliction. I'll call on you tomorrow to discuss further. In the meantime, have a peaceful sleep and wake up with good health and cheer, my friend."

With a deep sigh and another shake of his head, my father took my hand and led me out of the tiny room and into the warm evening air. Immediately, I primed my body for flight in the special way we had in *Ibaja-La* and willed my mind to lift my body into the air.

Nothing happened. My feet remained rooted on the ground. Each of my limbs felt as heavy as concrete blocks and flight completely eluded me—*Oh no, no! What new trouble is this? Please, please, don't take away my flight now on top of everything else.* Once again, I tried to levitate. But no matter how hard I strained, my feet remained land-locked like the cursed Ghost-Bride from The Wastelands, the one we knew as Gisèle-from-Paris.

At the thought, a sudden dread filled my heart with unease. Something teased the edges of my mind but refused to hold firm. I shook my head, shaking away the elusive thoughts. Beside me, my father walked along slowly, matching his long strides to my smaller, clumsy ones. For some reason, I struggled to hold my balance in this human realm after having glided in the fragranced air of *Ibaja-La* for a long time.

The sky was a purple hue of approaching nightfall and most of the houses were already lit up with wick-lamps. I could hear the happy and excited voices of children gathered for their Tales by Moonlight folk-story sessions, while the evening meals sizzled in various open fires. Their heady aromas brought a sudden rumble of hunger to my stomach—*Please let there be lots of food at my father's house when we get there. I'm so hungry I could eat a horse.*

As the word 'horse' slipped into my mind unbidden, another sudden chill slithered across my body. Yet another elusive memory teased the corners of my mind, but again slid away like a slippery snake. No matter how hard I tried to hold onto it, all I was left with was a fluttery image of something frightening and unpleasant.

Quickly, I pushed away the disagreeable thoughts and gripped my father's hand tighter—*Uh-uh! Bata, you have enough things to stress about without inviting more worries.* Instead, I stared down at the unfamiliar clothing I now wore, a blue and silver voile wrap-around that lacked the spectacular beauty of the hanbok that Jeong-from-Gwangju had gifted me. Somehow, I wasn't surprised to see myself in the strange attire. I was quickly discovering that everything in this human world was as unexpected as it was depressing—*Oh, Madison-from-Texas! Jeong-from-Gwangju! Emma-from-Quebec! Guadalupe-from-Mexico! And my beautiful Aaliyah-from-Dubai! I miss you all so, so, much! I wish I were back with you in our beautiful* Ibaja-La. *Please don't forget me till I return. And save lots and lots of nice cakes for me too.*

Night-time was rapidly drawing close as we walked past lamp-lit houses and deserted, dusty paths. I could hear the noisy barks of dogs and the noisier scolding of mothers, coupled with the happy squeals of children inside the numerous compounds we passed. There was a cosiness to the sounds that filled me with yearning and I would have given anything just then to be back at *Ibaja-La* with my friends and their delicious foods.

"We're almost home." Papa's quiet voice broke into my morose thoughts. "You'll soon see your mother and siblings. They should be back from the wedding by now." Instantly, my heart started to thud as sudden panic gripped me—*What if they see me and scream and run away from me because of my eyes and speech? What if they all hate me, these people that are my own family? Oh my bad luck! If only I had a mirror so I could see my eyes and what it is about them that's made my father and Dibia uneasy.*

A deep soul-weariness descended on me. I inhaled deeply—*Huh?* I inhaled again, deeper, longer.

My heart exploded with joy, little slivers of bliss dousing my flesh in goosebumps—*I recognise this smell! I know this place! I'm home! I've come back to my village! I remember everything!* I quickly turned to look at the tall man holding tightly to my hand—*Papa! It's Papa!*

"Papa! Papa!" I shouted his name, tugging his hand as I came to a sudden halt. "Papa! I remember! I remember everything now!" I beamed him a wide smile as I wrapped my arms around his waist. He gave me a startled look. Then his lips stretched in an uncertain smile.

"Akuabata, you're happy that I'm taking you home now, yes?" he asked in his familiar deep voice, his eyes looking down at me with a nervous kind of affection.

Disappointment descended on me, shrouding my heart with dull resignation—*He still doesn't understand my speech! Papa still thinks I'm a ghost. Oh please, Big Momma Mmuọ-Ka-Mmuọ; please give me back my speech and my eyes. I don't want to be a ghost when I meet Mama! Please let Mama love me; please let Ọla and Ada and Ejima and my cousins like me as before. Don't let them run away from me… please…*

"Papa..." As the word left my lips, an icy fist gripped my heart—*Huh? What is this evil I hear?*

For the first time, my ears opened themselves to human sounds and I finally heard what Papa and Dibia had heard, the chorus of voices that spoke the single word 'Papa'. It sounded as if ten Ghost-Brides from the cursed realm spoke the word simultaneously from my lips in their different voices, some raging, some loud, some shrill, others hollow, just like an empty drum. I was speaking in Mmuọ-Ka-Mmuọ's multiple voices. The sound filled me with sudden dread and when Papa looked askance at me, I shook my head and stayed silent, fighting the tightness behind my throat.

In that instant, I knew that I would never again open my mouth in speech till I recovered my human voice. I could not risk terrifying and alienating my family and friends. It was bad enough I had my unholy eyes to contend with without adding the curse of my voice—*Maybe I'll ask Papa to buy me some sunglasses till I recover my human eyes again? The children will laugh at me, but at least, they won't see my eyes. Yes, that's what I'll do. I'll stay inside my room until Papa buys me the sunglasses. Oh please, let Mama love me despite my curse...*

15

Mama was waiting for us just outside Papa's parlour when we arrived. As soon as she saw us, she shouted, "Jesus!" with great relief, and started to run towards us. The kerosene lantern in her hand wobbled as she ran, casting dancing shadows on the ground. Electricity was sporadic in our village and even though Papa had a small generator that provided emergency lighting, it was rarely used. The long journey to the nearest town with a petrol station, coupled with the endemic petrol scarcity, had turned the generator into a sitting decoration inside Papa's motorcycle shed.

"Our-Husband, where have you been with the child?" Mama asked Papa, dropping the lantern on the floor and pulling me into her arms. She held me close in a tight hug, and the familiar pomade scent of her body filled me with intense bliss as my memory-gates instantly flooded me with nostalgic recollections. I clung hard to her, inhaling deeply, my face creased in a wide smile.

"We were all starting to worry, wondering what had become of Bata. Where did you find her?" Mama drew me away from her embrace, her face stern. "And you, fool-child, how many times have I warned you never to wander away without telling someone where you're going, eh? It's a good thing your father found you and brought you home, otherwise I would've taken the birch to you. Come; off to bed with you and no supper either. You don't deserve it."

On hearing her words, I started wailing, loud, choked howls that stunned Mama into slack-jawed silence. Even while crying, my unearthly multiple voices rang eerily in the night and I saw Mama's eyes widen in panic.

"Our-Husband, what is going on? What has happened to Bata?" Mama asked in a fear-hushed voice. She picked up the lamp and held it aloft as she leaned low to peer into my face. A deep frown furrowed her brows and her wide eyes showed her fear. I quickly dropped my lids, hiding my eyes from hers. Her fingers pressed hard into my dry cheeks as she turned my face first to the left, then to the right, seeking something she could neither name nor recognise. All she wanted was a human answer to the supernatural affliction burdening her daughter. I hiccupped myself into desperate silence, fighting the sudden pounding in my temples.

Papa shook his head wearily. "Don't scold the child, woman," he said in a tired voice. "It's not her fault. I took her to Dibia's shrine for a cleansing ritual after what happened at Gabriel's house yesterday. However, there's something very important I need to tell you about her. But first, go into your kitchen and bring food for Akuabata inside my parlour. She must be very hungry after everything she's been through today. Go now; hurry."

Papa took the lamp from Mama and waved her away as she continued to stare gobsmacked at him. It was no secret that Papa had never cared much for my company in the past, and requesting food for me inside his private parlour was unheard of. As Mama hurried away to do as Papa instructed, he turned to me with a sad smile.

"Come, child. Let's go rest from your long journey." He took my hand once again and led me into his parlour. He sat on his fabric sofa, placing the lantern on the low centre table before him.

"Sit, child," he said in the same heavy voice, still smiling wearily. He patted the space next to him on the sofa. "You've been through a lot recently, haven't you? I know you must be as confused as I am, and no doubt very frightened too. But have no fear, my daughter. Your father is with you and will protect you from everything and everyone, okay?" He paused and looked at me again with the same considering look in his eyes that he'd worn since I woke up inside Dibia's shrine. Then he shrugged tiredly. "Akuabata, I'm not sure if you understand me, since I can't understand you, but it's okay. You're home now, inside the safety of your father's house. I'll explain everything to your mother and your stepmother, and they'll ensure nobody troubles you, neither your siblings nor your cousins. Is there anything you want to say to me? Just nod if you understand me."

I nodded. Papa gave me a startled look before a big smile broke over his face.

"You understand everything I say, then?" he asked in wide-eyed disbelief. Again, I nodded. "That is wonderful indeed, may the ancestors be praised." He paused briefly, a slight frown on his face. Then he nodded. "That's it! We need pencil and paper so you can write whatever you want to say. I'm hoping you know how to write a bit?"

Again, I nodded. Papa had never read my school report cards, seeing as he was illiterate, otherwise he would have known that I was the cleverest in the family. My determination to be as educated as my stepmother, Ọla, drove me to strive for good grades. My dream was to go to Germany one day and acquire the real German Success Walk. Then, I would build a storey-building for my family and buy Papa a Mercedes-Benz car, just like Engineer Tip-Toe's big German car.

"Good! I'll send your sister for your schoolbag. Wait a second." Papa got up and went outside to shout Ada's name. Soon my big sister came running over.

"Go and collect Akuabata's schoolbag at once," Papa instructed before Ada could fully enter the parlour.

"Huh?" Again I heard the stunned bafflement in my big sister's voice that echoed Mama's own.

"Are you deaf? I said hurry up and bring me your sister's schoolbag and don't waste my time. Tell Mama-Ejima to come over while you're at it."

Papa returned to his sofa as my sister hurried away on the errand. I sat shyly by his side even as my heart fluttered with pride at the unfamiliar positive attention I was receiving from him. I recalled it had been like this since the day I became my cousin Keziah's Bride-Sentinel—*Was it only yesterday as Dibia said? But how can only a day have passed when I know I spent several weeks in* Ibaja-La? The thought brought a heavy feeling once again to my heart, and by the time Ada returned with my schoolbag, I was ready to cry.

"Bata, are you okay?" my big sister asked in a concerned voice, ruffling my hair affectionately as she handed me my bag. I wanted to throw myself into her arms, but I was afraid to show her my eyes. Instead, I nodded and kept my head down. I knew Ada was probably thinking that Papa was scolding me again, as was his habit, and I was relieved by the thought. It was better she believed that rather than be confronted with my ghost eyes and unholy voice.

"Akuabata, find your pencil and write me what you want to say," Papa said, pulling the lantern closer to me as he waved Ada away.

I nodded and pulled out one of my notebooks, a small twenty-four-page writing exercise book with lined pages. I placed it on the low table and leaned forward with my pencil. With meticulous care, I wrote down my request, making sure to fit my words inside the lines. It was important I impressed Papa with my calligraphy, seeing as this was the first time he was seeing my handiwork—I WANT SUN GLASIS PLEASE.

I passed the note over to Papa just as Mama returned with a tray stacked with rice and chicken dishes for Papa and me, as well as a bottle of Fanta drink for me. Even before she placed the tray on Papa's table, my mouth was already salivating. My tummy rumbled noisily with intense hunger and Papa nodded at me.

"Go on and eat, child," he said, just as Ọla sauntered into the parlour. Her face was shrouded in bored irritation. "Here, read what the child has written and tell me what it says." Papa handed the notebook to Ọla. She stooped low to the kerosene lamp and read it out to Papa.

Papa's face creased in a wide smile. "Aahh! Sunglasses, eh? Yes, my child; I will indeed buy you a pair of sunglasses tomorrow, okay?" His voice was choked with laughter as he spoke.

I nodded as I fell on the food, wolfing it down with so much speed I choked after the third spoonful of Jollof-rice. I started to cough noisily and Papa smacked my back with the ball of his hand.

"Take it easy. The food won't run away. Here, drink your Fanta," he said, giving me the bottle of soda. I gulped it down with the same speed with which I had attacked the rice. It was a miracle I didn't choke for the second time, and Mama and Ọla were staring at me as if I were an alien entity. Still, I kept my head down as I ate, refusing to meet their eyes.

"Our-Husband, what is wrong with Bata?" Mama suddenly burst out, her voice loud, almost combative. "I've never seen her this hungry before. One would think she hasn't eaten for a week with the way she's gobbling the food. And why is she sitting here with you? Why are you buying her sunglasses? Is anything wrong with her eyes? I know something's wrong with Bata. I can feel it inside my blood. Oh, Jesus! Don't let anything bad happen to my child!"

Mama quickly weaved the sign of the cross before returning her accusing eyes to Papa's weary face. "In fact, Our-Husband, why did you even take Bata to Dibia's shrine in the first place? You know how much I dislike you involving my children in your pagan rituals, but you continue to disregard my wishes. I'm begging you, tell me what the trouble is otherwise I'll have no rest this night." Mama was almost in tears, and my heart was racing once again— *Oh please, don't let Papa tell her anything yet, at least, not now. Maybe after I finish eating. I don't want Mama to see my eyes yet.*

Papa heaved another tired sigh and motioned Mama over to the chair opposite his sofa. He waited till Mama perched at its edge before grunting loudly. He waved Ọla away, dismissing her from the parlour. She hissed in frustration as she turned to leave. I knew she was curious to hear what Papa had to say, but she dared not disobey him or usurp Mama's right as the first wife, despite being the mother of three sons. Papa waited till Ọla's footsteps faded away. Then he turned to Mama. When next he spoke, his voice was as heavy as his sigh.

"Woman, I want you to stop your snivelling before you upset the child further," Papa said, his voice hard. His gaze was fierce on Mama's face. "Now, I need you to pay careful attention to what I have to say, are we clear?" Mama nodded repeatedly, her eyes clouded in anxiety. "You already know that Akuabata is a Bride-Sentinel. What you don't know, however, is that the role comes with its own hazards. Our daughter was exposed to other spiritual entities when she guarded Keziah last night. Dibia says they were the ghosts of dead brides who latched onto her body, draining her life force. He ordered a cleansing ritual in his shrine to rid her of the entities. It didn't go as we planned. Akuabata died in the process and—"

"What!" Mama shrieked, leaping from her chair. "Our-Husband, what did you just say? Did I hear you say that my daughter died?" She stared at me incredulously where I remained frozen, my spoon halfway to my lips. "If she died, how come I'm looking at her right now?"

"Woman, if you'll let me finish, then you'll know why," Papa snapped. For several seconds, I sensed Mama's eyes on me, staring long and hard. I could hear her heavy breathing over my bent head before she slowly sank back into her chair. "I already told you to pay great attention to what I have to say. I don't want to be interrupted or made to repeat myself again; are we clear?" Papa bit out, his voice hard, icy.

Mama nodded reluctantly, wringing her hands with nervous frenzy.

"Good. As I was saying, Akuabata died briefly during the ritual. Dibia said she was supposed to die for two hours; however, something went wrong and she was dead for almost three hours. When she regained life, she came back drastically altered. Dibia says it's as a result of her spending a longer time in the dead-world than she was supposed to. Her speech is gone. She hears and understands everything, but she has forgotten how to speak in our tongue. Worse, when she speaks, her voice is not of this world. You heard it when she cried earlier. No one can understand what she says now."

Papa paused as Mama gasped, covering her mouth with her hand. Her eyes were saucer-wide as she stared at me and my now-abandoned meal—*Oh no, no, no!* I wanted to press my hand against my pounding heart as Mama had hers pressed against her lips, but I was frozen with panic.

Papa turned to look at me and nodded with a small smile. The gentle compassion in his eyes calmed my fright. "Akuabata's eyes also underwent a drastic change," Papa continued in his heavy voice. "Lift the lamp and see for yourself. That's why we need sunglasses to protect her from unkind words and stares."

With a trembling hand, Mama lifted the lamp and approached me. My heart raced faster. I wanted to run away, to hide myself from her seeking gaze. I lowered my lids but Mama grasped my chin, raising my head.

"Bata, open your eyes, my child," Mama said, her voice a tremulous whisper. With great reluctance, I complied.

I stared into my mother's eyes, her goggled, horrified, and terrified eyes that looked ready to drop from their sockets. Mama let go of my chin as if it were a rattlesnake and stumbled away from me.

"J-Jesus, have mercy!" Mama stammered, weaving the sign of the cross and shaking her head over and over like a cobra with a malfunctioned neck. "Wh-what evil is this?" She turned accusing eyes at Papa. "Our-Husband, what have you and Dibia done to my child, eh? Tell me the truth now. Have you used Bata for money rituals? Have you gone and sacrificed our child to a wealth deity? Oh, Holy Mother, save my soul! I know you don't favour the child as you do her siblings, but if you've done this evil to her, I swear by heaven that I'll—"

"Shut your stupid mouth," Papa snarled, fixing Mama a vicious glare. "How dare you accuse me of such unspeakable evil? Are you crazy? Didn't you hear a word I just spoke? And who says I don't favour Akuabata? That's how you foolish women go about creating discord in your marriage and family. In fact, I now regret saying anything to you." Papa made a disgusted sound before turning his face away from Mama. "Go this instant from my sight and woe betide you if anyone hears anything that transpired here tonight or should anything bad happen to Akuabata." Papa's face was like thunder as he turned to me. "Follow your mother and ignore everything she just said, alright?"

I nodded, rising from his sofa with trembling limbs. All the while I lived in *Ibaja-La*, I had longed for my mother, missed her and loved her desperately. But now I was finally reunited with her, I found myself wishing I could remain with Papa instead. Since my transformation, I felt safer with my father, he whose voice used to send me into petrified panic in the past. It was as if my affliction had altered my parents as well. Mama was now driven by fear and confusion, feeding my own terror, while Papa's calm strength and compassion soothed my heart.

A great weariness overcame me. My eyes were so heavy I was ready to drop to the floor and sleep for eternity. With dragging legs, I followed Mama out of Papa's parlour and into the cosy familiarity of the room I used to share with my big sister Ada. With a loud sigh, I fell onto my mattress.

"Bata; come, my child, tell me everything that happe—"

I was asleep before Mama could finish her sentence. And when I dreamt, my dream was all about the haunting, silvery beauty of *Ibaja-La* and its equally enchanting inhabitants.

16

I remained in my altered state for several months following my return from Dibia's shrine. In that period, I never spoke a word save in the privacy of my bedroom. Apart from my parents, Ọla, and Ada, no other person in the wider family knew of my cursed affliction. My dark sunglasses ensured the triplets were never frightened by my silver-glass eyes, and my self-imposed mutism hid my cursed voices from all. Not even my stepmother or big sister knew of the terrible transformation in my voice. Only Papa and Mama nursed that ghastly secret and they ensured I too kept it imprisoned behind the deep silence of my throat.

Mama and I tested my voice every morning to see if it still resonated with the multiple voices of the dead. It was a daily ritual we carried out with mechanical commitment, without any hope or joy. Since my transformation, Ada had abandoned our bedroom and now slept in Ejima's room. She said she had to sleep with Ejima to help them use the toilet when they needed to piss at night. But I knew she was uncomfortable around me, just like the rest of the adults in our house. I missed the security and cosiness of my sister's presence, but at the same time I was thankful for the privacy to deal with my affliction. In the mornings, I would quickly dress and put on my sunglasses, to ensure I didn't frighten Ejima should they dash into my room unannounced and accidentally stumble upon my curse. When I was done, I would sit down on my mattress to await Mama's arrival. In no time, her light footsteps would pause outside my door.

Today was no different. I waited in trepidation for Mama to enter my bedroom for her usual morning inspection, but she waited outside my door as she had done every day since my transformation, steeling herself to enter. I knew she was there. She knew that I knew she was there. I recognised her daily battles with herself, her fear of what she would encounter when she entered my room, her fervent prayers to the Virgin Mary to work a miracle and return me to normal, and her shame at having a daughter whose pagan affliction diminished her before her beloved Father David. I hadn't even attended Keziah's wedding as her flower-girl because of my affliction, something that filled me with regret and despair. Mama had made up a story about my sickness to hide her embarrassment. Mama's shame was my shame, her fears mine too. Guilt was my daily companion and the fear of permanent imprisonment inside our compound followed me everywhere.

After several minutes, Mama entered my room. She flashed me a bright smile and motioned me to my knees as was her norm.

"Bata, how are you today? Come; let's pray first," she said, bringing out her rosaries and sprinkling holy water on my head. I shut my eyes obediently and began to mouth the prayers silently along with her. I didn't want to frighten her with my cursed voice.

The prayers were empty monologues inside my head. They no longer touched my heart or held my trust. Since *Ibaja-La*, I knew a different reality, an afterlife that was real and blissful. I had seen Big Momma Mmuọ-Ka-Mmuọ and experienced her powers. I now knew that Papa's gods were stronger than Mama's own. If anyone could heal my affliction, I knew it wasn't the Virgin Mary.

"Bata, remove your sunglasses, let's see your eyes and hear your voice now," Mama said when we were done with our prayers. I obeyed. As she looked into my eyes, I prepared myself for what I knew would be the outcome: the fact that my day of salvation had yet to arrive.

Mama's eyes clouded in disappointment as they observed the solid silvery hue of my eyes. She shut her own eyes and sighed heavily.

"Let's hear your voice," she said dully.

Again, I obeyed with my usual mantra. "Good morning, Mama; I slept well and didn't have any nightmares," I said, trying to speak in a whisper.

She winced involuntarily at the creepy multitude of voices extruding from my lips. These days, my tongue had regained our language despite the unearthly multiplicity of its tone, so thankfully, Mama could now understand some of my speech despite the ghastly sound I made. There was still a garbled quality that hindered total clarity and I prayed that in time, my words would become clearer. Mama mouthed a quick prayer and sprinkled more holy water on me before hastily leaving my bedroom to report my condition to Papa.

I sighed wearily and stared blankly at my door—*When will this horror end? When will I be free from this curse?* Our lack of success now brought a sinking feeling in my heart whenever I heard Mama's soft footsteps outsider my bedroom door.

I remained cooped up inside my bedroom until Ejima called me out to play before breakfast. As I took my place on the eating-mat, I smiled a greeting at my stepmother.

Ọla blanked me out with her eyes. I hung my head, fighting the sudden tightness in my throat. Since my transformation, my stepmother no longer sought my company as in the past. When she was forced to address me, she spoke coolly to an empty space above my head. Her coldness was a deep wound that hurt me more than anything else, save my loss of *Ibaja-La*.

After breakfast, I withdrew to my bedroom to read my story books for the umpteenth time. Due to my affliction, Mama kept me away from school and kept our cousins and playmates away from me. She also kept herself away from me as much as she could without arousing any suspicion. But I sensed her terror and unease whenever she found herself alone with me. Gone was the old, baffled humour in her eyes when they now rested on me. Even without the dark sunglasses creating a natural shield between us, Mama's eyes would have still turned away from mine. It wasn't merely as a result of my unnatural eyes and forced mutism either. I quickly discovered that I returned from the land of the dead brides with another defect, a curse that quickly consigned me to a state of near-exclusion in our compound.

Everything started a couple of months ago on a bright Sunday morning. Mama was getting ready to attend Mass. She had finished having her bucket-bath and was busy applying pomade cream to her skin. I dashed into her wardrobe and brought out her red lace Bubu gown and red Enigogoro scarf for her to wear. Mama gave me a startled look as she stared at the items on her bed. A deep frown furrowed her brows as she quietly resumed her toiletries.

On the same day, I fetched a bottle of Coca-Cola for Ọla, together with one of the ripe bananas from the bunch in the kitchen while she sat reading one of her Mills & Boon books on her favourite wooden bench. Like Mama, my stepmother gave me a startled look before her eyes narrowed suspiciously. She waved me away from her presence without a word.

Later that day, I brought in Ada's laundry drying on the line and gave her the ripped red blouse and blue skirt, together with her sewing kit. Her stunned reaction mirrored Mama's and Ọla's and I ran away from her before she could speak. Later that evening, I noticed the three of them huddled together and whispering urgently. The sight surprised me, as it was rare to see such a degree of camaraderie between Ọla and Ada.

The next evening, I entered Papa's parlour and started massaging his feet after he returned from work. He gave me a startled look but smiled approvingly at me. When I was done, I dashed to his bedroom and brought him a bottle of Heineken beer from the carton behind the door. I also brought his tin money box and a thick brown envelope from inside his drawer. Papa's eyes looked ready to drop from his sockets when I presented him with the items.

I did all these chores for my family without being asked. Instead, I heard the thoughts inside their minds and complied with their wishes before they could speak the words. Not too long after I left Papa's presence, I saw Mama, Ọla, and Ada making their way to Papa's parlour. Their faces looked grim and their strides, determined. They were with Papa for a long time while I played with Ejima.

Almost an hour later, Ada called out to me. "Bata, come quick. Papa wants you now."

I abandoned our game and hurried over—*I know I've been good in recent days… I don't think I've displeased anyone.*

I entered Papa's parlour without my usual panic.

"Akuabata, I have something to ask you and I want you to tell me the absolute truth, alright?" Papa said, giving me a piercing look.

I nodded—*Oh no! What is it this time? What have I done wrong now? They all look very upset for some reason.*

"Can you read our minds?" Papa asked. "Be careful with your answer, child, and tell me nothing but the truth. Are you able to hear our thoughts?"

Aahh! Now I know. I nodded with a bright smile.

Papa did not return my smile. Mama, Ọla, and Ada did not smile either. They stared at me instead as if I had grown horns, tails, and feathers. They exchanged panicked looks with each other and Papa looked so angry I thought he might strike me— *But why? What have I done wrong? I'm only helping them by doing chores for them so they don't waste time saying what they want.*

"Oh, Jesus!" Mama wailed, weaving the sign of the cross frantically. "What new evil is this? When will this torment leave our family?" She started sobbing softly and Ada quickly wrapped her arms around her, eyeing me with malevolent rage.

"Akuabata, let this be the last time you sneak into our heads, do you hear me?" Papa snarled, pointing a threatening forefinger at me. "You are never, ever to spy on anybody's thoughts in this house again. Should I discover that you've disobeyed me, I'll send you over to Dibia's house permanently, so you can practise this evil habit with him to your heart's content, are we clear?"

I nodded, my throat tightening painfully with unshed tears. Papa waved me away from his presence and I ran into my bedroom in guilty mortification. From then, they addressed me as one would a stranger rather than family, with extreme politeness devoid of warmth. Even Ọla's best friend, Teacher Uzo, no longer smiled at me when she visited my stepmother. I wondered what Ọla had said to her, since I knew my stepmother was bound by the same code of silence Papa had imposed on everybody about my latest curse.

Only my younger siblings, ignorant of my affliction, continued to seek out my company with loving irreverence. No matter how much I tried, Ejima's thoughts came flying into my head of their own volition. In their minds, I read nothing but uncomplicated joy, together with the various games and foods they craved. And, as always, I granted their wishes before they spoke them aloud, endearing myself the more to them. The only wishes in their thoughts which I couldn't grant them were to remove my sunglasses for them to play with and to regain my former unrestrained laughter and chatter. Their joy in my mind-reading abilities left me confused over the frigid responses of the adults—*Surely they should be happy that I'm saving them the trouble of asking for things, just like Ejima.*

My mind-reading abilities were not perfect, which might perhaps explain their displeasure with me. During subsequent interrogations by Papa and Ọla, I told them with gesticulations and written notes that I could only hear their thoughts when they were close to me. But now, most of them kept their distance from me, as if I were plagued with the leprosy boils. Apart from Ejima, Dibia was the only other person that found favour with my thought-hearing. The medicine-man had smiled broadly when Papa first informed him of it, patting my head affectionately as he chewed his tobacco stick with slow relish.

"Child, can you tell what I'm thinking about now?" he asked me. Something in his dark eyes simultaneously doubted and challenged me. It made me both want to succeed and fail at the same time. The medicine-man was the only person I feared more than Papa. I didn't want to offend him by invading his mind or disappoint him by not accurately reading his thoughts. I lowered my gaze to my feet, trapping my words within the prison of my mouth.

"Come now, child; don't be afraid," Dibia cajoled. "I am thinking about something this very instant. I need you to tell me what you hear in my thoughts. We must know everything you brought back with you from your sojourn in the realm of the dead. Only then can I help you return to normalcy, and you want to be normal again, don't you?"

I nodded fervently—*Oh yes, yes... I'll do anything to return to how I used to be and play freely with my cousins and friends—unless I'm lucky enough to return to our beautiful Ibaja-La.*

"So, what am I thinking now?" Dibia repeated.

"I think she's worried about using the dead voices that came back with her from the dead realm," Papa said, looking at me with tired resignation. "Akuabata, don't be afraid. You can speak freely to Dibia. I doubt if there's any voice our esteemed medicine-man hasn't heard in his long and illustrious career. Don't forget he's already heard you speak when you first awoke from your dead sleep."

Papa's words and weary face emboldened me to speak. I forced myself to hold Dibia's fierce gaze through the dark protection of my sunglasses as I allowed my mind to flow into his head.

Huh? A deep frown creased my brows. *What is this I'm hearing? Whose thoughts reside inside Uncle Dibia's head?* I glanced up at him in surprise. The thoughts I heard inside the medicine-man's head were spoken in a female voice, not the familiar deep tenor of his spoken voice.

"What?" Dibia asked, a sly look in his dark eyes. "Are you struggling to read my thoughts then?"

I shook my head. "It… it's a woman's voice that I'm hearing inside your head," I stammered, hearing the multitude of voices coming from my mouth with renewed dread. "I hear your thoughts, Uncle Dibia, but you're thinking them in a woman's voice."

Dibia's eyes widened in shock. He gripped my arm and leaned forward till his face almost touched mine.

"Speak; tell me exactly what I'm thinking word for word." There was anger in his voice, as if he'd been caught praying the Rosary inside the church. "Remove those wretched sunglasses so that I can see your eyes and read any mendacity—quick."

I quickly complied with his command, awed by his immense powers that gave him the ability to think in any voice he wanted. I always thought with my own voice; I heard other people's thoughts in voices that mirrored their spoken words. Yet, Dibia could harness any voice he wanted in his thoughts—*I bet he can even think in a snake's or a mosquito's voice if he wants.* I shuddered involuntarily at the thought.

"Has a demon stolen your ears and your mouth?" Dibia demanded. "I told you to tell me everything you heard inside my head. I know you heard something. Your own words damn you. Now speak before I put a curse on you."

"You're thinking that the b-black goat you received from Ugo of Amadi clan might die before you c-can use it for your divination on his behalf, since it has refused to eat anything all day." I stumbled over my words, fighting the quaking of my limbs. "But you can't do the divination ritual before midnight, and it will be too late by then. So, you're angry with Ugo of Amadi clan for bringing you a sick goat. You're also wondering if you should return the goat to him without performing any rituals or punish him with a defective divination that will bring him poverty rather than the wealth he desperately craves."

I heard Dibia gasp.

"What? What?" Papa's voice was impatient. As Dibia began to tell him everything I said, I heard his own shocked groan. When I looked up, they were both staring at me as if I had transformed into a prowling two-headed tiger.

"I told you, didn't I?" Papa said to Dibia in a voice that held no triumph. He shut his eyes and shook his head before hanging his chin low on his chest. He inhaled deeply and exhaled loudly, cradling his head with hands that trembled. He stared fixedly at the ground, refusing to meet my gaze.

Several tense seconds passed in complete silence. My heart thudded so hard my chest hurt. Then Dibia whistled long and loud before leaning low again to look into my face. His eyes gleamed with wonder and excitement.

I shrank back from him, clutching my fists tightly to my sides—*Bata, you stupid, foolish girl! You should've just kept your* cursed mouth shut. Now Papa is very upset again and if you're not careful, he might just decide to send you to live with Dibia after all. I wanted to slap myself and vanish from the place.

Dibia was speaking once more, his voice now pitched in excitement. In fact, he was practically hopping on his feet.

"Okeke, you have really produced a true wonder of the world in this child," Dibia said, rubbing his hands gleefully. "Not only is she a Bride-Sentinel, but now, with her new mind-reading powers, we can rid our village of evil and mendacity. I think you should apprentice her out to me without delay, so I can help her develop and harness her powers. What do you say, my friend?"

I stared at Papa with horror, shaking my head violently—*No, no! I don't want to be anyone's apprentice! I don't want to live with Uncle Dibia in his dilapidated house. I want to go to school again and become educated like Mama-Ejima. Oh please, don't let Papa send me to Uncle Dibia's house!* My eyes burnt with the tears that wouldn't leak. My body shook so much from my terror that I couldn't move from my frozen spot by Dibia's wooden door.

Papa must have sensed my silent desperation. I was almost hyperventilating, gasping air desperately through my open lips. He lifted his head and stared at me for several tense seconds. Inside his head, I heard the warring voices thundering for his attention—*Send her with Dibia till he cures her. If anyone can cure her cursed affliction, it's Dibia.* BUT IT WON'T BE FAIR ON THE CHILD. EVEN NOW, I CAN SEE THE TERROR ON HER FACE AT THE PROSPECT. *Still, she needs to go with Dibia. It's for her own good. Moreover, I can't have her reading my mind and knowing my deepest secrets. And that terrible voice... Amadioha, save my soul! We must do something to rid her of this accursed voice.* BUT WHAT WILL I SAY TO HER MOTHER? THE WOMAN WILL DRAG IN THAT BLASTED PRIEST, FATHER DAVID, TO TORMENT MY LIFE. *Yet, the child needs to have her afflictions cured and only Dibia can help her.* YOU KNOW VERY WELL THAT DIBIA JUST WANTS TO USE HER POWERS FOR HIS OWN GAINS. IN NO TIME, HE'LL KNOW THE SECRETS OF EVERYBODY IN THE VILLAGE, INCLUDING YOU. *No! No! I can't let that happen. Better the child stays home with us where I can monitor her until she's healed. I just have to shut out my thoughts from her and all should be well… oh damn!* DID SHE HEAR ANY OF THIS?

Papa's head swerved around sharply. He stared hard at me with suspicion-narrowed eyes. I quickly dropped my head, fixing my gaze to the hard-mud ground of Dibia's visitors' room. Even so, my silvery-grey eyes continued to burn with unrestrained grief. My terror-doused face seemed to convince Papa. He grunted deeply and stood up from his wooden bench.

"I've heard everything you suggested," he said to Dibia in a hard voice. "I'll think it over. But for the time being, I think it's best we keep Akuabata at home. I don't want her mother worried more than she is already. Moreover, after what she's been through, I think it's better the child stays in the familiar surroundings of our compound. As you said, she might return to her normal self in time. We just need to be a little more patient. As our people say, a skinny goat can't be fattened overnight on the market day. We merely have to wait for a while longer. Goodnight now and may morning find you well and alive."

Papa left the medicine-man's house with me. His stride was long and fast and his mind was shut to mine. All I heard was silence, a dead silence that reminded me of the forest of tall silver trees in *Ibaja-La*. But I no longer wanted to hear Papa's thoughts; I had no desire to hear anybody's thoughts anymore—*That's why everybody avoids me… they are afraid I'll learn their secrets. Oh please, Big Momma Mmuọ-Ka-Mmuọ, take away this curse from me. Take it away so that my family can love me again. I don't want to hear thoughts anymore… please. I've changed my mind; I don't want to be a Bride-Sentinel anymore. I just want to come back home to* Ibaja-La, *please…*

17

Papa didn't send me to Dibia's house as I had dreaded, but his promise to think over the medicine-man's request hung over me like a sack of burning coal. I skulked around the house, avoiding everybody the same way they avoided me. Soon, a heavy lethargy held me in its thrall, stealing my strength and my will. All I wanted to do was sleep; just shut my eyes and dream of *Ibaja-La*. I fast realised that it was only in my sleep that I could once again find joy, dreaming of my beautiful bride-friends with an intensity that would have stained my cheeks with tears if I were still normal. Despite being with my family, I missed my bride-friends and their realm with great anguish. The collective ill-will of my family members drained the last vestiges of my joy at being back home and *Ibaja-La* pulled me like an Ubọ minstrel's song. Nobody knew of *Ibaja-La* or my wonderous experiences there. There was no one to share it with in my human family.

Sometimes, I wondered if I had dreamt it all, if my mind had conjured everything from my famed vivid imagination. Save for the dramatic physical changes in me and Dibia's words confirming my death inside his shrine, I would have consigned my memories of *Ibaja-La* to the realms of covert lunacy or the psychedelic malaria-dreams. Since my return, I no longer had the terrifying nightmares that used to ruin my sleep. I slept whenever I wanted with my head facing the door and without Dibia's charmed Jigida cowries to ward off my sleep tormentors. It was as if my visit to *Ibaja-La* had wiped away every evil in my sleep, and my nightly dreams of that beautiful realm helped me stay connected to my bride-friends and our wonderful companionship.

Sometimes, a vague memory of something unpleasant would tease the corners of my mind, an unsettling recall about Gisèle-from-Paris. Like all the other Ghost-Brides, I still remembered her with a vividness that didn't diminish with the passage of the months. The last memory I had of her was of our visit to the silent forest of tall silver trees. I remembered every minute detail of the forest. Yet, everything that happened after that forest visit had vanished from my memory. I could recall neither leaving the silver forest with Gisèle-from-Paris nor having any further interaction with her during the rest of my stay in *Ibaja-La*. In fact, my visit to the forest with Gisèle-from-Paris was the final memory of *Ibaja-La* that I had, which was sad, because I didn't want that horrid Ghost-Bride to be the last person I saw before leaving our beautiful realm.

As the days dragged sluggishly into endless months, my heart grew weary from my unremitting misery. I could see no freedom from my unhappy isolation. I started avoiding mealtimes and playtimes with Ejima. Instead, I lay inside my bedroom, rereading my Ladybird fairy-tale books with lethargic grit. The books were the only way I could continue keeping myself educated, since I wasn't attending school anymore. In the beautiful gowns of the princesses—Snow White, Cinderella, Sleeping Beauty, Rapunzel, and Beauty from *Beauty and the Beast*—I saw all my *Ibaja-La* bride-friends in their dazzling glory once again. The universal beauty of the princesses transcended worlds and skin colour. Both Madison-from-Texas and Aaliyah-from-Dubai were shrouded in the same mysterious and dazzling beauty of the Ladybird princesses, and with each passing day, I missed all my bride-friends and wanted nothing more than to be in their ethereal realm once again.

Soon, Mama started to worry about my health and began to spend more time with me; at least, as much as her unease allowed her. She prayed the Rosary with countless Hail Marys and the Lord's Prayer every time she entered my room. I knew that she hoped Our Holy Mother might exorcise the curse from me, and a part of me felt intense pity for her—*Poor Mama! If only you knew about Big Momma Mmuọ-Ka-Mmuọ and The Great Council of Guardians, you'll realise just how powerless the Virgin Mary is.*

Mama always said that before somebody could give you a helping hand, you first had to see the helper. But the Holy Mother had never showed herself to us save in her pictures and statues, so I didn't think she could do anything for us; whereas Big Momma Mmuọ-Ka-Mmuọ lived and cared deeply for me. I had seen her in the flesh and experienced her immense powers. To me, she was real while the Virgin Mary was now a white ghost that might show herself to Gisèle-from-Paris and other people that looked like her, but never to us; *never us...*

Nine months after my return from *Ibaja-La*, Papa finally summoned me into his presence. Ever since our disastrous visit to Dibia's house to find a cure for my mind-reading, Papa had avoided me as he used to do in the days that I dreamt nightmares. He sought information from Mama about me rather than ask me himself. His actions bred a mixed feeling of relief and despair in me. On one hand, I missed his new affection for me, brief as it had been. Yet, each day I didn't see him meant another day I got to live amongst my family members without being exiled to either Dibia's house or the big city as a domestic servant.

The previous night, I had once again slept alone in the bedroom I used to share with my big sister. Even though I hid myself away from them to avoid hearing their thoughts, they still kept their distance from me. The only advantage of my ostracism was the vast improvement in my reading and writing skills. With little to distract me, I applied myself intensely to my studies, terrified of losing the education I had gained before my curse. Now, I wrote without spelling mistakes and the written words held an easy familiarity to my sight.

I was about to dress up for the morning when Mama entered my bedroom. I smiled at her and prepared myself for our daily ritual—eyes, voice, prayer, holy water. But Mama looked distracted and an air of excitement hung over her.

"Bata, hurry now and dress up," she said in a hushed voice. "Your father wants to see you immediately."

My eyes widened as I stared at her in stunned disbelief—*Papa wants to see me? But why? Please, please, don't let him send me to Uncle Dibia's house after all.* I fought the sudden thuds in my chest as I pulled on my yellow dress with the puffed sleeves, a gift from my cousin Keziah, who was now the proud mother of a baby son. The dress was too long and loose, and it hung on me like a shapeless yellow sack. But tying the red belt from my old Christmas dress around my waist always gave the yellow tent some majestic pretentiousness, just like a fool's kingly robe.

I entered Papa's parlour with ill-suppressed panic, clenching my fists and hanging my head. Papa was sprawled on his favourite sofa, and as soon as I crept in he gave me a big smile and waved me to the space by his side—*Huh?* My heart started to race faster. A hard knot formed behind my throat. I started to shake my head frantically—*Oh no, no! Papa is sending me away after all. That's the only reason he's being this kind to me. I don't want to go... I don't want to go... I don't want...*

"Come, child, sit next to me," Papa said, his voice the kind and compassionate voice I had known from the day I first became a Bride-Sentinel. "It's been a while since we last caught up about your situation. Come; let's share my breakfast together while we talk."

I perched myself beside him as he scooped some fried plantain and goat-stew onto a plate for me. But I found that my stomach had closed itself to the delicious food. Despite the tantalising aroma teasing my nostrils, my mouth remained dry and the painful knot behind my throat repulsed even my own saliva.

"What is this? Why aren't you eating? Is it possible that our Akuabata isn't hungry, eh?" There was humour in Papa's voice and I knew the reason for it. My appetite almost rivalled that of Ejima, and in our immediate family, I was known to never decline any food or drink offered me. In fact, before she died, my grandmother used to warn me that a witch would feed me witchcraft one day if I wasn't careful. She said that despite their greater greed, Ejima were not considered at risk of the witchcraft food-hex, due to the fact that they were boys. Witches tended to seek greedy little girls like myself to infect with their evil sickness.

Now, as I looked at Papa's food offering, I made a silent promise to my late grandmother—*Please, Nne, please stop Papa from sending me to live with Uncle Dibia. I promise I'll never ever accept food from any stranger again if you stop him and keep me in our house. Better even: Nne, please send me back to Ibaja-La. I don't like living here anymore. Everybody hates me and I'm just so unhappy. Please send me back to Ibaja-La, Nne—*

"Okay, you don't have to eat if you're not hungry." Papa's amused voice broke my panicked thoughts as he returned the food to his own plate. "So, tell me: do you still hear people's thoughts?"

My heart plunged to my feet—*Oh disaster! Papa is setting me a trap. If I say yes, he'll send me to Uncle Dibia. But if I say no, he might catch me out somehow and punish me. Adults are so tricky and know how to discover everything from children. What do I do?*

"I c-can't hear yo-your thoughts anymore," I stuttered, hanging my head. "B-but I can still hear Ejima's thoughts when we play." I opted for the half-truth. "P-please, Papa, don't send me to Uncle Dibia's house… Please. I've done as you told me and haven't listened to anybody's thoughts. Ejima's thoughts just come to me of their own will and I can't stop them no matter what I do. I promise I won't ever listen to anybody's thoughts again, please. I've been locking myself in my room so I don't see them or hear their thoughts. I swear I'm telling the truth. You c-can ask Mama if you don't believe me. I'll be very good and you'll never see me; but please, Papa, don't send me away to Uncle Dibia's house… please…" My panic killed the usual unease the sound of my creepy voices bred in me.

Papa stared at me goggle-eyed. Then he burst into merry laughter. For several seconds, his laughter rumbled and boomed inside the parlour till I started to think he might never stop laughing.

"Is that what you think?" he finally said, still chuckling. "That I plan to send you to Dibia's shrine as his apprentice?" He chortled again, staring at me with laughter-wet eyes. "It's clear you really can't hear my thoughts anymore, otherwise you would've known my intentions about Dibia's request and why I've called you here today." Papa sounded very pleased with himself, and once again he looked at me with a look that was close to his old affection, but not quite. "But you can still hear Mama-Ejima's thoughts if you want, right?" Papa's voice was quiet, the humour all but gone.

I stared at him with a perplexed frown—*Why Mama-Ejima? Why not Mama and Sister Ada too?* My shoulders raised in an invisible shrug. I could not lie. I nodded slowly.

"Good! Very good!" Papa's voice held smug satisfaction. "Now, listen carefully, I need you to listen to Mama-Ejima's thoughts and report everything you hear to me, okay? I want you to tell me every single thought she has, are we clear? Most importantly, listen out for any thoughts about Ugo of Amadi clan, okay?"

My lids flew open—*Ugo of Amadi clan!* Papa saw the shock on my face and nodded grimly, a malicious gleam in his eyes.

"Yes, the same Ugo of Amadi clan that you heard about when you listened to Dibia's thoughts." He confirmed my suspicions. "The same one that you said gave the medicine-man the sickly black goat for wealth-rituals. That's the bastard I want you to catch inside your stepmother's mind. I've heard some disturbing rumours and need to confirm things for myself, and you will find out the truth for me. I am giving you permission to read Mama-Ejima's thoughts, are we clear?"

I nodded slowly again, my heart pounding—*Oh my cursed life, what is this that Papa is asking me to do? I don't want to listen to Mama-Ejima's thoughts, and I don't want to tell Papa about it. But if I don't, he'll get angry with me and send me away. What to do?*

"Ha! Woe betide that woman if the rumours prove to be true," Papa muttered viciously under his breath, a deep scowl on his face. The menace in his voice filled me with dread. Suddenly, I was very afraid for my stepmother. "Make sure you report every single thought inside that woman's head to me, and whatever you do, never reveal what we just talked about to anyone, not even your mother, alright?" Papa held me prisoner with his hard eyes. "I don't want to send you to Dibia's house, but if you push me to do so, then I might have no other choice. Do you understand?"

This time, my nod was fervent, driven by terror. I would do anything to avoid Dibia's house. My aversion to the medicine-man's house wasn't just because of the man's fearsome reputation and terrifying visage. The filthy poverty of his tiny compound, which reeked of fresh blood as a result of all the animals he butchered for his sacrifices to the ancestors and spirits, also caused my skin to crawl the few times I'd visited his shrine. For someone who had the ability to make other people rich through his powers and rituals, it baffled me that Dibia couldn't bring the same wealth to himself.

"You can leave now." Papa's voice broke into my befuddled thoughts. "From tomorrow, I want you to come every morning to report what you have heard to me, alright? And let me know if you need new clothes or shoes—anything. I'll give you the money so your mother can take you shopping. Off with you now, and remember, not a word to anybody."

I nodded and scurried out of his parlour with a sudden headache that threatened to steal my sight—*Please, Big Momma Mmuọ-Ka-Mmuọ, send me back to* Ibaja-La. *I don't want to be here anymore. I don't want to hear people's thoughts. I just want to be happy again… please…*

Reading Ọla's thoughts was the easiest, and yet the hardest, thing I had ever done since my return from *Ibaja-La*. Like everybody else, my stepmother avoided me save for times when our paths had to cross, such as during mealtimes. However, such occasions were rare as I had been missing my meals or eating alone inside my room to avoid their reproach and cold detachment. But with Papa's new orders, I had to force myself to return to the communal eating space in order to spy on Ọla's thoughts.

Everybody looked up as I skulked in with my head bowed, before lowering myself onto the mat next to Ejima. Guilt and shame washed over me as I sensed their suspicious eyes on my hunched body. I felt they could hear my thoughts the same way I could hear theirs, and it took everything in me to restrain myself from scrambling to my feet and escaping back to my room. But my fear of Papa and his subtle threat was greater than my guilt and the painful tension pounding my head.

"Bata, I see you have decided to join us for your lunch today." Ọla's voice was both hard and humorous, as if she sensed the reason for my presence. I glanced at her quickly under the dark shield of my sunglasses and nodded.

"See, Mama: I told you there was no need to fuss over Bata, that she'll come out when she gets tired of sulking inside our bedroom," Ada said, cracking her knuckles while eyeing me reproachfully. "You just like seeking attention, you girl. If you ask me, I think you should just throw away those stupid sunglasses. So what if your eyes have coloured themselves grey, eh? What's the big deal after all? Grey eyes, brown eyes, black eyes, blue or green eyes like Oyibo people; they're all eyes. I think you just like wearing the sunglasses because you want to feel special, huh!" Ada hissed and cracked her knuckles more viciously. "Mama, just take away the sunglasses, you hear? Me, I'm not frightened of her eyes anymore."

"Shut your mouth and eat your food," Ọla snarled before Mama could answer. "What do you know? You just run your big mouth like a motorcycle without thinking about anybody else, you selfish girl. Have you thought about Ejima? Have you thought how Bata's eyes might frighten them? Of course, no. Everything must be about you as always." Ọla hissed in annoyance and raised a spoon of rice between her red lips.

"Look who's talking," Ada screeched, jumping to her feet, arms akimbo. "Look at this baboon calling the monkey a wild animal! Who amongst us thinks the world revolves around them, eh? Who goes around doing what she wants when she wants it without bothering to take care of her own three children, eh?" Ada turned fury-reddened eyes on our mother. "Mama, I've told you not to feed this woman's kids, but you never listen to me. Let the lazy cow cook for her triplets and do her job as a mother, instead of dumping everything on you while painting her ugly Pancake-Face and gossiping with that stupid spinster, Teacher Uzo."

"Ada, sit down and stop talking nonsense, you hear?" Mama's voice was weary. "Everybody in this house is family. We live and eat as a family." She turned to me. "Bata, here's your rice plate. Let me know if it's enough for you, okay?"

I nodded, grateful for the end of the latest fight between my big sister and my stepmother. At least it had diverted Ada's attention from me. Since I became a Bride-Sentinel, Ada's former indulgent affection had turned to cold resentment. I couldn't tell the cause of this change of attitude in my big sister apart from my thought-hearing abilities, which had earned me the displeasure of everybody. But Ada already resented me even before my mind-reading awakened, and I was loath to invade her mind to find the cause of her annoyance. With each passing day, the distance between us grew. It left a gnawing pain in my heart which increased my sense of isolation.

After several seconds of standing and glaring at Ọla, Ada finally sat down with a loud grunt and resumed her dinner. She attacked her food as if she was fighting a rival in the playground and her loud chomping and angry sighs quickly soured our collective moods—apart from Ejima's. The triplets continued stuffing their faces while the fight raged, and soon they held up their empty plates, demanding seconds. Mama promptly obliged, smiling tenderly at them as if she were their blood-mother. Ada eyed them sourly, mumbling viciously under her breath, while Ọla picked at her food with silent delicacy and superior detachment, holding the ubiquitous book before her face. The transistor radio beside her played a popular song by the musician Sonny Okosun. I forced myself to concentrate on reading Ọla's thoughts, but the high beat of the music distracted me. Moreover, my emotions were everywhere and everybody's jumbled thoughts kept crowding my head at the same time, stealing my peace. My headache became more intense and my heart raced so fast that breathing became hard.

I jumped up from the ground and dashed away towards my room. Behind me, I heard Mama shout out my name while Ejima mimicked her in their happy mischievous shrills—"Bata! Bata! Come back here!"

I ignored them all and flung myself onto my mattress, waiting for my panic to subside. I couldn't tell why I felt this way. It was something that had been happening in recent times, this inexplicable sense of panic and weepiness that followed me from when I woke up to when I slept—*What do I do? Tomorrow, I must report Mama-Ejima's thoughts to Papa, but I haven't heard anything yet. How do I get close enough to her to hear her thoughts? What will Papa do to me if I don't report them tomorrow?*

18

Good fortune smiled on me because, without any reason, Ọla invited me into her bedroom later that night. I was playing Koso, the spinning snail-shell game with Ejima inside my room, when my stepmother approached us in her familiar languid sway. I knew she had come to take Ejima into their bedroom for the night and the triplets immediately started to resist with rumbunctious tenacity. I hurriedly stood up to leave my room to avoid lingering before her.

"Bata, come with us," Ọla said, smiling at me with the old laid-back smile that was part humour and part mockery. In all my years, I had rarely known my stepmother to smile widely or laugh boisterously. Everything about Ọla held a languid air of aloof superiority, as if she secretly mocked us while tolerating our presence. I guessed it was the way of educated women, and I yearned even more desperately to become as educated as her. More than anything, I wanted to have Ọla's superior ways and her dazzling beauty stamped on me by high education and powerful German knowledge.

With a light heart, I followed Ọla into Ejima's bedroom. The triplets chatted happily and raucously as their mother undressed them and tucked them into bed. On good days when Ada was on cordial terms with my stepmother, it would be my big sister undertaking the bedtime routine with the triplets. Moreover, since the manifestation of my mind-reading abilities, Ada had been sleeping with Ejima instead of sharing our bedroom as in the past, afraid of having me invade her mind in her sleep. But her fight with Ọla earlier in the day meant my stepmother now had to put Ejima to bed.

"I don't want to hear a whisper from you, do you hear?" Ọla warned the boys when she was done. "Go to sleep now and make sure you don't piss on your bed, alright? Bata, come, follow me to my bedroom." Ọla placed the kerosene lamp on top of the large cupboard that housed Ejima's clothes, leaving the room in a dim and cosy glow that soon had the triplets yawning loudly. I knew they would be asleep before we got to Ọla's bedroom. Ejima ate and played so much during the day that their bodies usually crashed from the abuse inflicted on them once their heads hit the large mattress they shared.

Inside Ọla's bedroom, I stood by her door awaiting her instructions even as I tried to read her mind—*I can't waste this opportunity or Papa will be furious tomorrow morning. I wonder why she's brought me into her bedroom after all this long while of avoiding me.*

"Sit down on the bed." Ọla motioned me to her double bed, which was littered with clothes. I perched myself at the edge, staring again with awe and longing at the small shelf of books nestled between her dressing table and her white wardrobe.

"Are you still wishing to read my special books?" Ọla asked, smiling at me through the mirror where she sat on a small stool re-applying her make-up for the night. I had heard Ada, during her frequent fights with Ọla, bitching about her Pancake-Face and telling Ọla to reveal her real ugly face without make-up. Nobody had ever seen my stepmother without make-up, neither when she was awake nor when she slept. Growing up, I used to think that was her natural face, till Ada disabused me of that belief. But even the knowledge didn't dissuade me from wanting to be like my stepmother. In my eyes, Ọla was still the most beautiful and intelligent woman in the world, and when she smiled at me with the familiar amused affection of old, a warm flush suffused my body.

I nodded shyly at her reflection in the mirror, wishing once again that I could borrow one of the books arranged on the small shelf. Despite my plethora of used copies of Ladybird fairy tales, my heart hankered after Ọla's special books on her bedroom shelf. Even if they weren't picture stories, I knew my improved reading abilities would give me a fair understanding of the stories. Plus, I could always fill in the rest I couldn't understand with my vivid imagination, which was usually more fun than the original stories in the books anyway.

Now, as I eyed the elusive books once again, my longing was stronger than ever. If nothing else, they would distract me from my restless thoughts and constant panic. With a heavy sigh, I leaned over and picked up one of the colourful items of clothing littering the bed, a purple lace blouse with a puffed sleeve—*Might as well fold them up into a neat pile for Mama-Ejima.*

"Oh my God!" Ọla exclaimed, leaning forward to peer at the calendar hanging on her wall. "November 29th! Bata, it's your birthday today! You're eleven years today! I can't believe we all forgot. It's because of all the troubles in our house since you changed." She sighed loudly and came over to me, holding a small pair of shiny earrings in her hand. "Here, let's put these on for you. They're my birthday present to you. Tomorrow, I'll buy you a nice dress, okay?"

A tight knot bunched painfully behind my throat—*I'm eleven years today and nobody remembered my birthday, not even me.* A wave of self-pity engulfed me, coupled with an intense feeling of gratitude and love for my stepmother. I inhaled Ọla's wonderful body scent as she leaned low to put the earrings on my lobes.

Ọla's thoughts hit my head without warning like a massive thunderclap.

I did not go seeking her thoughts, I swear that on my eternal soul. I wouldn't do that to her now, not when she was the only one who remembered my birthday and gave me a birthday present—not even for Papa anymore. Her thoughts just flew at me on their own volition, hitting my head like rapid, hard pebbles from a boy's catapult.

My breath caught in my throat and my hands froze. In a blink, my head started to pound as thought after frenzied thought dripped from Ọla's mind like a leaking basket, bombarding my head with horror. As I listened to her thoughts, I felt a tight fist punch a painful hole inside my heart—*Oh my cursed life! What is this wickedness I'm hearing?*

Then another thought hit me—*Mama-Ejima is trying to shield her thoughts from me, just like Papa does.* Except Ọla wasn't as smart as my father and her thoughts kept seeping through the buffer she tried so pathetically to build—*RED LIPSTICK... RED LIPSTICK. Ọla, don't let this cursed child read your thoughts. Think of your red lipstick... RED LIPSTICK... RED LIPSTICK... I wonder if Our-Husband suspects anything? RED LIPSTICK... RED LIPSTICK. Yes, I think I'll apply the new lipstick tonight. I don't like this particular colour. I need to entice Our-Husband to stupid distraction tonight so that I can steal the keys to his store and money box once he sleeps. Useless man always falls asleep once he's had his fun... RED LIPSTICK... RED LIPSTICK... Ugo had better be telling me the truth this time. I'm tired of waiting indefinitely for him to take me away from this wretched village to Lagos City... RED LIPSTICK... RED LIPSTICK. Once he raids the store, he can't say he doesn't have enough money for us to go to Lagos… Lagos! Wonderful Lagos City! Finally, I can live in a civilised place and mix with the white people and other educated people of my own class! But I must be sure that Ugo will come through this time. He's promised to marry me but he's been stringing me along for several months now and I'm near done with his lies. Bata must read his mind for me tonight before I hand over the store keys to him. The money from the money box is mine to keep, just for security… RED LIPSTICK… RED LIPSTICK… RED…*

Ọla paused, her body went still. Then, she stepped away from me and stared hard into my face. Her eyes squinted with suspicion. In her mirror, my panicked face revealed my guilt in crystal clarity: my dipped brows and open mouth. Even through the shield of my dark sunglasses, my stepmother could see my panicked expression.

"Did you hear my thoughts?" Ọla shouted, rage and terror darkening her eyes. "Tell me at once, you demon child! Did you hear what I was thinking right now? You read my thoughts, didn't you? Didn't you? Speak up before I strangle you." Ọla hulked over me, glaring down at me with unrepressed fury.

I shrank back instinctively, certain that she was going to strike me. In all my life, I had never seen my stepmother so angry, not even when she fought with my big sister. Before my return from *Ibaja-La*, Ọla had rarely raised her voice at me or looked at me without a kind smile. Now, her eyes glowed with a loathing and rage that killed my heart and brought sudden trembles to my body.

Ọla yanked me up from her bed and shook me hard, her fingers painful on my arms. Unshed tears stung my eyes—*Oh no, no, please! What to do? What to do? I'm so afraid… Mama-Ejima is really angry with me. If I say no, she'll know I'm lying and might even hit me. If I say yes, she'll be equally furious. What to do? Oh my bad luck, what to do?*

"Speak up before I break your head." Ọla's raging eyes bored into mine. "What did you hear? Didn't your father warn you never to listen to our thoughts, eh? Yet, you've gone and disobeyed him. Tell me every single thing you heard—NOW!" Ọla's voice reverberated inside my head. In my panic, I shook my head frantically. I kept shaking my head like a stunned lizard till reason gradually returned to her mind.

"That's right; I forgot you're now a mute." She barked a bitter laugh as she pushed me away. "Go to your room at once and bring your schoolbag. Hurry, and don't say a word to anybody, do you hear me?"

I fled from her bedroom. My heart was pounding so hard I could hear it as I entered my room—*I'm doomed… I'm doomed. Mama-Ejima will make me write everything I heard inside her head. She knows how well I can write; after all, she was teaching me for a long time before I changed. She'll know if I lie and will make Papa send me away.* Fresh panic gripped me. I thought about not returning to her room and perhaps sneaking into Mama's room. But Mama was already very displeased with me; everybody disliked me now save Ejima—*I daren't make Mama-Ejima angrier than she already is.* With a weary sigh, I picked up my exercise book and pen.

Ọla motioned me to the small table next to her bookshelf as I re-entered her bedroom. She picked up one of the four kerosene lamps in the room and placed it on the table near my exercise book.

"Now, write everything you heard." Her voice was as hard as her eyes. "Make sure you miss nothing. Don't bother about the spelling. I'll know what you mean."

With a trembling hand, I started to write—*You are planning to steal Papa's money box and shop keys for Ugo of Amadi clan because he will marry you.* I dropped the pencil and hung my head, folding my shaking hands between my thighs. I waited with a pounding heart for her fist to land on the back of my head. Instead, I heard the rustle of paper as she picked up my notebook. Then her stunned gasp filled my ears.

"Oh my G-God! Oh m-my God!" she stammered. I looked up and found her staring at me as if I were Echieteka, the deadly viper. "What kind of d-demon are you? Oh my God, what evil has taken over this girl?" Ọla shut her eyes tightly, inhaled deeply, and opened her eyes again. Once again, her eyes were full of rage as she glared at me. "What will you do? Answer me, you possessed child: what will you do with this?" She waved the notebook furiously at me before tearing the page I wrote on to pieces with frantic hands.

I heard and saw her fear in the trembling of her voice and hands, but my own terror was greater than hers and I could neither answer her nor grasp the jumbled thoughts roaring inside her head. I remained rooted on the chair, staring at her with terror-filled eyes, fighting the panic pounding my heart— *I'm doomed now... I'm doomed. Mama-Ejima will surely make Papa send me to Dibia's house. Oh my bad, bad, bad luck...*

As if she read my thoughts, Ọla inhaled deeply again and shook her head. She started to pace up and down her room, sighing loudly and mumbling softly underneath her breath. I sat very still on the chair, trying to still my breathing, anything to avoid drawing her attention to me. After what seemed like hours, she walked over and stood beside me. I felt her gaze hard on my bowed head. I pushed my sunglasses up with trembling fingers and shut my eyes tight, bunching my hands into tight fists between my thighs.

"Bata, look at me," Ọla commanded. Her voice was soft, yet hard.

I obeyed, lifting my head slowly till our gazes held. In her eyes, I saw a new resolve that killed her earlier fear and the sight further ignited my terror.

"I want you to listen carefully to me," she said, leaning low to speak into my face. "You will follow me out now and you will say nothing to anybody. Since you already read my thoughts,

you know what I want you to do. We shall meet Ugo tonight…
By the way, how did you know his full name, eh? How did you
know he's called Ugo of Amadi clan? I never think about him with
his full name. Have you met him before? Did you see us together
before? Answer me quick." She shook her head with little jerky
movements. "Actually, say nothing. I don't want to know what that
accursed demon mind of yours hears anymore. It doesn't really
matter what you know. The important thing is that you'll say
nothing to your father, or I'll make sure you don't spend another
night in this house, do you hear? I'll make your Papa send you to
work as a domestic servant in Enugu town if you talk; am I clear?"

I nodded over and over like a red-crested lizard, struggling to
stop the hard racing of my heart. A satisfied glint entered Ọla's
eyes and her voice became slightly softer, almost friendly. "Think
about it, Bata: even if you tell your father, who do you think
he'll believe, eh? You or me? You know I can make your Papa do
anything I want with my Pancake-Face, don't you?"

Again, I nodded fervently.

"Good. Now be a good girl and do as I tell you. Listen carefully
to everything Ugo thinks as I speak with him tonight and tell me
afterwards. If you do well, I'll buy you nice clothes and biscuits
and even pay for the hairdresser to braid your hair with beads
like mine. In fact, I might even let you read one of my special
books. You'd like that, wouldn't you?"

Once again, I nodded. There was no joy in my heart anymore
at the prospect of finally getting my hands on Ọla's special books.
Everybody wanted to buy me things and they all wanted me to
do bad things. I wondered who next might ask me to do more
bad things—*Perhaps Ada or Mama? Oh please, don't let Mama
ask me to do something bad, please…*

Ugo of Amadi clan was waiting for Ọla by the cluster of trees located on the route that led to the village stream. The path was deserted since nobody visited the stream at night, and under the murky glow of the half-moon, I made out the tall, slim figure of a man dressed in flared blue jeans and a black open-neck shirt that made him look like an actor in one of the American films I had seen occasionally on Papa's small TV set the few times we had electricity in our village. His head was crowned with a full afro that resembled the style worn by the members of the popular boy band Ofege, whose vinyl LP decorated Ọla's shelf. A thick silver medallion glittered against his exposed hairy chest, and under the gloomy skies I could see that Ugo of Amadi clan was a very good-looking man. Poor Papa would have no hope should this wickedly handsome man desire my stepmother the way she clearly desired him.

On sighting Ọla, Ugo's bright white teeth flashed in a slow smile that seemed to speak a secret language to my stepmother which only the two of them understood.

"Hello, sexy," he said, speaking to her in an English drawl that complemented his slow smile. He started to open his arms to receive my stepmother when he saw me trailing behind her.

The smile froze on his face. Then a frown replaced it. His eyes narrowed and his arms dropped to his sides—*What the fuck?* I heard the angry words inside his head and halted behind Ọla. I could tell the man's rage was directed at me. But when he spoke, he seemed to be angrier with Ọla than me.

"What the hell are you doing with the kid?" he asked in a raspy voice that sounded like somebody nursing a bad cold. "And why is she wearing those stupid sunglasses in the middle of the night?"

"Just relax, this man." Ọla laughed, taking hold of my hand and pulling me forward. "She's my little stepdaughter and I need her as a cover in order to avoid rousing suspicion, okay? She's got a bad eye infection, so we can't have dust or anything making it worse." She also spoke in English and I was surprised by how well I understood them despite my limited education. But the fact that I could read their thoughts helped me grasp the gist of their exchanges.

Ugo made a gruff sound and glared down fiercely at me in a silent threat. I shrank back against Ọla and quickly hid myself behind her—*I don't like Ugo of Amadi clan even though he is a very handsome man. I wish Mama-Ejima won't let him rob Papa's store and steal Papa's money.*

As the thought left my mind, a deep sadness overwhelmed me—*Poor Papa! What they're planning to do to him isn't fair!* A new thought superimposed itself in my head—*Lie, Bata! Lie to Mama-Ejima about this man and tell her he plans to betray her, so she'll abandon her plan to leave Papa for Lagos City. It's a sin to lie, but I'm only doing it to save Papa and poor Ejima, who won't have a mother anymore when their mother runs away with this horrible Ugo. I hate Ugo of Amadi clan. I really, really hate him and his nice afro hair and big medallion and...*

"Anyway, we don't have time to spare tonight." Ugo's sulky voice broke the chain of my thoughts. "Have you got the store key yet?"

"Not yet. I'll get it tonight, but you must first tell me how and when we'll leave for Lagos. I can't afford to spend the slightest time in that house once the theft is discovered. If my husband suspects me, I'm a dead woman. Everybody knows just how violent a temper Okeke brews. So, I need to know from you right now the exact plan for our escape." Ọla's voice was hushed and I felt the tension in her body as she spoke. Her hand holding mine squeezed it so tightly I almost gasped from the pain.

FUCKING DUMB BITCH! The thought shrieked from Ugo's head with a rage that contradicted the wide smile on his face. And even though I had no idea what the words meant, I understood the hostility directed towards my stepmother from this man she liked to the exclusion of all else.

"Hey, babes, don't you trust your man?" Ugo smiled, taking Ọla's free hand in his, the left hand that wasn't gripping mine. "Of course I plan on getting us away from this dump as soon as the deed's done and marrying you at the first opportunity. Listen: just have the key ready before dawn, and we'll meet up here again in a couple of hours, okay? I'll sort out everything and then we head out to the main road to catch the bus to Enugu town and then to wonderful Lagos City from there. Ooh yeees!"

Ọla squealed and let go of my hand. I had never seen my stepmother's face beam so brightly and her voice shook when next she spoke, as if she was about to cry, even though she had no reason I could fathom to cry. From what Ugo said, everything was going the way they planned—except his words were at odds with his thoughts. This time, as I listened, he spilled out his thoughts in our local language instead of the English in which they had been communicating. And with a heart that shrieked with horror, I heard every single, terrible word that dripped through the evil basket of his mind—*Stupid woman has to die, just like the other dumb bitches, Efuru and Gloria. I can't have her expose me after I leave for Lagos without her. The villagers will ostracise me for good if they find that I robbed Okeke's shop and stole his wife. Can't believe the sucker expects me to take her along with me and marry her. Ha! As if there aren't better single girls without bothersome kids begging for my attention. One stab in the heart with a knife once I have that damned key and she can sleep with her ancestors for good. Ha! Dibia sure knows how to do his wealth-charms. The goat I gave him wasn't a waste after all. It brought this dumb woman into my life, and now her rich husband's wealth will be mine. Ha!*

And for the first time in my life, I hated somebody with a rage that burnt a murderous inferno inside my heart—*I want to kill Ugo of Amadi clan… I want Ugo of Amadi clan to die and die and die…*

19

The night was still and heavy as a graveyard, shrouding our village in silent gloom. Ọla and I skulked our way back to our compound, hugging mud walls and cassava bushes to conceal our unusual loitering at such late hours.

"Did you hear Ugo's thoughts?" Ọla asked, her voice breathless and hushed beside me. I nodded. "Good; as soon as we get home, write everything you heard in the notebook. Tell me, was he thinking of me? Did he think I looked beautiful? Did he like my new hairstyle and red lipstick? Does he love me? Will he really take me to Lagos City and marry me? Just nod your head or shake your head."

I shook my head, over and over with fierce grit. Ọla halted beside me and grabbed my arm with hard fingers. Then she grabbed my other arm and turned me around to face her. Under the pale light of the half-moon, her face was dressed with shock and rage.

"What did you just say?" she whispered fiercely into my face. "Did you just shake your head? Are you saying that Ugo doesn't love me, that he doesn't plan to take me to Lagos with him? Don't you dare lie to me, you hear?"

Again, I shook my head to tell her Ugo didn't love her and planned to betray her. She swore under her breath and shook me harder. "Which one is it, you stupid child? Should you be shaking your head or nodding it?"

I started to cry. My shoulders shook with the force of my sobs and I couldn't control my despair. And, as was always the case since my transformation, no tears stained my cheeks and my face held no evidence of my pain. Everything about my situation weighed heavily on me, and in that moment, I wanted more than anything to disappear from my family and our village forever. It didn't matter where I went as long as I was removed from all the treachery and badness that now surrounded me. Looking at my stepmother's furious face was like seeing the face of a stranger, a stranger without the familiar halo of beauty and superiority. For the first time in my life, I had no desire to look like Ọla or be her child. The sudden loss of my icon crushed my chest, leaving me with the anguish of mourning.

"Stop crying, you hear? It's okay, this girl." Ọla's voice sounded tired, her fury slightly deflated. "Come, dry your tears, you hear? I won't scold you again. Let's just go home and I'll give you some roast peanuts and Fanta in my room. Then you must write down everything you heard in Ugo's mind, alright? You'll do that for me, won't you, my mini-me?" Her voice was coaxing.

I nodded, fighting the hiccups while pretending to wipe my face with the back of my hand. I was thankful that in the gloom of the night, Ọla couldn't see the absence of tears on my cheeks. After a few seconds of silent contemplation, her staring pensively into the sky and me staring numbly at my dusty feet, we resumed our journey. For the rest of the short walk back home she said nothing and I was grateful for the silence. My emotions were scattered everywhere and I still wasn't sure how to process everything I had heard and experienced. The only thing I knew for sure was that there was no way I would reveal the night's events to Papa.

Despite the guilt I felt about betraying his trust as my blood-father, I knew that Ọla's life mattered more to me than Papa's trust. Ọla was no longer my favourite person; her words, her education, and her beauty now left me cold. Yet, I knew that I would rather die myself than consign her to certain death at the hands of my father, just like Agnes, the owner of the village palm wine bar, whose jealous husband had doused her in kerosene and set her on fire when he caught her with her lover. Papa's temper was known across the clans and wider village. I had no doubt that Ọla would meet the same dire fate as Agnes, or even worse, should Papa ever discover her treachery.

I shuddered as my imagination played out numerous scenarios of murder, each one more horrible than the first—*What should I do? How can I escape this terrible trap? I'm now a bad sinner. I'm a liar and Satan's child now. Oh my bad, bad, luck... What should I do?*

Our compound was silent and dark when we finally sneaked our way into the house. Save for the dim light coming from Papa's parlour, which told us he was still awake, nobody else stirred. We tiptoed through the back of the house and through the outdoor kitchen before finally making it safely into Ọla's bedroom. Instinctively, we avoided the various buckets, brooms, and boxes that lined the long, gloomy corridor that led off to our different rooms. Papa's bedroom lay at the very end of the corridor, and I was thankful he was still drinking his usual night-time Heineken beer inside his parlour. With stealthy expertise, Ọla quickly locked the door of her bedroom behind us, making no sounds to alert anyone of our entrance.

"Here, sit down on the bed while I get you a nice bottle of Fanta and peanuts, okay?" Ọla smiled tightly at me as she turned on the wicks of the numerous kerosene lamps, once again flooding the room in brightness.

I perched at the edge of the bed and hung my head. My eyes still burnt from all the rubbing I gave them when crying and all I wanted was to return to my bedroom and lose myself in sleep and hopefully dreams of *Ibaja-La*. But I knew I still had a job to do: I had to let my stepmother know that the man she loved planned to kill her on this very night.

Ọla returned with a small bowl of peanuts and a bottle of Fanta. And suddenly I realised I was very hungry. My tiredness instantly disappeared as I grabbed the treat with greedy haste.

"Ha! I knew you'd not say no to food." Ọla barked a bitter laugh. "Go sit at the table and enjoy it. Then when you're done, you'll write everything for me in your notebook just like before, alright?"

Our eyes met and I saw an anxious and pleading look in her eyes, even as she tried to maintain a stern expression. Unexpected compassion filled my heart. I felt sorry for her. I wanted us to be friends again, for her to like me and call me 'mini-me' with affection as in the past. Yet, I didn't want to like her as I did before. She was now an adult no longer worthy of my respect, just my pity and contempt.

I nodded and sat on the high-backed wooden chair. I placed my snacks on the table and started to wolf down the peanuts with silent haste, savouring their crisp and sticky sweetness. In between mouthfuls I took long swigs of my Fanta drink, and soon a gentle mellowness shrouded me in tired contentment. I wanted to stretch out on my bed and sleep. My eyes felt heavy and I started to yawn, long and loud.

"Bata, don't sleep now, alright?" Ọla came over and pushed away the empty bowl of peanuts and bottle of Fanta. She opened the notebook before me and placed the pencil in my hand. "Now start writing everything you heard in Ugo's mind. As I said, don't worry about the spelling. Just write everything down and we'll take it from there."

I inhaled deeply and started to write, fighting the dullness in my eyes and the fogginess in my head. Ọla paced up and down her room as I wrote, wringing her hands and sighing loudly and frequently. With forced concentration, I allowed my mind to recall everything I had seen and heard at the clandestine night meeting with Ugo of Amadi clan. My fingers ached and trembled as I wrote, and when I was done I put down my pencil and bowed my head. Ọla rushed over to the table and grabbed the notebook.

She started to read it.

Then she screamed.

In my panic, I forgot my affliction. I opened my mouth and spoke.

"Mama-Ejima, please don't steal Papa's shop key and money box. You mustn't go back to Ugo of Amadi clan tonight or you will die," I pleaded with desperate fervour, hearing the multiple hollow voices spilling from my lips with renewed horror. No matter how many times I heard my voice, its discordant and jarring multiplicity always germinated goosebumps on my skin. "Ugo is an evil man. He'll stab you to death with a knife and escape to Lagos City without you after stealing Papa's money. He has already killed two other women called Efuru and Gloria. He's a bad, bad man. He doesn't want to marry a woman with children. He just wants to use you and then kill you too like the others. Please, stay with Ejima and Papa and me."

Ọla dropped the notebook and staggered back against the door. Her eyes bulged with terror and soft whimpering sounds issued from her lips. Under the bright light of her four kerosene lamps, I saw that the hand covering her mouth trembled like dandelions. She looked like somebody who had opened the door to death.

The truth hit me. I covered my mouth with my hand. But it was too late. Ọla had never heard me speak and the sound of my cursed voices and the terrible message delivered in their multiple ghastliness proved too much for her to absorb.

By the time Papa and everyone rushed into her bedroom, my stepmother had toppled to the ground in a dead faint.

"What happened here?" Papa asked, stooping to lift Qla into her bed. Mama rushed to cover her with a thin wrapper.

I shook my head, terrified by the situation unfolding before me. Papa's eyes glinted with unspoken understanding as he hurriedly dragged me by the arm out of the bedroom and down the corridor to his own room.

"Now tell me exactly what happened," he commanded once the door shut behind us.

"I thin-think she saw a gh-ghost in her mirror," I stammered, saying the first thing that came to my mind. I tried to speak in a whisper to avoid my sister Ada hearing my cursed voice, yet the unearthly voices echoed loudly in their creepy multitude, and I saw Papa's eyes widen in dismay as he heard their eerie resonance once again. In the silence of the night, they sounded louder, creepier. My body trembled violently, shaken by my lies, the night's experience, and Qla's collapse. It took everything in me to maintain my standing position before Papa's hulking presence.

"Is that all? Are you sure you didn't hear something else in her head?"

I shook my head frantically. Papa fixed his hard eyes on me for several silent seconds before stalking out without another word. I followed him with heavy legs, wishing I could disappear from the house and its inhabitants. As I re-entered Qla's bedroom, I saw Mama dousing every corner of the room and its unconscious owner with holy water. Papa eyed her sourly before striding out again. When next he returned, he brought Dibia and his juju-bag of occultic charms with him.

"Ha! Okeke, evil has entered your house tonight," the medicine-man said as he lifted Ọla's lids to peer into her eyes. "Your wife is a victim of a supernatural hex. She has clearly been possessed by the ghost she saw in her mirror. That's why I keep telling people not to look in mirrors at night. It's one of the easiest ways for malevolent spirits to enter our world, and as we all know, the night belongs to them, not to the living." He tutted disapprovingly as he placed his juju-bag on the floor by Ọla's bed. He wasted no time in commencing his exorcism rites. "Hurry up and bring a white male chicken to sacrifice to the malevolent spirit that has taken possession of your wife's soul."

Papa hurried to comply with his command. Soon, my stepmother's face was smeared with chicken blood, together with other unknown herbs from the raffia bag of juju-magic. Everybody waited with hushed breath to see the result. Half an hour passed without any visible change in my stepmother's malaise. In that time, every kind of terror quaked my heart as I stared at Ọla's blood-coated face—*What if Uncle Dibia discovers what occurred with Mama-Ejima? What if Papa learns that I lied about the ghost? Oh my bad, bad luck! Why won't Mama-Ejima wake up from her faint? What if I've killed her with my cursed voice?*

With each passing second that we waited inside Ọla's bedroom, the weight of my sins grew into bloated corpses, pressing me into a dark grave of eternal doom. I was so tainted by my wickedness that I knew the beautiful realm of *Ibaja-La* would instantly reject me should I by some unfathomable miracle find myself there again.

Just as I was about to give up hope, Ọla stirred on her bed. She coughed violently and groaned, her face creased in a fitful frown.

"Praise be to Our Holy Mother!" Mama said with great relief, weaving the sign of the cross over her shoulders, while Papa grunted in satisfaction.

"Woman, praise our medicine-man, not your holy mother who has done nothing to heal your sister-wife." Papa's voice was gruff with wry irritation. Everyone knew that even if a mango tree produced mango fruits or a dog gave birth to a puppy, Mama would still praise the Holy Mother for the 'miracle'.

"Okeke, I think you can now relax," Dibia said, nodding with self-satisfaction. "Whatever evil spirit afflicting your wife has now been vanquished by my powerful charms."

As Dibia stooped to pick up his juju-bag, Ola opened her eyes. My sister Ada gasped, gripping Mama's arm tightly as she stared at my stepmother with shock-widened eyes. My eyes met Ola's own and a sudden chill raised goosebumps on my skin.

"Great Spirit, your servant bows her head before your might," Ola said, scrambling from her bed to prostrate before my feet. In her eyes, I saw the unmistakeable fever of madness. "Don't punish me for my sins, oh most high spirit. I will serve you with my blood, flesh, and soul, to the end of my days if you'll only accept me as your faithful servant and bless me to eternity."

"Dibia, what is this madness, eh?" Papa gasped, staring at Ola with goggled eyes. Then his eyes narrowed as he turned to me. I wilted, inching away from my stepmother. But she grabbed my ankles with feverish hands and would not let me go.

"I fear the residue of her possession still lingers in her," Dibia said, also eyeing me with suspicious contemplation. "Okeke, you have to remember *what* Akuabata is, and understand why your wife holds unto her for salvation. The child has been tainted by the supernatural world, so it makes sense that your wife, who has just survived a possession by a supernatural entity, will recognise the otherworldly aura of your daughter and cling to her. Give her a few hours for the haze to clear and she'll be well again."

Dibia left with his juju-bag and ancient wisdom, leaving us alone with my stepmother and her new madness. Papa followed

Dibia out while Mama and Ada stared at Ọla and me with baffled and frightened eyes.

"Our-Wife, come; let's help you into your bed, you hear?" Mama finally said, leaning low to assist Ọla from where she was still sprawled on the floor, gripping tight to my ankles. "Bata, move your legs away so I can help her up."

I tried to move but Ọla tightened her grip.

"Ada, come and help me," Mama urged with a frown. Ada hesitated, as if afraid to be contaminated with my stepmother's madness. "Hurry up, girl," Mama snapped, dragging Ọla by the right arm.

Ada finally moved, taking hold of Ọla's left arm. As they pulled her, she howled in rage, holding so tight to my ankles that she almost cut off my blood supply. I began to moan in pain, biting my teeth hard.

"Mama-Ejima, you're hurting Bata's legs," Ada snarled, forcefully unclawing Ọla's fingers from around my ankles as I strove to maintain my balance. I staggered away as they dragged her to her bed and held her down by force. She fought them wildly like a caged animal, her face twisted with rage.

"Great Spirit, don't abandon your servant," Ọla howled from her bed, reaching out her arms beseechingly to me. "Speak to me again in your mighty voices and tell me your will. Your servant awaits your command, oh powerful spirit."

Ọla's demented voice followed me as I escaped from her room on trembling legs—*What have I done? Oh my wicked life; what have I done?*

The following morning, when she showed no signs of improvement, Papa rushed Ọla to the hospital in the big town. But all the Nivaquine malaria tablets and typhoid-fever antibiotics they gave her did nothing to alleviate her symptoms. For over a week following her collapse, Ọla lay sick in her bed, shivering under the attack of a high fever that left her drenched in sweat and rashes, mumbling incoherently in her delusion. She refused all foods and visitors, save myself.

"Great Spirit, please save me," Ọla would whisper to me in a frantic voice through fever-cracked lips, gripping my hand with her hot, moist palms. "I know you're not Bata; I know you're just using her body as a shroud to hide your true identity. I know you can strike me dead with one look from your deadly white gaze and put me under an eternal curse with a few words from your unearthly voices. But please, Great Spirit, pity me. Save me, heal me, bring Ugo back to me and make me your acolyte. I promise I'll serve you with every fibre in my body and my soul. Tell me what shrine to build for you and I'll build it once you make me whole again and return Ugo to me. But first, please tell me your name. Tell me the true name of this great spirit before me, that I may praise it and worship it faithfully." Her eyes were wide with mania as she pleaded from her sick-bed, quaking violently underneath her blanket.

My stepmother's words filled me with dread and panic. No matter how many times I told her my name was Bata, she refused to accept it. I tried to read the thoughts in her head, but the madness of their jumbled cacophony had me recoiling in horror. In her fever-reddened eyes, I saw that I had ceased to exist as her stepdaughter; I was now a deity in her twisted mind. She wanted to hear my multiple voices and see my silver-grey eyes to confirm her false belief about my spirit-identity. She promised me gifts: biscuits, sweets, trinkets, even the precious Mills & Boon books lining her shelf. All she wanted was my presence and my dubious blessings. Whenever Papa, Mama, or Ada visited her room, she feigned sleep and refused to engage with them. Even Ejima and her best friend, Teacher Uzo, failed to rouse her interest. She was only animated when I visited. Her fanatical attachment to me did not escape Papa's attention.

"Bata, tell me again what happened on the night Mama-Ejima fainted," Papa asked me for the umpteenth time as Ọla continued to suffer under her unknown affliction. "I know you said that she saw a ghost, but I need to know everything you saw. Did you really not hear anything she was thinking? Are you sure she never thought about Ugo of Amadi clan even for a minute? Why isn't she getting better and why does she insist on having you with her? What does she say when you're alone with her? You're not hiding anything from your father, are you?"

Papa's questions filled me with the familiar panic that had followed me since my stepmother's collapse.

"Mama-Ejima n-never thinks about Ugo of Amadi clan," I stuttered with a thudding heart. "Sh-she just wants me to read her my fairy-tale books, that's all."

Again, I forced away my guilt as I lied to my father. I was already a damned soul, my mouth filled with lies, spilling falsehoods to both my mother and father in order to hide my complicity in Ọla's treachery. I wanted desperately to spare my stepmother's life, but I also wanted to spare myself from my father's fury should he ever discover about my night trip with Ọla to meet that wicked man, Ugo of Amadi clan.

Once again, a hard knot twisted itself tightly around my heart—*I am doomed... There'll be no escape for me from the punishment awaiting me for my wickedness. How I hate Ugo of Amadi clan! I wish he'll be sick too and suffer and suffer and cry...*

Ọla started following me around from the day she recovered from her sickness, ten days later. Like a leashed dog, she trailed every step I took from the minute I left my bedroom to when I finally laid my head on my thin pillow at sundown. Gone were her lazy saunter and aloof smile, with the ubiquitous book and transistor radio held in her superior hands. Instead, she shambled behind me like a person drunk on Ogogoro brew, a manic grin on her face, chanting praises to me in a voice laced with madness. Her dirty clothing and unwashed body evidenced the slow decline of her sanity. Even her famous Pancake-Face had become an extinct sight in our household.

Seeing Ọla's face devoid of its famous make-up was like seeing an adult without their clothes in a public space. It roused intense pity and embarrassment in me on her behalf, even as I stared with awe at the marvel of her bare face.

"Great Spirit, your humble servant praises your might! Please, bestow your blessings on your faithful servant, I beseech you," Ọla wailed in a shrill voice, spraying her treasured Charlie perfume on me as she trailed behind me in that submissive manner that had become her habit since her recovery.

My sister Ada giggled maliciously, while Mama shook her head sadly before serving us breakfast.

"Our-Wife, why don't you sit down and have your breakfast, alright?" Mama's voice was gentle, as if she spoke to the triplets who were already busy stuffing their faces on plantain and Akara-beanballs.

Ọla ignored her and waited for me to sit down first on our breakfast mat. As ever, my heart wilted in mortification as I lowered myself to the ground. Ọla quickly plonked herself next to me instead of on her usual wooden bench and started fanning me with her colourful straw fan. Once again, Ada chuckled spitefully beside us, stuffing her mouth with several plantain slices before cracking her knuckles with vicious grit as she eyed us with contempt-laced eyes. Ejima looked up and smiled brightly before attacking their food with renewed gusto. Mama sighed deeply as she placed our plates before us. Ọla quickly pushed her plate over to me, offering me her food with a fawning smile. I shook my head and pushed her plate back to her, but she immediately returned it to me.

I looked at Mama helplessly as she sat on the mat next to Ejima, weaving the sign of the cross over her shoulders. She shook her head and cast another pitying look at Ọla.

"Give her permission to eat, since she will only do what you tell her to do," Mama said in a weary voice, turning away to focus on her food.

"Oh, Great Spirit, will I have a lot of customers today at the sewing shop?" Ada asked in a solemn voice brimming with mockery and malice. "Bless me, Great Spirit; please bless your servant with lots of customers and lots of money, oh, oh—"

"Ada, shut up and behave yourself." Mama cut her off, glaring at her with rage. Ada kissed her teeth and returned to her food, mumbling under her breath as was her habit. "Bata, when you're done, why don't you take Mama-Ejima to the bathroom and help her have a bath, alright? Your father says he wants to talk to both of you today when he comes back from work, so make sure she looks decent."

I nodded even as my head started swirling with frightful thoughts—*Why does Papa want to see us together? What does he want to ask me again? Oh my bad life; will I never stop lying and sinning? Will Mama-Ejima ever recover her senses and stop seeing me as a great spirit? I fear Papa suspects I lied about Ugo of Amadi clan. Since Mama-Ejima started following me around, he might think we've formed a wicked pact against him. Oh, Big Momma Mmuọ-Ka-Mmuọ, help me: heal Mama-Ejima so that she can go back to being how she used to be… please…*

That night, Papa returned to the house with Dibia. As Ọla followed me into the parlour, once again dressed in colourful flamboyance, I knew that both our fates now hung on a very thin line that could snap at the slightest breath. I had tried to apply her make-up, fortify her face with the weapon that would dazzle Papa and protect us from his anger. But I made such a terrible job of it that it was better to wipe it off and leave her with her new natural and powerless face.

As we entered Papa's parlour, I knew with a sinking heart that all my fears were finally realised. In the dark accusing eyes of both my father and the medicine-man, I saw our doom, Ọla's and mine. And for the first time, I knew that I must face my father's wrath without the protective shield of my stepmother's haughty beauty that had saved me on numerous dire times in the past. Now, Ọla was a ruined beauty and her powerful Pancake-Face grip on Papa's affection had finally run its charmed course.

20

Papa glared at me as I entered his parlour with my stepmother. In his eyes, I saw rage and contempt. I didn't need to be told that the rage was for me, and the contempt reserved for Ọla. Even in her madness, Ọla felt the menace oozing from Papa's taut body. Her hand, holding mine, tightened its grip as we sought to give each other desperate courage.

"Akuabata, you lied to your father, didn't you?" Papa snarled. His voice brimmed with rage and my pounding heart knew I could expect no mercy from him—*But how? How did he find out?*

Dibia cleared his throat noisily. I looked into his knowing eyes and shut my own in despair—*I should've known! Nothing escapes our powerful medicine-man.*

"Ugo of Amadi clan is about to marry the chief's daughter, Amara," Dibia said, looking intently at Ọla. "In fact, I just finished officiating the proposal rituals at the chief's house. She's a lucky woman to find a single young man ready to remarry her after the breakdown of her first marriage."

Ọla's body jerked. Her grip tightened, squeezing my hand so hard I winced in pain. I looked up and saw the fixed smile on her face as she stared at Dibia, a wide and desperate smile of manic despair. Her thoughts hurtled towards me, smashing into

my head and filling me with anguish and terror. I yanked my
hand away from hers, shutting my eyes, pressing my pounding
head with my trembling hands, anything to shut out the soul-
crushing agony of her silent, screeching despair.

She quickly shuffled behind me, falling to her knees and hiding
her face from Papa and Dibia, just like a child taking refuge behind
its mother's back; just as I used to do in the days she protected me
from Papa's rage with her invincible Pancake-Face. For the first
time, the full force of my predicament dawned on me.

"Crazy bitch!" Papa cursed, eyeing her viciously. He downed
his half-full glass of beer and banged the empty vessel on his table
with violent force. He turned to Dibia with blazing eyes. "Tell the
useless slut about her lover. Go on, tell her everything. Even in
her madness, I know she'll understand what you say. She's lucky
my ancestors have already taken vengeance on her and ruined
her mind, otherwise she would've returned to her family in a
coffin today, the filthy bitch."

Behind me, Ọla groaned softly, her hands gripping my dress
tightly. I turned to look at her. She stared wildly at me, her eyes
brimming with unshed tears—*Save me! Please, save me, great deity!*

Her frantic thoughts hit me again with sudden force. Her
wide eyes pleaded silently for my help. The bright, manic smile
was still fixed on her face, but it failed to hide the desperate
anguish in her darting eyes. Even now, she still believed in her
deity; she still had total faith in my omnipotence. Her faith in
me and my helplessness filled me with shame and guilt. It also
made me angry—*It's her fault... she's to blame for everything,
she and that horrible Ugo of Amadi clan. Oh my bad, bad luck...
What will I do now? Papa will surely send me off with Dibia to
become his apprentice!*

I groaned silently. All I wanted to do was run, take Ọla's
hands and escape from the double menace of Papa and Dibia.

But terror froze my limbs and Papa's icy gaze told me I could expect no mercy this time.

"Ugo's fiancée told my daughter, who happens to be her best friend, that you threw yourself at him and tried to buy his affection with your husband's wealth, even going as far as plotting to rob Okeke's store before escaping to Lagos City together." Dibia's voice was soft, yet icy.

Once again, Papa smashed his glass on the table and cursed loudly. "Mbarama! Prostitute! Ungrateful bitch!" He jumped to his feet and lunged at Ọla, shoving me aside with violent hands. Ọla whimpered and scrambled after me on her knees. Papa yanked her long braids and she screamed, wrapping her arms tightly around my waist, almost pulling me to the floor.

"What? What? Do you think Akuabata can save you again after you've corrupted her mind, took her to see your lover, and got her to lie to her own father for you, eh?" Papa smashed a hard fist into her head. She wailed pitifully and clung tighter to me. Papa tried to drag her from the floor.

Ọla bit his hand.

She sank her teeth so hard into Papa's flesh that she drew blood. Papa shouted and let go of her arm. Ọla ran, stumbling away from the parlour before Papa could recover his wits.

"The mad woman just bit me!" Papa shouted, turning panicked eyes to Dibia. "That slut just bit her madness into my bloodstream. Ancestors, save my soul!"

"Calm down, my friend," Dibia consoled with calm assurance. "I'm here, am I not? Do you think any harm can come to you while you're in *my* presence? Relax. I will remove the madness-poison instantly from your bloodstream. Sit down so I can treat you before it spreads. Unfortunately, your wife's madness is now too far gone to be cured. When they start biting like wild dogs, there's nothing anybody can do for them anymore. It's now just a matter of time before she goes naked to the village market." He tutted sadly, yet gleefully, as he reached into his ubiquitous juju-bag for his tools.

By the time I followed in my stepmother's steps and made my escape from the infernal parlour, Dibia was already making a cut into Papa's arm with his blade, to drain out the madness from Ola's bite.

Amara, Ugo's fiancée, and her band of gossiping friends, wasted no time in spreading the shameful story across the village. Mama equally wasted little time in telling Ola off later that night, after she heard the story from numerous village women who had rushed over to our house to share the juicy gossip, despite the late hour. Even before Ola and I stumbled out of Papa's parlour in panicked flight, Mama already knew everything about our crime.

"Our-Wife, how could you dishonour Our-Husband in such a shameful manner?" Mama admonished in a loud voice, her arms akimbo. In her face, I saw a rage that rivalled Papa's own. In all my eleven years of existence, I had never seen my mother so angry. "Is there anything you wanted that Our-Husband hasn't given you? Does he force you to cook or clean like other wives? Has he ever raised his hands to touch you in violence? What was it about the wretched pauper, Ugo of Amadi clan, that made you forget your pride and woman's honour? Even worse, you dragged my silly child into your shameful secret, exploiting her affection for you in the most wicked manner."

Mama turned to look at me with a mixture of resentment and pity before returning her attention to my stepmother, who cowered under the cotton sheet on her bed. Every bit of Ola, from her toes to her hair, was covered with her flower-patterned sheet. Through the thin material, I saw the violent quivering of her body.

"Anyway, I know your madness won't let you understand half of what I've said." Mama continued her tirade. "But I also know you've understood some of what I've said. In your heart of hearts, you know that you've done evil to this house that welcomed you with open arms. God is already punishing you for what you did. See the mess you've become, you who was once the most beautiful woman in the ten villages. I don't know how you can ever show your face in public again after the shame you've brought upon yourself and our family. Anyway, if you can gather some of your wits, try and get yourself to confession with Father David and pray your rosaries and novena in penitence."

Mama turned back to me where I stood cowering by Ọla's open door. "As for you, I don't want you to hang around Mama-Ejima anymore, do you hear me? If she comes near you in her usual madness, run away from her. Don't accept any more gifts from her. She's clearly a very bad influence on you and you need to reflect on what you've done and how you've betrayed our trust." She sighed deeply and walked away, clutching her rosaries like a lifeline.

I escaped to my room on trembling legs, my shoulders shaking in my tearless sobs. My shame and guilt were great and my only consolation was that my sister Ada had not been around to witness my humiliation and add her rage to Mama's own. Ada was out visiting with her friend and by the time she returned, storming into our bedroom after hearing the notorious story, I feigned sleep with a determination that refused to budge to her screams, shoves, or curses. Ada eventually gave up and withdrew to Ejima's room.

I spent the rest of the night trembling in panic and terror, wondering how I was going to face everybody the next day, what Papa would do to me, and what the future held for me. I was gripped by a deep sense of despair and my sense of isolation was complete—*Everybody hates me now. Maybe I should run away before anybody wakes up... but where will I go?* I thought of going to my auntie's house but Mama's sister lived in the neighbouring village which was almost a day's walk from our village. I wasn't even sure if I could make the long trek or find my way there on my own—*I might get bitten by snakes or scorpions in the dark or kidnapped for my body parts for rituals. Worse, the ten-headed ghost king might whip me with his snake hands and drag me to the dead realm inside his terrible boat made of human skulls. Anyway, Auntie Uche will probably send me away when Mama tells her what I've done, then I'll be in even bigger trouble.*

I shuddered, feeling cold sweat dampen my body. The night stretched out long and unending. Heart flutters and tummy cramps left me writhing on my mattress and my breathing came hard and fast. Nonetheless, I must have fallen into a fitful sleep, because by the time I woke up the sun was bright in the sky and our house was in uproar.

Papa didn't get infected with Ọla's madness, thanks to Dibia's superior juju. But he was still mad with rage at her betrayal. Early the next morning, he gathered his kinsmen to inform them officially of Ọla's infidelity and demand their verdict on her future within the family. They gathered inside his parlour, breaking Kolanuts and drinking palm wine as they mulled loudly and angrily over what to do with my stepmother in her present mental state: whether to return her to her people or to leave her in our house in shamed ridicule. The clanswomen and several village women had also gathered inside our compound to share the scandal and witness the Mbarama (slut), as they now called Ọla, get her just punishment.

Clothed in her manic smile and lunacy, Ọla trailed after me as I skulked over to our communal eating-mat to have my breakfast with Ejima. As always, the sight of her bare face stirred something painful inside me. From the faces of the gathered crowd and the multitude of clamouring thoughts coming from them to me in relentless waves, I knew I wasn't the only one affected by the disappearance of my stepmother's famous Pancake-Face. I tried to hide her away from their avid gazes as we rushed to join the rest of the family at our communal eating place. And after breakfast, which I could barely touch, I quickly led her back into her bedroom. Once there, I faked divine blessings for her to delay her exit back to the compound and its spiteful guests.

"Today, Mama-Ejima will be the favourite of her ancestors," I said in my myriad of spooky voices that both thrilled and frightened her.

"Amen! Iseh!" she shouted joyfully, falling on her knees and bowing down low to me, rubbing her hands together fervently.

"Mama-Ejima will get many gifts of gold and silver very soon." I carried on the ruse. I figured I wasn't doing anything really bad—*I'm just blessing her. Anybody can bless anybody. It doesn't matter if she thinks I'm a deity. At least she's safe and happy here, away from those horrible village women and Ada.*

I carried on with my fake divination for a long while before playing Snakes and Ladders with her. But eventually, my hold on her ran its course.

"I want to go outside now," she said abruptly, standing up and heading towards her shut door. I grabbed her hand desperately.

"Let's stay inside, Mama-Ejima," I said. "I think there might be some danger outside."

She flashed me a happy smile. "Uh-uh!" She shook her head emphatically. "Great Spirit, you've given your grateful servant many good blessings today, so nothing bad can happen to me." She turned to leave, intent on wandering around the compound. "I can do anything I like now; I'm fortified with the power of your blessings."

I sighed in despair. In her madness, I doubted she would cotton on to the mendacity of the meddling villagers loitering in our compound.

I was right.

Ọla greeted the gathered women with happy exuberance, as if they were all her long-lost friends. It was as if she had completely forgotten everything that took place in Papa's parlour the previous evening; perhaps she even failed to link the clanswomen's presence with her disgrace. Some of the women sneered openly at her, while others blanked her into invisibility. A few smiled back at her with wide smiles that failed to hide the gloating malice in their hearts. Ọla glided amongst them in blissful ignorance, her crazy smile fixed on her face. As the day progressed, villagers wandered into our compound in their droves, under different guises, to view my now notorious and adulterous stepmother, cloaked in nothing but her lunacy and natural face.

"So, this is what she really looks like." They giggled, their eyes glittering with spite. "Without her Pancake-Face, she's not half as beautiful as we thought. If Ugo of Amadi clan had seen her as she is now, he would've never touched her, even for all her husband's wealth."

Listening to their mockery and seeing my stepmother's guileless smile as she wandered amongst them, revelling in the unusual attention she was getting, my throat constricted painfully with unshed tears. I wanted to rush over to Ọla and hug her and shield her from their spite and Ada's relentless malice. Since discovering our crime the previous night, my sister had turned her tongue into bullets, shooting targeted venom at both Ọla and me with deadly accuracy.

"I always said the woman was as ugly and fake as they come, with all her stupid talk of Lagos City and her superior education," Ada repeated each time the villagers made a disparaging comment about my stepmother. "Only a fool like my little sister and the stupid one who calls herself Teacher Uzo would've fallen for her fakery. Now see what's happened. My poor Papa! Only God knows how he'll endure this wicked treachery. I hope the kinsmen chase her away naked and childless."

Ada's vicious words raised my anger, coupled with the feeling I always felt when Ejima hurt themselves. With a promise of new blessings, I quickly shepherded Ọla back into the safely of her bedroom and away from their unkind eyes and cruel lips. Once again, I tried reading her mind, to know what she was thinking, if she understood anything that was going on. But just as had been the case since that fateful night she lost her sanity, I was met with a blank wall of nothingness. I could neither read nor hear her thoughts unless she sent them to me, as she had done in Papa's parlour yesterday when we were both in danger.

As I watched her curl up like a child in her bed, I studied her face once again with wonder. Despite the vacuousness of her smile, Ọla's face still had a haunting beauty that held the eyes in its thrall—*Ada and the villagers are wrong about Mama-Ejima.*

The thought slipped unbidden into my head. To my eyes, my stepmother's Pancake-free face looked younger and kinder than her old glamorous face. Ọla might have lost her former sophisticated hauteur, but she had gained a sort of motherly, yet childlike warmth that made her more endearing to me and Ejima. Since her madness, the triplets sought her out more, enjoying her cheerful and crazy companionship with boisterous glee. Ọla now laughed freely and loudly and ran around playing games with us without caring about her dignity or superior beauty. As long as I was engaged in any activities, she too would do them to please me, her new deity. Even as I wished I had the power to return her to her old, sane grandeur, I wished she would remain the sweet way she now was, but without the madness.

The kinsmen decided that Ọla would remain in our compound after all. I heard the good news from Mama, as they discussed the day's proceedings later that evening when we gathered for our supper.

"The kinsmen said it would be a disgrace to our family if she's returned to her people in her current lunatic state," Mama said to my big sister, eyeing Ọla with the new pitying look that had been her norm since Ọla's descent into madness.

"Are they crazy?" Ada shouted, giving Ọla a vicious look. "What disgrace? She's the one that disgraced herself, Papa, and our family. Who gives a hoot if she's crazy or not? I say return her without delay to her people. Let them deal with her madness." Ada cracked her knuckles loudly and angrily, bringing an involuntary wince in me.

"Ada, I keep telling you that you must learn to have more Christian charity in you," Mama admonished gently, as she scooped more food into the near-empty bowls of the triplets to keep them busy. "You know how superstitious our people can be. If we return Our-Wife to her people in her present state, they'll accuse your father of using her to do wealth-rituals, sacrificing her sanity for his riches. They'll claim we fabricated the whole Ugo of Amadi clan scandal to cover our crime. No, it's better she stays with us as she is. At least Ejima will get to see their mother as they grow older, even if she's more their playmate now than their mother." Mama shook her head sadly.

"What? You mean she gets away without any punishment for what she did?" Ada looked incredulous, her eyes wide in stunned disbelief. "Are you telling me there'll be no reckoning for her and Bata for what they did?" She turned her furious gaze at me and I quickly lowered my head, feeling the sudden pounding of my heart. "What has come over Papa? Is he still held hostage by this woman despite her madness and the absence of her Pancake-Face? Even worse, have our kinsmen turned into clanswomen with nothing between their thighs? Even if Papa has become a weak woman-wrapper, the kinsmen ought to be able to insist on some form of discipline for these two." Ada hissed loudly before shoving a heaped spoon of rice into her mouth.

"If you had opened your ears more and used your mouth less, you would have heard the rest of the verdict," Mama scolded, shaking her head wearily. At her words, my stomach tightened—*Oh, Big Momma Mmuọ-Ka-Mmuọ, please don't let there be any punishment for Mama-Ejima and me. Don't let them send me to the big city or to Dibia's house… please…*

"Sorry, Mama," Ada mumbled, giving Mama a wry grin. They smiled at each other and resumed their conversation as if they were the only people present. Since Ọla's affliction, Mama and Ada tended to talk freely about her as if she were not there, or as if she were an inconsequential child, like Ejima and me.

"Anyway, the kinsmen decided that even though she'll remain in our house, she must be made to suffer for her actions, madness or not," Mama continued in a low voice. "So, tomorrow morning, they'll take her to the marketplace and flog her naked in the presence of all the villagers. Our clanswomen have already been given the task of collecting the wiry birch she'll be whipped with. If nothing else, her body will suffer the pain her mind can't receive now because of her madness."

I felt Ọla tense beside me. Her spoon instantly hung, suspended in a space between her trembling hand and her mouth. I heard the sudden, sharp intake of her breath and felt the violent quivering of her left thigh against mine where I sat next to her on the mat. When I turned to look at her, the fixed smile on her face was the brightest I had ever seen. Then once again she resumed eating, wolfing down the rice with manic frenzy like a person starved for months.

"Good!" Ada's voice brimmed with smug malice. "That'll teach her alright. I'll even contribute several whips to the kinsmen if they like." She turned resentful eyes in my direction. "But what about Bata? After all, she was complicit in deceiving Papa and all of us?"

Mama sighed deeply. "Your sister is just a foolish child who was manipulated by a wicked and shameless adult who should've known better." Mama's voice was bitter. I knew she would never forgive Ọla for involving me in her adulterous affair. "Moreover, in her current altered state, she can't be sent to be a housemaid in the big city. No family will accept her. They say Dibia wants her to live with him, but thankfully your father is against that idea. I'll not let any child of mine serve the pagan gods of that witchdoctor." Mama's face screwed up in disgust. "Anyway, for the meantime, Bata is banned from having anything to do with Our-Wife and will no longer attend school even if she eventually recovers her eyes and her voice. After the harm that schooling did to Our-Wife and her best friend, that pathetic spinster, Teacher Uzo, who wants their daughter to acquire an education and lose out on a good marriage and a good moral compass? Bata will stay home instead and take care of Ejima. She has done enough schooling now."

No! No! No! Oh please… no! Not my school! I must get a good education! I must visit Lagos City one day… I must go to school… I must…

"Now we're talking," Ada gloated, eyeing me with spite. My big sister was contemptuously referred to as 'Itibọlibọ', the illiterate, by my stepmother. It was a slur she bitterly resented and I could see her glee at having me join in her nescience. "After all, it won't be fair on the other kids if Bata uses her mind-reading abilities to steal answers from the teachers' minds. Home is the best place

for her, especially now that her icon has become a fallen god."
Ada's gleeful voice heightened my despair.

My shoulders started to shake with the force of my hoarse sobs.

"Shut up, you," Ada snarled. "You should be grateful you're
not being sent out of the house after everything you did. After
all, you only want to go to school so you can be like your precious
Mama-Ejima. Well, look at her now and tell me what's so precious
about her. By the time they're done with her at the marketplace
tomorrow morning, let's see if you still want to be like her." Ada
kissed her teeth in disgust before resuming her meal. Beside
her, Ejima continued stuffing their faces, oblivious to the threat
facing their mother. My full plate of rice exposed my vanished
appetite, and soon Ejima were fighting rowdily over it.

I stood up and stumbled into our house. Ọla quickly stood up
to follow me. I looked back and saw Ada jump up as if to chase
after us. Mama pulled her back by the arm.

"Sit down and let them go." Mama sounded weary. "It's
only for tonight. Let them spend their last time together. After
tomorrow, everything will fall into its natural state. By the time
they're done flogging Our-Wife, I doubt she'll be in any state to
follow anyone around."

Inside Ọla's bedroom, I quickly lit up her four wick-lamps and
turned to guide her into her bed. I looked up at her and caught
my breath. Tears streamed down Ọla's face, and in her eyes I saw
the water-crystal clarity of total sanity. She stooped and folded
me in her arms in a tight embrace.

"My mini-me, thank you," she whispered into my ears. "Thank
you, you hear? Thank you, Bata, thank y—" Her voice cut off as
she began to cry softly, hard sobs that quaked her shoulders and
drenched her face.

Before I could speak, she pushed me away violently and flung
herself onto her bed. The dazzling smile was back on her wet

face and the madness glazed her eyes once again. I crept out of her room on shaking legs and shut the door gently behind me. I thought I heard the sounds of soft sobbing again, but I couldn't be sure.

Soon, I too stretched out on my mattress and waited for sleep to claim my churning mind and free it from its troubled thoughts. The last thing I remember thinking was—*Why won't they flog Ugo of Amadi clan too? Why is it only poor Mama-Ejima who'll be stripped naked and whipped in the marketplace tomorrow, in the presence of the entire village? It's not fair... not fair...*

21

Ọla died before the rooster crowed in the next dawn. Ejima found her corpse when they went to say their obligatory "Good morning, Mummy" to her. They ran out when she failed to respond to their greetings and told Mama that their mummy refused to wake up. Mama thought Ọla was hiding away in shame from everyone following the revelations about her affair with Ugo of Amadi clan; or perhaps, despite her madness, she'd somehow cottoned on about the impending public flogging. By the time Mama decided to check on her when she failed to appear for breakfast, Ọla's body was cold and stiff.

Ada's painful kick on my thigh was the first thing I felt before my mother's screams pierced through my grogginess.

"Get up, you," Ada said, glaring at me with swollen eyes reddened by tears. Then she screamed at me, "How dare you sleep when you caused all the trouble and killed Mama-Ejima, eh?" She looked ready to kill me.

I stared up at her from my mattress, trying to make sense of her words. Beyond my open door, Mama's shrieks, now joined by other screams, continued to fill the air—*What's happening? Oh please, don't let it be that they've started flogging Mama-Ejima already... I don't want to see it... I don't want to see blood and see Mama-Ejima crying...*

"Get up at once, you wicked girl, before I strangle you with my bare hands." Ada started to drag me up from my mattress as she spoke. "I hope you're happy now that you've finally killed Mama-Ejima. First you spied on her thoughts, then you made her mad and turned her into your slave. Worse, you helped her deceive Papa even after you met up with her boyfriend, that useless Ugo bastard. Yet, you said nothing, you wicked freak. You kept it all to yourself while spying on our thoughts for your own evil entertainment. I hope you're happy now that Mama-Ejima is dead. I hope her ghost torments you to the end of your days."

Ada dropped me to the floor and ran from the room, fresh tears streaming down her face. I lay frozen on the spot, my heart pounding so hard I struggled to breathe—*What does Ada mean? Why is she saying I've killed Mama-Ejima? I didn't kill anybody... Mama-Ejima isn't dead. I left her sleeping in her bed last night. Ada is just being her usual mean self.*

I felt the tenseness leave my shoulders. My limbs loosened and once more I could breathe freely. I pulled myself up from the ground and started walking towards the door. Another piercing shriek halted my steps. Once again, my heart started its manic race—*Why am I hearing screams? Something is wrong in our house. Oh please... please, don't let anything happen to Mama-Ejima.*

I started to run. A great impatience drove my steps—*I have to see... I must know... Mama-Ejima, please be well... please don't let them flog you.*

Out in our corridor, I came to a sudden halt. A great throng was gathered outside Ola's door, a crowd of wailing clanswomen. The pounding in my heart was now deafening. A melting weakness came over my limbs. My body started trembling like wind-danced leaves. I stumbled against the wall, gasping, struggling to take in precious air. A painful knowing filled my soul even before I caught the thoughts of the women—*Mama-Ejima is dead... Pancake-Face is gone... Poor Ọla! To die so young...*

Somehow, I managed to drag my shaking legs to Ọla's door. I squeezed myself through the soft bodies of the clanswomen and entered the crowded room, overheated by the crowd and reeking of Charlie perfume, sweat, and death. Another piercing wail almost deafened me. Ọla's best friend, Teacher Uzo, stood next to her bed, keening and beating her chest with hard fists. I forced my reluctant eyes towards Ọla's bed.

I gasped softly. My eyes widened in awe. Goosebumps layered my skin in a cold, damp blanket. On the bed, stretched out in an elegant poise, lay my stepmother, clad in her former glory. Decked out in glittering jewellery and an elaborate lace Ashoke gown, Ọla was a sight to bedazzle. Her famous Pancake-Face was back, more colourful and striking in death. The perfection of her make-up showed that a very sane and steady hand had applied it. I could swear a small secret smile twisted her red lipstick-coloured lips. It was as if she were giving the villagers the middle finger, a final act of proud defiance to her detractors and Ọwu, the Death Lord himself.

In that instance, I knew that Ọla must have regained a brief spell of anguished sanity before she took her life. The empty bottles of Phenergan stood ominously on her side table. In the end, my stepmother had reclaimed her old glamour at the hour of her death and protected her educated superiority—*There'll be no humiliating flogging in the marketplace for her after all. Good...*

At the thought, a slight burden was lifted from my heart, but the pain remained. Thoughts and images flashed in my mind and the past became my present. I saw Ọla as she used to be before the madness took over, before my fateful sojourn in *Ibaja-La* ruined everybody's lives. I recalled the countless times she'd bought me presents, taught me how to read, sang along to

'The Naughty Little Flea' song with me, told me stories about Lagos City, took me to see Engineer Tip-Toe's German wife and almost-white son, called me her mini-me with pride, dressed me in her trinkets and fed me delicious treats. In many ways, Ọla had been my one true companion and best friend in our family. And now, it was all over. Never again would I hear the music from her transistor radio, smell the heady scent of her perfume, or see the soft swaying of her elegant walk.

My shoulders began to quake with the force of my grief. My throat constricted with the pain of the tears that would not flow. I squeezed my way out of the room, sucking the thoughts and words from the bodies I touched—*She'll be buried in Ajọ-Ọfia, the bad forest... She's a suicide who has died a cursed death... No way will she get a Christian burial... The kinsmen won't allow for her body to be buried inside this compound now... She's a cursed corpse and no ancestor will welcome her in their realm... Poor woman! Why did she have to take her life like this and abandon her three small sons? Why couldn't she just take her punishment at the marketplace today and be done with it instead of taking her own life? Chei! What a curse... Okeke's house has truly been cursed...*

I dashed out of the room and fled to the safety and agonised privacy of my bedroom. In the unremitting anguish that blighted my heart throughout that terrible day, one thought kept playing in my head, over and over with bitter grit—*I hate Ugo of Amadi clan... I hate Ugo of Amadi clan...*

Ọla was not given the dignity of a lying-in display to receive the final goodbyes from the living. As a suicide, there was no funeral feast or wake; no prayers or hymns; no mourning clothes or dug grave inside our compound. Instead, all her personal items were collected and burnt, to prevent her ghost from returning for them. From her glamorous clothes to her Mills & Boon collection, everything ended up in the heaped, blazing pile. Even her numerous framed photos were smashed from their frames and burnt, while her jewellery was pounded into a fine, colourful mess inside the wooden mortar used in pounding yam-fufu meal for Papa.

While her corpse lay in her bedroom through that fateful day, Papa wandered around the compound as if he had been infected with Ọla's madness after all. His eyes were wild, yet vacant, and his thick kinky hair looked unkept and uncombed. When the mourners commiserated with him, he responded with a kind of bewildered silence that caused them to shake their heads with pity. I wondered if he was sorry for hitting my stepmother and pulling her braids the previous day—*I hope Papa kills Ugo of Amadi clan… I hope Ugo of Amadi clan suffers and dies too… I hate Ugo of Amadi clan… It's all his fault… Everything is his fault…*

Later that night, Ada came into our bedroom to collect some personal items before returning to Mama's bedroom, where she was spending the night. Save to use the toilet and a brief spell outside to observe the burning of Ọla's belongings, I had not left our bedroom all day. Nobody had come to seek me out either, not even to call me out for a meal. I doubted Mama would have had time or the mind to cook anything. Ejima were likely fed at Uncle Gabriel's house.

"Huh! So, this is where you've been hiding all day," Ada said, eyeing me sourly through swollen lids. I didn't need to be told that Ọla's death had hit her hard. Despite their famous fights, there had been a twisted affection between them, the type that cats share with dogs, each needing the other to torment in their various ways. I knew that my sister would miss my stepmother almost as badly as I would.

"Wh-what have they done w-with Mama-Ejima?" I stuttered, squeezing my hands tightly between my thighs.

Ada snorted and carried on packing her stuff. I sighed deeply, resigned to being ignored. When she was done, she turned to leave. At the door, she paused.

"Mama-Ejima's body is still inside her room," she finally said in a bitter voice. "At midnight, Dibia and the kinsmen will collect her corpse and dump it at Ajọ-Ọfia. Are you now satisfied, eh?" Ada walked out, slamming the door behind her.

Ajọ-Ọfia! I shuddered, recalling the morbid thoughts I had stolen from the clanswomen earlier that day. Ajọ-Ọfia was the cursed forest at the outskirts of our village, the designated burial ground for cursed corpses such as Ọla's own—executed criminals, murderers, suicides, lightning victims, and a host of other corpses considered as cultural rejects. To think that such a place would be the ignominious end for my stepmother, once the most beautiful and feted woman in our village, was too much for me to bear.

I began to cry once again as I had been doing intermittently all day, the choking dry sobs that hurt my chest and burnt my gritty eyes. Sleep and I parted company that night and terror became my chilling companion—*What if Mama-Ejima is still angry with me and comes to haunt me?* All manner of scary thoughts filled my head and I kept hearing Ada's parting words: *"Mama-Ejima's body is still inside her room."* I craved the company of another living person, even a dog would have been enough to chase away the terror gripping my heart. With manic repetition, I kept glancing up at the small wall clock, watching the needle crawl towards that ominous hour of midnight—*Maybe when they take away Mama-Ejima's body, her ghost will follow them along and leave the house.* Every second, I expected to see my door squeak open, see her floating apparition enter my bedroom, feel her cold, dead hands on my clammy skin, and hear her hollow voice calling my name. *"Mini-me... Mini-me... Mini-me..."*

Just before the clock struck midnight, the kinsmen entered our house with Dibia. From my bedroom, where I was still crouched against the wall quivering in terror, I heard their heavy tread and muted voices as they removed Ọla's corpse from her bedroom and sealed up her room with a heavy lock. Soon, a deep silence descended in our house and my shoulders slumped in relief—*It's over... over... Mama-Ejima will be buried in the bad bush after all, just as the clanswomen had predicted.* A great sadness and weariness overcame me and once again, hard tears choked behind my throat. With weighted limbs, I crawled onto my mattress and pulled the thin cotton wrapper over me. I shut my eyes tiredly, and in seconds I was lost to the world and its troubles.

When I woke up the next morning, all the mourners had vanished and our compound lay in a heavy shroud of silence. Everybody spoke in hushed tones, and even Ejima muted their voices when they played, infected with the gloom in the air. Nobody had told them yet that their mother was dead. When I read their minds, all I heard was food thoughts. Occasionally, they wondered when their mother would return from the market or stop sleeping and open her locked door and let them in. Otherwise, their thoughts were the same joyful and clueless jumble of innocent childhood. I was thankful for their sake, even as I envied them their ignorance.

And later that night, when the terror entered my life once again, I wished I had been born blind and deaf.

It was the smell that first woke me up, the distinctive fragrance of Charlie. The deep sleep of extreme grief and fatigue tried to hold me in its dark and oblivious cocoon. But my nostrils sought and inhaled the familiar scent, filling my head with its sweet familiarity. Sudden consciousness returned to me, dragging me into the chilling reality inside my room.

I opened my eyes and screamed.

In the unearthly glow illuminating my room, I saw Ọla. Dressed in the glamorous Ashoke she had died in, she stood at the foot of my mattress staring silently at me. Her beautiful polished ebony skin was now a ghastly ashy hue that heightened the night-blackness of her eyes. Tears poured down her pallid face in an endless flow that dampened her cheeks, now devoid of their former Pancake-Face pink glow.

"Help me... help me... I don't want it..." The ghost reached out its arms towards me. I shrank back, whimpering, quaking underneath my cotton bedcover with my eyes squeezed shut.

"Bata! What now?" Mama's voice pierced through my terror. "Are your nightmares back again? Oh, Mother Mary, what have I done to deserve all this trouble? Why can't we ever have peace in this house?"

Mama pulled the cover off and I opened my eyes. The unnatural light and my stepmother's ghost had vanished, together with the smell of Charlie. My room now glowed once again with the familiar dull light of my wick-lamp. I scrambled up from my mattress and flung myself into Mama's body. She leaned low to fold her arms around me. The familiar scent of her Dax hair pomade chased away the terror of Charlie and I held tight to her with desperate arms.

"Bata... child, it's okay, you hear?" Mama's voice was soft, kinder than I'd heard it since my transformation. "It's only a dream; everything is alright. Come; let's go to my room. Ha! Everybody is sleeping in my room tonight, so you might as well join them all."

I wanted to tell her that I had seen Ọla, but I feared her displeasure—*I can't sleep alone in this bedroom... I can't! Oh, Big Momma Mmuọ-Ka-Mmuọ, save me from Mama-Ejima's ghost.*

She has come to torment me as Sister-Ada predicted and I don't know what to do now... Help me please... Help me...

I spent the rest of the night in Mama's crowded bedroom, sharing her bed with Ejima, while Ada slept on a mat on the floor. Sleep and I parted company and my mind whirled with ghastly thoughts that kept my heart thudding and my limbs trembling. I kept seeing Ọla's ashy face and weeping eyes, the terrifying light that shrouded her body and illuminated my room. Just before sleep finally stole my sight, a final thought sneaked into my head—*Mama-Ejima asked me to help her... She didn't come to take revenge on me after all. But how can I help her? What does she want me to do? What is it that she doesn't want? Maybe she doesn't want to be dead but how can I bring her back to life? Big Momma Mmuọ-Ka-Mmuọ, please keep Mama-Ejima's ghost away from me... Please...*

22

For three weeks following her death, Ọla's ghost continued to visit me daily. In the bathroom, in my bedroom, outside on the eating-mat, even when praying with Mama, her relentless haunting stole my peace. The lingering smell of Charlie, which was now the most terrifying smell in the world to me, always signalled her presence. Her voice was a constant whisper in my ears—*Help me… Help me… I don't want it… Help me…* Terror became my constant companion and Mama now allowed me to sleep in Ejima's bedroom instead of risking the return of my nightmares in my own bedroom. She feared Papa's reaction, just as we all did.

Since Ọla's death, Papa had become a near-recluse. He left for work and returned in silence. It was a silence that bode no good for anyone. His brows were dipped in a perpetual frown and he exuded an air of menace that caused even the pesky flies to avoid his presence. He ate his food, drank his Heineken, and listened to his radio in the same brooding silence. He turned away visitors and kept even Ejima from his parlour. We all tiptoed our way around the house when he was home. There was an air of a thunderstorm brewing, ready to explode over our heads. Nobody wanted to be the trigger and Mama knew my nightmares could easily bring his repressed rage on me and the entire household.

As for Ejima, since their mother's death they preferred my company above all others and would insist we played the games we used to play together during Ọla's brief spell of madness, when she became a joyful and playful child, just like us. They now knew their mother was dead but struggled to grapple with the meaning of this. When I read their minds, I heard thoughts such as, "I wonder if we can go to heaven to visit Mummy one day?" or "I wonder how long Mummy will stay in heaven before coming back?" or "I hope Mummy brings us lots of heaven's foods when she comes back."

No matter how many times my mother tried to explain to them that Ọla was singing for Jesus with the angels in heaven, that she was waiting for the glorious day they would join her when they grew into blessed old-age, Ejima still believed that their mother would make a surprise visitation from heaven one day bearing lots of peanuts and treats—*If only Mama-Ejima would remain in heaven forever and stop visiting me or, even better, visit her sons who are desperate to see her...*

Three weeks after her death, my wish was granted.

The afternoon was the hottest it had been in a long time. Everything and everybody roasted under the unusually intense Harmattan-season sun. Even Mama had withdrawn to her bedroom for an impromptu afternoon siesta. Ejima and I abandoned our outdoor games for an indoor game of Koso in my bedroom. It was a popular game that required each of us to spin an empty snail shell and count down as it twisted furiously on the ground. The person whose shell danced the longest won the game.

I had just spun the empty snail shell into a dancing spin, when the insidious smell of Charlie hit my nostrils—*No, no, no... Please!* The familiar chill doused my skin in sudden goosebumps.

My heart started its terror-race while my wide eyes flickered frantically, searching for the spectre across every corner in the room. The scent of Charlie was so overpowering that I knew Ọla's ghost was very close to me. Yet, no matter how hard I searched for it, I couldn't see the loitering ghost with its ghastly, ashen pallor.

Ejima did.

"Mummy?" Ejima-One whispered, his brows dipped in uncertainty. The other two followed his wide, gawping eyes towards the open door of my bedroom.

"Mummy!" they screamed in unison, terror shrilling their voices. Like frightened mice, they scrambled towards me and buried their faces in my clothes. I felt the quivering of their bodies and heard the harsh gasps of their breathing. Soon, they were crying, then howling. Mama came dashing into my bedroom, her brows dipped in irritation.

"What is it now?" she barked at me. "Can't you watch your brothers without making them cry? Can't I even take a brief siesta without being disturbed? Do you expect me to cook, do laundry, clean up, and watch you and Ejima round the clock as well?" She turned to Ejima. "Boys, what is it, eh? Come; don't cry, alright? I'll soon have food ready for you."

"M-Mummy... Mummy just came down from heaven... She was standing b-by the door... but her face is scary... We don't like Mummy's heaven-face..." they said, completing each other's speech as was their norm before resuming their wailing. Even Ejima-One, who rarely cried, was bawling his eyes out.

The hair at the back of my head spiked, ruffled by skeletal fingers. My head swelled into a giant coconut—*Ejima saw their mother's ghost... Mama-Ejima has really turned into a proper ghost. I'm not the only one that sees her now!*

Mama gasped, her eyes widened into bulging balls of horror. "Wh-what nonsense are you talking?" she stammered, glaring at us. "Your mother didn't come, you hear? It is hunger making you see things that are not there. Come; I'll give you peanuts and Fanta to keep you busy while I finish cooking nice rice and goat meat for you."

She looked at me suspiciously before leaving the room with Ejima, who had now quit crying at the prospect of the treats awaiting them. I sniffed hard and glanced around the room frantically, praying I wouldn't see the terror I sought. But the scent of Charlie had vanished and I suddenly realised I was the only occupant of the room.

I ran out of my bedroom fast on Mama's heels, like one escaping a rabid dog. I stayed close to Ejima for the rest of the afternoon, right to their bedtime, and despite my terror, there were no further hauntings from my stepmother. From that day, Ọla's ghost finally ceased its visitations. I figured she didn't want her little sons to witness her terrible, ghostly visage. I kept myself glued to Ejima, whom I now viewed as my new guardians, even though it was now my full-time job to watch and care for them—*As long as I'm with Ejima, their mother's ghost won't haunt me and I'll never smell that horrible scent of Charlie again*. The thought brought me some solace in the gloomy months following Ọla's tragic death.

The explosion we feared finally happened on Christmas Day, a sunny Sunday morning, as the Christian villagers prepared to attend Christmas Mass at the Catholic church hall. Like the rest of our household, save Papa, I dressed in my new Christmas dress even though I wasn't going to mass due to my curse. But it made me feel better to dress in nice clothes for that one special day.

I also dressed Ejima in their new suits, clipping their identical red bow ties to their equally matching white shirts. Christmas this year was a muted affair in our household due to Ọla's death, but

Mama ensured she bought us children Christmas clothes, just as she always did every Christmas. I was also glad to see the big Christmas ram tethered to the cashew tree in our compound. I expected some of the clansmen to arrive later in the morning to kill it as was the norm and take their share of its meat back to their families. The bulk of the delicacy would be given to Mama to prepare our Christmas lunch. Christmas was one day in the year that we ate enough meat to satisfy our craving for months to come.

As I clipped a hair band on my head, I wished I could go out and join the all-girl dancing group as I'd done in previous years. But just like everything else, my curse prevented me from rehearsing with the rest of the group this unlucky year. It was a dance group made up of twenty girls from our clan, aged between eight and twelve years. We would rehearse the dance moves in the 'ber' months preceding Christmas, and then borrow our mothers' wrappers as our uniform to dance on Christmas Day. Immediately after Christmas Mass, we would go around the village, visiting various compounds to perform our dance routine for them and be rewarded with money and treats.

The clans-boys had their own acrobatic dancing group too and the two groups always competed every Christmas over who would get more money and treats. Now, with yearning regret, I imagined all the treats and money they would receive from all the compounds they visited—*Maybe next year I'll be able to dance again... Please, Big Momma Mmuọ-Ka-Mmuọ, please remove my affliction before next Christmas, please...*

When I was done dressing Ejima, I ushered them towards Papa's parlour to greet him before they headed for Christmas Mass with Mama and Ada. I lurked outside, waiting for them to join me when they were done. Like I had done since Ọla's death, I avoided Papa like a woman would avoid the fearsome Ijele Masquerade, the great king of all masquerades. I knew

Papa blamed me for Ọla's untimely demise, just as my sister Ada did. Day in and day out, I feared his retribution when he finally recollected his senses—*If only he would flog me with the wiry whip instead of sending me to live with Dibia... anything would be better than living with Dibia.*

Just as Ejima dashed out of the parlour, I heard their name called from beyond the short Ixora hedge surrounding our compound. I looked over and saw Teacher Uzo waving at Ejima. My stepmother's best friend was all decked out for Christmas Mass, except the clothes she wore belonged to Ọla. My late stepmother had been in the habit of gifting her clothes to her friends whenever she tired of them. The flowing, sequined Bubu gown Teacher Uzo now wore had been one of Ọla's favourites for a long time before she discarded it. It did not fit her dumpier best friend as beautifully, despite its glamorous cut and design, and seeing the Bubu on Teacher Uzo's rotund body brought a sudden lump to my throat—*Poor Mama-Ejima... I wish you hadn't died... I'm so sorry. I really miss you... Not your ghost, you hear? Just you, the real you.*

A sudden roar from Papa's parlour doused the air with panic. In a blink, Papa dashed out of the house and tore across the hedge towards Teacher Uzo.

"Mbarama! Prostitute!" he screamed, his voice fuelled by rage. He yanked the scarf from Teacher Uzo's head and began dragging her into our compound by the arm.

Teacher Uzo shrieked, resisting him, clawing at his hands. One of her high-heeled shoes fell from her foot, together with her handbag.

"You dare wear my wife's clothes to mock me, eh?" Papa snarled, his face livid. "It's not enough that the two of you connived and deceived me and now you dare to rub in my humiliation?"

"Okeke, let go of me, you hear?" Teacher Uzo begged, tears staining her cheeks. "I didn't do anything to you. Was I the one that told Qla to have an affair with Ugo? What did you expect me to do? Tie her up with a rope?"

"Yes, tie her up with a rope, that's what," Papa barked. "You should've stopped your friend from her amoral acts by every means, or told me about it." Even as Papa spoke, a great crowd, including Mama and Ada, quickly gathered, and the din outside our compound was great.

"What? Betray my best friend to her husband? What do you take me for?" Teacher Uzo managed to finally wrench her arm free from Papa's grip. I could see a rage similar to Papa's own now reddening her eyes, her courage buoyed by the presence of the crowd. "Every sane person knows better than to interfere between a husband and his wives. The next thing you know, they'll use you to settle their quarrel. If you're looking for someone to blame for your wife's infidelity, then go find Ugo and fight him man-to-man instead of bullying a poor, helpless woman like me. Would you have dared touch a single hair on my head if I had a husband to protect me?" she hissed loudly and stooped to pick up her discarded scarf.

Papa's foot landed on her hefty backside, knocking her to the ground. Mama screamed and grabbed hold of Papa's arm.

"Our-Husband, please... enough!" Mama begged, her voice tremulous. "Let the woman go, you hear? The dead are now buried together with their sins. Don't dig them up again, please. Come; let's return to your parlour. It's Christmas and we don't want to make it a miserable day for the children." She tried to lead Papa away but he yanked his arm from her hand.

"That garment you're wearing was bought with my money," he snarled at Teacher Uzo. "Strip this minute; remove it now and give it back to me."

"What?" Teacher Uzo stared at him with goggled eyes. "You want me to return this Bubu to you this minute?"

"Yes, now."

"You expect me to naked myself before everybody?"

"Yes, let them all see your shameless body. Tomorrow, you'll think twice before encouraging a married woman to commit adultery. Quick; strip before I pull it off you."

"Okeke, have mercy, okay?" the crowd begged. "Do Christmas for the woman, you hear? Just a little Christmas charity, please. Allow her to go home and change. Come, Teacher Uzo, go home quickly and remove his wife's gown and return it to him immediately. You're a very foolish woman. You should've known better than to wear his dead wife's clothes and flaunt it before his grieving eyes."

They hurriedly pushed Teacher Uzo away as others led Papa back into his parlour. My father's shoulders were now sagged and his face looked defeated, older than I had ever seen it. Mama left him to the care of his kinsmen as she hurried away to church with Ada and the triplets, while I retired to the eating-mat to await their return. I would have preferred to retire into the privacy of my bedroom, but I no longer felt safe within the house. I feared the renewed visitation of my stepmother's ghost, especially on a day like this when Papa had harassed her best friend—*I hope now that Papa has raged against Teacher Uzo he'll finally let go of his anger towards me and abandon his plans to send me away to Dibia's house...*

Later that night, just as sleep was about to claim me, a faint, malodorous whiff filled my nostrils. At first, I wrinkled my nose, wondering if Ejima had farted in their sleep as was their habit. But there was something different about the smell, something unwholesome and evil, a putrescent stench of raw chicken, wet dog, rotten eggs, and bad breath combined. And in that instant, from a long-buried memory, total recollection returned. I remembered; *I knew.*

My heart began racing—*Oh my cursed luck! I know this foul smell! Oh please, don't let it be them... I don't want to see them ever again... I don't want to come near their evil presence again.*

My body started to raise itself from my mattress even as I resisted the terrible pull of the unholy stench. My feet grew light, leading me towards the shut door of Ejima's bedroom. Now they were gliding, guiding my suddenly feather-light body beyond the corridor and outside our house. The sky was awash with twinkling stars and the night air should have been fresh. Yet *their* corrupt reek pervaded everywhere, giving me no respite— *No, no, no! Why? I don't want to be a Bride-Sentinel anymore. I want to be normal again! Oh please, no more... no more...*

Hot tears poured down my cheeks. Even the miracle of my returned levitation failed to bring me solace. Unlike the first and only time it had happened, I was fully aware this time of my supernatural transformation. I didn't need to look down to see that my body, my now naked body, from my hair to my toes, had turned a chalky hue that glittered like white paint in the dark night.

A sudden cacophony of unnatural sounds filled the air above me. I looked up and saw a sight that stunned me into terrified awe. Eight flying geladas whirled around our compound, each flapping a pair of dazzling red wings. Even their famous red-hued chests glowed as if infused with a supernatural bulb. The sky above them was lit up by the fiery light of their wings. The sounds they emitted were so terrible that our household and the neighbouring compounds were soon awakened. People gathered outside, staring with horror at the band of gurgling, glowing baboons whirling over our house in their diabolical flight.

"What new evil is this that has entered Okeke's compound again?" the villagers asked, staring with terror-filled eyes at the flying geladas. "How in God's heaven can baboons fly? This is evil sorcery beyond human powers. Oh, Jesus!"

Then, they saw me in my gliding whiteness and shrieked.

"Jesus Christ, save our souls!" Their screeching voices were laced with terror and disbelief.

Pandemonium struck.

The crowd started to run in all directions like senseless chickens. Some of them ran away from our compound while others fled into our house in mindless terror. In their midst, I saw Papa. He ran towards me instead of away from me like everyone else. His eyes were free of the fear that crippled the rest, and for the first time in a very long time, I saw the old compassion and love return to his face. He reached out his hands to me.

"Come, child," Papa said, his voice gentle, coaxing. "Float down to your Papa now. It's enough, you hear? You've done enough for this stupid village. You don't need to torture yourself by helping anyone else or their haunted brides. Let them deal with their troubles and their own ghosts. Come now, my daughter; don't fly away. Come down to Papa."

Papa stretched his arms up to pull down my elevated feet. One of the geladas dived down with a piercing shrill that brought screams to the people's lips. Even Papa shouted as he tried desperately to hold onto my ankles. The fiery baboon scratched his arms viciously, forcing him to let go of my feet with a howl of agony. The din inside our compound was deafening as more villagers arrived to witness the strange events of the night. The women were crying, while the men shouted at each other to arm-up and attack the unholy primates. Others screamed for Dibia and his powerful juju, while a few brave ones joined Papa in the melee. Papa was still flailing his bloodied arms, trying to scatter the flying geladas swirling above him and save me from their fierce grip.

The geladas wrapped their glowing wings around my body and drew me away from our compound in a slow, gliding motion.

I heard the awed gasps of the villagers as they observed our departure. Their bewildered thoughts hit me in a thundering wave that would have toppled me to the ground had I still been in my human state.

Out!

With a single thought, I banished the cacophony of their thoughts from my head. I needed to hear the message from the flying geladas, the words that flowed from their mouths in a familiar voice I instantly recognised—*Big Momma Mmuọ-Ka-Mmuọ!*

Bliss washed over me in warm waves that brought a sudden tightness behind my throat—*Oh, Big Momma Mmuọ-Ka-Mmuọ, you've finally come for me… finally! You've remembered me again! I'm finally going back to* Ibaja-La! *It's over; my suffering is over at last!* I cocked my ears eagerly, ready to receive Mmuọ-Ka-Mmuọ's message. I expected any second to see her mighty zebra frame, her long beard, and four obsidian eyes spinning in her multiple cascading faces.

"Child, what a heavy burden you've carried; what dire trials you've endured." Her voice, extruding from the lead gelada's mouth, was the beloved rumbling boom I remembered from my sojourn in *Ibaja-La*. "We thought we could wait for you to be older and grow into your powers. We didn't reckon on other factors that would create the anguish you've had to endure. We let you down, child. The Great Council of Guardians apologises to you for the unfair burden we placed on your young shoulders."

Mmuọ-Ka-Mmuọ paused as the flying geladas navigated me over houses and trees, farms and roads. I started to panic— *Please don't leave me! Big Momma Mmuọ-Ka-Mmuọ, please take me with you. I don't want to be a Bride-Sentinel anymore…*

"Have no fear, child. I am here now to set things right and set you free." Her voice broke through my panic, restoring temporary calm. "But first, you must fight your final battle and annihilate the Ghost-Brides awaiting you. It will not be easy: four adversaries await you tonight. Some of these Ghost-Brides have been sorely wronged and therefore come with the righteous protection of Ọfọr n'Ọgu—clean hands and justice. The others lack innocence and have come with vengeance and hatred in their corrupt hearts." Mmụọ-Ka-Mmụọ paused as the blazing geladas soared higher underneath the bright glow of the full moon. The night breeze was warm on my naked body and my skin tingled from the delicate touch of soft fur.

"You must annihilate these evil Ghost-Brides without harming the innocents amongst them." Mmụọ-Ka-Mmụọ's voice returned to the gelada's mouth. "You're already equipped with the weapons to battle them. The Eight Faces of Devastation you received from The Great Council of Guardians must be used in order for them to leave your face and set you free. You may not remember your powers now, but once you confront your foes, full recollection will come to you. Go now, child; proceed without fear. Go and face your destiny and set yourself free."

And the flying geladas opened their claws and let go of me. I began to fall. With a loud gurgle, the charmed primates exited the dark skies in a blaze of powerful, dazzling wings. A sudden stillness shrouded the night. With a slow and silent flight, I glided down and landed inside the bedlam that was Chief Omenga's compound.

23

The first person I saw on landing inside Chief Omenga's compound was his daughter, Amara, the young woman betrothed to Ugo of Amadi clan. In all my eleven years, I had seen Amara just a handful of times in the village. As the precious only daughter of our chief, she was far-removed from the vicinity of most of the lowly villagers. Even after she became a divorcee as a teenager, she managed to retain the shroud of superiority that came with great privilege. I remembered her as a beautiful, curvy woman of quiet and demure disposition, blessed with a shy smile and a sweet voice. I heard someone once mention her age, twenty-two years, but she never looked older than my big sister Ada in my eyes. Save for a distant admiration, I never had any feelings one way or the other towards her—*Until she shared the vicious rumour about Mama-Ejima's affair that resulted in her suicide.*

At the thought, rage flared in my heart, hot and murderous—*Stupid, basket-mouth woman! I hope you die for what you did to Mama-Ejima!* I couldn't count the number of times since Ọla's death that I had wished Amara and her friends ill for the harm they had brought to my stepmother. Save for her revealing Ọla's affair to Dibia's daughter, my stepmother would still be alive today. Now, as I observed the ensuing madness inside the great chief's compound, I knew my wishes had finally been granted.

Amara was being dragged across the dusty grounds of the compound by invisible hands. From one end of the vast homestead to the next, she was hauled furiously on her back in a trail of dust, her body outstretched, long braids gathering dust and dirt. She was shrieking, spewing foul and corrupt filth from her lips, her face twisted in a lascivious smile.

"Ugo! Come on down; fuck me good!" she screeched with shameless lechery, cackling with wild abandon. "My King-Ram, pump it up and fuck me down!"

Amara tore the garments from her body with violent hands, exhibiting private parts that had the crowd gasping and shutting their eyes in shock and repulsion. Her stunned clanswomen dashed over to reclothe her and cover her corrupt mouth with frantic hands. Her naked shame was their shared shame and a dishonour to their clan.

Amara fought them like a ferocious hellhound, and despite their great numbers, they could not restrain her. She displayed a supernatural strength that defied their puny, human efforts. The vulgar shrieks she emitted curdled the blood of all who heard her. The desperate and terrified thoughts of her family members filled my head in relentless waves—*Oh, Jesus Christ, have mercy! What evil is this? Which jealous enemy has hexed our daughter with this wicked juju? What have we done to deserve this shame? At this rate, Amara won't even live to celebrate her wedding tomorrow morning. Even if she survives, our people enjoy malicious gossip and will spread tonight's shame across the ten villages. What groom would wish to yoke themselves with such a damaged bride when they learn about this? Oh our cursed fates! We're facing dishonour and disgrace of monumental proportions!*

I dragged my attention away from their distressed thoughts and returned my eyes to the tortured young woman. Already, my nostrils were filled with the stench of corrupt decay. The familiar cloying reek of raw chicken, wet dog, rotten eggs, and bad breath almost caused me to gag. With my supernatural gaze, I could see something nobody else present could see.

Two malevolent Ghost-Brides had taken possession of the young woman; two ghouls I instantly recognised as the enemies I had to vanquish tonight. One of the Ghost-Brides had already gained entrance into Amara's body while the other fought to dislodge it and claim the woman's body for itself. In their unholy battle, they inflicted great damage on Amara's body, leaving a litter of bloodied cuts and fractured limbs in their wake. I saw the trapped soul of the possessed woman inside her body, crying and cowering, her face clothed in terror and anguish. Her petrified thoughts rang loud inside my head—*It's not my fault... I didn't make Ugo murder you... I didn't know he was a serial murderer and romance-rat or I would've never agreed to marry him... Oh please, let me go and I'll have nothing to do with the evil man again... please...*

I shuddered, recalling the murderous thoughts I heard inside the accursed man's head on the night Ọla took me to her clandestine meet-up with him. I had no doubt that my stepmother would have died at his hands, just like these two scammed and vengeful Ghost-Brides had—*Not that it made any difference in the end. Mama-Ejima still died, thanks to this loose-tongued Amara. I'm glad you're suffering now. That'll teach you a good lesson. Next time, you'll think twice before gossiping. I hope Ugo of Amadi clan suffers like you and is tormented by evil Ghost-Brides for the rest of his useless life.*

In that second, a light bulb exploded inside my head. Memories came rushing in like a burst dam, bearing blinding images and old wisdoms from a realm beyond our own—*Big Momma Mmuọ-Ka-Mmuọ! The magical globe-shaped hall with walls of cascading, shimmering rainbow waterfalls! The singing golden table, shaped in a half-moon and adorned with mythical creatures! The Great Council of Guardians, eight powerful women deities all wearing Mama's face! The eight flying faces of power and terror*—The Petrify Face, The Soothing Face, The Fire Face, The Skinning Face, The Melting Face, The Vanishing Face, The Healing Face *and* The Annihilation Face!

My head almost exploded from the recollection. Pride and glee like nothing I had ever known filled my heart—*Vengeance! I'm as powerful as The Great Council of Guardians! I can kill all of them with my power-faces, including this stupid Amara and the two evil Ghost-Brides tormenting her. Yes! I can even kill Ugo of Amadi clan and Dibia, and forever free myself from ever being his apprentice. In fact, I can kill everybody I don't like in the village and...*

The Bata-me vanished before I could complete the thought. A fearsome darkness descended in my consciousness. I quivered in terror, my former bravado gone in a blink. Fear and panic became my companions. An intense heat seared my head, bringing a sharp gasp of pain to my lips. My face began to burn up like an out-of-control bushfire. I moaned softly, my breathing hard and laboured.

I felt something crawl its steely way through my body, from my head down to my toes. I thought I knew the presence, yet I couldn't tell its identity. There was a familiarity to it that terrified, even as it drew me in. A feeble resistance from me and the struggle was over. It found me where I cowered and it swallowed me whole. I yielded my soul to the presence and the Bride-Sentinel took dominion over my body and my soul.

An inexplicable strength flowed into my limbs as if my bones were wrought of steel. The burning inside my head vanished, replaced by a birring sound that filled my ears with sudden ancient knowledge. In a blink, all my terror died out like a tired storm. A cold calm filled my heart. I smiled as I flexed my steel muscles with languid deliberation. Then, I walked into the blazing night.

And the horror began.

I am changing. Underneath the bright glare of the generator-powered bulbs strung around Chief Omenga's compound, my body begins to stretch. The muscles ripple tautly against my bones and immense power surges inside me. The crowd finally catch sight of me and their awed gasps fill my head.

"It's Bata, Okeke's daughter! Look at her unnatural white skin and white eyes! She's turned into the Bride-Sentinel again! Bata has come to save poor Chief Omenga's daughter! Christ be praised!"

My lips twist in a disdainful smile—Fools! Even with the truth staring you in the eyes, you continue to give honour to the wrong god.

I continue to stretch and expand. Soon, I am a great giantess, taller than the one that goes by the name of Iroko, the tallest man in this village. I stand almost as high as the roof of Chief Omenga's storey-building and my girth is wider than a cow's length. A thick, long beard sprouts from my chin, dropping all the way to the ground like a black waterfall. I feel a delicate touch on my skin, and in a blink my body births the most stupendous Nsibidi body-artwork that streaks down my chalk-white skin in a riot of red, black, and yellow symbols, shielding my nakedness in dazzling rainbows. I raise my hands to my face and feel the cascading faces of power lighting up my head and my body. The birring sound in my ears announces the presence of my four obsidian eyes, spinning furiously inside their cavernous sockets. And I know that my transformation is complete.

The crowd shrieks. Their petrified voices pierce the air as they shrink back in terror, gawking, pointing, quivering. All eyes are now fixed on me. Even the possessed bride, Amara, has ceased her lewd shrieks. She lies prone on the ground, panting heavily, her near-naked body coated with filthy sweat. The evil Ghost-

Brides tormenting her turn their raging eyes at me. Their reek is overpowering and icy malevolence oozes from them.

"Foul ghouls! Corrupt souls! Release the human bride or face your annihilation!" I command, pointing a forefinger that sparks and sizzles with fiery threat. I speak with the multiple voices of the dead, except this time, the volume and menace is tenfold.

With a curdling shriek, the possessed bride hurls herself at me. Even with her puny size, Amara is intent on annihilating me. I can see the Ghost-Bride inside her powering her rage, together with the other ghoul clinging desperately to her arms. The villagers are blind to what I can see and Amara's brothers rush over to drag her away from me.

She flings them off with a casual flick of her arm. The three men crash against the crowd as if their bodies are wrought of feathers. I see the bewilderment on their faces, together with the stunned disbelief of the spectators as they gasp in awe and terror.

*I am faced with a sudden dilemma—*I must annihilate these two ghouls without harming the human girl. *But the evil Ghost-Brides cling onto Amara with malicious grit and will not leave her body without a fight. My first instinct is to raise* The Annihilation Face *and reduce the vile entities into an instant, ashy dust-pile. But Mmuọ-Ka-Mmuọ's instructions ring clear and loud in my head—*I am the Bride-Sentinel and I must not harm the human bride.

With icy resolve, I let my mind prowl through The Eight Faces of Devastation, seeking the right face that will vanquish the two Ghost-Brides without harming the tormented woman or the gathered villagers. Soon, illumination brings cold decision.

I pull The Melting Face *and turn it on the Ghost-Bride clinging to Amara's arm. It is the ghost of the married woman who was known as Efuru in her lifetime. Blinded by lust, she had poisoned her husband to escape with her lover into a new marital bliss. Ugo had taken every last penny she stole from her late husband before dumping her dead body under the Eko Bridge in the vast jungle that is Lagos City.*

The Melting Face *goes to work in its ghastly devastation. The arms clinging to Amara begin to melt, dripping gooey clumps of rotten, ectoplasmic matter in seconds. The Ghost-Bride lets out a horrified shriek as it quickly lets go of the possessed woman, cradling what is left of its ruined arms against its chest. It starts to levitate rapidly in a desperate flight. I am ready for it. I pull* The Petrify Face. *In an instant, I freeze the wicked ghoul into an icy statue, a frozen hologram of unimaginable horror that suddenly becomes visible to the horrified villagers.*

Their panicked screams fill the air. Seeing the evil Ghost-Bride in its ghastly pale malevolence, limbs skewed in inhuman positions, brings total chaos to the terrified crowd. It also frightens the other Ghost-Bride lurking inside Amara into frantic flight and it exits her body in a furious whirlwind of rage.

I know the cursed history of this second ghoul too. It is the one known as Gloria, a night-woman that sold her body to countless men in her lifetime, wrecking marriages with unrepentant glee. She had even lured her own adolescent niece into her corrupt trade, leading to the young girl's early demise to the AIDS scourge. Ugo of Amadi clan had promised her marriage in exchange for her ill-gotten wealth. Instead, he left her with a knife buried in her chest in the seedy motel room in his favourite hunting ground, Lagos City.

In a wink, the foul ghost dives into one of several black goats tethered to the nearby mango tree. The black goat instantly turns a pale white hue. It starts to kick and dash itself against the tree in manic frenzy like a rabid dog. The piercing bleats emanating from its mouth are like nothing ever heard from any living animal. The torture inflicted on it by the malevolent bride is too much for the poor creature to endure and it starts foaming at the mouth.

I pull The Fire Face *and blast the crazed animal with its fiery bolts. The goat topples to the ground in roasted death, charred back to its original black hue.*

I am not fast enough.

The diabolical spirit escapes into a second animal, this time a sturdy ram whose skin is as white as its own. It hopes to hide its presence within the white camouflage of the beast. But I can see what the humans can't see: its insidious, lurking presence inside the ram. Unlike the goat, this white ram does not break into a frenzy. It is as calm as the cunning spirit hiding inside it, who lulls it with a lullaby in its own bleating language. The wicked ghost is waging a war of attrition, hoping to shroud its presence inside the animal till I depart.

I turn my back on it and pretend to walk away. With a rapid whirl of faces, I pull The Vanishing Face. *In a blink, I disappear from the sight of everybody, human and spirits. The crowd gasps at my vanishing stunt before falling into tense silence, uncertain of what to expect next. Somewhere in their midst, Amara lies unconscious, now free of her tormentors. But I have no interest in her or the traumatised throng. I walk back towards the ram till I stand mere inches from it. I await the Ghost-Bride with unhurried alertness—It is only a matter of time.*

I am wrong. I wait and I wait. Time is seeping fast from its great vault and still the vile ghoul clings fast to the ram, which is now in a deep sleep. I have no other choice. I pull The Skinning Face *and turn it on the unconscious animal.*

The fur-coated skin covering its body starts to peel. I see the skin slice open in a lateral line from its head down the middle of its back and right to the tip of its tail. As the skin begins to slowly peel away, it reveals the bloodied soft flesh and skulking ghost underneath. Instantly, the ram leaps in panicked frenzy to its feet, finally realising its unholy possession. It starts bucking, thrashing, and bleating pitifully, its glassy eyes wide with terror and pain. Like the dead goat, thick foam fills its mouth.

The Ghost-Bride realises its camouflage has been discovered. Blind terror shrouds its raging features as it quickly flows out of the tortured ram like a decayed white cloud, seeping putrid funk. Its stench is overpowering and my multiple faces are cascading furiously to birr away the stink.

I do not delay. As the accursed bride separates itself from the doomed animal in desperate flight, I pull The Petrify Face and freeze it into a suspended hologram of horror. Then, with a blitz of blue bolts from my four obsidian eyes, I consign the tortured white ram to a charred corpse. I observe my handiwork with icy detachment as I sheath The Vanishing Face and reveal myself once again in my terrifying, mammoth glory.

The shrieks of dismay and terror in Chief Omenga's compound are deafening and harrowing. The sight of the two Ghost-Brides, suspended mid-air in their ghastly, frozen malevolence, is beyond anything they can comprehend or digest. They shudder and curse with riotous revulsion. Some scream "Amadioha, save us," flinging their arms over their heads and clicking their fingers to click away the evil. Others weave the sign of the cross over their shoulders and shout the names of Jesus and the Holy Mother for protection.

Soon, however, their curiosity overcomes their terror and they inch forward to gawp at the two frozen Ghost-Brides in their chilling, unearthly poises. Amara's clanswomen quickly carry the exhausted and injured woman into her bedroom. She is unconscious, but free from the vile possession that stole her modesty and pride. I know she will recall nothing of what happened to her when she awakes, but the stories she'll hear from the villagers will ensure she lives in shame for the rest of her life.

I am done with the evil Ghost-Brides. With a furious cascade of faces, I pull The Annihilation Face *and blast them into an ashy pile of phantasmagorial dust.*

A sudden scream rends the air. It is coming from inside Chief Omenga's sprawling storey-building. I let loose my mind and it finds the new terror wreaking havoc within. The chaos is concentrated solely in the west-wing, the section that houses Amara's bedroom. Doors and windows are slamming by themselves and lights are rapidly winking out, despite the generator that continues to power the rest of the compound with brightness. The west-wing of the house is now shrouded in solid darkness, while the east-wing blazes brightly in silence and serenity.

I see a radiant light break the pitch darkness in the mansion. It is a moving light, a living glow that glides slowly towards Amara's door. Within its halo, I see a new Ghost-Bride. This latest spectre is dressed in a pair of blue jeans, white T-shirt, and a white veil that trails several feet behind her. Tears stream down her chalky face, and a brilliant light cloaks her in a shimmering haze that almost blinds the sight. Her eyes glow with the familiar silvery hue of the Ibaja-La *brides and I notice that she is very young, possibly in her teens.*

I delve into her soul, and instantly her tragic story begins to play out to me in its painful totality.

Ugo of Amadi clan was her first love, the man to whom she bequeathed her virginity and heart. He promised her marriage and then abandoned her when she got pregnant. She died on the abortion table, her doomed infant bleeding away with her life. Of all the Ghost-Brides I must confront, I know that this unfortunate spirit will be the hardest to evict. I can neither petrify nor annihilate her. I can only coax her away from Ugo's new bride. Already, my mind tussles between The Healing Face *and* The Soothing Face. *I reckon one of the two faces might solve my dilemma—Even so, will she depart without a fight?*

I shake away the gloomy thought and will myself to shrink. My great height diminishes and I become leaner till I can finally fit into Chief Omenga's house. Still, my head almost touches the high ceiling and my girth fills the width of the narrow corridor. I can hear the shrill cries of the clanswomen cowering in darkness inside Amara's bedroom with the unconscious girl. They know they're doomed. No matter how firmly they lock the doors and windows, the teenage Ghost-Bride opens and slams them with inhuman force. The fierce wind swirling around the entire west-wing is like a hurricane, and its whistling noise shatters both glassware and eardrums.

I position myself outside Amara's open door and await the weeping teenage Ghost-Bride. Before she can get any closer, I pull The Petrify Face *to freeze her and halt her advance—Perhaps I can reason with her while she's frozen and coax her back to* Ibaja-La.

She glides through its powerful waves with ease, her face wreathed in anguish. I stare at her in disbelief as Mmuọ-Ka-Mmuọ's words return to my mind—"Some of the Ghost-Brides will come with the righteous might of Ọfọr n'Ogu, clean hands and justice." With sudden dismay, I realise there's nothing my deadly faces can do to her.

"Ugo... Ugo... Ugo..." she wails pitifully, her cries a ghastly groan that would chill the heart of the bravest warrior. As she drifts closer to me, I notice the pool of blood dripping down between her thighs, staining her blue jeans the terrible red hue of an aborted foetus.

I do not tarry. I pull The Healing Face *and stretch out my arms to her in an act of compassion my cold heart neither feels nor knows. It is merely the action that* The Healing Face *forces from me.*

Instantly, the bleeding between her thighs vanishes. She pauses in mid-air and stares at me with her wide, silvery eyes. Then she bends and looks at her thighs. She feels between her legs, her stomach, and her breasts with fragile pale hands before lifting her face to me again. There is incredulity and joy in her eyes, even as she continues to whine pitifully. With another cascade of faces, I quickly replace The Healing Face *with* The Soothing Face.

In a blink, the hurricane winds die and the slamming doors still. All is silent, save for the weeping Ghost-Bride and the gibberish prayers of the cowering women inside Amara's bedroom, as well as the murmurs of the anxious crowd huddled outside the building.

"Unfortunate spirit, weep no more," I say, my multiple voices coming out in a gentle lullaby that halts her plaintive moans. "Look into my face and calm your hurting soul. All is well... All is well."

Miraculously, I get through to her. She pauses again, staring at my new face. Suddenly, the light around her explodes into a kaleidoscope of shimmering rainbows. She glows so bright that she almost dazzles my quartet of dead obsidian eyes. Her tears dry and the pain leaves her tortured face. Serenity replaces her agitation and her eyes glow with calmness. She hovers before me, swaying in a gentle dance like dandelion spores.

"Return now to the happy realm of Ibaja-La," I croon gently. "Go now and thrive in the company and love of your fellow Ghost-Brides till your second, joyful reincarnation arrives."

Still, she stays. She will neither leave nor cease her plaintive calls for Ugo of Amadi clan. She smiles serenely at me and continues to sway gently in the air.

"Ugo... Ugo... Ugo..." she wails again in a pitiful howl, though I notice that the terrifying timbre in her voice is no longer present as she calls her lover's name.

The name stirs something inside me. I feel I should rage and curse the man, yet an icy indifference blunts my heart. There is no hate or judgement for him inside me. My business is with the brides, not the grooms.

I repeat my instructions to the moaning Ghost-Bride. Again, she blanks me out with her gentle smile and pitiful calls for her faithless lover. Each time she wails Ugo's name, the clanswomen shielding inside Amara's bedroom scream in terror. I hear them fiddling with the windows, seeking escape through that route. But every door and window in the west-wing is now sealed by the teenage Ghost-Bride. Until she departs, they are trapped. Nobody, save me, can enter or leave the building. Yet I cannot exit this haunted house without vanquishing the restless dead within. We are all prisoners of the grieving Ghost-Bride.

I contemplate the situation with icy deliberation—I must vanquish this Ghost-Bride without harming her. Yet, none of my faces can fight this righteous battle. I rack my brain, seeking a way out of my dilemma.

I see something approaching along the long corridor, something white that has a female shape. I am already expecting it—The final Ghost-Bride! I steel myself for the encounter. Mmuọ-Ka-Mmuọ had told me I shall battle four Ghost-Brides, and now I finally see the last spirit.

Ọla materialises before me in a wedding gown that dazzles with its glamorous sparkle and beauty. Sequins, beads, and lace blend into a shimmering, silvery creation that hugs Ọla's slender frame, accentuating her perfect figure. An overpowering scent of Charlie fills the corridor. Despite the chalky whiteness of her skin, her face now wears its famous Pancake-Face glory once again, and her eyes sparkle with silvery despair.

"Bata, set me free," she whispers with the hollow voice I remember from our previous encounters. But I am no longer frightened of her voice or her ghastly mien.

"What do you want from me?" I ask her, my multiple voices like thunder inside the building. The wailing Ghost-Bride pauses her moans and observes us in silent impassivity.

"I am to take the baton from you," Ọla says, looking at me with the same despairing eyes. "The Great Council of Guardians

have decreed my punishment and atonement. I am a bride; Ugo promised me marriage. Yet, I am also a married woman, with a living husband I betrayed. So, I can never live in Ibaja-La. The Great Council of Guardians decreed I be sent to The Wastelands, but due to her great affection for you, Mmuọ-Ka-Mmuọ offered me a lifeline. I must become the new Bride-Sentinel. The role of Bride-Sentinel shall once again return to the dead, and you will relinquish all your powers to me." Ọla's voice breaks and she reaches a beseeching hand towards me.

"Bata, help me... please help me. I don't want to be a Bride-Sentinel; I want to live freely in Ibaja-La till my next reincarnation. I don't even mind if I never reincarnate as long as I can live in Ibaja-La in peace. Mini-me, you're the only one that can set me free. Mmuọ-Ka-Mmuọ is only doing this because you want to be free. Please accept your destiny and remain the Bride-Sentinel of the ten villages. You already do the work so well. Please, mini-me, do this favour for me, you hear? Help me... please help me."

Ọla's words birth no feelings in me. She means nothing to me. It matters nought to me if I remain a Bride-Sentinel or relinquish the role to her as Mmuọ-Ka-Mmuọ instructs. All I care about is sending both her and the teenage Ghost-Bride away without harming them. If granting her wish will do the job, then I am more than willing to do so.

"If that's what you want, then I'll—"

My voice sticks suddenly behind my throat. A great shuddering quakes my body and a deep pain grips my heart in a steel fist. I want to cry and yet, I have no idea why I feel this inexplicable emotional overwhelm.

"Mama-Ejima, I don't want to be a Bride-Sentinel anymore." A small, tremulous voice extrudes from my lips. I recognise the child's voice, yet I do not remember who it belongs to. "Please, Mama-Ejima, become the Bride-Sentinel so I can go to school. I *want to be like you and become educated. I want to play with my friends and talk in my normal voice again. I don't want to wear the sunglasses anymore. I don't want Uncle Dibia to make me his apprentice. So, please, Mama-Ejima, become the Bride-Sentinel so I can be free, you hear?"*

As the child's voice dies away, Ọla's ghost bows its head and sighs heavily. Her long veil shrouds her face and her shoulders remain stooped in a defeated slump. Then she shakes her head and lifts her face to mine. In her eyes, I see a sudden resolve. The despair is gone and a dark rage replaces her former gloom. She reaches out and takes my hands in her cold ones.

Something flows from me to her. My light starts dimming as her own brightens. The colder her hands become the warmer mine grow. There's a burning, itchy sensation in my face as The Eight Faces of Devastation begin to flee from me.

With dizzying speed, they detach themselves from my face and hurtle over to their new mistress. As the last face, The Annihilation Face, *exits my face, the coldness in my heart begins to thaw. Memory starts to return to my head and tears pool in my eyes. They pour down my face in a rivulet, as if making up for all the long months they had remained frozen behind my lids. I am no longer in a dark place. I am alone; my body hosts only my own soul; me, Bata. When I look at my arms, my skin has returned to its former human brownness.*

In a blink, I begin to shrink. I grow smaller as Ọla stretches taller, bigger, mightier. Four dead obsidian eyes replace the silvery ones in her cascading faces. And suddenly, I am in the presence of the new Bride-Sentinel. Terror returns to my child's heart with terrifying suddenness, quaking my limbs.

"Summon Ugo of Amadi clan," Ọla commands, her chilling multiple voices icy and hard. "He must answer for his crimes tonight before we can depart from this house."

I don't tarry. I dash outside the building with jellied legs, crashing into a great number of villagers gathered outside. Dibia grabs my arms, staring at me with wonder.

"Get Ugo of Amadi clan, now," I say, my voice the old child's voice I remember from my pre-transformation days. "The new Bride-Sentinel wants him immediately. He has to answer for the deaths of all the women he murdered, otherwise the Ghost-Brides will not leave Amara tonight."

*Even before I finish speaking, I hear the thunderous roar of the crowd as they gasp in horror. They surge towards Chief Omenga's tall gates, calling out Ugo's name with rage. I scurry back into the house, fearful of offending my stepmother's ghost. My heart is pounding, yet a small thrill of excitement courses over me—*Finally, that horrible Ugo of Amadi clan will get his comeuppance. I hope Mama-Ejima turns him into a very ugly man, so he can no longer trap other poor women with his handsome looks.

There's a scuffling sound behind me and I see Dibia dragging the screaming philanderer into the house. I know the crowd are too frightened to enter the building and confront the haunting spectres. Ugo of Amadi clan is blubbering, shrinking away from Dibia and glancing around wildly. His face is twisted in terror and his good looks have vanished. I know the ghosts are invisible to him, but not to Dibia. The powerful medicine-man instantly sees them and gasps.

*Dibia bows low to Ọla in reverence and quickly averts his eyes from the hovering teenage Ghost-Bride by her side. I feel a sudden thudding of my heart, panic once again weakening my limbs—*I wonder if Mama-Ejima remembers what Uncle Dibia and Papa did to her? Oh please… don't let her take revenge against them now that she's a powerful Bride-Sentinel with the killing faces of power.

The young Ghost-Bride sees Ugo and sudden pandemonium breaks out. She shrieks his name in a piercing howl, and in a blink, the hurricane winds return, slamming doors and windows

with raging force. Light bulbs, mirrors, and glassware shatter
and the clanswomen cowering inside Amara's bedroom resume
their terror-screams. With a furious shriek, the teenage Ghost-
Bride grabs Ugo's thick afro hair and starts to drag him along the
corridor. Her face is contorted in manic rage and deadly sparks fly
from her eyes. The former healing of The Soothing Face is undone,
and red vengeance rules her heart.

Ugo is shrieking as he finds himself suspended near the high
ceiling. Red welts appear on his skin as the Ghost-Bride scratches
him with sharp talons, goring into his flesh with unrestrained
fury. The burning sparks from her eyes blister his skin, exposing
bloodied flesh and damaged veins. He glances around him
wildly, searching for his invisible assailant as he howls in agony
and terror.

"Die! Die! Die!" she shrieks as she tears his ears from his head
and breaks every last finger of his hands. Then, she exposes herself
to him, materialising before his terrified gaze with a suddenness
that steals his sanity.

Ugo lets out a curdling scream as he crashes to the ground,
breaking more limbs and teeth. Dibia turns to flee, his eyes wide
with terror. The door slams in his face.

"Stay and watch," Ọla commands in her new multiple voices.
"This snivelling snake before us will meet his fate tonight and
answer for his crimes. Be a witness to his judgement and ensure
his vile corpse is discarded in the same place where mine lies."

Ọla sheds her cascading faces and Dibia screams. Up till then,
he had thought that Ọla was Big Momma Mmuọ-Ka-Mmuọ. Ugo's
shrieks are reduced to pathetic whimpers.

"Yes, it is me, Ọla, late wife of Okeke," she says, staring the
petrified medicine-man in the face. "You know exactly where you
discarded my corpse, don't you? So, make sure to give the same
treatment to this wicked creature here."

She turns to Ugo of Amadi clan and her mien is a terrible sight to behold. "Vile snake, tonight you answer to us for your wickedness." Her voice drips with rage and I see the bright light of her Bride-Sentinel aura dim. She reaches down and drags Ugo up till his face is close to hers. The smell of Charlie is all-pervading and Ugo's voice is now a hiccupping whine. His body drips blood and his swollen eyes lower their lids to shut away the horror.

My heart thrills at the sight—Good! Horrible Ugo of Amadi clan is finally going to get his overdue punishment. I hope he dies a very horrible death.

As the thought leaves my mind, a sudden panic engulfs me. An ancient knowledge flows into my head, bringing a soft gasp to my lips—Oh no, no, no! A Bride-Sentinel can't destroy anyone that isn't an evil Ghost-Bride. Her business is not with the grooms, only the brides. If Ọla kills Ugo of Amadi clan, she'll lose her powers. Then I'll become the Bride-Sentinel again. I don't want to be a Bride-Sentinel anymore. Oh, Big Momma Mmuọ-Ka-Mmuọ, no, no...

I dash over and grab Ọla by her mighty legs. It's the only part of her my puny size can reach. Her neck swivels violently and she glares down at me. There's murder in her eyes and her body pulses with rage.

"Mama-Ejima... no... You can't kill a groom... you're the Bride-Sentinel now. Remember: The Great Council of Guardians took an oath never to harm a groom again after their great sacrifice. Please, let him go. I don't want to be the Bride-Sentinel anymore... please." *Tears trail down my cheeks and Ugo's agonised moans join my pleas.*

"F-forgive me... P-please, babes... f-forgi..." *Ugo is trying to speak through his delirium, his words an almost incomprehensible mumble.*

He never completes his sentence. With a wild shriek, the teenage Ghost-Bride sinks her hand into his chest and gores out his heart.

Ọla lets go of him and he crashes to the ground. He's dead before his head hits the hard cement. Dibia is making little whimpering sounds like a small puppy and my soft moans join his own. The teenage Ghost-Bride giggles gleefully and her bright light is once again a kaleidoscope of dazzling rainbows.

Ọla sighs wearily and turns to me. Once more she is the Bride-Sentinel and her four obsidian eyes are cold and distant.

"It is over now," she says, speaking in the multiple voices of the dead. "I am the Bride-Sentinel. Live freely and joyfully, child. May our paths never cross again."

She takes the teenage Ghost-Bride by the hand, and in a blink they vanish. Ugo of Amadi clan's tortured corpse is all that remains in the gloomy corridor, together with Dibia and me.

And all is silent.

24

The grey lights of dawn layered the skies by the time Dibia and I exited Chief Omenga's house. We were accompanied by the terror-numbed clanswomen, whose red-rimmed eyes wore a dull and vacant look, like people who had spent the night in Satan's mansion amongst his hordes of demons. As we stepped through the entrance door, we were instantly surrounded by a crowd of stunned villagers, whose raucous voices almost deafened my eardrums.

"Bata! Great Bride-Sentinel! The protector of her people! Great medicine-child, we hail you!"

Uh-Uh! You're wrong! Hot tears trailed down my cheeks once again—*It is over! I am free! I'll never be a Bride-Sentinel again. I can go back to school and play with my friends like before.* I held tight to the cotton wrapper covering my nakedness. One of the rescued clanswomen had given it to me inside the supernatural battlefield of Chief Omenga's mansion. Until she did so, it never dawned on me that I was still naked from my transformation; that the unnatural chalky hue that had shrouded my skin when I was Bride-Sentinel no longer hid my brown nakedness. Behind me, I heard Dibia instructing some men to go and withdraw Ugo of Amadi clan's corpse for a cursed burial in Ajọ-Ọfia, the bad bush—*Good!*

The wicked man has killed his last woman. Now, he'll rot inside that
cursed burial ground. I hope the snakes bite his corpse every day.

I felt myself engulfed in a hard embrace. I turned and saw
Papa's face coated with the same tears that stained my cheeks.

"It's alright, my child," Papa crooned, rocking me gently in his
arms. "Don't cry, now. You did an amazing job last night. Look
and see the dead goat and ram lying in the compound. They
were all alive and kicking yesterday, sturdy animals that were
bought for the wedding ceremony of Chief Omenga's daughter.
Now, they're mere ashes, killed by the evil Ghost-Brides you
vanquished last night, my amazing daughter." Papa's voice
brimmed with pride and awe.

In no time, I was passed from arms to arms, as Mama and my
extended family all hugged and feted me. Even Ada came over
and enfolded me in a warm, yet shy, embrace.

"My special little sister, I saw with my own two eyes what
you did last night," Ada said in a shamed voice, stroking my
face gently and looking at me with the old love she used to have
for me before my transformation. The warmth was back in her
voice and tears brimmed in her eyes. She struggled to hold my
gaze as she spoke. "I didn't know who you really were… I had
no idea what you've had to deal with all this while. You are truly
incredible, Bata. I am so proud of you that I want to shout to the
whole world that you are my little sister."

In typical Ada fashion, she instantly followed her words with
action. "People, this amazing child is my little sister, Bata! You
hear? She is my wonderful little sister and the best-bester-bestest
sister in the whole wide world!"

The crowd cheered and clapped with humorous goodwill. I
shrivelled within Ada's arms, mortified, yet thrilled. To be once
again back in my family's good books was a dream come true
for me.

Dibia materialised before us, armed with his ubiquitous leather juju-bag. His eyes wore an expression I had never seen in all the time I had known him. He stared at me like somebody that answered a knock and found their own ghost standing at their door. When he spoke to me, there was reverence in his voice, as if I had become his master, and he the apprentice.

"Great Bride-Sentinel, we welcome you back to our fold," he said, his voice tremulous, overwhelmed with emotion. "You may not recall the great feats you performed last night. Never... never in the history of mankind has anyone witnessed the freezing of ghosts, exposing the inhuman to human eyes in their chilling and ghastly totality. But you..." Dibia paused, shut his eyes and shook his head, still in stunned disbelief. When he opened his eyes, they glowed with manic fervour. "Great Bride-Sentinel, you made the impossible possible. You showed us the invisible threats lurking amongst us. You exposed and vanquished evil and showed us we can sleep with our two eyes shut in the knowledge that a great sentinel watches over us. I can now return to my ancestors in peace when my time comes, knowing that one greater than I has arisen." Dibia's eyes brimmed with unshed tears, and in that instant I knew that I had become a supernatural entity in his eyes.

The gathered crowd broke out in louder cheers. They surged closer to me, their faces alight with goodwill and awe.

"Bata! Bata! Our Bride-Sentinel! Saviour of Brides! The eyes of our village!" they chanted, clapping and singing and dancing with unbridled joy.

"But, Uncle Dibia, I'm no longer the Bride-Sentinel," I said, holding his arm with fierce desperation—*Uh-uh! I won't let him make me his apprentice. He can't force me to be a Bride-Sentinel.* "You saw Mama-Ejima inside the house. She's now the Bride-Sentinel. I'm now free to return to school. You heard Mama-Ejima, didn't you? You did... you did..."

I was almost in tears and Papa turned incredulous eyes at Dibia, grabbing his arm in a tight grip.

"Dibia, what is this she's saying about my late wife?" Papa asked, his voice barely above a whisper. "Did you encounter Mama-Ejima's spirit inside that house? Quick; tell me the truth. Don't even try to hide anything from me. Come; let's go to a private place and talk."

As Papa led Dibia away, Amara's mother arrived with several of her family members. I had still to see the former bride who would have been celebrating her marriage today but for the harrowing events of the previous night. I guessed she was still sleeping away the traumatic effects of the torture inflicted on her by the two evil Ghost-Brides.

Amara's mother offered me every delicacy and drink in their house and kept bowing down to me as if I were a deity, just as Ọla used to do in the days of her madness. But she wasn't mad like my poor stepmother, neither were the other villagers who imitated her actions. Like my sister Ada, they were merely awed and overwhelmed by what they witnessed during my battle with the Ghost-Brides.

Before I finished my meal, Amara awoke. She asked for me and I was led into her bedroom where she lay in her bed, swathed in bandages. She looked twenty years older than her twenty-two years, and despite her great pain she managed to hold fervently onto my hands, calling me her saviour and eternal friend. Her bruised face was damp with tears and her eyes smiled shyly into mine. The mortified look on her face, coupled with her soft voice and kind words, brought sudden compassion in my heart and killed my former resentment—*Maybe she won't spread bad gossip about people anymore after everything that happened to her. Now, she'll become a victim of gossip herself and will have to live with the shame for the rest of her life.*

Chief Omenga turned the aborted wedding ceremony into a celebration and thanksgiving event for the life of his only daughter, Amara. Soon, the villagers were treated to the sumptuous feast and great entertainment originally meant for the wedding event. Musicians and dancers entertained, while endless gourds of palm wine brought drunken cheer amongst the people.

As the merriment continued, I found myself suddenly overwhelmed by intense tiredness. All I wanted was to go home and sleep the day away in my bedroom. But Papa and the rest of my family were having such a good time that I felt guilty about making a fuss.

Halfway through the celebrations, the wealthy Chief Omenga stood up and addressed the crowd through the loud microphone.

"Our people, I greet you all!" he announced, beaming a benevolent smile at the guests.

"Money-Tree! Great generous chief! Your subjects salute you!" the villagers responded enthusiastically, buoyed with goodwill and affability from all the good foods they had consumed. The chief lapped up their praise before speaking once again into the microphone.

"You all witnessed what happened inside this very compound last night, so I will say no more. All I can say is that our ancestors and Jesus Christ have blessed us with a gift beyond anything we can imagine. That gift is the child standing before us, the one you all know as Bata, Okeke's daughter." Chief Omenga pointed towards me as he paused, awaiting the crowd's response.

They did not disappoint. They cheered and clapped enthusiastically once again, calling out both Chief Omenga's and my name in hearty praise. I wanted to hide myself from their benevolent gazes and I held tight to Ada's hand for support. My sister hugged me briefly and ruffled my hair affectionately before joining in the clapping.

Chief Omenga turned to Papa and addressed him directly. "Okeke, I want to train your daughter in the top secondary school in our country, Queen's College, Lagos," he announced, speaking loudly into the microphone to ensure the whole village heard about his benevolence. "I intend to send this wonderful child to any university she wants to study at and pay all expenses for her. Even if she wants to study in America, I will sponsor her studies."

Chief Omenga paused as the crowd roared. Even Papa gasped. *America!* The word reverberated in the crowd and all eyes turned on me once again in awe. I was glad I could no longer hear their thoughts. My head would have exploded from the deluge of their frenzied excitement.

"I hear the child is a very intelligent student and I can't think of any other way to reward her for the great feat she performed yesterday for both my family and our village at large," Chief Omenga continued. "Without her, my only daughter would be a living corpse by this morning. Worse, we wouldn't know about the wickedness that lurked inside the heart of one of our own, the dastardly snake called Ugo of Amadi clan. May his accursed soul rot forever in hell."

"Amen! Iseh!" The villagers jeered and cheered wildly on hearing the chief's announcement. I knew the jeering was for Ugo and the cheering for me. The pride on Papa's face completed my bliss. People came over to pump his hands vigorously. They praised him for raising such a great daughter and many bowed in reverence before him.

I thought my heart would explode from joy as I listened to Chief Omenga's announcement—*Oh my blessed life! I'm going to school! I'm going to study in Lagos City. I will finally become educated like Mama-Ejima and talk properly like the white people. Maybe I'll even go to Germany instead of America to learn how to walk The German Success Walk and become as rich as Engineer Tip-Toe and finally build a storey-building for Papa...*

Fantastical images flashed inside my head and it took everything to stop myself from dancing and singing like the rest of the villagers were doing. My face remained stretched in a wide smile through the day following my great feat at Chief Omenga's compound.

My good fortune continued in our house. For the rest of that day, my eyes and skin remained their natural brown colour, while my voice continued to speak with the high pitch of an eleven-year-old human girl.

The following morning, after the events at Chief Omenga's compound, Mama hurried into our bedroom to carry out her old checks. Beside me, Ada slept once again on her mattress. The sight of her returning to share our room for the first time in a very long time had overwhelmed me the previous night. She had held me in her arms as my shoulders shuddered in silent, hard sobs and told me several folk tales before I finally slept. Even with our close proximity, I heard neither her thoughts nor those of any other person as in the past. And that night, my accursed nightmares didn't return. Best of all, the ghastly scent of Charlie didn't haunt my nostrils either.

Mama dashed into our bedroom before Ejima woke up and shook me hard, dragging me into fuzzy wakefulness. As I opened my eyes, she stared at me with eyes the size of oranges. She leaned in to get a better look. Then she jumped to her feet and stretched her arms up, tilting her head and shutting her eyes in fervent prayers.

"Holy Mother! Thank you! Thank you, Our Blessed Virgin, for this great miracle!" Mama cried, tears pouring down her face. "I thought what I saw at Chief Omenga's house yesterday was a fluke, that the curse would return again. But Mother Mary has heard my prayers finally!"

At her words, my heart skipped joyfully. Before I could speak, Ada opened her eyes and stared around her groggily. "What? What? Mama, what's going on?" Ada asked, cracking her knuckles loudly as was her habit whenever she woke up.

"It's your sister; her eyes are back to their human brown colour." Mama's face was wreathed in smiles. Then her eyes narrowed. "Bata, quick my child; open your mouth and say something. Let's see if your normal voice is still back."

Oh please... please, let my voice still be okay... please. Heart pounding, I obeyed Mama's instruction.

"Good morning, Mama." I said the first thing that came into my head. I was chuffed to hear my normal child's voice once again, just as it had been since yesterday—*Yes! Yes! Finally!* "Good morning, Mama! Happy morning, Mama! Good, good, wonderful morning, Mama!" I chanted the greeting over and over, my voice thrilling in great happiness.

"Yes, child; speak! Shout! You are free! Our Holy Mother has set you free!" Mama started dancing, shaking her buttocks and clapping her hands. Tears of joy rolled down her face as she pulled me up from my mattress to join in her dance. Then she folded me in her arms tightly. Her shoulders shook with the violence of her sobs and my tears soon joined her.—*Thank you, Big Momma Mmuọ-Ka-Mmuọ! Mama and Ada love me again! Papa is proud of me! I am cured! I'm normal again!* Tentatively, I reached my mind once again into their heads, seeking their thoughts—*Just to be sure I'm fully free.*

Silence: nothing came into my head. There was a blissful silence that I never appreciated till I lost it. All I heard were my own thoughts, my joyful, excited and thankful thoughts—*It is really, really over! I am finally free... free...*

Later that evening, Papa killed a goat in an impromptu Salaka (thanksgiving) ceremony to the ancestors, to celebrate my freedom from possession. Our clan and friends gathered for the party despite not knowing the reason for it. They assumed Papa was merely thanking his ancestors for Chief Omenga's generosity and my Bride-Sentinel powers. The only face that wasn't happy in the crowd was Dibia's own. I knew the medicine-man had harboured hopes that Papa might one day relent and send me to him as an apprentice. With my return to normality, that dream had been crushed and Dibia did not tarry long in our compound after having his bowl of goat pepper-soup and palm wine. I was pleased to see him go, and for the rest of the day I played with my cousins with manic frenzy, shouting, jumping, running, shoving, dancing, and doing everything I hadn't done in months since my transformation. I happily abandoned my detested sunglasses to the rowdy possession of Ejima, finally granting their long-held wishes.

By the time I slumped down joyfully on my mattress later that night, I could barely wait for the next morning to arrive— *Finally! I'll return to the classroom again to become educated like Mama-Ejima!* I knew with unquestionable certainty that waking up every morning would now become an endless joy without Mama's former daily checks. I also knew that the scent of Charlie and the terrible nightmares that had blighted my peace, had vanished permanently from my life. I was finally free.

Father David made an unscheduled visit to our house four weeks after the events at Chief Omenga's compound. The sight of the priest's imposing presence, brimming with holy righteousness in his long white cassock, was enough to send my heart plummeting—*Oh, Big Momma Mu—uh-uh! Holy Mother Mary, what have we done now?* Father David was known to only visit homes for funerals or last sacraments, so his unexpected visit to our house filled everyone, save Papa, with great curiosity and anxiety.

My thoughts were like scattered ants, running everywhere and nowhere—*When was the last time I went for confession? What sins have I committed since then? Or maybe Ada has done something bad? After all, she's the one with the bad temper in the family…*

Father David stomped into Papa's parlour with great purpose, clutching his Bible firmly against his chest. Mama and Ada exchanged puzzled looks, before hurrying towards Papa's parlour, bearing bowls of ripe aghara (garden-eggs) and peanut paste as refreshment for the priest. I knew they were all going to spy out the priest with their refreshments, and a part of me wanted to accompany them to feed my curiosity. But another part dreaded any interaction with the fierce priest. Just like Dibia, I feared Father David's omnipotence and the guilt their presence always wrought in my heart.

I busied myself by playing with Ejima, trying to distract my thudding heart and frantic thoughts. Just then, I heard my name called out with loud urgency. I looked up and saw Ada waving her arms impatiently, urging me towards Papa's parlour.

"We go too," Ejima-One said with bossy determination before dashing off to Papa's parlour before I could stop him.

"Me too." Ejima-Two cackled with glee before dashing after his sibling.

"Wait for me." Ejima-Three's voice was already wobbly with tears as he ran off to catch up with his brothers.

I sighed and wiped my panic-damp hands on my dress. My feet dragged as I made my way towards Papa's parlour. Father

David's frowning face did little to alleviate my unease as I hovered near the door.

"*Bene, Bene!* Come closer, child," Father David said, waving me in imperiously as if he owned Papa's parlour. Already, Ejima were huddled by the centre table on their knees, stuffing their faces with the ripe aghara and peanut paste Mama had prepared for the priest.

I inched closer till I stood near Mama's chair. I looked anxiously into their faces, but I read nothing in them. Papa looked bored, as if he wanted the priest gone. My father was an adherent of Omenaanu, the ancient spiritual religion of our people before the arrival of Christianity. Consequently, he had little patience with the Church and its priests. Mama's face was wreathed in anxiety, but then, she was always anxious in the presence of Christ and his earthly priests. Even the wooden crucifix caused her to worry in case there was an unconfessed sin still clinging to her. Ada cracked her knuckles with impatient curiosity and the familiar sound restored some of my calm.

"Good evening, Father," I whispered, curtsying reverently to the priest.

"*Buonasera*, my child," Father David said, dusting invisible dust from his Bible. As usual, he interspersed his words with some Italian to show his importance as a priest who had visited the Vatican. Father David was from a different village from ours and I guessed he was the equivalent of our Engineer Tip-Toe to his people. "I was just telling your parents that our school can no longer support the disruption caused by your continued presence. I've heard about the heathen feats you supposedly performed and I must say I am disappointed in you." He turned his fierce gaze to Mama, who wilted under his reproving glare.

"You call it heathen, we call it a blessing," Papa snapped, scowling at the priest. "So, what do you expect us to do? Do you want to send the child away from your school even though she is one of the brightest kids in the village? You may not know this, but Chief Omenga has promised to fund her schooling at Queen's College, Lagos, as well as in any university of her choice, even in America." Papa's voice brimmed with pride as he glared at the priest.

Father David grunted and flicked more invisible dust from his Bible. My stomach tightened in panic—*Send me away from school? Oh no, no! It's not fair! Why am I still suffering when I'm no longer the Bride-Sentinel? Everything was supposed to be normal again, so why are things still the same? It's not fair... not fair.* In the one month I'd been back in the classroom again, nosy visitors seeking the famous Bride-Sentinel had been invading my school on a daily basis, resulting in some friction between the children and me. Some of the pupils mocked me, while others called me a liar and a fake. I was called a freak by former playmates and totally excluded by others. Even some of my cousins had started turning their backs on me out of embarrassment. School was now a place of tears rather than fun for me.

"I know about Chief Omenga's generosity and that's why I'm here today," Father David said, his gruff voice breaking through my gloomy thoughts. "The chief sent for me a few days ago and advised me about his incredibly generous offer. *Molto generoso!*" The priest nodded in approval, as if he were the one making the donation to my school fund. "He asked me to look into getting Bata into Queen's College and I think I have come up with a good solution. With your permission, I shall arrange for her to live with one of our nuns in Lagos City, where she will attend one of our primary schools before taking her exams for Queen's College. Sister Mary-Therese is a wonderful nun. I can personally vouch for her, and I assure you she'll be as kind to Bata as if she gave birth to her. Chief Omenga will be paying the school fees and her upkeep, of course. In fact, he has very kindly offered to fund the roofing of our church building as well. *Bellissimo!*"

For the first time, I saw a smile crease the priest's face. Papa's brows dipped and Mama started to twist her hands frantically, looking from Papa to Father David with anxious eyes. As for me, I was ready to sprout wings and fly—*Lagos City! I'm finally going to see Mama-Ejima's Lagos City!*

"L-Lagos City?" Mama stammered, looking at me with a panicked expression. "B-but, it is such a far place for Bata to go at her young age."

"*La Cinacia!* Nonsense! She's eleven years now and will be entering secondary school in less than a year's time. So, she will only spend a couple of terms in our Lagos primary school before entering Queen's College's boarding school. The education she'll get in Lagos will be superb, beyond anything she'll ever receive in our village school. I worked very hard to secure this great opportunity for the child because Chief Omenga personally asked me for the favour. Plus the fact that Bata is a very bright child, of course. So, don't hold your child back with your unchristian fears. Where is your faith in Our Lord's mercy and protection?"

Mama bowed her head in silent mortification.

Papa grunted and looked at me. "Akuabata, what do you think about all this?" he asked.

I wanted to run over and hug him. He was the only one that sought my opinion in this crucial discussion about my future. "I want to go to Lagos City, Papa," I said without hesitation, nodding over and over to emphasise my answer.

"Bata! Are you sure?" Ada asked. In her eyes I saw an emotion that twisted a painful knot in my chest. She looked as if she was silently pleading with me not to go, even as she tried to hide the sudden tears brimming in her eyes.

I nodded, giving her a reassuring, yet apologetic, smile.

"That's settled then," Father David said, rising to his feet. "I shall begin making the arrangements and will let you know once everything is sorted. It shouldn't take long. In fact, I'm confident Bata will be in Lagos City before the end of this month. *Ciao!*"

Father David nodded to my parents and exited our house with his ubiquitous black Bible. I was ready to do one of Mama's happy jigs. I felt the happiest I had ever felt since my sojourn in *Ibaja-La,* and later that night, as Ada snored softly into her pillow, I rummaged through my meagre clothes, picking out the dresses that were worthy of the great city of Lagos.

And two weeks later, on a bright and sunny morning, I hugged my family goodbye and left our village for my long-awaited journey to that city of dreams, Lagos.

Epilogue

Our compound heaves with a crowd never before seen in the history of our village. People have come from every corner of the ten villages that make up our wider community to celebrate this auspicious day with my family. There are also guests who have travelled all the way from Lagos City and from Abuja, our country's capital. The day is bright, and music and laughter thrill the air space.

From my upstairs bedroom window, I observe the colourfully garbed guests with a heart overflowing with happiness. I'm surrounded by my cousins and friends who have come to dress me up and prepare me for my special day. Very soon, Mama and Ada will arrive to lead me out into the compound to greet my in-laws and my handsome groom, Falk.

Today is my thirty-third birthday. It is also my traditional wedding day, a day I never envisioned would happen. Against all odds, I've survived the night, the eve of my wedding day, to see this most wonderful of days. If anybody had told me in my childhood that I would find my own handsome groom and live to witness this wonderful day, I would have laughed at them in derision— Who in their right mind would want to marry a creature such as myself, one known to be possessed by the spirits at intermittent and unexpected times? *Worse, my earlier life as a Bride-Sentinel had created in me a terror of bridehood that stayed with me, even after I relinquished that role. I only have to see a bride to begin trembling, overwhelmed with fear and grief. I'd long decided that I would never become a bride for as long as I live.*

Yet, against all odds, the miracle happened.

Lagos City had proven to be everything Ọla said and more, while Sister Mary-Therese had been everything Father David promised and better. Under her kind nurturing, I progressed through primary school in total serenity before passing my entrance exam into the prestigious Queen's College, Lagos, with flying colours. I returned to my village during the school holidays and was treated almost with the same reverence as Engineer Tip-Toe. In fact, Chief Omenga treated the great engineer and me to a special dinner during one of my Christmas holidays, resulting in the beginning of an unusual friendship between me and his family. Soon after that dinner at Chief Omenga's house, Engineer Tip-Toe began to invite me to his Ikoyi mansion, located in one of the exclusive sections of Lagos City. In no time, I began spending most of my holidays with him, his German wife, and their almost-white son, whose name I finally discovered—Falk.

Despite the five-year gap between us, Falk and I gradually grew closer through the years, a closeness that my studies in America, and his own in Germany, didn't break. With my law degree, I had unbelievably ended up surpassing my stepmother in education, a feat never achieved by any woman in our ten villages. By the time Falk returned to the country with a German degree in Architecture, I was already a seasoned lawyer with an established chamber in Lagos City. I was also the daughter of the third man with a storey-building in our village.

Against all odds, I finally fulfilled my dream to build Papa a storey-building, a feat I achieved with the help of my three brothers. Papa's new house is neither as big as Chief Omenga's mansion nor bigger than Engineer Tip-Toe's own. But it's still a storey-building and that is all that matters. These days, my father wears the proud title of 'Papa-Lawyer', and people tell him he could demand ten cows for my bride-price come the time. I've become the de facto pro bono village lawyer, as well as Chief Omenga and Engineer Tip-Toe's special advocate. The only regret I have is that Ọla didn't live to share this house with the rest of our family. It's a house that is worthy of her beauty and would have brought her great joy and pride.

Falk turned up at my Lagos flat two years ago in a surprise visit that almost knocked me unconscious when I opened my door and saw his tall, lanky frame leaning against my doorframe, oozing mega sex-appeal. With his tanned mix-race skin, lazy green eyes, and deep raspy voice, he had me quivering helplessly under his mesmeric spell. In no time, we were wrapped in each other's arms in a steamy embrace that lasted through the long, unforgettable night, and by the time he left, we both knew we'd been bitten by the forever-bug.

Now, this incredible day of my marriage has finally arrived, a day I never knew would occur in my wildest dreams. Already my three brothers have taken charge of all preparations. What I had long expected finally became reality. With their mother's early demise, they transitioned easily into Mama's care and I doubt if they remember that they ever had any other mother than Mama. At twenty-eight, the same age as Falk, Ejima have finally learnt to use their own individual names. The oldest, Nnamdi, has taken over Papa's shop and expanded it into several branches across our state. Nnamdi never made it past primary school, but that didn't stop him becoming a successful businessman, bullying his way through every obstacle posed by educated bureaucracy to make it big in the local business world. Ejima-Two, better known now by his professional name of Vascot, has become a professional footballer whose fame goes beyond our village and all the way to Lagos City. I take great pride in telling people that I'm the big sister of the striker Vascot, and Papa never misses a game by his club on the big television screen adorning his upgraded parlour. The only one of my brothers to make it to university is the weepy Ejima-Three, now known as Nonso. Like Falk, Nonso also studied Architecture, albeit in a local university. It pleases me no end to see the strong bond between my little brother and my fiancé.

Through the years, I've sometimes wondered with great anxiety about my own wedding should the day ever come—*Will I be safe? Will the evil Ghost-Brides come to take their revenge on me for the times I worked as a Bride-Sentinel? Oh, Big Momma Mmuọ-Ka-Mmuọ, who will be my Bride-Sentinel come the time, if it ever happens? Will you even remember me?*

Last night, on the eve of my wedding day, I finally received the answers to my questions.

I am alone inside my large bedroom in Papa's new storey-building. It is a much grander affair than the tiny room I used to share with my feisty sister Ada, now long married and gone to Chief Omenga's compound as a wife to one of his sons. I should be thinking of Falk and our wedding the next morning, but instead, my heart keeps pounding with terror. Every little sound outside my door brings the swelling of terror to my head. A sense of dread lies heavy on my soul—Oh, Big Momma Mmuọ-

Ka-Mmuọ, where are you? Please come and save me tonight. Please be my Bride-Sentinel. Keep the evil Ghost-Brides from me tonight. Let me be a successful bride tomorrow, please!

Hot tears drench my face as I stare at my shut door with terror-glazed eyes. Ghastly images of every evil Ghost-Bride I've ever battled now return to haunt me with devastating effect as I crouch at the furthest corner of my bedroom, quivering with terror. I don't know why my old terrors have risen to torment me so badly tonight, yet sleep eludes my eyes and there is no rest for my soul—I just need to get through the eve of my wedding safely and all will be well. *I try to hold onto that thought but it does little to dispel my terror. I've already sent my cousins and friends away, insisting on my privacy before my wedding. I'll not expose them to harm should the evil Ghost-Brides come for my soul tonight. Now, I wish they were with me, that someone else would hold my hands and share my dread.*

In the midst of my terror, a familiar scent wafts into my nostrils. I smell them. Even before I see them, I inhale the wonderous fragrance of fresh fruits and flowers. And when my bedroom suddenly illuminates in a dazzling, silvery light, I release a loud shriek of overflowing joy.

In a blink, they surround me—Jeong-from-Gwangju! Guadalupe-from-Mexico! Emma-from-Quebec! And my beautiful Aaliyah-from-Dubai! Oh, Big Momma Mmuọ-Ka-Mmuọ, is this miracle real? *I cry and squeal with unbridled bliss, transported in an instant back to our wonderful, idyllic days in the silvery enchantment of* Ibaja-La.

"Little Amina-from-Enugu! See how big you've grown! And finally you'll become a real bride, you wonderful child!" *They hug and kiss me, their silvery eyes glowing with love and kindness. Despite the passage of the years, they have not aged a day, and the sight of their beautiful, tragic faces fills me with intense love, awe, and bliss.*

I quickly notice that one bride is missing. I search frantically for my best friend and protector, Madison-from-Texas.

"*She finally became a bride when her beloved Cedric remarried,*" *Jeong-from-Gwangju informs me.* "*Mmuọ-Ka-Mmuọ said that she's already been reincarnated, the lucky girl.*" *I hear the yearning in Jeong-from-Gwangju's voice. The news brings tears to my eyes—* Oh, Madison-from-Texas! Dearest friend, I wish I could see you just one more time!

"*Amina-from-Enugu, go open your door,*" *Emma-from-Quebec says, her eyes gleaming playfully. I shake my head—*Uh-uh! *Even with my bride-friends with me, I know I'm not safe. They're ordinary Ghost-Brides with no powers to act as my Bride-Sentinel. The evil Ghost-Brides will destroy them as easily as myself should they decide to make an appearance.*

I hold my ground inside the dubious safety of my bedroom. But my friends won't hear my objections, and with playful yet determined arms they push me towards the shut door.

"*Just open it,*" *they urge.* "*Don't be afraid. Open the door.*"

Finally, I obey.

With a trembling hand, I turn the knob and open the door.

*I inhale the long-forgotten smell of smoke and burning wood. A loud gasp escapes my lips and I am stunned into slack-jawed disbelief. My skin tingles and intense warmth suffuses my body, filling my heart with indescribable bliss—*Big Momma Mmuọ-Ka-Mmuọ! *The mighty guardian stands sentinel before my door, together with my stepmother, Ọla. In their mammoth, terrifying glory, they fill the breadth and length of the wide corridor, daring any malevolent Ghost-Brides to risk their deadly might.*

*And when they look at me, even with the grim determination on their terrifying, cascading faces, their gentle smiles, the tender smiles of a loving mother, fill my heart with perfect peace. Tears fill my eyes, trailing down my cheeks—*I am safe! I have the greatest of Bride-Sentinels watching over me tonight! Thank you, Big Momma Mmuọ-Ka-Mmuọ! Thank you, Mama-Ejima! I am glad you finally entered this house that was truly built for you. Thank you once again, great guardians of dead brides!

Acknowledgements

With immense gratitude to so many people behind the successful publication of this book, including my indefatigable agents, Bieke Van Aggelen, Debbie Van Der Zande and the entire team at the African Literary Agency who worked tirelessly to find the right publishing home for my book.

My awesome Editor Cath Trechman, who believed in the story and sold the dream to Titan Books.

The entire team at Titan Books who worked flat-out to bring this book into the world; George Sandison, Elora Hartway, Olivia Cooke, Katharine Carroll, Valerie Gardner, Kabriya Coghlan, all the extra editing team, including Louise Pearce and Dan Coxon and so many others too numerous to mention but who are truly appreciated.

My incredible book cover designer, Natasha MacKenzie, who gave me my dream cover.

My wonderful peers who humbled me with their amazing endorsements including, Tim Lebbon, Irenosen Okojie, Cynthia Pelayo, John Langan, A. C Wise, V. Castro and Tananarive Due.

My dear special friends who remain my backbone and biggest cheerleaders; Ted Dunphy & the entire Redditch gang, Eugen Bacon, Acep Stuart Hale and Chidi Ejikeme.

And my two beautiful daughters, Candice Uzoamaka and Carmen Jija, who continue to give me an unbreakable reason to hold on to life. Girls, you are my past, my present and my future. You are EVERYTHING! xxxx

About the Author

Nuzo Onoh is an award-winning Nigerian-British writer of Igbo descent. She is a pioneer of the African horror literary genre. Hailed as the 'Queen of African Horror', Nuzo's writing showcases both the beautiful and horrific in the African culture within fictitious narratives. Nuzo's works have featured in numerous magazines and anthologies. She has given talks and lectures about African Horror, including at the prestigious Miskatonic Institute of Horror Studies, London. Her works have appeared in academic studies and been longlisted and shortlisted. She is a Bram Stoker Lifetime Achievement Award® recipient. Nuzo holds a Law degree and Masters degree in Writing, both from Warwick University, England. She is a certified Civil Funeral Celebrant, licensed to conduct non-religious burial services. An avid musician with an addiction to Jungyup and K-indie, Nuzo plays both the guitar and piano, and holds an NVQ in Digital Music Production. She resides in the West Midlands, United Kingdom. Find her on Twitter/X and Instagram @NuzoOnoh

For more fantastic fiction, author events,
exclusive excerpts, competitions, limited editions and more

VISIT OUR WEBSITE
titanbooks.com

LIKE US ON FACEBOOK
facebook.com/titanbooks

FOLLOW US ON TWITTER AND INSTAGRAM
@TitanBooks

EMAIL US
readerfeedback@titanemail.com